Highland Destiny

Laura Hunsaker

Historical/Paranormal Romance
New Concepts   Georgia

Be sure to check out our website for the very best in fiction at fantastic prices!

When you visit our webpage, you can:
* Read excerpts of currently available books
* View cover art of upcoming books and current releases
* Find out more about the talented artists who capture the magic of the writer's imagination on the covers
* Order books from our backlist
* Find out the latest NCP and author news--including any upcoming book signings by your favorite NCP author
* Read author bios and reviews of our books
* Get NCP submission guidelines
* And so much more!

We offer a 20% discount on all new Trade Paperback releases ordered from our website!

Be sure to visit our webpage to find the best deals in e-books and paperbacks! To find out about our new releases as soon as they are available, please be sure to sign up for our newsletter (http://www.newconceptspublishing.com/newsletter.htm) or join our reader group (http://groups.yahoo.com/group/new_concepts_pub/join)!

The newsletter is available by double opt in only and our customer information is *never* shared!

Visit our webpage at:
www.newconceptspublishing.com

Highland Destiny is an original publication of NCP. This work has never before appeared in book form. This work is a novel. Any similarity to actual persons or events is purely coincidental.

New Concepts Publishing, LLC.
5202 Humphreys Rd.
Lake Park, GA 31636

© copyright November 2010 Laura Hunsaker
Cover art (c) copyright 2010 Melody Lane

All rights reserved, which includes the right to reproduce this book or portions thereof in any form whatsoever except as provided by the U.S. Copyright Law.

If you purchased this book without a cover you should be aware this book is stolen property.

NCP books are available at special quantity discounts for bulk purchases for sales promotions, premiums, fund raising, or educational use. For details, write, email, or phone New Concepts Publishing, LLC., 5202 Humphreys Rd., Lake Park, GA 31636; Ph. 229-257-0367, Fax 229-219-1097; orders@newconceptspublishing.com.

First NCP Trade Paperback Printing: January 2011

Prologue

She looked across the room of dancing guests and swirling colors, and stared into the cold, hard eyes of her betrothed. This was undoubtedly the most terrifying moment of her entire life. Her death was imminent, and unstoppable. And she knew. She *knew* that it would not be enough. Her death would not stop the pain and destruction that she'd so desperately fought to end. Her hopes had crashed the instant she had stared into those flat eyes. There was no hate, or anger, like she'd been expecting; they were just empty. And it scared her. But she refused to let the fear weaken her; she would meet her death with a stoicism she'd never dreamed she possessed. Before she could stop them, her fingers fluttered to her churning stomach betraying her nerves, but she straightened her spine and dropped her hand. With a careful expression of boredom, she walked forward, and sat down next to the man she'd agreed to marry, the man who would kill her by midnight. And she prayed without much hope that her death would be enough.

Chapter One

Scotland- present day 2010

It was the same dream. Mackenzie was exhausted and jet lagged, and had figured she'd sleep like the dead, but it was the same dream. There was nothing remotely frightening about it, but she still woke afraid. Every time. It felt too real. The man was too real. He had cold blue eyes and blond hair and glared at her from across a crowded room. People danced in colorful costumes, but she never could make out anyone's face...all she could see was the anger and *hate* radiating from the man with the blue eyes. And she was drawn to him like a magnet to steel.

She'd been having the same dream since she was a teenager, but it still left her with that familiar feeling of fear when she woke. Today, Mackenzie woke up in an unfamiliar room, and to the misty grey light of a Scottish morning. Scotland! She was on vacation in Scotland! How could she possibly have forgotten that? The joy of her vacation released her from the annoying fear of a non-nightmare. That's what she'd taken to calling the dream, for it wasn't really a dream, but neither was it a nightmare. The excitement was apparently too much for her best friend Jenna, who was in the neighboring suite, because she knocked, well banged, really, on the door and hollered,

"Wake up Sleeping Beauty! Don't make me drag you out of bed!!! Our tour of the castle starts in less than ten minutes! Did you know that they've filmed movies at this castle? I want to see the sets

"I'm up, I'm up!" Mackenzie smiled as she let her impatient friend into the room. "Gimme five minutes, and a cup of coffee...then we can go. Deal?"

"Deal. And I brought you a cup of coffee." Jenna held the coffee towards Mackenzie, knowing her best friend needed at least a pot to get going in the morning.

"You know me so well."

Really it was more like fifteen minutes and two cups of coffee since Mackenzie made more coffee with the complimentary coffee pot in her room. But Jenna and Mackenzie had been friends since elementary school, so she knew it wouldn't bother Jenna in the slightest that they were a little late joining the tour. Mackenzie had even sacrificed her fashion sense by wearing tennis shoes rather than the trendy wedged espadrilles that had cost more than the last tune-up on her car! They hustled off to the lobby, where the receptionist had told them in her lilting Scottish accent...so musical to American ears...that the group should be in the castle's Art Gallery by now, and pointed the way.

The art gallery was really the second floor of what was probably the ballroom, or billeting room according to the tour guide. On one side was the balcony looking down over the ballroom, which was now a five star restaurant, and on the other side were floor to ceiling bookshelves with oil paintings of every lord and lady who had ever resided in the Eilean Donan Castle. It was a half circle that had benches and arm chairs scattered every so often. Once they had walked through what Mackenzie thought of as a loft, they approached the tour, which was halfway across the gallery.

"Wow," gushed Jenna, "I can't believe that we're in a real castle! They say it's haunted by the ghost of the last laird, whatever that is. Supposedly, he died miserable and alone, pining away for his lost love. No one knows what happened to him." She sighed dramatically. "It's so romantic. Maybe we'll meet a handsome prince and he'll sweep us away into a fairy tale romance!"

Mackenzie smiled patiently at her friend's enthusiasm. Ever practical, Mackenzie said, "But if there's only one prince, how will we decide who gets him? Besides, I think the last guy who lived here was a lord or an Earl or something, not a prince."

Jenna stuck her tongue out at Mackenzie and retorted, "Fine, I get to keep the prince since you're being a pessimist!"

"No, just a realist. But alright, fine, if we should meet any handsome princes here, they're all yours." Her voice dropped to a whisper as they approached the tour group.

"I only need one." Jenna's wistful comment was cut off as they were hushed by someone in the group. She stuck her tongue out at his back.

Mackenzie was in no mood to look for handsome princes. She had just recently broken off a serious relationship with her own handsome prince who had been sleeping with his boss for the majority of their relationship. He'd only wanted Mackenzie for the image she presented on his arm at fundraisers. He had felt that Mackenzie was the kind of girl he should marry, but not the kind of girl he wanted in bed. The few times they had come close to getting intimate, he would tell her it was her fault he couldn't perform, or that she wasn't adventurous enough for him. Eventually they had quit trying. Once Mackenzie had caught him in the act with another woman, well she hadn't looked back as she walked away. She'd been an accessory to him, nothing more. She was tired of being treated like a thing, an inanimate object. Besides, she didn't really think that she was all that beautiful. She knew she was pretty, and when all dressed up, she knew she could turn a few heads, but her hair was too unruly to be beautiful, and her nose was straight, rather than turned up like Jenna's cute little nose. She was tall, as well. Jenna was a petite, adorable girl who tugged at most guys' instinct to protect. Mackenzie had been comparing herself to Jenna for too long, and shoving that train of thought out of her head, tried to focus on the tour.

"Wow, who is that?"

The question came from a teenage girl to the left of Mackenzie and Jenna, and everyone turned to look at the oil painting that was hanging on the wall next to an immense bookshelf. Mackenzie's heart stopped. He was the most attractive man she had ever seen in her twenty three years! No, not attractive, but drop dead gorgeous! He had sapphire blue eyes, and dark hair that touched his shoulders. The bright blue was in stark contrast with the dark hair and bronzed skin. He stood brandishing a two-handed claymore, the standard weapon of choice for the Highland warriors, with one leg braced on a rock. His white shirt and kilt made him look like a gentleman, but the look in his eyes was that of a fierce warrior. It was those eyes that caught and mesmerized her; they seemed to stare right into her soul. Mackenzie couldn't hear one word the tour guide said about him because her heart had restarted and it was pounding double-time in her ears.

Jenna whispered to Mackenzie, "I'll take him, prince or not!" Mackenzie barely managed a smile for her friend, and just nodded wide-eyed at the painting. "Hello? Earth to Mackenzie? Are you there?" Mackenzie shook off her mental stupor and turned to Jenna.

"Huh?"

"The tour moved on a couple minutes ago, are you just going to stand here and stare at this hunk of a man who died like 200 years ago? Not that I blame you; he is totally HOT!" Jenna giggled, and grabbed Mackenzie by the arm to drag her back toward the group.

"You know what? I think I *will* just sit here and ogle him for a while." Jenna gave Mackenzie a look that clearly questioned her sanity, as Mackenzie pulled her camera out of her purse and snapped a few photos of this handsome warrior.

"Whatever, Kenzie. I'm moving on to reality. There's a super cute guy who is vacationing with his two roommates, and they are both just as hot. Ooh, and they have sexy Italian accents."

"Okay, go have fun. I think I'll sketch this painting."

"And I thought you were the realist," Jenna teased. But when Mackenzie just turned back to the painting, Jenna grumbled, "Whatever. Enjoy your painting, I'm going to make plans with the hot Italians."

Mackenzie mumbled something incoherent to her and turned back toward her room to grab her sketch pad.

Sitting in the art gallery, sketching, and staring into those fierce blue eyes, Mackenzie lost track of time. It wasn't until someone tapped her on the shoulder and said a polite "Pardon me, lass?" that she even glanced around her.

"Hmmm…yes?" Her vague expression focused on two men dressed in period garb. She didn't remember the tour guide wearing a costume, strange. Were they employees making sure she was where she was supposed to be? Where was she supposed to be? What time was it? It looked dark out.

"Would you be Miss Stewart?" The man who spoke to her was old, no, *ancient* would be a better word. He was hunched over and his wispy white hair hung past his shoulders. His face was creased with paper thin skin that looked brittle, as if it would tear if he smiled or frowned too quickly. His partner was middle-aged, and non-descript. There was nothing interesting about him; average height, medium build, brown hair. Both had dark cloaks draped around them and black boots that went up to their knees, *like pirates*, she thought absently. And both had the same excited light in their dark squinty eyes.

"What can I do for you?" Mackenzie asked by way of answering their question.

"You can come with us," the middle-aged man demanded.

"Why? Is something wrong?" Her thoughts turned to Jenna and her Italian lunch dates. "Is it Jenna? Is she alright? If those men did anything to hurt her…" she trailed off at the looks on their faces. They both looked slightly uncomfortable, as if they were about to say something unpleasant. "What? What is it?" her voice strained as she worried about her friend.

"You shall follow us. My son will lead the way." The elderly man definitely looked uncomfortable.

Concern colored her tone, "Where?"

"Follow us," the plain man answered, and he turned without waiting for her reply.

Mackenzie did follow, more out of curiosity than anything. The two men led her to a wall at the far end of the loft in the gallery. But before she could question their sanity, the old man pushed a tapestry aside and pulled on a lever causing part of the wall to swing open. Mackenzie gasped, and stepped back. The old man walked into the dark passage without hesitating, and the other man looked at Mackenzie briefly before grabbing her upper arm and pulling her in behind them.

Chapter Two

Scotland 1792

The carriage was unbearably unforgiving. The horses flew along the craggy road (if it could indeed be called a road, Mackenzie had her doubts) as if the hounds of hell were chasing after them. Mackenzie sat on a wooden bench covered with a velvet pad that did nothing for her sore bottom as she felt every pebble and bump. "The Princess and the Pea" came to mind, and she almost smiled. Almost. The carriage's other two companions, the elderly man and his middle-aged son, gave her looks begging her forgiveness.

Mackenzie still couldn't believe it. She, Mackenzie Stewart, born in 1987, who just this morning had woken in the year 2010, was actually in a carriage in the Highlands of Scotland! And that was not the crazy part! It was now the year of our Lord, Seventeen hundred and ninety-two. This time, the wave of nausea that encompassed thinking of the date didn't take as long to pass. She was getting used to the idea. Maybe she just figured that she was dreaming. Either way, her stomach only lurched this time due to the jostling of the carriage.

When the Nutty Professor here and his son had literally pulled her through the secret passage, she had screamed bloody murder. After a couple of good screams, Mackenzie had seen the concern in their eyes, and had thought them harmless. She'd figured them to be part of the castle tour, dressed up in period garb and speaking of Highland lairds and curses; so she'd played along. So, harmless indeed, she'd almost dropped to her knees as the secret passage gave way to the main entrance. It exited out by the front of the castle, where she had been dropped by taxi the day before. There was nothing resembling the paved drive that had been there just that morning. It must be as the two men had said; another time and era.

She noticed the subtle and not so subtle changes in the outside of the castle, it looked smaller and brighter. And the sky…it was clear and sunny, not at all the grey overcast sky of an autumn day that had greeted her just hours ago. Then she had been bustled into a carriage, and a lump of soft wool had been thrust into her arms.

"You'll be needin' to change your garments, Miss Stewart." The older of the two had spoken first, while she eyed what turned out to be a cloak and gown.

The look Mackenzie gave them was incredulous. Like she was really going to change her clothes in front of two perfect strangers! Right. They had some explaining to do. So she pulled the cloak around herself and pursed her lips instead, waiting.

Perhaps sensing the reason for her hesitation, the older man spoke again.

"Please forgive our methods, my Lady, however, we have great need of your assistance. It was foretold by the stars; the Stewart lass from a different time shall come through the gate and end the curse."

She played along, "And just how do you know that I am the right 'Stewart lass?' There have to be a million of us."

"We know it is indeed you, else you would not have been able to pass through the gate. Our clan has endured strife and war for far too long, and it is for you to be ending." The fevered light was back in his eyes. It reminded her of a religious zealot speaking of his god.

"You are the answer to the curse that has plagued our lands."

This time it was the younger of the pair who spoke.

"How?" It was stated so flatly that it almost wasn't a question. Mackenzie was afraid that she'd been kidnapped by a couple of crazies, what with their talk of the stars foretelling of her little time travelling adventure. But how could she deny what she'd already seen? Was *she* the crazy one?

"Why, you are the Stewart lass, it is to be." The younger man answered her again, in a tone that was so sure of the statement that Mackenzie raised her eyebrows and blinked. His father took over.

"On Samhain, or as you would call it, All Hallows Eve, you shall help to defeat the Campbell laird and stop the end of his cruel vendetta against the neighboring clans. You are to break the curse your ancestors put upon these lands. Then our lands shall prosper without bloodshed once again."

"What do you mean 'my ancestors,'" Mackenzie demanded. "What curse? And how on Earth am I supposed to help defeat some bloodthirsty tyrant? It's not as if I'm a ninja or a Navy SEAL. What exactly am I supposed to do? What is it you expect from me?"

Mackenzie thought that the elder of the two seemed a bit uncomfortable with her directness. *Well, too bad*, she thought, *it was their turn to feel out of place.*

He cleared his throat, and glanced furtively at his son before answering her.

"Well, we have foreseen that you'll be distractin' the Campbell with wedding and feast details, so that he will not be as intent on" he cleared his throat, "attacking the other clans."

"Excuse me? You expect me to be able to distract him from killing all of his neighbors with wedding plans?!" The incredulity was evident through the sarcasm. *What man has ever been distracted by wedding details?* "You pulled me from my century to discuss wedding plans with an evil dictator? Right. This is going to work soo well…"

"It will work." The authority of the old man rang in each word. "You are going to pique his curiosity enough that he will be so intent on being with you, that it will delay his other" he hesitated "plans." He added quickly, "Then Gregor and I shall use the distraction to gain access to and study the sacred texts." Then he muttered under his breath, "And we shall do so before he sacrifices you."

"Who's Gregor?" Mackenzie asked faintly before his words sank in, "Wait, WHAT?"

"Oh, have we forgotten to introduce ourselves? I am Morvern, and this is my son Gregor. We are the sorcerers of John Campbell. This is how we know of his plans, and how we hope to thwart his unpleasant plots."

"*Unpleasant?* That's what you call his plot to sacrifice me? You two are insane!" Mackenzie was almost shouting at them. "You brought me here to have me *sacrificed?* No, uh-uh, no way, you can just take me right back home. Now. There is no way in hell that I am staying here to pretend to marry a man who wants to kill me. Absolutely not!"

Morvern and Gregor shifted in their seats during her rant, but Morvern calmly stated, "Of course we shall return you to your time before he kills you." He was trying to soothe her, but Mackenzie was still freaked. Not only was her mind being asked to process time travel and magic, but now she had to act like a girl who was in love with the man who wanted to kill her. She felt nauseous again. Morvern continued, "Once we have an idea of what exactly it is that we need to do to accomplish this, we shall contact his most hated enemy, who is also the laird of the most powerful of the clans, Connor MacRae. The MacRae has been looking for a way to end the feuding and to dispose of the Campbell for years. He will help our cause."

Mackenzie thought that Morvern sounded like he was hoping this Connor guy would help, rather than being certain of the fact. She had no idea how she was supposed to believe these magicians, or whatever they were, when they didn't even sound too sure of themselves.

"Wait, wait, wait. Let's just think about this." Mackenzie was holding her hands out, palms facing them, and emphasizing each word with her hands. "You don't even know if this guy will help you or not? And you want me to agree to an engagement that has me being killed at the end rather than happily married? And why does this Campbell person want to kill me? He doesn't even know me," her fear was seeping through and she was done trying to remain calm.

"We will do what we can to protect you, of course." Gregor pulled a heavy piece of jewelry from his cloak, and handed it to her. "This amulet has been charmed with a protection spell and it is also the key to getting you back to your time. It will open the portal on Samhain and you will be returned to your time as if nothing ever happened."

The talk of her going home calmed Mackenzie enough to find her voice.

"And what if I refuse to help you?"

Morvern looked staggered by her soft question, but Gregor looked smug, "The time when the gate opens again is set. There will not be another opening until All Saints Day, the first day of November, and after that not until the end of the year."

"So I don't really have any choice in this, do I?" her tone was sour, even under the anger at being roped into this.

Morvern tried to placate her by saying, "We will not force you into our feud. If you choose not to help us, we shall find a way to hide you until the gate opens."

"And that's what, a month away?"

"Yes."

Mackenzie's mind was reeling. She closed her eyes, pinching the bridge of her nose and hunching her shoulders, while she so casually discussed her fate. She figured that she really had nothing to lose; besides, she wasn't altogether convinced that this wasn't a dream. She exhaled forcefully, and straightened her shoulders; might as well face this head-on.

"Okay, I'm here, I might as well do a good deed. So, you've dragged me 200 years into the past, now what?"

Gregor spoke up, "Now you will play your role. You shall use your middle name, it is Isabella, is it not?" At Mackenzie's hesitant nod, he explained, "Your given name is quite unusual in our time. Then you shall play the part of a woman excited at the prospect of a smart match. He is wealthy and titled, and in this time, that is enough for any bride-to-be. Your distractions must center on having him show you his lands and meeting his people. It will be time consuming, and a safe enough topic. You will need to dress accordingly. I hope you do not mind that we have taken the liberty of sending a trunk of clothing ahead for you?"

Mackenzie shook her head, feeling dizzy that they had this all worked out to such a degree. Something was nagging at the back of her mind. What about the fact that she was nothing at all like a proper lady of this time? Her mannerisms and her manner of speech, wait, she wasn't even Scottish! Panic made her voice come out a little higher than normal,

"But I'm not Scottish. How am I supposed to explain how I behave and talk? And I know nothing about this time, and what do I call him? What's his first name? And what about…" Mackenzie's voice trailed off as the fear clawed its way up her throat.

"Calm down, please. It is common in this time for men and women to know nothing more than each other's names before marriage. He has been told that you are Isabella Stewart. Your mother was English and your father Scottish. Your parents liked to travel, so you were raised abroad…that should explain your, ahem, *muddled* accent. You will be introduced to your betrothed as Miss Stewart and you will address him as *My Lord*. You are expected to be spoiled, and demanding. Your reputation is of great beauty."

Mackenzie rolled her eyes at that and muttered, "Right, this should be a piece of cake."

"Might I continue?" At Mackenzie's chagrined nod, he resumed his description of her character. "You are a little older than the average bride, so the story is that you were betrothed to a Frenchman whom you left on the day of the wedding. Although your reputation has not been tarnished, you chose not to marry any of the other potential suitors." He handed her something long and sparkly; a knife with jewels on the handle.

"Here is a *dirk* for your protection. You must hide it on your person once we have reached his keep."

"And once we reach his 'keep,' what then? It's the middle of the night!" Mackenzie was really nervous at the idea of meeting this Campbell guy, and she doubted that waking him up in the dead of night was the way to start off their relationship. Especially one where she needed to hide a dagger under her gown, and pray he didn't kill her on the wedding night. With that thought resonating in her head, she tucked the dagger into her waistband.

"We won't arrive until well into the day," Gregor spoke in a patronizing tone, as if to a child.

"Oh."

Morvern continued in a gentler tone, well it was a raspy, dry whisper, but Mackenzie assumed it was supposed to be soothing.

"My Lady, please do not fret. You will be the distraction we so desperately need, and it will work splendidly. Once we are able to vanquish him, you will be sent home immediately after. You need only act as a besotted bride for a few weeks and all will work itself out."

Right, act like a spoiled, obnoxious, brat to make the evil warlord like me, this'll work. Mackenzie was having trouble wrapping her head around the whole scheme. She blew out a long breath and squared her shoulders. At least she didn't have to do anything dangerous. This Highland warrior they were hoping would help was supposed to do all that stuff. All she had to do was visit a lord in his castle. And survive. Well, it wasn't like she was going to be held prisoner against her will. She was going in completely aware. Besides, she would be treated as a lady, with the privileges and graces afforded to one who would marry a man of that station. Mackenzie felt slightly hopeful that this whole crazy plan might work.

Chapter Three

The jarring motion of the carriage did not steady, but it seemed to shudder now. Actually, it had halted. *Strange.* Why would they be stopping here? Mackenzie was under the impression that it would take all night to reach their destination. She heard men shouting, and what sounded like a scuffle. Were they being robbed? In the brief second that someone shouted "Highwaymen!" and the carriage door was thrown open, Mackenzie was suddenly very grateful that she hadn't changed into the gown they'd given her. She was still dressed in her plaid Bermuda shorts and gauzy white tank top. She glanced down at her Nikes and was doubly thankful she hadn't worn the less-functional espadrilles, just in case she had to run. She pressed herself against the carriage wall, and held her breath.

When the door was yanked open, Mackenzie didn't know what to expect. Probably a man yelling "Give me all your jewels" or something equally clichéd like that. Whatever it was, it definitely was not a long, muscular arm reaching in for *her* of all things! The strong arm dragged her out of the carriage and brought her up hard against a wall. No, against a rock hard muscular chest. The man had his arm wrapped around her ribs, just under her breasts. Mackenzie had never before been so aware of her breasts before. Ever. And she was hot. There was heat everywhere that he touched. Odd that this man was so warm against her back. Although she wore the cloak, she could still feel his heat radiating into her body, forcing her senses to notice every solid inch of him.

And there was a lot of him to notice; six foot plus, easy.

Mackenzie shook off the odd feelings and thought of the dagger she'd tucked into her waistband. Mentally thanking Joséf, her kickboxing trainer, Mackenzie stomped the man's foot as hard as she could, drove her elbow into his ribs, and twirled into him with her arm raised to stab him. But as she looked up and locked eyes with her attacker, she gasped and stepped back.

It was him!

The Highland warrior from the oil painting that she'd been so fascinated with! In that brief flash of recognition, Mackenzie hesitated, and the man saw her intentions; the dagger had glinted in the moonlight. Nevertheless, Mackenzie swung, but he'd blocked her swing and she'd only grazed his forearm, dropping her dagger in the process. He swore, and reached for her again, but she danced out of his reach. While it didn't incapacitate him as she'd initially planned, it did buy her precious time.

She took off sprinting full-out for the trees on the left. She didn't know what she would do once she reached them, but perhaps just getting to cover would help buy her more time. What did this guy want with her anyway?

As she ran, she tore off the cloak; it was tangling in her legs and the last thing she needed was to trip right now. Once more thinking grateful thoughts to still be dressed in 21st century clothes, she ran as fast as she could across the too open meadow. Not hearing any sounds of pursuit behind her, Mackenzie turned once, losing her hair clip in the process, and couldn't see anyone giving chase. The relief was almost staggering. She stumbled to a stop, bracing her hands on her knees and panting, she glanced around to get her bearings. Wrong move. She felt the impact before she heard him. The man had tackled her around the waist and drove her face down to the grass. Mackenzie wryly thought that an NFL linebacker would have been easier to avoid.

He pinned her to the ground, letting her feel helpless for a moment, before roughly rolling her onto her back. His hands were all over her, and they were not gentle. He was running his hands across her breasts, ribs, stomach, thighs…was *this* what he wanted? Had Mackenzie been naïve in thinking it was jewels? The thought made her eyes widen in fear and then narrow with determination.

"NO!" she shouted, and tried valiantly to free herself. Her thrashing only made her more aware of his strong muscular body pressing along every inch of hers. Instinctively, in a timelessly female move, she freed her knee and brought it up to his groin. Her attacker was one step ahead of her though, and shifted his weight so that his hipbone ground into her soft abdomen, and she inhaled quickly with the pressure. He captured both of her wrists in one of his large hands and put a dagger to her throat; her dagger. She swore, and froze.

"Smart. Now Miss Stewart, lie still."

He spoke softly with the same lilting Scottish burr she'd heard from the receptionist, except rather than sounding musical to her American ears, it sounded seductive. Mackenzie was so annoyed that she found anything seductive about her attacker, that she missed his familiar use of her name. Her anger at herself helped her as she renewed her struggle by yanking her wrists free and hoping he didn't actually want to slit her throat. In the same instant that she freed her hands, Mackenzie grabbed for the blade at her throat. His eyes widened as she tried vainly to push it away.

"While I admire your courage, lass, my patience only extends so far." *Damn his voice was sexy.* It was throaty, and raw, and dark, and reached places deep inside her, and what was she thinking?

The man recaptured her wrists and then pulled her to stand up with him, the blade never leaving her throat. Her wrists were seared with the heat from his one hand. He held them in front of her, as if she were handcuffed. She frowned as she realized her breathing and heart rate had yet to slow. Mackenzie hadn't realized how tall he was; she had to tilt her head back to meet his steely gaze. He was not only tall, but he had broad shoulders and muscles to spare. The plaid tartan and kilt he wore only seemed to emphasize just how very muscular he was. He made her feel small. Since there weren't too many men out there who could make her feel small, this frightened her a bit. It actually frightened her more than the huge sword slung across his back. Mackenzie started thinking of ways to get him to drop the blade at her neck, but the only thing that kept coming to mind was her original plan. So she tried once more, shifting her weight slightly enough that she didn't think he would notice, and swiftly bringing her knee up towards his groin. But the man must have been a mind reader, because just as swiftly he sidestepped her, yanked her arms above her head, and pressed the dagger into her skin hard enough to make swallowing impossible.

"Lass, if you try that again, I'll tie you to my horse." Damn him, but he sounded amused.

Mackenzie did not doubt that he would. His clear blue eyes were almost silver in the light of the moon, and they sparked with his annoyance at her. She lost her breath for a moment.

"What do you want from me?" she demanded, however it came out so quietly that it lost all power.

His eyes narrowed at her breathless question, "To make sure that you are unarmed."

His eyes dropped for a second and Mackenzie realized that with her arms restrained above her head, her breasts were moving conspicuously with her ragged breathing. She almost rolled her eyes at that. Only helpless damsels in distress were supposed to have heaving bosoms. She was normally far from helpless. Of course, normally she didn't have a dagger at her throat. *What a weird dream*, she thought, because she was now thoroughly convinced that this was a dream. She must have hit her head and passed out on the tour of the castle and was now understandably dreaming about the man she'd seen in the painting. Right? Mackenzie tried to calm her breathing. Dreaming or not, she was not about to become some clichéd damsel in distress. But once his eyes had finished their insulting perusal of her body, and his gaze came back to hers, she almost gasped. The sparking anger was gone, and in its place was some emotion that had turned the blue flashes to molten sapphire. No one had ever looked at her like this in her life, with such open desire. It was like he wanted her, right there in the meadow. Mackenzie forgot how to breathe.

His voice broke the spell his eyes had on her and she sucked in a shuddering breath.

"You will come with me without complaint." He raised an eyebrow as if to dare her to run again.

She glared at him mutinously. He would probably just *love* an excuse to tie her to his horse. The man ignored her glare, and instead his eyes swept down her body as if he were appraising a horse. The look he gave her was beyond incredulous; in fact Mackenzie couldn't help the smile that tugged at her lips in response to the shock on his face.

"Where are your clothes? You canna be seen in this undressed state!"

It wasn't so much his question, but rather his tone, high-handed and arrogant, that got under her skin. "There's nothing wrong with my clothes!" Mackenzie snapped at him. "And just because some pushy Scotsman decides he doesn't approve of my outfit, which is by the way, perfectly normal for an American tourist, it doesn't mean that I will automatically change them!" she huffed. Her anger caused her to speak her thoughts without censoring them, forgetting that she was playing the part of *Isabella* Stewart who would be from this era, and who would be dressed in a gown, a modest gown.

The man simply shook his head and put her dagger in his waistband. Then he started to tow her towards the line of men and horses that waited in front of her carriage. Mackenzie stumbled along behind him because he still had both of her hands in one of his, and that hand was causing electric sparks to shoot up her arm. *Yep, I'm definitely dreaming*, Mackenzie thought. *There's no way some random hot guy is going to show up in the middle of nowhere to kidnap me and drag me off to his castle and…and then what? I don't even know who this guy is!*

"Who are you?" Mackenzie's question caused him to break stride long enough to look down at her with suspicion, but seeing only curiosity in her eyes, he answered.

"I'd be Connor MacRae, Laird of Castle Eilean Donan, Earl of Kintail."

Eilean Donan? The same castle she had booked a room in? This was definitely a dream. It was too coincidental; the same man from the painting, the same castle, she must have fallen asleep or something. But wow, what a dream!

Connor seemed to be watching her face carefully. He must be wondering why she was smiling, little did he know…

"Now stop trying my patience and come."

Mackenzie didn't know what made her do it, whether it was his high-handed behavior, or the way his gaze seemed to unnerve her, but she dug in her heels and yanked her hands free. "And if I don't?"

Connor's eyes darkened a fraction and he warned her softly, "Then I would bind your hands and throw you over my shoulder." His answer irritated Mackenzie, there was no way this was a dream, she would never dream up some guy who would treat her like she was beneath him. She looked poised to run again, and Connor saw that.

"I'd just drag you back," his seductive voice made her even angrier. "Besides, lass," he said gently, "Where would you run? I know these woods inside and out, do you?" And as if to prove his point, he did throw her over his shoulder and quickly crossed to his men. Connor dropped her to the ground in a heap and glanced at one of his men. The man threw him a length of rope, and when Connor advanced on Mackenzie, rope in hand, she scrambled up and pleaded,

"No, no please, it's unnecessary. I won't try to run again. Please..." her voice broke. She knew now that she was definitely not dreaming. This was far too real, and far too scary.

"I have your word on that?" Connor stared into her eyes for a second longer than was necessary.

Mackenzie bit her lip and looked down at the ground, before she breathed out, "You're right; I have nowhere to run." As she said it, her anger fled and she realized just how true those words were. She hugged her arms around herself. If she was really in the 1700s, 200 years before her own time, then did it really matter who she was with? That thought made her so incredibly sad, that Connor must have seen something on her face.

His voice gentled when he replied, "Good. Now, come along. We have a long ride ahead of us."

Mackenzie's head whipped up at that. "A horse? I get to ride a *horse*?!" She'd loved riding as a kid, and she was excited to be on a horse again. It must have showed on her face because Connor was looking at her as if she were slow.

"Aye," he drawled out the word as if she were stupid. Of course, people here rode horses out of necessity, rather than out of sport like people of her time. But she didn't care, this was the first thing to happen today to make her happy, and she was grasping at it like a lifeline. It was something familiar and safe. Horses hadn't changed in 200 years, and she'd been good at riding. She'd even competed a bit in some barrel racing as a teenager. Mackenzie went straight to a huge black war horse, he was much bigger than her quarter horse had been, and approached him with her hands out, palms up so he could sniff her. She nuzzled his soft nose and cooed in his ears. She stopped short after agilely mounting the large black horse. All of the men had stopped to stare at her. Some of them stared aghast, others ogled, and she couldn't figure it out. Her confusion cleared as she realized that women of this time would have ridden sidesaddle, and in gowns that covered, well, everything that her outfit from the mall didn't. Her sheer tank top suddenly felt invisible. When Connor came up to her she bent down and asked,

"Should I ride sidesaddle?"

"Aye, lass you should, however, 'twill be easier if you stay astride. We have a long ride ahead of us, and we need to ride quickly. You'll also need to cover yourself." He handed her the grey cloak, and asked her if she had anything warm.

"A gown, in the carriage, I think," she trailed off as one of Connor's men was already walking toward the carriage. They followed his commands without his even having to speak them aloud. This man was powerful. That shouldn't have surprised Mackenzie, by now nothing should surprise Mackenzie, but nonetheless, it did.

As soon as she had fastened the cloak around her shoulders, Connor vaulted up behind her, his arm encircling her waist. Mackenzie stiffened and turned, her green eyes wide.

"I assure you, I am quite a capable rider! There is no need to for you to ride with me." She didn't want to tell him that she hadn't ridden in years, she knew he'd use it against her. Her shock was amusing to Connor, though, she could tell because he looked as if he were trying not to smile.

"You ride in carriages, I am not at all confident that your riding skills would be a match for my mount. Therefore I shall ride with you. Nor am I convinced that you would not try to run again. I doona relish the idea of chasing after you." He bent to whisper in her ear, "And I would chase you down, my Lady, doona forget that."

Mackenzie's eyes narrowed and she ignored the shiver his breath caused. "I gave you my word that I wouldn't try to run away again. I don't appreciate being called a liar." She also didn't like how in order to talk to him, she had to turn into his body and crane her neck to meet his eyes. For her taste, it was entirely too intimate.

Connor sighed and tried a different tactic: sarcasm. "My Lady, I am exceedingly sorry," his mock bow was not lost on Mackenzie, "but as you can plainly see, there are nay extra horses. Now, seeing that there are highwaymen about, I shall ride with you to guarantee your safe passage." The false sincerity was not lost on her either. So Mackenzie turned away and put as much distance between them as the saddle would allow. His smirk became more pronounced as she glared at him over her shoulder one last time before turning stiffly forward and straightening her spine for what was proving to be an uncomfortable ride.

* * * *

Mackenzie's bottom hurt from Connor dropping her rather unceremoniously on the ground earlier, and this hard ride didn't help either. She remembered saddles being more comfortable than this, but apparently feeling one's rear while riding was unimportant in this day and age. As she shifted in the saddle again, she brushed against Connor and felt that strange heat again. It was like nothing she'd ever felt before; like he ran a few degrees warmer than she did. She heard his swift intake of breath and assumed that he'd felt it too. Weird that she should feel such a magnetic pull towards this man who had actually just abducted her. It was too bad that she'd given up her dream theory, because this just seemed too much like a dream to pass as reality. A wry smile touched her lips as she thought that Jenna would be much more suited to this time-travel thing than she was.

Mackenzie glanced down as his arm brushed hers and she saw blood. Actually she saw quite a lot of blood. It took her a second to realize that he was bleeding because she actually *had* stabbed him earlier. She hadn't just grazed him as she'd initially thought, but rather gouged him. She felt awful, she hadn't been in a fight since the fifth grade when Meredith Baker stole her My Little Ponies lunch box. She peeked up at Connor from the corner of her eyes, and noticed that his face gave nothing away; no hint of pain, not even a reaction to the fact that he was bleeding. She thought he'd make an excellent poker player.

"I'm, uh," Mackenzie cleared her throat and tried again, "I'm sorry I stabbed you." Connor didn't do more than look down at her, then his eyes flicked back out toward wherever they were riding. She continued a little nervously, "I didn't mean to hurt, well, I guess I did mean to, er, well, you were attacking me after all, and I didn't know who you were, and umm…" She stopped babbling, and took a deep breath. "I *am* sorry," she said softly and as sincerely as she could.

"You defended yourself." This time he didn't even glance down at her.

Connor didn't say much, she'd decided, and when he did, it was usually sarcastic or cryptic. This was neither. Was there —dare she think it— a hint of admiration in his tone? *Figures*, she thought, *it was just like kindergarten: you punch a boy in the face, and he likes you.* Except Connor didn't like her, he just respected the fact that she hadn't been a helpless victim, she guessed.

"Does it hurt?"

Connor's eyes rolled up towards the dark sky, "You talk too much."

Mackenzie narrowed her eyes. *So that was how it was going to be? Fine, two could play at that game.* She straightened up and faced forward, trying to ignore all the havoc his proximity was wreaking on her already overloaded system. It was harder than she'd thought it would be since every movement of the horse brought their bodies into contact. They were riding at a hard gallop, and Mackenzie was tired from holding her muscles so stiffly in a vain effort to not touch Connor. Her whole body was exhausted from the entire ordeal. She had finally given up her dream theory for good. This was real. There was no doubt in her mind that it was real. If it were a dream, she and Connor would be in a sunny meadow with nothing but the sun and a nice breeze for their companions, not riding through the night with a dozen men as their escort. Sooner than she would have thought possible, her body sagged against Connor, and she fell asleep; her mind needing the protection of oblivion to sort through and accept all that had happened.

Chapter Four

Connor MacRae exhaled roughly as the tiresome woman in his arms fell asleep. She was leaning against his chieftain pin, so he gently rolled her head to the other side. He wore his usual *breacan feile* over a linen shirt, with trews beneath the belted plaid. He had an iron penannular brooch, open to one side, to fasten the plaid at his shoulder. Connor knew that it was the annular brooches that were worn now, and his wasn't in fashion, but what did he care for fashion? It had been in his family for several hundred years; the clan chieftain had always worn it. His *claidheamhmór* was slung across his back, and he had his bow on his massive *destrier*, just in case.

She shifted a little, and he could feel her rear pressing against him, her spine having relaxed from its rigid position to lean back into him. Her head fell right at his shoulder; she was not small, this one. Her head had lolled to settle against his throat. He could feel her even breathing against the skin of his neck. He'd never noticed anything as mundane as breathing about a woman before. Connor found himself noticing quite a bit about this spirited woman.

Dougal, his captain, had ridden up beside him, and cocked an eyebrow at the sleeping woman. Connor nodded his head. The silent conversation was merely Dougal asking if she was going to come willingly; he clearly thought the lass was daft. Not that Connor could blame his first, she hadn't behaved like any woman he'd ever known. He'd never been stabbed by a lass, nor had to chase one down for that matter. Of course, he'd never abducted a woman before, either.

When he and his men had attacked her carriage, all had gone according to plan. No one had been harmed. *Well*, he amended, *nothing that wouldn't heal*. No one had been seriously harmed. It had been easy. But Connor still felt that twinge of unease. Had it been *too* easy? Something didn't ring true about the simplicity of the abduction. His senses had been honed by years on the battlefield, and they had never let him down, so it was unusual for him to feel uneasy about a victory.

His attention was brought back to the girl in his arms as she shivered. Unthinkingly, he unraveled his plaid and wrapped it around the Stewart lass, for she must be cold with naught but a cloak on. She was practically naked underneath, he recalled. American, she'd said, and while Connor knew nothing of ladies' fashions, he was fairly certain that they wore gowns in America. She must have lost her gown, though he knew not how. He preferred a woman in a simple sark to the unusual and confining undergarments this woman wore. The thought of her in a sark had him thinking of how her body had felt when he'd landed on top of her. She was made of lush, soft curves, but he'd seen her legs wrapped around his horse, and he knew they were solid muscle. He'd also chased her, and he knew she was fast. He'd never been so surprised in his life as when the Stewart lass had stomped down on his foot and turned with her dagger.

And those eyes.

He hadn't missed the split-second hesitation that she'd had when their eyes connected. He had been able to read every emotion in her eyes as if they were spelled out on her forehead. They had been wide, frightened, and they were emerald green. He'd never seen green eyes so deep. Connor felt that he could stare for hours into her eyes and he would never understand her secrets. Oh he knew for certain she had them, for in that short moment when their eyes had met, he had seen her secrets. And he wanted to know them. Something else though, he had seen the flare of recognition in her eyes. Had they met?

He looked down at her as her head lolled against his shoulder, and he studied her face. She had beautiful alabaster skin; it seemed luminescent in the moonlight, which contrasted with the dark, thick lashes that swept her cheeks. She had fine bone structure, with a straight nose. Her chin was pointed, and her lips were a bit too full for her heart-shaped face, but those lips were so incredibly sultry that he doubted any man would think them unattractive. She sighed and a slight smile turned her lips up. Connor's thoughts drifted down an entirely different path as he watched them. There was no denying she was beautiful. Her reputation had not been exaggerated.

When her hair had come unbound while she'd been fleeing, and the moon had turned the golden locks to silver, he'd thought her a wood sprite or a faerie. The pale moonlight had her skin glowing like a luminous pearl. But she was no faerie, she was real. Her very real warm body had proved that. She was also betrothed to his enemy, the Campbell lord, and Connor would stop at nothing to ensure his demise. Even abducting the bride-to-be before she entered Campbell lands. She was a means to an end, nothing more. Connor would do well to remember that.

After he had launched himself at her, Connor wrapped his arms around her waist and pulled her to the ground. When he stayed on top of her he wanted her to feel his weight; to understand that the best way out would be acquiescence. And when he'd flipped her over, he'd merely run his hands over her to see if she had any more weapons hidden; ravishing her was the furthest thought from his mind…until she'd renewed her struggle. He'd suddenly become acutely aware of every voluptuous curve against his body. Those expressive eyes of hers had shown him that she thought his intentions impure, and his thoughts quickly followed along those lines. Impure thoughts around her would be natural, especially when her ragged breathing drew his attention to her breasts. Thinking of her breasts had him shifting farther away from her in the saddle, but she made a little sound of protest at his movement, and Connor frowned. With a sigh, he wrapped one arm around her waist and pulled her back against him. She fit into the curve of his body perfectly, and he rested his chin on her head.

The Stewart lass smelled delicious, mouthwatering, actually. He'd never smelled anything like it. It was decidedly floral, and every time the wind stirred strands of her hair into his face, Connor had to fight the urge to bury his nose in it. He thought of the reactions his body had to just her scent alone, and wondered what it would be like if he had the time and the right to enjoy her. The weight of her breasts on the arm he had wrapped around her ribs caused his body to tighten. He passed the time trying not to think of her, and thinking instead of not running his horse too hard with the extra weight. Connor frowned as he felt her ribcage. She really wasn't that much extra weight. His thoughts turned toward the girl again, and he had to force his mind to the job at hand; to take her to his castle, and keep her as far away from the Campbell as possible. He wasn't completely sure what the Campbell had planned for Miss Stewart, but he knew it would indeed irritate him to have Connor steal her away. The thought of the Campbell's irritation with Connor had a smile playing about his lips.

Besides, the Campbell only needed a bride at all because the brutal clan Mackenzie was pushing for a chief who was married; he would be a safer alliance for them if he had a woman and sons at home. They had been pushing for a marriage to a Mackenzie lass, so it had been quite a surprise when he'd announced his betrothal to the Stewart lass, however, since everyone knew about the curse, the Mackenzie allowed the soon-to-be alliance. There had been rumors of the Campbell playing at the dark arts, and Connor knew that the man would go to any lengths to destroy the MacRaes. A man such as that was deadly in his unpredictability. Who knew what he had planned for this unsuspecting girl? It was just sheer bad luck that she was the only direct descendant left in the Stewart line. He'd heard tales since he was a lad about how a Stewart lass would break the so-called curse. Really, it was quite ingenious of the Campbell to choose a Stewart to unify the clans; it was said if the Stewart Curse could be broken, the lands would once again be fruitful. Unfortunately for Connor, those lands had belonged to him.

Dawn was breaking as his attention shifted to the sleeping girl in his arms once more. He had spent the majority of the ride trying to ignore the way her soft body fit against his, and deny the uncharacteristic surge of lust he'd felt at every bump and jostle. At one point, her head had turned into his neck, and her lashes had fluttered against the skin of his throat. Connor swallowed hard, trying to tamp down the unreasonable flare of heat. Similar to his hyper-awareness of her breath coming and going, he noticed everything about her.

She stirred. He felt first her confusion, and then the dawn of understanding as she remembered where she was. It was natural that she should be afraid of him, he thought, after all, he had abducted her on the way to meet her betrothed. He almost wanted to laugh at the naked panic on her face as she glanced back at him. If she only knew that he was definitely the lesser of the two evils.

"Sorry, I didn't mean to fall asleep." She quietly cleared her throat.

"Where are we?"

Her voice was husky still from sleep, and very arousing. She hid the panic from her voice, but he knew that it would be there in her eyes. For some reason, it was important to him that she not think the worst of him; he wanted to assuage her fears about his abducting her. That worried him; Connor did not want the complication of caring what this chit thought of him.

"We'll dismount soon and break our fast. We should be there before the noon hour," he cautioned. And then he couldn't resist teasing her, "How did you sleep?"

She peered up at him through her thick lashes before answering, "Well. Thank you."

They rode in silence for another half hour before Connor spoke again, "We'll stop here." He glanced at his captain, Dougal, who rode to his left, and they all pulled off to the edge of the trees. Beyond that, there was clearing where one could see where the three lochs met: Loch Alsh, Loch Duich, and Loch Long, with his castle on the northwestern island. Connor looked down sharply as he both heard and felt her gasp. There was a look of sheer delight on her face, and his lips turned up as he followed her gaze. She was staring at the loch, and the mountains that surrounded it. It pleased him that she found his lands beautiful. But it shouldn't. Connor's smile fell as he reminded himself that his duty was to his clan. He didn't have time for distractions, and this Miss Stewart was unequivocally a distraction.

His voice was sharp as he told her, "Take a moment, Miss Stewart, tend to your needs, but be quick about it. Doona take too long, or I might think you've run off; I'd rather not chase you down."

Connor leaped down from his horse, and raised his hands to her waist to pull her down. He slipped the plaid from around her shoulders, wrapping it quickly around himself. Her scent was overpowering. If she noticed the internal battle, the way his hands wanted to stay against the smooth skin of her neck, she didn't show it. His hands lingered at her hips, but she broke the contact by storming off in a huff. *The lass has spirit*, Connor thought. *Verily, she'll need it.*

* * * *

Mackenzie felt so cozy and snug that she almost didn't want to open her eyes. But she did, and as she woke up her first thought was, *Wow, it really all was a dream, a really elaborate strange dream.* She sighed, at least she hadn't had her nightmare again. And then reality set in. She felt the very real horse beneath her, and the strong and very real arm around her waist. Definitely not a dream. There was a male hand resting on her thigh and holding the reins. That hand was burning through the wool of her cloak like a branding iron. The day before came rushing back; the castle tour, the first kidnapping, the second, Connor…Mackenzie turned to look at him and he was staring down at her. His lips twitched; he looked as if he was trying to keep from laughing at her. It was probably because he could feel her embarrassment at having fallen asleep in his arms. And one of those arms was wrapped around her, pulling her close against him, his hand splayed across her ribs. She could feel every single bump in the road, and she imagined he could feel her breasts with every one of those bumps. She had to break the silence.

"I'm sorry. I didn't mean to fall asleep." Nothing. "Where are we?"

Connor told her that they'd stop to eat soon, but she really didn't mind if they had to ride for a while longer, she was really quite cozy. *Woah, wait, what?* Her thoughts were slightly incoherent as she scrambled to figure out where that traitor thought had come from. Just because she found him attractive didn't change the fact that he had kidnapped her, and he still hadn't told her why. What was it he wanted from her? Connor interrupted her scattered thoughts by asking how she had slept. Was he messing with her? He was! He'd smothered a smile, and that man knew, he *knew* how she had felt waking up curved so snugly into his body. She feigned indifference and answered him that she had slept well.

Mackenzie intended to ignore him, but after about thirty minutes, she saw a break in the trees and was stunned by the beauty of the lake. It was bordered by thick trees and jagged, snow-capped mountains. Farther out Mackenzie saw a beautiful ethereal sight; a tall grey and white stone castle surrounded by mists. It was hard to distinguish any details of the castle, the fog was too thick. She gasped audibly at the staggering beauty of it all. Being raised in the desert, this was unlike anything Mackenzie had ever experienced. The air smelled clean, and crisp, so unlike the dry, smoggy air back home. She had always found the desert beautiful, in its own way, but the lush greens of the Scottish Highlands were undeniably breathtaking. There were three lakes that met at a small island and it reminded her of where she'd spent her first night.

The landscape was unspoiled by modern, well, by modern *anything*. It was magical. There was no other way to describe the view of this lake: it was magical. And Mackenzie no longer doubted the existence of magic in the world; not just the Lance Burton or Siegfried and Roy type of magic, but the real thing. She had no clue what other fairy magic existed, but her mind was now wide open after everything that she had recently been through.

Mackenzie noticed that during the night the previously warm air had dropped in temperature considerably. Grateful for the wool cloak, she pulled it closer to her neck, only to have it whisked out of her grip. Looking down at Connor, who had just dismounted, she watched him intricately twist his plaid over his shirt and leather pants. It hadn't been the cloak at all keeping her from freezing, but this rough Highland warrior had tucked her into his plaid so she wouldn't get cold. Strangely thoughtful of her kidnapper.

And she felt it down into her bones as his hands had brushed her neck before tugging off the plaid.

After being unnecessarily warned by Connor not to go too far, Mackenzie wandered to the meadow to look around. She dropped the cloak at the edge of the water, and washed her face and arms. The cold water felt refreshing to her overheated skin. She walked along the edge of the lake and marveled at the way the fog danced across the water, and idly wondered if the Loch Ness Monster swam in these waters. Mackenzie sighed as she pushed her hair behind her ear before the wind whipped it around her face. She had spent so long carefully straightening her curls out the day before, and she'd used her flat iron to flip out the ends. It seemed so silly now, here, in this place. It made her realize how so many of her day-to-day troubles were rather insignificant when compared to the grandeur of this land. Another gust of icy wind made her shiver as it lifted her blonde strands off her neck and swirled them around her face. Her white camisole fluttered around her, and she thought that Bermudas and a tank top seemed so normal for her, and in just seconds of looking into Connor's eyes last night, she'd felt naked. It was funny how that worked.

Her reverie was interrupted as a tall shadow appeared next to her. Connor, of course. He was well above six feet tall, at least 6'4" and strong. Very strong. He had lifted Mackenzie off the horse as if she weighed nothing, and his large hands spanning her waist had made her feel small and dainty. She was 5'9" neither small nor short, and yet Connor easily made her feel tiny. She glanced up at him and could see his ancestors' Norse influences in his high cheekbones and blue eyes. The dark hair should have looked out of place with eyes so bright, but it fit him. It added a rugged quality to this handsome man who exuded sexuality. But there was no doubt in her mind about what he was. He was dangerous.

"Are you ready?" he passed her a canteen of water, no, Mackenzie mentally corrected herself, a bladder, probably sheep…eewww…oh well, she was pretty thirsty. She held it bravely to her lips and drank deeply. Then she sighed, well it wasn't her usual brand of bottled water, but it worked.

"Thank you." She handed it back to Connor, noting the way he was staring at her mouth. Did she have something on her face? She nervously darted her tongue out to moisten her lips, and she watched Connor's eyes follow the movement. He gave nothing away though, his face was masked as if through years of keeping everything inside himself. She briefly wondered what it would be like if Connor were to look at her without his guard up; if he caused this much havoc to her senses with his unfathomable gazes, how would she withstand a straight dose?

"Come along, Miss Stewart. We must ride." He put his hand on her wrist to pull her along.

"Where are we going?" The searing heat from his hand made her question less of a demand and more breathless than she liked. She frowned. It seemed a bad habit she was picking up just by being near him. Perhaps he'd put it off to the fact that she was trotting to keep up with him.

She could tell that Connor didn't like to have his commands questioned. He raised an eyebrow at her and placing both hands on her shoulders, spun her around to face the lake. He pointed.

"There." Monosyllabic, typical.

Mackenzie followed his arm. The heavy fog rolled away from the castle she'd been looking at. *Typical, even the elements follow his commands* Mackenzie grumbled to herself. Her grumbling was cut short by the mythical sight before her. She gasped. A whitewashed castle stood prominently on an island jutting out into the water. The gray waters danced beneath the mist, and the medieval castle slipped out of sight behind the rolling fog. The glimpse she'd caught earlier through the fog had nothing on the beauty of a clear view.

"We're going to a castle? Wow, is that *your* castle?"

She didn't want to admit it, but she was impressed. She never really knew what to expect from Connor; he kept surprising her. The castle looked exactly like the one she'd been staying in just the day before. Had it really just been yesterday? Mackenzie shook her head a little, still a bit dazed. This time there wasn't any accompanying nausea with the thought of where, and more precisely, *when* she was. She didn't know if that was good or not, that she was getting used to the idea that it was the 1700s. Perhaps it had something to do with his lairdship's blue eyes? He didn't answer her, and she didn't like the silence, it made her uncomfortable. Perhaps that was why she felt the need to ask him,

"Is this where you live?" Her hand encompassed the whole area; lake, forests, and mountains. It suited him. He hadn't answered her, so she turned to him, "It's so beautiful."

He stared at her for a long time before he answered her, "Aye."

Monosyllabic again. Great. She was annoyed, she was trying really hard here, he could at least make an effort to be civil. She tried again,

"Has it been in your family for very long?"

"For several generations, off and on. You are trying my patience Miss Stewart."

"Mackenzie," she answered automatically, a reflex to being called "Miss."

She'd been studying the lake, thinking, without really paying attention to the fact that Connor hadn't yet answered her, when the grip on her wrist tightened until she winced. Her eyes flew to his, confused, and she gasped. The black fury on his face had her trying to yank her hand free and step back. Her forehead creased in her confusion.

Connor growled at her, "Your name is Stewart, is it not?"

Still trying to free her wrist, "Ow. Connor, you're hurting me. Please…" she trailed off at the glare on his face.

"Your name, lass." He was still glowering at her, but at least his grip had loosened fractionally.

"Mackenzie Isabella Stewart. Why? What's the matter?" She was whispering now.

"Your given name is Mackenzie?" For a brief second she thought Connor looked confused, but she couldn't be sure; he hid his emotions well and his poker face was back.

"Yes." Her voice was stronger now, and impatience flashed in her green eyes. He hadn't said anything. Her chin tilted a fraction, and she challenged, "Is that a problem?"

She should know by now not to challenge him. His anger was palpable, and she knew he was dangerous. He'd noticed her irritation, of course. She realized that there probably wasn't much this Highlander would miss. Mackenzie didn't know too much about Scottish history, but she'd seen enough movies to know that Highlanders liked to fight. They'd fought to the death for their laws and principles during the Jacobite Risings, so she really shouldn't antagonize Connor. They reminded her of the Vikings they were descended from. He was a warrior. Perhaps he'd honed his skills at reading people on the battlefield?

"We have been at war with the clan Mackenzie for years." Whatever she expected, it wasn't his softly spoken answer. "They are a brutal people who care not for whom they hurt, or from whom they steal. We had been allies for a long time, but now, they are backed by your betrothed. Surely you are aware of this?" He raised a dark brow as if to dare her to deny it.

"Actually, no, I wasn't. I'm not from here, in case you can't tell, and my Scottish history is minimal." Mackenzie was furious at the assumption that she would approve of any violence or cruelty. "So please forgive me, my *Lord*, as I am not familiar with your little feud." Her sarcasm was not overlooked, which she would have noticed by the narrowing of his eyes, if she'd been looking. But she had yanked her wrist free and was stalking away. For a split-second, she remembered that she was supposed to use her middle name, and thought that perhaps his over-reaction might be the reason why, but she was interrupted by a long arm catching her about the waist and dragging her back to him. Her breath hitched as her breasts grazed his chest.

"You'd best guard your tongue, lass, or I'll be forced to help you do so." His threat was so soft and low that she almost missed the menacing tone.

Mackenzie was weary and annoyed, and the idea of being chastised for her lack of etiquette and knowledge had her at her breaking point. She had been asked to accept quite a bit on faith, and her mind was rebelling at the idea of being scolded for her understandable ignorance.

"Oh, right, and what'll you do, cut out my tongue? You need me and we both know it, so cut the bullshit, and tell me what your problem is?" She was breathing heavily after her tirade, and her breasts were pressed up against Connor's chest, making her aware of just how close they were. She tried to put some distance between them, but when she stepped back, Connor pulled her up to his eye level as if she weighed nothing! Mackenzie gasped in outrage… and something else…as he lifted her against his body.

"I warned you to control yourself."

Connor's anger was obvious in the fierceness of his kiss. When his lips slammed down on hers she gasped. It gave him the perfect chance to slip his tongue into her mouth. With one arm wrapped around her waist, crushing her up to him, and the other tangled in her hair, holding her still, it left his mouth free to ravish hers.

It was unnecessary, anyways, since she couldn't have broken free if she'd wanted to. She'd placed her hands on his chest to push him away, but he was immobile, a rock. And through his anger, there was something else, something, more… passion. That's what it was. Mackenzie felt the moment his kiss became more hungry than angry, because at that exact moment, she was kissing him back. A low burn started smoldering in her belly, and her hands slid up to his shoulders, and then crept behind his neck until she was clutching his hair as if by letting go she would lose her balance, when in reality it was Connor who was holding her up.

Once she'd weakened, it was obvious Connor felt it; his muscles bunched under her hands with restraint, as if he struggled with something. Then his head snapped up, and he stared down into her eyes for a moment. His eyes were clear. If he'd been as surprised by the heat behind their kiss as she, he didn't show it. If anything, it was the opposite; he was collected and slightly distant, where she was scattered and mussed.

"We'd be needin' to leave. Now." He released his hold on her waist, but gripped her wrist again, and she let him tow her behind.

Mackenzie didn't say anything in response; her mind was too busy trying to figure out his motives. She must have imagined the passion she'd felt in the kiss; Connor was just too cool. He'd even seemed annoyed that she had responded, well, *she* was annoyed by how she'd responded to that kiss. It hadn't even fazed *him*, and here she was, dazed, disoriented, and still thinking about it, over and over. That must have been his game all along. Mackenzie growled in irritation in her head. She hated arrogance. Connor was definitely arrogant. And he must have known how she would react to his kiss. He was attractive, no doubt, and he obviously knew his appeal to women. There was no way he was ignorant of the fact that he was incredibly hot, so he must think that if Mackenzie were attracted to him, she'd be more likely to follow his orders. It was the only reason that made sense. Well, Connor would see that she was not some schoolgirl who would cave at a mere kiss. Although to be fair, it had been more than a *mere* kiss. Her body had never actually melted into someone else like that before. But it was probably just the strain of the trip and the magical backdrop of the lake. She sighed. She was over-thinking everything.

When they reached his destrier, Mackenzie stepped ahead of Connor to mount his horse, rather than let his warm hands span her waist again. She had regrouped her scattered thoughts, and was firmly in control of herself once more. She was resolved that Connor would not get to her like that again; if he even kissed her again. Which he wouldn't. She wouldn't let him, besides he didn't think of her like that. But how *did* he think of her? And what exactly was it that he wanted from her? He had some questions to answer when they got to the castle. She folded her arms across her chest. And he would answer them.

After she had situated her cloak around her, now understanding that her legs were bared to these men and that she was riding astride, she knew how that must look to them, Connor leapt up behind her. One hand was on the reigns of his horse his arm brushing her waist, and the other was tucking her hair behind her ear. She felt his lips against her ear, and she couldn't repress the shiver that ran down her spine.

"Once we arrive at my keep, you will dress accordingly. I doona care how you dressed in America, but while here, you'll dress appropriately." His voice was so low she mostly felt his breath rather than heard his words, causing the hair on her arms to stand on end. But the implicit threat in his command got under her skin.

"And if I refuse? My clothes are perfectly fine." *Fine for the 21st century.*

"Doona test me, lass. Your state of undress is an invitation, and be careful someone doesna take you up on it." Connor trailed his fingers from where he was holding her hair back at her ear down her neck, sliding underneath her cloak, to her shoulder, slipping her spaghetti strap down as his fingers continued down her arm to settle at her waist. His light touch was a hot brand on her skin; she felt the heat through her clothes. His voice was husky as he breathed in her ear, "You are a beautiful woman, Mistress Stewart, and not many men have my honor or self-control in the face of what you so blatantly offer."

"Self-contro...huh!" Mackenzie huffed, and shrugged her strap back into place. She glared straight ahead and prepared to give him the silent treatment.

* * * *

When Connor had gone down to the loch to offer the Stewart lass some water, he'd been stunned by how her blonde hair was swirled about her face by no breeze he could sense. The dawning sun streaked the skies and her hair with golds, and yellows, and reds. The red in her hair was undetectable normally, but when the sun peeked out from behind a few clouds, her hair had been ablaze with the fiery colors. He'd been stunned by the ethereal beauty of this girl. As her filmy white shirt, something akin to a shortened sark, had lifted in the unfelt breeze, it showed a tantalizing glimpse of skin. Something glinted in her navel, but before he could see what, her shirt fell around her once more.

He was irritated with himself for being so distracted with her, but he knew she must be thirsty. Connor stepped up next to her and handed her the water. When she drank, his eyes never left her lips. He was imagining what those lips would feel like on his, and what they could do. Dangerous thoughts. He almost groaned aloud as her tongue flicked out to catch any drops left on her incredibly sensual lips.

He grasped her wrist and told her that it was time to leave. He should have known she'd be defiant. She did nothing that a proper lady should. And he did not like having his commands questioned. So when she questioned him as to their destination, he spun her back towards the loch, and pointed at his home. She didn't turn when she asked him if that was where he lived, and he wondered what he would see in her eyes. She turned toward him then, and he realized that he hadn't answered her. She stared up at him, a little nervously, he thought, when she said his land was beautiful. But on the last word, *beautiful*, she sounded wistful. What did *that* mean? So when Connor finally answered her, he was more abrupt that he'd meant to be, but she was not what he had expected. He'd thought she would be a spoiled, simpering, silly girl. Instead she was intriguing, headstrong, and brave. But when he'd heard her correct his use of her name to *Mackenzie*, his temper had flared. If she were related to the thieving, murdering clan Mackenzie, well he would make sure she would be sorry for that lie.

Her little tantrum had eaten away at his unusually firm resolve. He had never encountered anyone who was so maddening in his entire life. His "little feud" as she'd so dismissively called it, had eaten away at his men's spirits, and crops and livestock for two years now. Even now, as he and the Mackenzie were at a tentative peace, he'd known that something was being planned to out maneuver him. But he'd gotten Campbell's betrothed. It had been so simple. His informant had been accurate with the information of when and where they would find the girl. He had been unsure as to why there hadn't been an escort with her; thought that it might have been a trap, however, all went smoothly.

Connor knew there would be repercussions, but the question was how soon?

She definitely evoked emotions he didn't want to admit he felt, and didn't understand why; frustration, an urge to protect, an urge to crush her to him, the urge to wring her neck when she questioned his authority….

Her emerald green eyes were so easy to read; she would be an awful liar. Connor frowned as he thought *Either that or she was a very good actress.*

He'd given in to the temptation he'd been fighting since he'd first dragged her against his body the night before.

He kissed her.

It had been meant as a warning, but when Mackenzie wound her arms around his neck and responded so passionately, it surprised him. Her sweet scent floated around him, making him want to take her right there. But Connor forced himself to remember that she was strictly a bargaining chip with his enemy, and could only ever be that. So he forced his expression cool and aloof as he broke the kiss. Her pupils were dilated, her green eyes darkened with passion, and her face was flushed from the rush of blood to her cheeks. He wanted to run his thumb across her swollen lips; he felt disgust at himself that he had been so rough that he'd bruised her lips. She looked so soft and fragile, with her fair skin; she brought out protective instincts in him. Looks were deceiving, though, as remembered her initial reaction to being abducted. Instead of touching her lips as he wanted to do, once more, he picked up her wrist and pulled her towards his charger. When Mackenzie had gracefully mounted the horse without waiting for his help, he couldn't hide his amusement, and his lips twitched upward. But he'd noticed when Mackenzie stiffened as he vaulted up behind her.

She wasn't as immune as she'd like to pretend.

Connor couldn't resist; her scent pulled him in and he wanted so badly to bury his face in her neck and hair. Instead, he swept her hair back away from her ear, and put his lips close to remind her that upon arrival at his keep, she would dress according to custom. His lips brushed the skin of her ear as he spoke, and while he delighted in the response from her, his own response shocked him. Connor forced his attention to what she had said.

"And if I refuse?" Mackenzie raised a delicate eyebrow. This aggravating lass dared where most men feared to tread.

At her petulant refusal, Connor reminded her of what happened to women who wandered around nearly naked. Connor ran his fingers down her neck, and slipped her strap down off her shoulder, but he couldn't resist her silky skin, and his hands trailed down her arm. The pink flush that followed where his fingers brushed pleased him more than it should; she was not indifferent to his touch. So he continued down her arm until his hand rested on her waist.

Most men would take what she put on display without hesitating, but Connor was not most men. He was controlled. He was a chief, the leader of his clan. He could not afford to take what she offered; no distractions. However, he could not control the reaction his body had every time Mackenzie shifted in the saddle. With her bold tongue and expressive eyes, she was unlike any woman he had known before. It would be a long ride home. Connor warned her that someone would take her up on her offer; he'd offended her if he was reading her reactions correctly. What he was really thinking was that he would be the man to accept that invitation. The thought of another man touching her made him curiously angry; he felt strangely protective of her. She was momentarily saved from the Campbell, and Connor *would* protect her, but now the question was would she need protection from him?

Chapter Five

Mackenzie's eyes were the size of saucers as she took in the castle. It looked so similar to the castle she and Jenna were staying in. Could it be the same castle? It looked the same, just smaller, somehow. The more she studied the castle, the more she realized that it was too similar to be coincidence. Of course, she thought wryly, nothing was coincidence anymore. It didn't have the renovations that took place after the first World War, but she was certain that this was the same castle where she'd spent her first night in Scotland, except that would be 200 years from now.

"Connor, what did you say the name of your castle is?" she said faintly, shock winning as the dominant emotion.

"'Tis the Castle Eilean Donan." There was pride in his voice, and it was understandable; he was the lord of a castle. "This is the Isle Donan. On a clear day ye can see to the Isle of Skye, the stronghold of the clan MacLeod."

"That's what I thought." Mackenzie whispered. The reality of the fantasy was closing down on her. The feeling only intensified as they rode into the courtyard. Everyone who was there stopped and stared. Some cheered as they saw their lord, but most were silent when they saw her, staring with open curiosity. She unknowingly cringed back into Connor's chest at the blatant hate coming from some. Connor murmured something soft and low in her ear, something soothing, she imagined, but she couldn't understand it. All of her original feelings from the day before came back with a vengeance. Mackenzie felt very trapped and very alone.

A young boy of maybe thirteen or fourteen came up to them as Connor reined his horse in. He dismounted and reached for Mackenzie. This time she let him help her down, and she didn't complain when he took her hand. Mackenzie was sure that her face showed her apprehension, and hoped that the fear was hidden, but mostly she just prayed that she wouldn't throw up. One woman was glaring daggers at Mackenzie and when Mackenzie met her glare with very wide eyes, the woman turned on her heel and stalked off. The only reason Mackenzie could think of for the blatant hostility was because of her engagement to the Campbell. Maybe it was something else, but she just didn't have the time or energy to expend on thinking of more than keeping her feet moving. With her free hand she clutched the cloak to her throat, and let Connor drag her by the other hand. Her breathing had accelerated so much that in order to keep from hyperventilating, she was matching each breath she took with Connor's. Nonetheless, she was dizzy.

Above the barred and studded door, something was inscribed in Gaelic. Mackenzie idly wondered what it meant. When they reached the door to the castle, someone opened it for Connor and said, "My Laird" as they passed. *Laird*? Mackenzie vaguely thought that must be his title, and she filed it away for later. For now, though, she just looked around with wide, slightly unfocused eyes. She noticed that they were in a large room with tables and chairs...the Banqueting Hall? Connor just towed her toward a stairway. He must have noticed her quiet apprehension, because he stopped at the bottom of the stairs, and asked her if she was feeling well.

"Fine," Mackenzie just stared up the stairs, feeling a dizzying sense of déjà vu from her castle tour the other day. She'd really thought she was over the feelings of hysteria from crossing time, but seeing the castle that she'd slept in a day ago as it looked now, well....

"You look ill. I'll have a bath sent up once you are settled in your bedchamber."

He sounded worried about her. She looked ill? She felt ill. That couldn't possibly be from the fact that she was now in the same castle she'd just visited, only it was just much newer, or that she had, gulp, time-traveled? The nausea came back. Mackenzie just nodded weakly and let Connor lead her up the stairs, and followed him to a hallway where there was yet another set of stairs leading up into the tower. *Perfect*, she thought, *of course it would be the tower*. Connor took her up three flights of stairs until the narrow spiral staircase opened up into a much larger and more open hallway. Connor took her to a wooden door in the middle of the hall, and its twin was about two feet away. He opened her door for her and released her hand.

"These will be your chambers, Miss Stewart."

"Thank you." It sounded stiff and strangled to her own ears—who knew what Connor heard.

"Are you all right?" This time she looked at him; he was peering at her as if she were insane. He was probably wondering if she were mentally competent. She didn't feel like going into it with him, so she lied.

"Fine."

Mackenzie could see that he didn't believe her, but he probably didn't care enough to press the issue. So she walked into what was now her room. She looked around and walked into the middle of the room, not seeing anything, just wanting Connor to leave so she could go to pieces alone, and wallow a bit in her misery. When she heard the door shut, she assumed Connor had left, and needing something familiar, she tore off the cloak and threw it across the bed. Her own clothes helped lift her spirits a bit. She stepped out of her Nikes, and turned to explore the room, only to almost turn right into Connor. She gasped and stepped back. He caught her elbow to steady her, smiling wryly at her surprise.

She'd expected Connor to leave her, but there he stood holding the grey gown that she had been given in the carriage. He laid it on the bed, and told her that he would have a bath sent up, and to be dressed *appropriately* afterwards. She didn't miss the emphasis on how she should dress. He would be back in an hour and then they would go down to dinner. Connor paused at the door, and repeated,

"One hour, Miss Stewart, doona make me wait."

This time, Mackenzie waited for him to leave before sagging to the bed in relief at finally being alone. But it was not to be. A knock sounded and before Mackenzie could stand up, a young woman with red hair and her arms full of what looked like a corset walked in.

"My Lady."

"Hello," Mackenzie was wary; so far no one had looked upon her with any form of kindness or sympathy.

"I am Bronwyn, and the laird said ye'd be wantin' a bath?"

At Mackenzie's hesitant nod, the girl called Bronwyn rushed out, and then back in followed by several servants, two of whom had a tub between them. The rest of them hauled buckets of water in until the tub was full. Mackenzie felt a little sympathy for them thinking that it must be quite a lousy job to haul buckets of water up three flights of stairs, quickly followed by a twinge of guilt, realizing that she was the reason they had carried the heavy buckets of water. But the tub was full and it smelled really inviting; like a spa she'd been to once, with essential oils and scented candles. Bronwyn tsked here and there as she first took in Mackenzie's outfit, and then helped undress her. Mackenzie wryly remembered that she was practically naked to the girl. Then Bronwyn helped her into the tub and immediately began scrubbing her and pouring water over her hair. When she was immersed in the water and smelled of lavender, Bronwyn started a fire in the large fireplace, then turned to Mackenzie,

"I'll just fetch ye some wine."

"Thank you," Mackenzie said quietly, wondering if she should really drink while she was here. Her already swimming head probably didn't need any outside help.

"My Lady." At that, Bronwyn nodded and bustled out the door.

Mackenzie hopped out of the bath, feeling slightly embarrassed that she had just been washed by someone else. So she dried quickly and dressed in her own clothes to await Bronwyn's return.

She sat on the bed, finger-combing her wet hair and looked around. There was a large trunk by the far wall, and a door next to that. A large oval mirror stood in the corner; it reminded Mackenzie of an antique her grandmother had kept in the guest bedroom. This one was probably new, she half-smiled at the thought. There were two chairs set in front of the fireplace, and the huge bed she sat on with a bedside table to the right of it. In between the fireplace and the wall the bed was on was a tall arched window with a window seat.

Mackenzie walked to the fireplace and shook her hair out towards the welcoming warmth. Her hair would be unruly curls without her trusty blow dryer and flat iron. Ugh. She'd always hated her curls; in the desert, it was so dry that they never curled right, and her hair was so heavy it weighed down the ringlets so they just looked funny. To her anyways. Jenna had always loved to play with her hair. But Jenna was a hair stylist, so she always made Mackenzie's hair look fabulous. Besides, Jenna had straight hair, she'd never understand.

She glanced toward the dress and the corset-looking undergarments with dread. Hopefully Bronwyn would help her get dressed when she returned. There were a lot of ruffles, she'd seen wedding dresses with less ruffles. But ever brave, Mackenzie wandered toward the bed and picked up the dress, then froze. *Yes!* Her purse had been salvaged along with the dress! *Lip gloss here I come!* Mackenzie grabbed her purse and dug through it til she found her compact. She opened it and reached for her lip gloss. She stuck her tongue out at her naked face, and sighed, wishing for mascara—she loved mascara; she would miss mascara. Her sigh turned into an exclamation of joy as she saw her cell phone. Then she immediately felt like an idiot; of course there was no service. *Besides, who would I call?* she thought, her lips twisting into a grimace, *Merlin?*

The knock at the door barely captured her attention as she tossed her purse on a chair, not sure she wanted anyone to discover it yet, and resumed trying to scrunch her curls by the fire. They'd be a tangled mess if left to dry on their own. She'd thought it would be Bronwyn, back with the wine, to help her into the pile of clothes on the bed. She was wrong.

"Why are you not dressed?" Connor's demand had Mackenzie jumping and turning wide, startled eyes to him.

The anger emanating off him was palpable, but rather than being afraid, his high-handed manner infuriated her. Fury was good, it distracted her mind from the uncomfortable emotions that were surfacing at his freshly-shaved-looking-hot-in-a-kilt-self. And he must have bathed as well, because he smelled amazing. He smelled clean; of soap and man, and something else. Something spicy and exotic. She tore her mind from his scent and focused on the black glare he was directing at her. She knew he didn't like to be disobeyed, but this wasn't something she could help. It wasn't her fault that she didn't know how to put all those clothes on. She bit her lip, thinking that while he may not like to be disobeyed, *she* didn't like to be bossed around, especially not by some 18th century highland laird.

So instead of telling Connor that she'd just been waiting on Bronwyn to help her get ready, Mackenzie got annoyed…and bold.

"I'm not going." Chin tipping defiantly, she crossed her arms across her chest. She knew she was being stubborn, but she didn't really care.

"You're damn well going down to dinner."

"No." It sounded petulant even to her own ears. His eyes narrowed.

"You'll come to dinner, and you'll do it dressed properly, or you'll dine alone with me and ye won't be dressed at all."

"You wouldn't," Mackenzie dared.

His voice was flat as he said, "Try me lass," but he injected a leer into it when he followed with, "I'd enjoy stripping you of your garments."

The memory of his hands sliding her strap off of her shoulder earlier was still fresh in her head, and she did not doubt he would do as he threatened. So Mackenzie glared at him and snapped, "Fine." She stalked to the bed and lifted the gown off the bed and looked at the long white nightgown-looking thing with ruffles on the sleeves and at the neck, thinking that it might not be too hard for her to dress herself. But Connor still stood in front of her door, arms crossed and feet planted. Mackenzie stared at him expecting him to leave, or at least turn around, or *something*, but he looked immovable as a statue. She raised her eyebrows and looked at him expectantly, waiting; she refrained from tapping her foot. But his eyes dared her right back. Her eyebrows snapped down in confusion, and then back up as her eyes widened and she grasped his dare.

Fine she thought, and pursed her lips. *Enjoy the show*.

Mackenzie slowly unzipped her shorts and stepped out of them. Her shirt slipped over her head, and she stood in her sheer white lace bra and matching bikinis. By modern standards, it wasn't that sexy, if anything it was boring in comparison to Jenna's collection. But he stiffened and she felt slightly braver. She heard his swift intake of breath and never letting her eyes drop, even as she felt the heat creep up her cheeks, she unclasped her bra, and tossed it on the floor with her shorts and shirt. Mackenzie figured she might as well go for broke, took a deep breath and slipped out of her panties.

So she stood there naked, daring Connor to look away from her eyes, to look down. And he did. Boy did he ever. Every inch of her naked body felt touched by the heat of his gaze, as if it were his hands on her skin instead of his eyes. Those blue eyes lingered on her belly ring, and when they dropped lower, his eyebrows shot up. She thought it might be because she had recently waxed, but couldn't be sure. Yet he never said anything, his eyes just continued down. Then once his eyes had finished their appraisal of her figure and were locked back on hers, he looked smug the jerk, she lifted the nightgown-looking garment up over her head, and tied the ribbons at her breasts in a bow. It fit snugly, emphasizing the curves it didn't hide. Covered in a modest, but sheer shift, Mackenzie felt only slightly better as she looked at the rest of what she would wear. Did the gown go on first, or the stays? And how on earth would she ever lace herself up? Mackenzie bit her lip and ventured a peek at Connor from the corner of her eyes. He was smirking at her, and much as it rankled, she didn't have a choice; she'd have to ask him for help.

"Umm…what goes next?" her hand encompassed the clothes on the bed.

His smirk became more pronounced, "Are you asking for my help?" He was making fun of her.

"I, uh, no. Of course not! I only meant that perhaps you could send Bronwyn back in. She was supposed to help me get dressed…" Mackenzie stammered out her excuse, but lost steam at the look in his eyes. He looked like he was trying not to laugh. He'd reached her in two strides.

"But I'm already here." His voice was like velvet.

Connor had spoken softly, practically purred, but Mackenzie still heard the implicit threat…or was it a promise? *Damn that man's sultry voice!* She shuddered as he lifted the stays to her body, his fingers brushing her collarbones. He gripped her shoulders, turning her to face away from him, and began to tighten them. The first tug of the strings brought her back hard against him. Her eyes were wide as she turned her head to look up at him.

"Hold the bedpost." Connor was definitely amused.

Mackenzie turned and put both hands on the bedpost, bracing herself for the next pull. He was finished quickly, although his hands lingered at the small of her back. Mackenzie pressed her hands to her ribs, just under her breasts. Every breath was much shallower than usual, since she was strapped into this corset thing. However, it wasn't as tight or uncomfortable as she'd thought it would be. It was just really stiff. Connor lifted the grey gown above her head while Mackenzie brought her arms through the sleeves, and he let the gown settle around her until it fell to the floor, brushing the tops of her feet. The laces on this gown were in the front, but Connor's hands were on them before Mackenzie could lift hers. He tied them at her breasts, and when he tucked the ties into the gown, his large hands brushed the tops of her breasts. The shiver of excitement that ran up her spine was echoed in Connor's eyes.

Mackenzie stood perfectly still like that, with his hands at her breasts, but not actually touching her. They were both frozen for a few seconds before Connor's head descended slowly to hers, his lips briefly brushing hers. The kiss was so soft, that if it weren't for the unmistakable heat, Mackenzie wouldn't have been completely certain that his lips had touched hers. Her lashes fluttered as her eyes opened and focused on Connor's face. Her breath caught in her lungs as all the amusement faded from his eyes. He looked at her hungrily as if she were a sweet to be devoured. As if he could mold her will to his own with that look. As if she would let the heavy drowsy feeling coming over her take charge. The naked desire caused her legs to turn to jelly. She swayed toward him and he caught her lips in a fierce kiss that crushed her body to his, and his lips to hers.

The spark that had been smoldering for the past day was igniting in slow burns wherever Connor touched her. His lips were unmercifully possessive, as they staked his undeniable claim without her permission to do so. This feeling was unlike anything she had ever experienced; Mackenzie had never wanted a man this much in her life. And the heat…the burn was not uncomfortable, it had the opposite effect. Mackenzie wanted more; she wanted to burn. She was amazed by how one kiss from this man had her knees giving out. As if he sensed it, or maybe he just knew his affect on women, his arm was around her waist, both supporting her and dragging her up to her toes. Her lush curves were pressed up against his hard unyielding body, and yet it wasn't close enough for her. Mackenzie pressed herself closer still, and it wasn't until Connor's fingers were on the laces he'd just tied, that reality came rushing back to her.

"Wait!" she exclaimed wide-eyed and tore her lips from his.

Connor stared into her eyes for a moment, before deciding what he saw there was encouragement enough. His lips brushed hers, his tongue traced her lips.

She stepped out of his embrace and pressed her hand to her lips, her breathing ragged. Connor stepped with her though, and gently pulled her hand from her mouth. Before he tugged her back into his arms, Mackenzie vaguely realized that his flawless control had slipped. This time his kiss was more demanding, more insistent. His lips were harder, bold and possessive, claiming her. She was right; he was losing control. While a part of her was thrilled that she was the cause of his loss of self-control, another part of her still couldn't shake the fact that he was her captor for all intents and purposes.

"Please don't," she said softly against his mouth, brushing his lips with each word.

As Connor pulled back, slowly, she could hear his uneven breathing, and once more reveled at being the cause. He felt this sizzling desire as much as she did. Although the distance he put between them was minimal, it was enough for Mackenzie's swimming head to regain reason.

"Why not? You want me." He stated, rather than asked.

"No," her response was tremulous, and not at all convincing.

"I doona believe you." His head descended once more.

"Please?" Mackenzie whispered desperately, and closed her eyes. When he paused, she opened them slowly, warily, and asked him, "What do you want from me?"

Connor stared into her eyes for a long moment, as if he were looking for the answer to some unknown question. His hands were still around her waist, and she felt his fingers tighten, gripping until they dug into her flesh. Finally, he spoke.

"You are engaged to the Campbell."

"Y-es," Mackenzie drew it out slowly, trying to see where his line of questioning was heading. Connor wasn't asking, he had stated, once again. "But you know that." Mackenzie was confused by this. What was he getting at?

"Do you know much about your betrothed?" Bitterness had twisted his features and his hands dropped from Mackenzie's waist.

"Like what?" Mackenzie narrowed her eyes, trying to understand his sudden change, wondering what he expected from her.

"Perhaps how he has burned my lands and raped our women when he canna best my men? Only a coward uses women to get to a man." His disgust was evident, as he continued on about the flaws of her intended. "Or how he only wants to marry you to unite with the neighboring Mackenzie clan? If he were backed by the Mackenzie, he would be nigh unstoppable. He uses what and who he can for his own designs. He is a cruel man, Miss Stewart, you'd do well to nae forget that. And for the good of my clan, I canna allow either union."

"So you kidnapped me to keep me from marrying Campbell." Connor's silence encouraged her, "But I don't understand why that would matter to him? Why *I* would matter to him? We've never even met. Plus, I'm not a Mackenzie, per se, I'm a Stewart. So why does marriage to me get him the support of the Mackenzie tribe? And even if all that you say is true, then won't he come after me, you know, try to steal me back?" Mackenzie realized that she had asked several questions, and paused, to see how he would reply.

"The Campbell is a proud man, and he will retaliate. When I abducted you, it was an insult to his *honor*," Connor sneered the word, curling his upper lip slightly. She guessed he didn't think the man too honorable. "You matter because you are his, and I've taken you from him."

"I am not *his*…What am I, a chair? I am not a piece of property!" Mackenzie fumed. She stalked to the fireplace and stared at the fire.

"Aye, you are, or at least you will be his upon marriage." Connor's tone was unapologetic. "In accord with your father, you will marry the Campbell. And you being a woman, will do as your father commands. Women are supposed to do as they are told. Do you ever to as you are told? I wonder if in rearing you abroad, your father made a mistake?"

Mackenzie glared at the fireplace, realizing that he was right, at least in his views on women's position in life. After a moment, she flipped her hair over her shoulder, running her fingers through it to further dry the damp curls. "This sucks! Stupid 18th century values, and lack of women's rights!" she muttered to the fireplace.

She whirled on Connor with a fierce light in her eyes, "You know, one day, women will have just as much a right to decide whom they marry as men do. And we'll be able to own property and vote and work and have a say in our own lives!" Was she allowed to tell Connor her secret? She figured probably not, and kept the rest of her feminist thoughts to herself.

Connor seemed amused by her little tirade, if not confused. "Well, until that day comes, you'll have to do as your father says. Who, if I am not mistaken, says you shall marry the Campbell. A marriage I canna allow to take place. As I have said, he is a cruel man, so perhaps you should thank me, for saving you from a fate worse than death, rather than stomping about the room." He was definitely amused.

"I was not stomping around the room." She pouted, then she smiled, "Well, maybe a little," and she chuckled. "I am sort of behaving like a child." And she giggled again. Then she sighed. "So, how much do you know about me?"

"Enough," he dismissed.

"So nothing, then?" she challenged.

"You are engaged to my enemy. 'Tis all I need ken." He said this so dismissively that Mackenzie bristled instantly.

"And that's all I am to you? A..a..a *pawn* to be used against him? That's so chauvinistic!!!" Her bitterness seeped through and she wasn't guarding her speech. "You know, there's a lot more to me than what you think you see. In my time…"

"What mean you, 'Your time?'" he interrupted.

"Nothing, never mind." Mackenzie suddenly felt the need to bite her tongue. "What of my travelling companions? What happened to them?"

Connor registered the subject change with a slight narrowing of his eyes, but let it go. "They were set free, of course. By now they should be back at the Campbell's keep. I assume they have reported of their failure to deliver you, and I assume the Campbell will no' be happy." He sounded smug.

"You assume a lot." Mackenzie muttered.

"You doubt me?" Connor sounded incredulous, as if anyone would dare doubt his word, let alone Mackenzie, a mere woman.

Mackenzie paused to gather her thoughts. "No, I just meant that you don't know for sure what has happened to them, so how can you be so certain that your little plan has worked?"

"And what do you think happened?" the sarcasm was heavy, with an implied *as if I care about your opinion* tacked on to the end.

"Well, what if they never made it back? Or what if this Campbell guy doesn't really care that his fiancée went missing? If you're hoping to pick a fight with him, am I really the way to do that? I mean, he's never even met me, for crying out loud. And I've heard the rumors; I'm supposed to be one of the most beautiful ladies at court. I'm pretty enough, but I'm no Helen of Troy."

"Doona underestimate your worth to him." Connor said this softly.

"What does that mean? How is he supposed to value someone he has never seen or met? You said before that you insulted his honor, but I still don't understand any of this. Is it because of the rumors? Because from what I've heard, I'm not exactly your average blushing bride; I've stood a man up at the altar, I'm too old, and I've romped around Europe for the last couple of years. Doesn't that 'de-value' me, so to speak?" She used her fingers to make air quotes, and the frustration was making her tone sharper than necessary, but Mackenzie didn't really care. None of this made any sense to her. And it was time someone explained this all to her. Now.

"It means, that for reasons known only to your father, he has made a devil's bargain with the Campbell to wed you by the end of the month. This will appease the Mackenzie clan, and your father is probably just happy you are still wed-able." Mackenzie folded her arms across her chest and glared, but otherwise ignored the jibe. "Now through that bargain, you are his, and I have stolen something of his. Were I in his place, I would retrieve what was rightfully mine, and seek justice against him."

"You mean vengeance."

He shrugged, "Whichever."

"So I could be ugly, but he wouldn't care, because you are both testosterone-fueled men who would rather fight it out, than resolve this peacefully, or let me choose what I would like to do?"

"And what is it that you would like to do, Mackenzie?"

It was the first time he'd called her by her given name, and the sound of her name rolling off his tongue sent chills through her. That smoldering fire in her belly flared at the seductive burr caressing her name. She noticed that he'd ignored her first question.

"I would like to know if I would matter to either one of you if I were an ugly old hag," she stubbornly refused to let it drop. She wanted to stamp her foot, but figured that it would be way too childish.

His smile was patronizing, as if he were speaking to a child. "Of course no'. Your appearance does not matter, your position does. Now answer *my* question; what would you like to do?"

Her eyes widened at the implication, but thought she wanted to look away, she held his gaze. "I would like to go eat." Mackenzie said it slowly, and he smothered a smile as she glared up at him.

"Then by all means, my Lady, let us go down to supper." And he chivalrously, if not a bit sarcastically, held his arm out for her.

Chapter Six

Dinner was a much larger event than Mackenzie expected. The whole clan was here, Connor had told her. It was an occasion; Connor had returned the victor. He had the Campbell's betrothed, and everyone was celebrating that. Mackenzie sat next to Connor, and on his other side was an empty seat. She idly wondered who it was saved for. He wasn't married, she was sure of that; he wouldn't have kissed her if he was married. Of course what did she know? Connor could have a wife and ten kids and she would never know, it's not like he confided in her. It didn't matter, though, because she was going to pretend to marry someone else, and then go back to her time (and reality). Hopefully. Right now, she wasn't really sure of anything. If Connor was right, and this Campbell guy came for her, would Connor give her up? Or would he fight to keep her? And then what? Mackenzie's imagination was getting away from her, she was imagining staying here with Connor. She knew he wanted her, but she also knew that was all he wanted, and for her it wasn't enough. He didn't really even like her, she thought. She knew that desire and lust were very different emotions from caring and affection. But that was a dangerous train of thought. So she let her eyes wander around the room.

The meal was in the Hall and it was set up with long tables and chairs. There were humongous oil paintings of men with swords, women in gowns, battles, which were spaced every few feet around the hall. She and Connor sat at a table raised up on a platform which reminded her of the seating arrangements at a wedding. They would be at the head table, with the other more important guests. And the whole clan was part of the audience. Mackenzie felt that audience was a good word, seeing as she felt like an actor in a very strange fantastical play.

Her musings were interrupted by the music. The loud wail of a bagpipe caught her attention, and she turned her head until she could see the piper. Being that Granny Mackenzie had always played her folk records whenever Mackenzie had visited, she was used to the sound of bagpipes…her brother however, couldn't abide the sound for the same reason; Granny always had Scottish music on. She sighed wistfully. How Granny would have loved to see this.

Connor was staring at her, and she hadn't noticed, until she looked at him.

"Are you enjoying yourself, lass?" He sounded as if he genuinely wanted to know. She put a smile on her face.

"Yes, thank you." She picked up her fork, noticing that someone—Connor?—had filled a plate for her. Some foods were recognizable, beef, potatoes, bread, others, not so much. Ever brave, Mackenzie tried one of everything on her plate.

"And the food's to your liking?"

"It's really good, thanks." Had she forgotten her manners? He was really staring at her. What was he waiting for? "What?"

"You seemed sad, a moment ago."

"Oh."

He pressed on. "What were you thinking about?"

She sighed again. This was still a sore topic. "My granny. She would have loved this. After she moved to America, she never got the chance to visit her home again. We were supposed to go together, but she died recently and we never got the chance. I was thinking that she would have appreciated the music better than I."

"You doona care for the pipes?" He sounded so astounded that she smiled.

"It's not that. It's just that she loved them."

He gave her a long look, that to her felt as if he could see straight to her soul. As she got more and more edgy, he stared harder and harder. *What? What did he want? What did he see?* But he turned back to the entertainment and she let out a long, unsteady breath.

Mackenzie was feeling very alone in a room otherwise full of people. She glanced shyly at some of the other tables in the Hall. Everyone was staring at her; it was a repeat of the earlier scene when she'd entered the courtyard that afternoon. Many stared with awe at Connor, and then when they'd look at her it would be with anger or hate or even disgust. The best she could figure on that aspect was that they were disgusted that she would agree to marry the Campbell. Maybe they all thought she wanted to marry him, or that she felt some loyalty to her fiancé. She half-smiled, *If only they knew*, she thought, *if only*. She glanced at Connor out of the corner of her eye to see he was staring at her too. Oh, that's right, she was smiling. He probably was wondering why. *Oh well, too bad for him*. That thought made her smile more widely. She liked thinking about all the ways she could tell him about where, or more precisely *when*, she was from. Mackenzie wished she had some cool piece of technology, like a laptop, or a TV that she could show him. His jaw would drop. She almost giggled at the thought of Connor's jaw hanging open as she showed him something like a movie, or a car. That line of thinking had her wishing she could tell him everything. She wanted Connor to know her. Was that against the rules? She'd never really gotten the whole story from Morvern or Gregor. How was she supposed to act now? They obviously hadn't *foreseen* this situation. She sighed. Oh well, she'd just have to play it by ear.

****

She walked in silence with Connor to her room, and at her door, she turned on him, "You don't need to walk me to my room; I've already told you that I'm not going to run away."

"I still feel better knowing that you are safe in your chamber." He barely glanced down at her as he said this.

She figured that this would be all she would get from him tonight, and sighed before opening her door. His hand caught her elbow before she'd taken a step, and turned her to face him. There it was; that heat that she always felt around him. Her arm felt scalded.

"Are you unhappy here?" His eyes were searching hers.

Mackenzie gaped at him for a moment before she found her voice, "Does it matter?" His question had caught her off guard and made her tone sharper than she'd meant.

"I'd rather you weren't unhappy."

"Why? What does it matter? You've made your stupid, barbaric intentions clear; you need me to start a fight. So I'm your prisoner. Until I get to go home, I'm a prisoner." She shrugged his hand off and turned once again to walk into her room.

"And where is home, Mackenzie? With your betrothed, the Campbell?" It was said so sardonically and condescendingly, that Mackenzie wanted to cry. As it was, she felt the pressure build behind her eyes, and the sharp sting of tears just waiting to sneak out.

"No," she turned slowly and looked at him, deciding how much to tell him; she already felt she'd told him too much. "I meant America. My home is in America." She wondered what he was thinking.

"But your father has sent you to marry the Campbell, America is no longer your home." He wasn't trying to be cruel, but Mackenzie suddenly felt the moisture in her eyes threatening to overflow.

"You're right. I guess I don't have a home. Good night, Connor." Her voice was very low, and the sorrow had seeped out into her words.

"Wait, please." He seemed unsure if she would actually listen, so she turned and sighed.

"What is it Connor? I'm exhausted; it's been a very long couple of days for me," he had no idea, "and I'd really just like to get some sleep." Dreamless sleep.

His eyes searched hers for a moment before he nodded once and said, "Then dream sweet, Mackenzie."

And he walked through the door next to hers. *Oh great*, she thought, *of course his room is right next door!* She trudged slowly into her room and closed the door behind her. Now that she was alone, the panic and the pain were overwhelming. The tears overflowed, and she sat down on the bed and let them come. Why did he have to remind her that she was currently homeless? She really just wanted to go to sleep and wake up in her own bed, or at the very least in her own time! But, if she was to believe the wizards, that wouldn't even be possible until Halloween.

Why her? Was it all really about her lineage?

All she knew about her Scottish heritage came from Granny Stewart, who had married into the family. She'd been a Mackenzie and this was who she'd been named after. After her parents had died, Granny had taken care of Mackenzie and her brother. She'd taken them to Highland flings and caber tosses when she was a child, but it had never been more than a fun outing. Mackenzie had even taken Highland dance lessons, and done the traditional sword dances to appease her, but that was the extent of her knowledge. This was insane. This was one giant farce. She had been sent out on stage without knowing not only her lines, but her character!

And what if this Campbell guy actually succeeded in capturing her, or getting Connor to trade her to him for some land, or sheep, or whatever it was he wanted? What would happen then? He was supposed to be a cruel man, did she really want to go with him? Her head hurt from all that had happened to her, and all that she'd been thinking about, so Mackenzie decided sleep was the antidote. She took off the gown, and pulled unsuccessfully at the stays for a while, with her arms twisted in an unnatural position. When her arms fell asleep from being bent backwards, she sucked in, turned her stays around, and untied it that way. She had no pajamas, so she figured she would sleep in her shift, and crawled between the covers.

Mackenzie knew sleep would evade her that night, no matter how tired she might be. Connor's eyes stayed with her as she tossed and turned. She checked her watch; it was barely 8:30. Ugh, way too early to go to sleep, but her mind was tired. Eventually, Mackenzie fell into a fitful sleep, full of Connor. Connor happy, Connor angry, Connor naked…and of course the inescapable nightmare. Mackenzie was grateful to escape the dreams when she woke.

But something was wrong. It was way too dark to be close to morning. And there was something heavy pressing down on her. A rustling noise caught her attention and her arms were gripped in an unforgiving vise before she could think.

It was dark, but as her eyes adjusted, Mackenzie could see a man standing on her bed, straddling her with a booted foot pressing against her chest holding her down. He dropped to his knees, one knee on either side of her, and raised a sword above his head. There were two other men, one pinning down her feet, the other holding her wrists above her head. As she realized the first man meant to impale her, Mackenzie sucked a breath in and screamed. Her scream only lasted a fraction of a second, as a hand clamped over her mouth and nose. Her lungs screamed for oxygen, and she heard the man by her arms say to the man with the sword,

"Be done with it, and do it quick."

He muttered something she didn't understand and then pointed the sword down at her abdomen. By now, her vision was swimming from lack of oxygen, and Mackenzie closed her eyes in the hope that she would black out before he stabbed her. She squeezed her eyes and tensed, waiting, but she only heard a gurgling sound before the hand was removed from her mouth. In the same instant, the man who'd been straddling her slumped down over her, and the small breath she'd managed to take in whooshed right back out of her. She shoved at the body on top of her, and felt warm when she'd shoved him off enough to sit up. It was his blood. Mackenzie swooned, still lightheaded, and tried to pull her legs out from under him, but he was very heavy. As she freed her legs, the sound of swords clanging against each other filled her ears and she strained to see in the dark. But her eyes couldn't see much more than the shapes of two men fighting with swords.

For the first time since her adventure had begun, Mackenzie felt real fear. Not the kind she'd been able to control before when two strangers had dragged her through time, or the kind of fear she'd felt when Connor had kidnapped her and she'd stabbed him. This was real, fear-for-her-life fear, and it was paralyzing her. She froze on the bed, next to a dead man, and waited to see who would be the victor of the next fight.

Chapter Seven

Connor had just slipped into his bed, when he'd thought to check on Mackenzie. She'd looked so sad when he'd left her, and he really didn't harbor any ill will toward her. It was just bad luck that the Campbell had chosen her. It could have been any girl. Well, any girl named Stewart. She really must have had a different up-bringing, if she didn't understand the politics of marriage. There was no doubt in his mind that the Campbell would send men to fetch her back. That was the whole purpose; keep him from gaining power, and insult him at the same time. He would come. That was how this worked.

Connor silently entered her room through the doors that connected the two chambers, and saw a sight that made his blood run cold. He'd expected to see her sleeping, or sitting by the fire, but he had not expected Mackenzie to be held down by two men, while a third prepared to impale her with his sword!

Connor had no sword on him, but he had her dagger still in his waistband. He also had the element of surprise, for they had not heard his entrance. He moved stealthily toward the man with the sword, and slit his throat before he could kill Mackenzie. The man holding her feet had his back to Connor, so he was able to break his neck, but the man at her head saw Connor and put up a fight. By this time, Connor had picked up the dead man's sword from the bed, and after a brief scuffle, Connor knocked the man unconscious.

His first priority was Mackenzie. He'd seen her struggling to push the dead man off of her, and he rushed over to her. She was frozen in shock, so he shook her shoulder to get her attention. She didn't even look at him. Her eyes were on the unconscious man on the floor. He didn't hesitate; Connor just scooped her up and strode to his room. But the second he lifted her into his arms, Mackenzie snapped out of it and gasped, her eyes flying to his. In the dim light, he saw fear, and then relief.

"I thought it was you," was all she said in a low voice. Her lips trembled a little as she stared up at him. "I thought it was you."

Connor was confused, had Mackenzie thought he was the one attacking her? That didn't make any sense; he'd had better opportunities to kill her, if he'd wanted to. Or was she worried that he had been harmed? She was concerned about him! He hadn't expected that her fear was for him, and not herself. What an extraordinary creature. When the light from his room enveloped them, she pressed her face to his chest and started to sob.

"Oh, oh God Connor, he…he was going to…to *kill* me!" He held her close and stroked her hair while she wept.

"Shh…it's all right now. You're all right."

She took a tremulous breath and looked back up at him with her wet eyes. It nearly made his heart stop as he gazed back into their wide, watery green depths.

"Are they," she gulped, "dead?"

"Aye, lass, shh…doona think about it." Connor gently placed her on a chair in his room, and draped his plaid over her shoulders. "You'll be safe here."

She wiped her damp cheeks with his plaid and smiled, "I know."

Before striding away to wake his captain Dougal, he turned back to her and ran his fingers from her cheek to her chin, and noticed that her lips trembled again. He ached to hold her in his arms and kiss her until she forgot the awful scene in her room. Instead, Connor cupped her chin in his hand, noting how satiny smooth her skin felt against his calloused fingers, and tipped her face up to his. Her eyes were huge, they dominated her face, but the fear was gone. Now there was only trust. She trusted him. And he wanted to deserve that trust. What he didn't understand was, why? Pressing a soft kiss to her forehead, he left her in his chambers.

By the time the unconscious man had been taken prisoner, and the dead bodies removed from her room, it was well past midnight. He'd worried about her the whole time that he'd been talking to his men, and giving instructions on what to do with the prisoner. Connor hadn't meant to leave Mackenzie alone that long. She must be so scared.

But she was asleep. Connor smiled as he saw that she had wrapped herself in his plaid. Then he noticed her sark discarded in a bloody heap on the floor. It dawned on him that she wasn't wearing anything underneath his plaid. His body tightened as he remembered exactly how she looked without anything on. He took a deep breath and gently lifted her from the chair. Mackenzie turned her head to rest her cheek on his chest, and she gently sighed, he could feel the warmth of her breath. Connor knew that she was asleep, but still the gesture touched something in him. He couldn't ignore her lush curves cradled in his arms and pressed against his chest. He finally gave in and buried his face in her lavender scented hair, inhaling deeply. She stirred and snuggled even closer to him (as if that were possible), and Connor groaned. His body tightened in response to her, and the sigh that escaped her lips this time was almost his undoing. He could feel her breath coming and going against his suddenly overheated skin. Connor wanted nothing more than to throw her down on his bed and ravish her. He imagined how he would kiss her awake, gently parting her lips with his. Once awake, he would run his hands down her tempting naked body, taking her up on that invitation she'd flaunted earlier. He stopped that dangerous train of thought, but it didn't change the knowledge that it would happen. The only question now was when?

Connor laid her down on his bed and pulled the covers up over her. He warred with himself, but the struggle was in vain; he gave in and kissed her gently on the lips, saying,

"Rest now, for tomorrow we may have a war on our hands," and he sat down in the chair she'd previously occupied.

Connor knew that the Campbell's pride was smarting from Mackenzie's abduction, but he had underestimated the swiftness of the response as well as the brutality of it. He'd tried to kill his own betrothed! Connor was disgusted. There must be something more, something that he didn't know. A small part of him wondered if Mackenzie would now believe how cruel a man her fiancé really was, and he wondered what kind of father would betroth his only daughter to a man such as the Campbell.

He took a long swig of the whisky he kept in his room, as he settled into the chair, and stared at the fire. This would be a long night. He glanced over at Mackenzie as she rolled onto her side in his bed. She was facing him now, and the blankets had shifted and rearranged to barely cover her breasts. Those full, high breasts, and her light pink nipples...he had no problem remembering what she looked like undressed. Connor groaned and shifted in the chair.

She rolled over again, this time facing away from him, with her back to him. Her bare back. The blankets were tangled around her waist, and Connor knew that this meant her breasts were bared to the other side. He thought about sliding into bed with her; there was no reason he shouldn't get some sleep too. Only Connor knew he wouldn't sleep. He'd keep battling with himself about putting his arms around her, or about burying his face in her hair which was spilling across his pillows. One touch wouldn't be enough. He shifted in the chair again. He stared at the fire again, and took another swig of whisky, trying to ignore the feelings that were surfacing due to Mackenzie's presence in his bed.

Once, he actually stood up and walked to the bed, intending to join her. Never before had a woman released such conflicting desires within him, such primitive thoughts unleashed. He wanted her. He felt the urge to take her, make her his in an undeniable way. But he also wanted to protect her, not just from the Campbell, but from anyone and anything that had ever thought about harming her. But his honor prevailed. He didn't slide in between the sheets with the object causing such turmoil inside his usually controlled self. Besides, what if she were a maid? What if she wasn't? Connor didn't know which thought bothered him more. Connor stared at her back, replaying the past day in his head, one hand extended toward her, as if he would touch her. *One stroke of her downy soft skin, that would be all,* he told himself. However, he knew once he laid his hands on her, he wouldn't want to stop. Finally, disgusted with himself, he returned to his chair and went back to glowering at the fire. The fire was safe; he couldn't see her back moving with each breath when he stared at the fire, or imagine what her face looked like, softened in sleep, her long dark eyelashes dusting her cheekbones...Connor exhaled in a gust and gave in, letting his mind wander back to Mackenzie.

He'd never wanted a woman like this. And he'd almost convinced himself that it was because she belonged to another, because she wasn't his, but he knew that was only part of the attraction. A small part. The majority of it was the beautiful, naked woman sleeping, unaware, so trusting, in his bed. She trusted him. That's what ultimately kept Connor from joining Mackenzie in his bed; he wanted to deserve that trust. He'd never really cared much what women thought of him. Women had always found him attractive, and he'd never had to work at it. For him to care so much what this girl thought of him was annoying. Why should it matter? Some chit who belonged to another had piqued his interest and he was acting like a schoolboy. So he passed the next few hours glaring at the fire, drinking whisky, and trying his damndest not to look at Mackenzie.

Chapter Eight

Mackenzie woke up this time because she was cold. No wonder, the blankets had slipped down to her waist. Brrr...she pulled them up to her chest only to realize that she was naked. She never slept naked. She sat up quickly, pressing the sheets to her chest, as the previous night came back to her in a whoosh, pushing sleep far away. She shoved her unruly curls out of her eyes, and found Connor's plaid beneath the twisted sheets. Connor! Mackenzie's eyes found him sitting by the fire. He was holding a bottle of something, probably whiskey, she thought, and he was staring blearily into the fire. At her rustling the covers, his eyes sharpened and he turned to Mackenzie. He looked like hell.

"Have you slept?"

"Nay."

His terse reply would normally have irritated her, but she felt so grateful to him, that she let it pass. She would try to behave, she owed him that much, if not much, much more. Besides, he hadn't slept, and it was who knew how late. Ugh, she ran a hand over her face and checked her watch, pushing the light button. 3:15. Double ugh. He didn't say anything, but she glanced up to see Connor's eyes following her movements. Oh right, the watch. What year was it again? Did they have watches here in the 1700s? She thought that the pocket watch had been invented in the 1500s, but wasn't sure. Her grandpa's pocket watch was from the 1700s; it had been in the family for generations, so she was pretty sure that Connor would have seen a watch before. But definitely not one that lit up. So she rolled out of bed and wrapped his plaid around her like a towel in one quick movement, then padded softly to kneel in front of him.

"Here," she offered him her watch. "Go on, take it," she coaxed, extending her arm toward Connor. "It tells time, see? This button makes it light up."

Connor didn't move at first. He slowly reached for it, and their fingers brushed. It took all she had not to jerk her hand back. It felt as if an electric current had just passed from him through her and it almost burned. The spark was undeniable. No matter his feelings, or his motives, the spark was there. The desire to touch him again was so strong that she clutched the plaid tighter around herself to keep her hands from reaching out again. She watched him do nothing more than glance at her watch before handing it back. She reached for her watch and tried not to touch his fingers this time. Mackenzie fastened the clasp and peeked up at Connor from beneath her lashes. The firelight danced over his features. The harsh angles of his face, high cheekbones, bronzed skin, straight nose, wide mouth…her eyes strayed to his mouth just long enough to see the lines tighten around his lips. She looked into his eyes and saw…desire. It was hot, blatant, big bad wolf desire. He wanted her. While the thought thrilled her, it also scared her. Big time.

Her hand tightened on his plaid as if it were a lifeline. Connor noticed and his eyes dropped to her breasts. Her heart pounded in her ears as her heartbeat increased under his gaze. She wondered if he could see her pulse; it felt like her heart would jump out of her chest. Mackenzie dropped her gaze and lowered her face, hiding in her hair. Her hair was curling around her face and shoulders shielding her eyes from him. A strong finger lifted her chin until she met his eyes.

"Doona hide from me, lass."

Her eyes widened. Damn, she knew she had expressive eyes, and she really didn't want him to see how the simple touch of his finger under her chin wreaked further havoc with her pulse, and how it felt like she had electricity running through her veins instead of blood. Mackenzie shivered and changed the topic.

"How did I end up in your bed?" Mackenzie could guess, but she had to say something to break the tension she felt building.

"You fell asleep in the chair and I carried you to my bed. I thought it would be best until your linens were changed." His eyes flashed and his chin lifted a bit; she remembered that Connor didn't like to explain himself, "Your honor is intact."

Her forehead creased, "My hon–" Why would he say that? "Oh!" Mackenzie blushed, "I didn't mean to insinuate, that is, umm, I mean, Connor, I know you wouldn't take advantage of me…," she trailed off lamely.

"How?" Was it a threat?

"Excuse me?"

"How, Mackenzie, how do you ken I didn't climb in beside you and run my hands down your soft, tempting, naked body?" he husked.

Mackenzie blurted out the truth, "Because you look like hell."

Connor actually laughed out loud. His whole face changed with the happy sound. He looked years younger.

"You should laugh more often," Mackenzie said softly, before her brain could edit.

"I should?" He looked surprised and curious.

Mackenzie tried not to blush again under the weight of his stare, and dropped her eyes. "You just should, that's all," she mumbled.

Again, that finger tilted her face until she met his gaze. The sapphire blue gave nothing away. His poker face was back, so it surprised her when he leaned his face down close to hers and paused just a breath away from her lips.

"Mackenzie?"

"Yes?" she breathed out. Where was her voice?

"Your plaid is slipping." His lips twitched with the laughter he withheld.

"Oh!" Mackenzie looked down to see that her grip had indeed loosened on the plaid she held around her naked body. A creamy swell of breast was peeking tantalizingly over the top of it. She hugged Connor's plaid closer to her breasts and when she looked up with wide eyes, his hands gripped her by her shoulders and he hauled her up onto his lap.

His kiss was demanding and insistent and brought liquid desire to pool in her belly. He ran his hands over her bare back; the plaid had slipped loose again, and while it covered her breasts, it dipped low to her waist in the back. His hands were gently skimming at first, brushing down her sides and the sides of her breasts. Then they were on the small of her back, pressing her closer. His kiss became more urgent. He tugged on the plaid until she let go of it, and he crushed her bare breasts to his chest. His chest hair felt scratchy and rough, but it only added to the thrill, gently scraping against her nipples, and heightening her desire. Connor's hands didn't stay in one place for long, now they were on her hips, gripping her tightly, and it felt natural for Mackenzie to turn and straddle him. She wanted nothing more than for Connor to stop this overwhelming need she felt for him. She was hot, so hot. Her skin was on fire, and sensitive to his every touch.

She'd never felt this way about a man before, and she'd never let a man get so close to her before either. Not physically, but in a different way, Mackenzie felt closer to Connor than she had any of her previous boyfriends, and she didn't know why. Maybe it was the way he looked at her? It made her heart stutter when she stared into those blue eyes of his. He seemed slightly surprised when she'd turned towards him and shifted to straddle his bulging erection. She could feel the pent up desire in him but she also felt that he was holding tightly to his control.

"Don't" she breathed against his lips. He pulled back confused, and Mackenzie clarified, more boldly, "Don't hold back. That's not what I want."

His "What do you want, Mackenzie?" was whispered along her neck. He trailed his lips back and forth from the line of her jaw to her collarbone. Then he paused at the hollow of her neck, waiting, his lips hovering. He wanted to hear it. He wanted her to say it.

"Oh, God, Connor, this. You. I want..." she couldn't finish the sentence because his mouth had taken hold of one of her nipples. He sucked, licked and scraped gently with his teeth until she thought she'd go crazy with need. And the heat...her whole body felt like it was on fire. She was instinctively rubbing against the *trews* he wore in a splendid agony. Mackenzie didn't know what she wanted, but she knew she wanted this burning to end. She was playing with fire, but she wanted to burn. It was so acute, it was almost painful, but she didn't want him to stop. He knew what she wanted though, because his fingers that had strayed from her hips to her thighs, paused to brush against her. She stilled. Then he slipped one long finger into her and she gasped in the exquisite shock. Connor groaned. His one finger gave her more pleasure than anything she had ever experienced in her whole life!

She'd had boyfriends before, of course, but there had never been this kind of heat with any of them. He brought her so forcefully to climax, that she wanted to just lean against him for a moment. But he gathered her in his arms, and strode to the bed, placing her gently against the pillows. When his hands dropped to the laces on his *trews,* a sharp rapping on the door startled Mackenzie. Connor growled in irritation. Mackenzie gasped. She was floating in fantasy one minute, the next she'd dropped like a stone back into reality, such as it was for her. Her eyes flew to his and then to her naked body. The panic started to build and she scrambled off the bed to wrap herself in his plaid once more, and she hid behind the door.

* * * *

When she'd knelt before him to show off the timepiece, he'd been unable to tear his eyes from hers, until the plaid she'd been clutching to her breast started to slip down. She had tucked one end into the other, and it had barely covered her. Then he'd been unable to tear his eyes away from the tempting ivory swells peeking above his plaid. When he'd collected himself enough to take her small clock, their fingers had touched and the attraction was undeniable. He knew she felt it too.

So with the fire glowing behind her, and Mackenzie kneeling in front of him, her little clock held no interest to him. It paled in comparison to the things he was thinking of her lips doing to him. When he'd pointed out that her plaid was slipping down, it was her blush that had killed his resolve. The color of her creamy skin with the pink touching the tops of her breasts; he almost groaned as he watched her reposition herself. And before he could think, he reacted; he pulled Mackenzie up onto his lap and kissed her until he was breathing hard. He wanted her skin against his; he tugged at the plaid until her hand released it, and pressed her against his chest. Connor trailed his lips down her neck to her breasts and when he finally drew her nipple into his mouth, it felt like destiny was calling him home. That's what Mackenzie felt like; home. That thought both scared him and thrilled him.

Then Mackenzie had turned to sit on top of him, and Connor knew that she wanted him too. And knowing that such a bold move meant that she was not a maid, he felt relief that he would soon take her. For there was no doubt that this was leading to his bed…if they made it that far.

"Oh," she moaned and her head fell back, her hair brushing the tops of his thighs. Connor tangled his hand in her silken curls and brought her mouth back to his at the same time as he slid one finger into her. God she was wet. In the most primitive way, her body welcomed him, encouraged him. He felt her gasp against his lips and pulled back just enough to watch her eyes drift shut. He wanted to make her call out his name over and over again.

The emotions that crossed her face as he stroked her were an incredible aphrodisiac to him. He wanted more, he needed all of her. Now. And in that instant, he knew she was his. She'd been made for him. He stared into her heavy-lidded emerald green eyes as she looked back at him with the unfocused gaze of passion. She was his. And he would claim her. He shoved all the new emotions he was experiencing out of his mind, and instead watched her dazed eyes flicker with desire. He was as surprised by the force of her climax as she seemed to be. But when Mackenzie leaned her forehead against his, he scooped her up with every intention of taking her to his bed.

This time, he would join her.

But fate had other plans; when he placed her against the pillows, someone knocked on the door. *Damn!* He glanced down at the woman lying naked in his bed, and saw her panic at being caught.

He dressed quickly and growled out, "Aye?"

"Forgive the interruption, my Laird, but ye are needed. Our prisoner has broken and ye need to hear his news." Connor recognized Dougal's voice through the door. Mackenzie had tucked his plaid around herself once again, and hurried to stand behind the door, so when Connor opened it, she wouldn't be seen. Connor opened the door to his captain, but didn't open it fully,

"I'll be right down."

There was a pause before Dougal answered, "Aye me Laird, we'll await yer arrival."

Connor shut the door and turned to Mackenzie. She looked so beautiful with the firelight behind her, catching her curls in its glow. He rather liked seeing her with his plaid wrapped about her shoulders; the expanse of bare leg it afforded him was incredible. It was a shame to leave her. He bent his head to kiss her and his lips tingled from their kiss.

"I must go."

"Oh," Mackenzie looked down at her bare feet, her metallic aqua blue nail polish in "Skinny Jeans" still on from her pedicure with Jenna pre-time travel. Jenna had chosen a muted hot pink called "It's all about me," how typical Jenna.

"But I canna go yet," Connor's voice snapped her head up.

"Oh?" He smiled at the hopeful look on her face.

"Nay, I need…" he trailed off suggestively.

"Yes?" her voice was barely a whisper.

"This." Connor stripped her of his plaid in one smooth movement and began to pleat it around himself.

"Connor!" Mackenzie gasped, futilely covering herself with her hands.

He tried not to laugh at the stricken expression in her eyes. But he quickly turned serious, "Rest, now, you'll need it."

Her brow creased, "Why, what's happening later?" His abrupt mood change from teasing to somber confused Mackenzie.

"Tonight, you're mine" he breathed it against her parted lips before succumbing to one last, long, lingering kiss. Then he turned to walk out the door, leaving her with his fingers trailing along her cheek.

Chapter Nine

The second the door clicked shut, Mackenzie let her breath out in a gust. She hadn't even realized that she'd been holding it. And she leaned against the cool wood. It felt rough against her naked back. She looked around the room, wondering if she'd have to wrap the sheet around her toga-style, or if there was something else in here that she could wear? She stepped over her ruined shift in disgust, and thought of returning to her room, wondering what awaited her there. She sighed and settled for the sheet, tucking it over one arm, and around her chest like a sarong. Mackenzie took a deep calming breath and opened the door to her room.

Luckily, no one was in her room, alive, or otherwise. It was apparent that her room had been cleaned as well. Her bed was freshly made, and there was even a fresh linen shift on top of the brocade cover. She hadn't really looked at the bed before; it was a huge wooden canopy bed with the duvet matching the canopy in a golden brocade. No one would ever know that there had been two dead bodies lying there just a few hours before.

Mackenzie mentally thanked Bronwyn, or whomever, for the clean shift and threw it on hurriedly, tossing Connor's sheet on the chair. Connor had said to get some rest, but she could see the pale light from the sunrise streaking through her window. Glancing at her watch she saw it was after five. Ugh, she ran a hand across her face and wished for some coffee, or an energy drink, or some other form of caffeine. She wasn't sure what they would eat here, or when breakfast would be, so she tried to dress herself so she could go explore. Hmm, the stays were much harder to do herself than she'd expected. So she passed the time by digging through her purse. Oh! The amulet! She'd forgotten about that. She put it around her neck, and stuffed it down into her shift.

When Bronwyn knocked on the door, Mackenzie half expected to see Connor standing there. But she let Bronwyn in with a bright smile; she was, after all, the only person who hadn't looked at her with hate or anger.

"Good morning, my Lady. Have ye slept much? I heard about all the excitement last night."

A wry smile twisted Mackenzie's lips as she thought of Bronwyn's understatement; *excitement. Hah!* "Not much, Bronwyn, thank you for asking." She was determined to make friends with Bronwyn. She needed a friend.

"I'd imagine not, dearie. Here ye are; I had Cook make some scones and eggs for ye. We thought it best to introduce ye to our foods slowly. Tonight we'll serve haggis; it's not for the faint of heart." As she said this, she'd gone to the large trunk and pulled out a lavender gown with some more undergarments that looked bulky and uncomfortable. Mackenzie sighed as she thought wistfully of jeans and a t-shirt. "Here we go, dearie, this one will look lovely on ye."

Mackenzie smiled at being called "dearie" by a girl her own age, if not younger. But she preferred it to "My Lady" by far. This time, Mackenzie watched how Bronwyn laced up her stays, and wrapped a full skirt thingie around her waist.

"What's the difference between what I'm wearing, stays is it? And a corset?"

Bronwyn's forehead creased, "I'm not sure what yer meanin' by 'corset,' my Lady. Is it that what the French are wearin' nowadays?"

"I guess so." She'd made a mistake in asking, but she wanted to know what they were called. Bronwyn didn't seem to have as many articles of clothing on; a simple dress to her ankles, and the unavoidable stays, plus an apron, with a cap the same color. *Hmm... must be the whole people dressing according to their stations type of thing.* "And what is this?" Mackenzie lifted part of the heavy puffy skirt.

"Yer petticoats, my Lady?" Bronwyn was giving her a look as if she were crazy.

"Ah, yes, of course. I'm sorry, it's just my father had new gowns made for my trip here, and I'm not used to such confining garments." Mackenzie lied with an aura of distraction, as if it didn't matter to her, hoping Bronwyn would let it drop.

"Well, yer father must have spent a pretty penny to have these dresses made for ye. I have never seen their equal in material or design." She fingered the fabric almost reverently. "They must be the latest fashion from London."

Mackenzie had no idea, so she let Bronwyn assume what she wanted. This gown was a little more difficult to get on, and a little more uncomfortable than the grey wool gown from the night before. It had a bodice that laced in back and front, and the square neckline smooshed her breasts up under her chin. One deep breath and Mackenzie thought she might fall out! Between the heavy skirts and tight stays (Bronwyn pulled them so tight Mackenzie had trouble breathing!) Mackenzie felt bulky and confined. The shoes, however were a different story altogether; for a shoe-a-holic, Mackenzie felt like Cinderella in her glass slippers. They were matching lavender satin, with little shimmery beads all over them, and they reminded her of the most beautiful ballet slippers she'd ever seen. Both she and Bronwyn gasped aloud as they admired the matching shoes.

"Oh my, these are quite lovely, my Lady, quite lovely." Bronwyn's whispered statement was understandable to Mackenzie.

"Wow," she agreed.

Bronwyn straitened up and was all business again, "Let me plait your hair before I leave ye to yer morning meal. Oh, and the Laird asked me to see if there might be anything ye'll be needin'? Are there any foods ye'd like?"

"Do you have any coffee here?" It was a long shot, but she'd try anyways. Coffee had to have been exported from South America by now, right?

"Aye, m'Lady, I've got a small pot on yer tray here. With cream and sugar?" Bronwyn actually went over to the tray and poured the cup for Mackenzie.

"Oh, here I can do that. You don't have to serve me." Mackenzie felt guilty for even asking.

"No trouble at all dearie, here we are."

Mackenzie took the beautiful teacup that reminded her of her grandmother's good china with a thank you, and inhaled the fragrance. It was much stronger than she was used to. But she knew it was exactly what her caffeine-deprived system needed. Plus, it smelled like it would be a better eye-opener than walking into a café early in the morning. One sip and she was right! Wow! This didn't taste anything like her normal skinny vanilla latte. But it was good in its own right. Bronwyn told Mackenzie that the library was on the first floor, if she wanted, and that if she needed anything else, she would be in the Hall dusting. She then ducked her head and opened the door to leave.

"Wait, please don't go just yet!" Mackenzie called out to her, and bit her lip. She didn't know if this was proper protocol or not, but she really wanted the company. "Would you mind keeping me company for a while? I'm still a little confused as to my..." she wanted to say *role* but settled for "position here. I mean, everyone must know who I am and how I got here, right?" At Bronwyn's wide-eyed nod, Mackenzie continued, "What am I supposed to do here?"

"My Lady, there are many books in the library, or I am sure I could find some needlepoint for ye if ye prefer..." Bronwyn was unsure of what Mackenzie wanted, she could tell, but she didn't want to be alone just yet; the fear and panic might come back.

"Would it be alright if we just chatted? Talked, I mean."

"What would ye like to talk about my Lady?" Bronwyn still sounded unsure, but she came back into Mackenzie's room and sat in a chair by the fire.

Mackenzie sat across from her, and started, "Well, maybe you could tell me why everyone hates me so much." Mackenzie looked down at her beautiful shoes as she asked. Bronwyn waited so long to answer that Mackenzie looked up and met her brown eyes. They were full of sympathy, which was both encouraging that Bronwyn at least didn't hate her, and a little disheartening that she was right; everyone else did.

"Well, m'Lady, ye are engaged to the Campbell. That doesn't put ye in the good graces of many here."

It was exactly as Mackenzie had thought. "But I didn't choose him! It was an arranged marriage!"

"I ken that dearie, but not all of our people are as sympathetic." Bronwyn patted her knee. "The Campbell is a cruel mon who has brought nothing good to this land. Most feel that anything that the Campbell has touched should be destroyed. Ye are his betrothed, and he'll be wantin' ye back. That means retaliation, and it means that a lot more of our men will die. The women doona like to think of their men dyin'. While the men are itchin' for a fight, they doona like the idea of defendin' ye...they'd rather kill ye along with the Campbell." At Mackenzie's strangled gasp, Bronwyn squeezed her hand and said, "Now doona fash yerself, dearie, the laird of this keep is a good mon, and he won't let any harm come to ye. He is an honorable mon." Mackenzie could hear the pride she took in that last phrase.

"Thank you for being straight with me, um I mean, I thank you for your honesty, Bronwyn," she amended. "I don't like feeling confused."

"Of course not, dearie. If 'tisn't too bold, might I ask ye a question?" At Mackenzie's nod, she continued, "They say that ye were reared abroad?" Bronwyn's question was timid, at odds with her bold explanation of her clan's dislike for Mackenzie.

"Yes." She forced a smile, expecting her to ask about her accent, her strange behavior, her lack of seemingly common knowledge.

"Where have ye travelled?"

"I've been around Europe; Germany, France, Spain, Italy," she didn't even have to lie; she and Jenna had backpacked through Europe after high school. "And then more recently I've been living in America." A real smile touched her lips and she glanced at her new friend.

"Oh my, the Americas! Is it true that they are a savage place with a savage population of natives?"

Mackenzie laughed, "No, no more savage than you or your clan" Mackenzie quickly searched her mind for what she remembered from her American History class. How much to share? "It only seems uncivilized because it is different. New England and the East Coast are fairly similar to London, and people are constantly exploring towards the west. Eventually it will all become like what you know."

"Oh, well, mayhap one day I might travel to the Americas." Bronwyn stood and said, "If ye'll excuse me, m'Lady, I've chores that need to be done."

"Oh, of course, I didn't mean to keep you. And thank you, truly." She paused and called out, "Oh, wait, one more thing. What does it say above the door downstairs?"

"*As long as a MacRae is in, a Fraser will never be out.* It is from before the MacRaes came to Kintail. In return, the Fraser stronghold states *As long as a Fraser lives within, let not a MacRae remain without.*"

"Thank you." She pondered that and figured that the MacRaes and Frasers must be friends. Once again, she wished she knew more Scottish history.

Bronwyn nodded and bustled out the door.

Mackenzie finished her coffee and thought maybe she could go explore the castle, but the Fates had other plans. She turned at the sound of something sliding under the door. It was a piece of paper, no parchment, she corrected, as she turned it over in her hands.

She only hesitated an instant before sliding her finger under the intricate wax seal. A ring crest perhaps? Her eyes widened, then squinted as she tried to make out the fancy script:

My Dear Miss Stewart,

Please forgive your rude welcome to my country. The Highlands are a barbaric place full of a barbaric people. I myself am English and much more civilized. I hear that you are being treated well. If I hear that you are treated as anything less than the fiancée of a man of my position, then Connor MacRae shall pay dearly. Please give my regards to your captor. And as our wedding is still set for the end of the month, I intend to see you soon. And, my Lady, if you are not a maid upon return to me, you will pay for that insult. It would be a shame to kill such as you. I look forward to seeing you in person and seeing if the rumors of your beauty do you justice.

With Fond Regards,

John Campbell

Chapter Ten

"Oh no! Oh crap!" Her hands were shaking as she re-read the letter. "There must be a spy here! Connor needs to know!" Mackenzie said it to herself as she ran out of the room, and down the tower stairs. She hiked up her gown and tried not to stumble down the stairs as she hurried. She jumped down the last three steps and ran for the door to the Main Hall. That was how she'd entered the castle the day before, didn't that lead outside? She hadn't really been anywhere in the castle yet, so she tried to remember the way. Of course, though, she got turned around, and searching blindly, Mackenzie followed the sound of swords clanging against each other.

She ended up in a training yard of some sort, but the ever fickle fates were on her side as she saw Connor in the middle of the yard. He was surrounded by men and they were coming at him from different sides. He was amazing.

He was shirtless, despite the crisp October chill, and wearing just his *trews*. She had seen him like this before, but here in the sunlight, she could see his muscles ripple with each movement of the sword, and she could see all of the scars along his back and chest. However, they only added to his sensuality, rather than detract; they hinted at danger. He was no metrosexual peacock like some that she met at clubs and bars; he was all man. A warrior. His bronzed muscular chest was on display as much as his skills were. He swung his claymore in a high arc, bringing it down with a resounding clang against his clansman's sword, and her eyes appraised him with lust. The flex of his muscles brought an undeniable feminine flare of excitement into her belly; he wanted her. She remembered the way his chest had felt pressed up against hers, the slight scratch of hair, the heat, and felt a slight flush color her cheeks…but she tore her gaze away from his sculpted body, and looked for a way to interrupt without making a scene. Unlikely, though, as there were no other women out there, and seeing as she was already famous, or infamous as the case was, she was sure to cause a stir. Mackenzie hated to interrupt, but he had to see this letter. So she gulped in a big breath, and walked out into the sunlit training yard.

Making her way to Connor, she saw all the men stop and stare at her. *Maybe women weren't allowed down here?* Well, she had more important things to worry about than just committing a social *faux pas*. The men moved out of her way as if the Red Sea had just parted. Connor's eyes found hers at the commotion, or lack of commotion, of her entrance. And he looked annoyed. Really, really annoyed. Mackenzie took a deep breath and smiled anyway, and walked directly to him, stopping only when she was close enough to feel the heat coming off him and smell the scent that was his alone.

"What?" He was definitely annoyed. Well, tough, she had news for him.

"I need to speak with you immediately."

Connor looked as if he was going to chastise her for the interruption, but decided against it and instead bent to pick up his shirt before taking her hand.

"Come with me." He dragged her in silence for about five minutes until they were out of earshot of his men, she guessed. They reached a clearing with a small pool of water.

"Oh, it's beautiful," she breathed, her urgent news momentarily forgotten.

"Why did you feel the need to interrupt my training?" He was so distant and sarcastic that she jerked her head around to look at him. What a different man than the one who had left her just this morning.

"Oh," his shortness with her caused her words to come out in a rush, "Connor, I think you're in trouble; there's a traitor here!"

"I ken."

"You do?" she was incredulous, her eyes bugged out of her head.

"What do you mean that you know?"

"The man whom we captured in your chambers last night told us all about the plot to kill you. That is what tore me away from you this morning." His voice softened, "Doona be afraid, Mackenzie, I will na let any harm come to you." His blue gaze was running up her body as if she weren't wearing several layers of clothing, and Mackenzie knew the man was remembering their parting that morning. This one man had seen her naked more in a few days, than most of her boyfriends had in a few months. Her skin flushed wherever his gaze lingered.

"Stop."

"Stop what?" His eyes were too wide and innocent; he knew what she meant.

"Stop looking at me like…like…like I don't have any clothes on!"

Connor raised an eyebrow, smiled, and taunted, "Embarrassed?"

"No," she glared, but her blush gave her away.

"Doona be, you're a beautiful woman, Mackenzie," his voice was husky as he drew her into his arms.

"No," she mumbled half-heartedly against his lips.

"Nay?" Connor hovered tantalizingly close to her mouth, and she could feel his warm breath against her lips. God he smelled good. Why had she said no again? Oh right, the spy.

"Umm," she had trouble focusing, "your spy?"

"My what?"

"Uh, the traitor?"

"That's right," his eyes narrowed. "What is it that you feel is so urgent that you ran down to interrupt my training?"

"Someone left me a note in my room."

Connor froze. "Show me," he demanded.

Mackenzie handed it to him wordlessly.

"'Tis in Scots." Connor ground his teeth together.

"What does that mean?"

"It means that the Campbell thinks me an ignorant barbarian too uncivilized to read Scots, the tongue of the Lowlander, if I can read at all. 'Tis his way of insulting me. 'Tis also why he goes by the English 'lord' rather than his own Scottish 'laird,' he thinks himself too good for his own people."

"What does he think you speak?"

"Erse."

"What is that, like Gaelic or something?"

"Aye." His terse reply had her biting her lip.

"I'm sorry, it's just that I don't know that much about your people."

"'Tis Scottish Gaelic. The English are trying to drive us out, and require that we speak their language and present ourselves in Edinburgh once a year to report on our clans. Your betrothed is the primary promoter of the Clearances. He has said quite publicly that in the

Highlands, the Irish language should be forcibly suppressed as the stronghold of ignorance and rebellion. He takes it upon himself to suppress it." He explained it impatiently, but at least he didn't insult her for not knowing her Scottish history.

"Oh." She paused, "You understand that I never chose to marry him, right?" She wanted to be clear on that. She was already in way too deep as far as her attraction to him went, and she wanted him to understand that she'd been sucked into this plan without her permission; she wanted him to know her.

Connor looked at her with surprise, "Aye, lass, I ken. 'Twas the Campbell who chose you. He knows of your background, and he might think that you are connected to the Mackenzie tribe as well. 'Twould only be natural." He almost smiled.

"No, he thinks my name is Isabella." Mackenzie corrected his assumption.

"The man you are set to marry does no' know your given name?" his voice was incredulous.

"No, his sorcerers, my travelling companions, told me to go by my middle name. They said it was more common in this era."

"This *era?*"

Oops! Connor had noticed her slip.

"Umm…this *area*. You know, the Highlands. Probably for the same reasons you thought." She could tell he didn't believe her, but she didn't really know what to tell him. What would he say if she told him she was not going to be born for over 200 years? He would probably lock her in the tower.

"What are you hiding from me, Mackenzie?"

She turned away from him and said, "Nothing."

A long arm caught her about her waist, "Doona lie to me, Mackenzie."

"Trust me when I say that it is 'need to know' only, and you don't need to know. In fact you probably wouldn't even want to know." Mackenzie was suddenly very sure of that fact. Connor seemed to only believe what he could see, and touch; like most people. She didn't think he'd even give the slightest credence to her fantastical story. Realistically, she wouldn't have either if their positions were reversed.

"You speak in riddles. Tell me plain, what are you keeping from me? Is it something to do with the Campbell?" His hands were gripping her upper arms painfully. "What do ken you of his plans?"

There was a fervent light in his eyes that had her cringing mentally at the thought of lying to him. So she thought of the best way to tell him as much as she could without revealing the main detail she was dancing around.

"As far as I know," Mackenzie spoke slowly, still gathering her thoughts, "The Campbell thinks that he has made a normal, typical marriage bargain with my father." Mackenzie had taken to calling him *the* Campbell as Connor did. She assumed that it must distinguish him as the chief. "He knows that I am the first female Stewart born since my ancestor who cursed the lands. He thinks that in marrying me, he will end the curse, if not in reality, then at least superstitiously. All of the people will believe that the curse is broken, so therefore the lands will prosper. No longer would they be able to blame anything on the curse. He also hopes that it will make them follow him more willingly." She could tell that Connor was not only shocked that she was so well informed, but also that he hadn't known some of this. "You see, Connor," she laughed blackly without any humor, "The Campbell has something much darker planned than even you know. He has been dabbling in the black arts, and he plans to sacrifice me on our wedding night, in order to produce his heir through dark magic."

Connor swore through clenched teeth. "And your father agreed to marry you off to this swine? What manner of man would do that to his only daughter?"

She had to lie again, "Umm, I don't think he knew all of this. I only found out when I arrived here."

"And you agreed to this?"

"No! Hell no!" she insisted. "Well, not at first," Mackenzie qualified. "I didn't really have much choice in the matter. Once it was all explained to me, I sort of agreed, tentatively, but only on the part where I am supposed to distract the Campbell. By then his sorcerers are supposed to send me back before the wedding night."

"Send you back where?"

"Oh, uh, America?" It came out as a question.

"But what of the agreement with your father? The Campbell will na take losing you again so lightly."

"Oh, umm…I don't really know all of the details," she was a horrible liar, so she went back to half-truths, "Besides, they were kind of interrupted mid-way through by this really bossy Highlander who dragged me out of the carriage during their explanation." Mackenzie smiled a tiny smile, hoping Connor would take the teasing in stride, rather than getting angry. He did.

"Hmm…and would you be speakin' of me?"

"I would." Mackenzie grinned. She liked that the topic had shifted slightly away from the lies. "But seriously, Connor, I don't understand his note. It's like it's full of innuendos for you, and not me. Is he the reason those men tried to kill me last night?" She shuddered at that thought. "Is he telling you to back off? Or is he telling me he knows I'm going to side with you?"

"You talk too much." And Connor silenced her with his lips.

It was a very effective distraction. Mackenzie lost her train of thought, and could barely remember to breathe, let alone what she'd been asking him. His lips were warm and soft, and in such contrast with the solid strength of his body. She made a helpless sound in the back of her throat, and pressed herself closer to his strong body. She felt him tighten his hold on her, but was surprised at how gentle his fingers were on her jaw, urging her lips to part. As his tongue stroked hers, stoking the fires he had awakened in her, she gave up on any rational thoughts and just concentrated on not burning to a cinder in the flames he had ignited. Once again, her whole body felt like it was pulsing with heat. When his hand found her breast, she moaned and her legs gave out from under her. If it hadn't been for Connor's strong arm around her, she surely would have melted into a puddle on the ground.

Wow, she thought, *two minutes of kissing him and I'm a puddle at his feet. This can't be healthy.* But she wanted more. She wanted to feel his skin on hers. She tugged at his shirt, lifting it just enough to put her hands on the small of his back. He inhaled sharply at her tentative touch, then yanked his shirt off in one swift motion. Next, he put his hands to her laces, but before he could pull them loose, he stiffened.

Mackenzie lifted her head and opened her dazed eyes. "Wha-?"

"Get behind me lass." He breathed in her ear, and pulled her tight to his body so he was shielding her. *But from what?* Mackenzie couldn't see or hear anything. She tried to peek under his arm when he lifted his massive sword from the ground. What was going on? Then she heard a twig snap behind her and she froze.

Before she could blink, four men also with giant swords, jumped out from the surrounding trees. It all was so fast, but her eyes took in everything. Connor caught the closest man off guard and sliced his arm off. The sound and accompanying scream were hideous. The man floundered on the ground.

Next he fought against two men, all the while he never let go of Mackenzie. The last man looked for an opening to separate Mackenzie from Connor, who had just taken a rough blow to the kidney. One of the two brought his sword up to impale Connor from behind but Mackenzie darted out from Connor's hold, and kicked the man in his groin as hard as she could. She then took a kick boxer's stance and punched him in the nose with the heel of her hand, driving upward. She felt the cartilage break and was instantly queasy. Her heart was pounding in her ears so loudly that it drowned out the sound of his nose crunching. Mackenzie was intensely grateful that she hadn't heard that. Even as the man was still doubled over in pain from the groin kick, she snagged the humongous sword out of his hands, and barely able to lift it, she pressed the blade to his throat. Her back was to Connor, but she could hear noises that sounded like he was killing or mortally wounding the others. Not wanting to see which, she turned her attention back to her captive. He glared at her but spoke.

"My Lady, if ye would but let me speak? My lord Campbell has sent us to rescue ye. Ye will not be harmed. Come, leave with us. We shall see ye safely home to your betrothed."

"As you can see, I am not in any need of a rescue. Send my regards to your master."

Connor whirled around at the man's voice, ready to defend Mackenzie. What he saw was Mackenzie holding a blade to the bleeding man's throat. He felt such relief that she was safe, and a strange swelling of pride that she had defended herself yet again. She was magnificent. A warrior goddess. Her hair had come unbound, the honey-colored curls were tumbling in the wind, and her cheeks were flushed with the exertion.

"Well done, lass." Connor came to stand by her side. "Rise," he spoke to their prisoner. The man glared daggers at Connor through his swollen face, but he lurched to his feet, nonetheless. He staggered, but it was just a ploy to retrieve his sword from Mackenzie. Connor moved faster and ran him through before he could touch her.

A scream tore from Mackenzie's throat as she watched his eyes roll back into his head and gag on his own blood. Her fingers involuntarily dropped the sword, and she backed away from him with her hand over her mouth. When she backed into another man, she whirled to face him. It was just Connor. And her adrenaline was gone. He could tell she looked faint; the color was gone from her cheeks and her breathing was coming in shallow gasps. She looked as if just standing was taking all of her energy.

He lifted her into his arms, and carried her back to the training yard where his men seemed oblivious of what had just passed. He never stopped moving as he spoke his order,

"Dougal, Robbie, take the men and search the grounds." His men wordlessly obeyed, some eyeing the silent girl in his arms. They armed themselves and went for their horses.

"Can you walk?"

"Yes." And he slid her down the length of his body until she stood on her own feet, but he didn't let go. She could feel his heart pounding.

"Are you all right lass?" his voice was thick with emotion and his lilting brogue caressed her ear.

Mackenzie just nodded, trying not to spill the tears she so precariously held back. Connor saw her bright eyes and pulled her gently against him, speaking soft unfamiliar words against her temple. Gaelic, she assumed, or Erse, as he'd called it. Either way, the soft musical words soothed her stretched nerves. He stroked her hair down her back, and finally pulled away enough to tip her face to his and drop a light kiss on her lips.

"I need to join my men..." Connor sounded torn. Did he really want to stay with her? Mackenzie couldn't be sure, but it *sounded* like that's what he wanted.

"I've never seen anyone die before, and now since last night..." Mackenzie couldn't finish her sentence without seeing their lifeless faces.

"Sshh...I ken. This is why women stay home instead of fighting. But woe befall any man who comes at you, lass. You were magnificent," his voice was that of awed respect. He smiled and ran his fingers down her cheek before grudgingly walking toward the stables for his horse. But he hadn't even made it halfway there, before his second in command rode up to him. They spoke in low intense tones, but they could have shouted for all Mackenzie could understand; it was in Erse. Connor's whole body stiffened, and then he glared murderously at Mackenzie. She'd never seen him look like that, even when he'd been fighting; he'd never had such a steely, flinty look in his eyes. He said something to his man, and never taking his eyes from Mackenzie's confused expression, he strode back towards her.

"You lied to me lass." His words carried an unmistakable threat with the seductive burr she'd become so familiar with.

"I did no such thing." She said warily. He was so angry and she had no idea why. "What do you think I lied to you about?" Now she was not only confused, but she was a little frightened; he was really mad at her.

Connor gripped her upper arm painfully, and reached his hand down the bodice of her gown. Ignoring her indignant gasp, Connor pulled the amulet she'd been given out from her cleavage and snarled at her,

"Then what, pray tell, is this?"

"An amulet. I was told that it was my only way out of this," Mackenzie shrugged; she didn't see where he was leading her with this.

"'Tis the crest of the Campbell. Only a Campbell may wear it, and 'tis given to a bride only after the marriage is consummated." She could see that his anger was barely controlled by the tightly clenched jaw muscles. "You lied to me."

It all hit her at once; the strain of what she had just seen, and what he was saying, accusing her of. Her eyebrows shot to her hairline, "You can't seriously think that I slept with him?!" She could see from the set of his jaw and the flash in his eyes that he could. "I've never even met him!" Connor was towing her behind him to the door that entered the Great Hall. "Connor, you kidnapped me within hours of crossing into this time. *You* kidnapped *me!* You were there! Connor..."

They had entered the castle by now, and he was dragging her to the tower stairs, to her room.

"Connor, think about it! Why would I do—"

"Enough of your lies!" He yelled at her, cutting her off.

She cringed back away from his black fury. The tears that had been threatening to spill earlier now fell silently down her cheeks. "I...I don't know what you're talking about," she couldn't make her voice above more than a whisper.

He gritted his teeth, speaking through them, "I almost believed you!"

Connor shoved her roughly into her room, where she stumbled before righting herself, and he slammed the door. She turned against the cool wood and pressed her forehead to the door. While she yanked the unforgiving handle, Mackenzie heard him shout to someone named Robbie that she was not to leave, and no one was to come in apart from Bronwyn or himself. She heard him stomp away, listening until she couldn't hear the echo of his boots. Only then did she finally crumple to the floor and cried her eyes out.

Chapter Eleven

He left her alone for almost three days, with only Bronwyn coming in with her meals, and once a bath. Bronwyn hardly spoke to her, but on the second day, she placed a book on the table for Mackenzie, and with a sympathetic look over her shoulder, she left her alone again. She was grateful for the distraction the book provided, and her spirits were lifted slightly by the fact that Bronwyn seemed to care enough to bring it to her. But still, she felt unwanted and unwelcome, and while she and Connor had never spoken aloud their feelings, she'd thought that besides the mutual attraction, that they were at least becoming friends. She was wrong. She was nothing more than a tool; a means to an end. And she'd been naïve enough to stay willingly. Well, that would change.

Mackenzie thought about climbing out the tower window, but after one look down, realized that it would be impossible. It was a very slick wall with no foot holds and it was way too high to try to shimmy down without the foot holds. Besides that, the castle itself stood on the edge of a cliff, and even if she could shimmy down, she'd have to swim for it.

She thought about just walking out the door, but the glimpses she'd caught of her guard had her rethinking that plan. He was nearly as tall as Connor, but bigger, burlier. He reminded her of a lumberjack; just really big. At one point she realized that she had become a helpless damsel in distress, and she hated that fact. There had to be something she could do to free herself. If she could only talk to Connor and explain everything. Mackenzie sat down and tried to figure the best way to go about this. Apart from their mutual attraction, they had nothing in common; Mackenzie didn't know if Connor even liked her for crying out loud! The only thing she was certain of was that Connor wanted her. He just found her desirable. Her face twisted with pain at the thought that he could very well sleep with her and think nothing more of it than that. And she really knew very little about him. She didn't like how much she cared about what he thought of her; it was unnerving.

Her dreams became more and more vivid during her isolation. The one familiar nightmare now had some new twists. She also had some new dreams, and these were getting progressively more frightening. The first night, it was just the familiar fears of knowing she was going to die that had her screaming into her pillow. The second night, there was the addition of Connor staring at her from the opposite side of the room, and she was afraid for Connor this time, rather than herself. And that fear for Connor only grew stronger and stronger with each recurring dream. She had that same dream several times that night, so she figured that there must be some significance to Connor's appearance. It was especially strange since she'd been having that same dream since she was an adolescent, and never once had it deviated from the same plot. Connor's starring role confused her. Why was he there at all? And she'd always known that her death was a given. Did his presence in her dream mean that he was going to be killed too?

Mixed into her nightmares were other, more unwelcome dreams; dreams that also starred Connor. In these dreams, however, she was in his arms, and his touch was gentle, his expression tender. These dreams only made Mackenzie frustrated and angry. More often than not, she woke with hot tears streaming down her face. She knew she was attracted to him, but these dreams left her with the feeling of emptiness, knowing that he didn't even like her at all. He hated her now, for some unknown reason. For her unconscious mind to show her that she desired him to care for her made her angry with herself, and mad at him for being so unfair.

She had to do something to keep from going insane. She wanted to try to escape, but even if she miraculously found a way to break out, she didn't know where she could go. Maybe she could play a prank on her babysitter? She thought about all the things her brother used to do to her when they were kids, and an idea formed.

The first night, she feigned an illness, and when her guard ran down to call for help, Mackenzie took advantage of the situation and sprinted out into the hallway. Unfortunately, though, he hadn't actually left, he just stood at the top of the stairs and hollered down for Bronwyn. Before he could see her, she darted into the next room, and pressed her back against the door with a sigh of relief. She looked around the room and came eye to eye with a hostile pair of brown eyes! She was in someone else's room, and that particular someone else was in bed with a man!

She was taken back to her room, and it was humiliating.

The next time, she asked her guard if she might have some needlepoint, or mending that needed to be done. Robbie brought her some of Connor's mending, and Mackenzie stitched one shirt together, one she shorted a sleeve by a couple of inches, and she cut the sleeves off of one entirely. See him wear these!

Yet even after all of her annoying and admittedly childish pranks, Connor never came up to see her. Mackenzie had thought that cutting the sleeves off his shirt would have brought him in here itching for a fight. But he was still ignoring her. And that bothered Mackenzie much more than it should.

So after two and a half days of nothing but her own thoughts and the inevitable dreams for company, Mackenzie was exhausted, and annoyed, and confused, all at the same time. Annoyance at Connor primarily won out. After all, it was his fault that she was alone with her stupid fantasies. She squared her shoulders and decided that Connor could go to hell! The next time the Campbell sent an attack party, she would go with them, sticking to the original plan of staying with him. And screw Connor MacRae! Maybe then he'd realize she wasn't part of this stupid scheme.

The door opened, but instead of Bronwyn, Connor stepped in! But she forced herself not to care. Rather than the speech she'd had planned for him the day before, her new decision to ignore him fresh in her mind, Mackenzie stared at him without smiling, stood and walked to the window, her back to Connor.

"You'd do well to never turn your back on an enemy."

That broke through Mackenzie's new-found resolve, "And is that what you are, Connor? My enemy?" she turned agonized eyes on him.

He stared into her wide eyes for a moment before answering, "You have made it necessary."

Cryptic, great. "Nice, Connor. I have no ulterior motives. Believe the bad guys." She sighed, "Whatever. So to what do I owe the great *honor* of your presence? I was under the impression that I was to rot away in here until the next century."

"A lady should no' use sarcasm." His eyes narrowed.

"I'm no lady." She sat down on the chair closest to the window, and sat on her purse! She'd forgotten about her purse, how could she forget her purse? And all the fun 21st century toys she had! Oh well, it didn't matter. The way he was behaving, she didn't care anymore about what Connor thought; or so she told herself. "So, I repeat, why are you here?"

"I need the amulet ye are wearing. I plan on sending it back to your *husband.*"

Her eyes narrowed at the sneered word, but she didn't say anything immediately. "What if I told you that I need it more than you do? That it is my way to freedom, my way home…would you care at all?"

"I would still ask that you give it to me."

"Ask?! Since when do you *ask*?"

Connor's smile was not a friendly one, "All right, I would prefer no' to take it from you, I would prefer that you give it willingly to me."

"And you would have no problem taking it physically from me?"

He crossed his arms and raised an eyebrow.

"I didn't mean it that way," she said exasperated. "I know you are stronger than I am," she rolled her eyes. "I meant that you would have no problem *morally* taking this from me?"

He watched her fingers twisting and untwisting the pendant before meeting her eyes and answering, "Nay, *my* conscience is clear."

Mackenzie thought for a long moment, and some of the speech she had previously planned the day before came back to her. "All right, Connor, I'll give it to you, in order to prevent you from physically taking it off me." Connor held his hand out and stepped forward, only to freeze as she continued her thought. "But only on the condition that you listen to something I need to say first." She waited much more patiently than she felt.

"I could just take it from you and be done with it," he was clearly annoyed at the condition of surrender.

"Ah, but then how would you keep your conscience clear?" She smiled a frigid smile at him. "Please, sit down," and she gestured to the chair on the opposite side of the fireplace.

"I'll stand."

He was going to make this difficult. Well she hadn't really expected any less of him. "All right, then. Hmm, how to start? Well, I'll be blunt. Connor what year is it?"

"'Tis the year of our Lord Seventeen-hundred and ninety-two." He answered her slowly, as if he were trying to figure out why the date was relevant.

"All right, so bearing that in mind, here goes." Mackenzie took a deep breath and continued, "I won't be born until the year 1987. Please don't interrupt." She held up a finger to caution him. "I was touring this castle, your castle as it turns out, in the year 2010, when two men kidnapped me from the Gallery, and told me a crazy tale about a curse and an end of the bloodshed that has plagued their lands. They then pulled me through a secret passage in the wall, and next thing I know, I am in a carriage a little less than 200 years before my birth. The amulet they gave me is my ticket home. I guess it will open the door to my time or something, they never got to finish their crazy scheme.

"Because then another man kidnaps me," she glanced at him meaningfully, and then turned her gaze out to the window. She softly continued, as if he weren't there. "And this man tells me something similar, but with a different angle; with him it's to prevent the farce of a wedding. And then I end up back in the same castle where it all began, with no way home, no place here, and no idea how to proceed. So now, here I am, Mackenzie Stewart from Las Vegas, Nevada, stuck in the past with absolutely no hope of ever seeing my home again." She had to take a deep breath to steady herself, because she suddenly felt how true those words were. "And if you don't believe me, I just don't know what I'll do, because for some unknown reason, your opinion matters to me." By now a few stray tears had made their way down her cheeks but she ignored them, turning back to face Connor.

"You expect me to believe this? You have lied to me from the beginning. Now why should I believe anything you tell me?"

"Believe what you want." She shrugged, and turned her wet eyes back to the window. "I have not lied to you, Connor, not once."

"What I doona understand is why?" He went on as if she hadn't spoken. "Why would you do this? Agree to all this, and then try to seduce me? Is this something that you and your husband will laugh about later in your bed? Was that part of the plan? Perhaps gain some weakness on my part? To seduce me and then laugh at how easily I succumbed?" Connor stepped closer to where she sat, and his voiced dropped to a seductive purr. "All you had to do is ask…I have no qualms against bedding you, lass, but know this: when it happens, when we do come together, it will only be because you are begging me. And any time his hands touch you, you will feel only me. You will wish it was me." Connor strode to the front of her chair and pulled her roughly to her feet. "The fire you feel is for me, and he will never make you feel like I can." To emphasize his point, he traced a finger from her wet cheek to her lips, parting them as he drifted toward her neck, coming to rest on her throat. Her frantic pulse beat erratically against his hand.

Mackenzie struggled slightly, but gave up and let her tears fall unchecked down her cheeks. But she refused to look away. She wouldn't back down; she met his gaze unflinchingly.

He caught a tear on his fingertip, and brooded over it for a short moment. "Such pretty tears…wasted. Your tears do not move me. It seems that even a whore can cry."

Mackenzie sucked in a harsh breath through her teeth. "Now hold on just a damn minute. You want to believe the worst in me, fine, let John Campbell win. But do not mistake me for him. I haven't even been with a …." She took another deep, steadying breath, "I am not now, nor have I ever been a *whore,*" she spat the word back at him. "How naïve of me; I thought that maybe, just maybe, in this crazy mess, I had found a friend. But even you admitted that I am no more than a pawn in your stupid war game. And I'm such a sucker that even after I knew this, I still wanted to help you! God I'm an idiot! Well guess what? I don't care anymore, Connor. I don't care about your cause, or your war, or *you!* If you are too blind or too stupid to see what's in front of your own eyes, then that's your problem. I'm done. For you to stand there all 'holier than thou' and call me a whore? Especially when I've never…well, you can go to hell, Connor MacRae!" She yanked herself free, and tore the amulet from her neck. "Take the damn amulet! *I don't want it*!"

She threw it to Connor, not bothering to see if he caught it, and turned her back to him. Storming across the room, she opened the door, stood motionless, and very deliberately said, "Please leave."

"Nay." His soft refusal made no sense.

"Excuse me?" She raised an eyebrow.

"This is my castle."

"So that's how it is? I get no privacy?" She laughed, a bleak humorless sound. "Fine, Connor, whatever game you're playing, you win. Now *go*. I think I need to be alone. I don't think I'm alone enough here." Her voice was dripping with sarcasm.

"Doona do that again." His voice held an unmistakable threat.

"Do what?" Her irritation was making her bold, her words coming out harsher than she intended.

"Behave so disrespectfully."

"Why? What are you going to do to me? What more *can* you do to me?" Her fury had her shaking, her voice rose with her anger. She wanted to pound his chest with her fists, but she'd probably only hurt her hands. "I am stuck here, do you understand that? I am stuck here in this stupid backwards time, with my family, my friends, my whole *life* in a far too distant future. What the hell do you think that you can do to me that would be worse than that?" At least the anger kept her from crying. She took a steadying breath to keep the tears at bay.

"You are a better actress than I gave you credit for," he murmured. "So what is the point of such a tale? I wonder… If you need this so badly" he was twisting the amulet in the sunlight so that it glinted, "if it is so important, why do you give it to me?"

Mackenzie blew her breath out noisily, "Because that was our deal; plus I have no doubt you'd take it from me, and I am pretty much at my breaking point Connor. Have you given one second of thought to how this has affected me? I mean, I'm asking you to believe something pretty crazy, I know, but what about me? I was dragged through time and told that I have to pretend to marry an evil warlord who wants to kill me after conceiving his spawn. How do you think I feel? My head is still spinning! And to top it off, I only have until Halloween to pretend to get married to this man I've never met, then end a years-long feud somehow, and still make it back to my own time. All of this is looking less and less likely. I can't get back to my time without that amulet, but I don't even know how to go about that. So, you can have it!

"You know, at first I thought this was a dream, that you were a dream, but now I realize that either I hit my head and am in a coma somewhere, or I really am insane! I just don't care anymore. This sucks!" The tears were streaming down her cheeks and dripping off her chin.

Connor walked to her and gripped her hand, gently tugging her back into the room enough to shut the door. He stared at her as if he were deciding what to say. "Have you any proof of this?"

Her mouth fell open. "Do you mean you actually might believe me?!" burst incredulously from her lips.

He paused for a long moment before saying softly, "I want to believe you."

She gaped at him, "You do?"

"I'd rather no' believe the worst in you, however, I've no proof that you are an innocent in all this."

"I don't know how to prove any of this," she said sadly, her wet eyes dropped to her toes, studying her slippers. "Unless you could contact Morvern and Gregor?" she sounded hopeful.

"Perhaps, however, I was thinking of something more immediate. What can you tell me of the future?"

"What would you like to know?" She eyed him warily. Was she allowed to tell him about the future?

"Will the Scots win our freedom from the English?"

"No, not in the way you mean. I'm so sorry."

"What happens? Do they succeed in clearing out the Highlands?"

"To an extent," she hedged.

"Can we change that?"

"I think so, but again, only to an extent; by destroying the plot Campbell has. I think that's why his magicians came to get me. Apparently I am the first girl born to the Stewart line in 200 years." She smiled wryly. "I'm sorry my knowledge of Scottish history isn't better, but I only really know what my Granny told me in the form of bedtime stories as a child. I don't really know what I can do to help, other than just keep to the original plan, in which case I need to speak with Morvern and Gregor."

"If you think that I am going to send you back to the Campbell…"

"Back? As in you still think I've been with him before?" She interrupted him, and shook her head sadly. "You don't believe me at all then, do you?"

"'Tis a difficult tale to believe."

"You have no idea," she muttered, eyes downcast. Her tears were flowing freely, but silently. She didn't think she'd be able to stop the sobs that were sure to follow, so she freed her arm from Connor's grip and walked slowly to stare out the window. "You have what you came here for, Connor, you can leave now." She said it flatly, hoping that none of the strain she felt came through in her voice. But her nerves betrayed her as she jumped when Connor's voice came from right behind her.

"And if I doona want to leave?" he said it against her ear, his breath sending shivers down her spine.

Mackenzie turned around warily, "What else can you possibly want from me? I gave you the stupid amulet. Take it and go start your war!"

"And if that isn't all that I want?" Connor raised an eyebrow.

"What? What else is there? I've got nothing left to give!" Her eyebrows were drawn down in confusion, her lips pouting slightly. At least the tears were checked…for now.

Connor ran his fingers along her collarbone and under the line of her bodice, and Mackenzie gasped as she understood his meaning. He smiled and stepped closer to her until they were standing chest to chest, but not touching. She could feel the heat rolling off of him in waves. Mackenzie took a step back, but Connor followed her, still chest to chest, not allowing any space between them. She took another step back, and he stepped with her, as if they were dancing. She backed into the wall next to the window. Connor braced his arms on the wall, one on either side of her head. So close that she felt his skin brushing her cheeks as she looked at each arm. He leaned forward, and she shrank back even closer against the wall. She was almost tempted to duck under one arm, but he anticipated that, and pressed his body to hers, keeping her pinned there. She turned wide, slightly scared, eyes on him and whispered,

"Why are you doing this?" It was almost a plea, her eyes begged him to stop.

"You are a beautiful woman, Mackenzie. I'd hate for you to return to him without accomplishing what you set out to do." His lips were right against hers. She could feel the words as he said them, and she could feel the now familiar flames on her skin wherever his body touched hers. She didn't want this. He hated her, and no matter her own feelings, no matter that he wanted her, she couldn't do this. She wanted more. She brought her hands to his chest and pushed, but it was like pushing on a statue.

Her mumbled "Please don't" was lost in the kiss, as was her willpower. Mackenzie felt like such an idiot, but she couldn't force her traitorous body to stop him. She had stopped caring about anything except for Connor's lips on hers. The heat was incredible. It no longer felt like her skin was burning, because the fire was concentrated to her lips now. When his hands moved from the wall to her waist, she threw her own arms around his neck and kissed him back with everything she had. He was slightly surprised by the fierceness of her response, but he slipped one hand up to cup her chin, and angled her head up so he could trail his lips along her jaw line. The arm around her waist was crushing Mackenzie to him so that she could barely breathe, and yet it still wasn't close enough for her. She pulled his head back up to hers and his lips found hers again with an intensity that she hadn't felt from him before, his tongue slipped against hers in a sinfully erotic mating of her mouth.

The kiss changed and her breathing was coming in gasps. One of Connor's hands slid down to her thigh, and lifted her leg up to his hip, his other hand pressed against the small of her back. As he lifted her up against him, Mackenzie could feel how much he wanted her. It was unmistakable. He pressed her closer against his arousal, and she moaned, her head tilting back against the wall. His mouth was feverishly pressing against her décolletage, and the swell of her breast. Connor had pulled her skirts up to about mid-thigh when the cool air on her skin brought her sanity rushing back.

"Oh, no! Please stop!" It was so breathless, she was afraid he wouldn't listen, but he lifted his head and stared at her with burning eyes.

"Nay." His mouth pressed down her throat and back up to her lips.

If he didn't stop now, she would lose the grip on her tenuous resolve.

Mackenzie was frantic now, "Please, please, you have to stop!"

He glared at her, his eyes still burning. The blue was molten, liquid desire. "What game are ye playin' at, Mackenzie?" His brogue roughened with passion.

"It's not a game, I just, I…I can't do this!" Her pleading eyes were staring into his, and he slid her leg down the side of his, keeping his hand on her bared thigh.

"You want me." A muscle flexed in his jaw.

She dropped her gaze from his, and softly admitted, "You know I do."

"Then I fail to see the problem." He flexed the fingers on his hand holding her thigh.

"The problem is that you don't even like me!" her voice was rising. "How am I supposed to…" She shook her head slightly to clear it, took a deep breath, feeling her breasts rise and fall against his chest, and started again, "If you don't respect me, how can I respect myself in the morning?"

Connor slowly pulled his fingers down her jaw, her throat, and across her collarbone, tracing the edge of her bodice. Mackenzie's lips parted, and her breathing halted.

"Your body betrays you."

And his mouth swooped down once more to hers.

"I can't think like this," she pulled her lips away, clutching at his linen shirt. Connor stared into her eyes, her eyebrows meeting in the middle, and slanting up above her nose in confusion.

"What is there to think about?"

And again his lips touched hers, this time more lightly, teasing at her lips. He would seduce her in no time, the way her body melted into his, her limbs so heavy there was no hope of moving away from him. He was right; she would beg for it. Heat pooled in her belly and lower still between her legs. She wanted him so badly, but she couldn't…

When his lips left hers, it was only to kiss along her jaw, but it was enough for her to choke out, "God, Connor, I feel like every time I'm near you I could burst into flames." He lifted his head, the smoldering desire still in his eyes made it harder for her to form a clear thought. "Why? Why you? Why now, 200 years before my time? No man has ever affected me like this; you muddle my brain and I…I can't think when you're so close. I don't understand! What is fate trying to throw at me?" Her desperation seeped out and her voice trembled.

He stared into her eyes for a very long time before finally stepping back and giving her the breathing room she so desperately needed. Her head was far from clear, but it was clearer without him so close, without his scent in her nose, his hands on her skin. Her breathing was slowing, and she could see that his breathing was almost even as well. She took comfort in the fact that at least she seemed to have the same confusing affect on him as he did on her.

They stood staring into each others' eyes for a while, each looking for the answers to different questions. Eventually Mackenzie found her voice.

"What is it that you want from me?" Her eyes were searching his, looking for some small measure of feeling. If she thought for one second that he cared for her, even in the slightest, she would throw herself into his arms and never look back, damn the consequences. But all Mackenzie saw was that the molten blue of his eyes had cooled to a hard sapphire now, and she knew he didn't think of her that way—he just wanted her in his bed.

"Supper will be served in the Hall, I'll fetch you in an hour."

"I'm going down for dinner?" Shock replaced the sadness on her face. Then skepticism. "Why?"

"One hour." He ignored her question, and strode out of the room.

Mackenzie sagged against the wall and caught her breath, mentally preparing herself for the inevitable contact she would have with Connor in an hour.

* * * *

Connor replayed the past events in his head as he strode downstairs. When Robbie had told him that Mackenzie was part of the plot to invade his castle, he'd lost it. She had lied to him! She had claimed no knowledge of the Campbell's plans, and he had believed her to be an innocent in all this, but in reality she was central to the plot. He had thought all his men loyal to him, but he'd never once thought the girl he'd stolen from his enemy would be a ruse.

He had always prided himself on being able to read people. Living by the sword, one found ways to read the smallest changes in expression, the barest hint of deception in one's eyes. He had never doubted Mackenzie's wide sincere gaze. He didn't like to be wrong, in fact he was rarely ever wrong, but he had been very, very wrong about this girl. And when the clan chief made mistakes, people died. He was very lucky that the man captured had told them of the Campbell's plots. To think! Mackenzie's abduction had been so easy because it had been a set up! Connor did not like to feel like a fool, and she had without doubt played him for a fool.

So he locked her in her room and tried to forget about her.

But the past few days he'd spent angry at her had been some of the worst of his life. It was the irritating attraction he had for his enemy's woman that was the problem. He'd wanted to barge into her room and demand an explanation. He'd wanted to kiss her senseless, forcing her to admit what was between them was more than just attraction. And most of all he wanted to be wrong about her.

When Dougal, his captain, had suggested that they send the amulet back to the Campbell, Connor couldn't admit to himself that he really just wanted an excuse to see Mackenzie again. Which was completely stupid; she was the Campbell's wife, and therefore the enemy. Especially since she had the key role of distracting and seducing Connor. He was grateful that his men had gotten that piece of information from the Campbell's toady so quickly.

So when he had walked into Mackenzie's chambers, he'd really had no intention of bedding another man's wife. But when she had turned her lying emerald green eyes, swimming with tears on him, imploring him to believe her tale, he'd thought, *Why not?* She was here to do just that, so he might as well be in control. It wasn't as if she were a maid. He now knew that to be false.

He'd given in to temptation and kissed her. It had surprised him a little when she had kissed him back so hungrily, but in truth, he found it hard to concentrate on anything when her tongue tangled with his. She seemed eager enough for his kisses, but what he didn't understand was why she kept stopping the inevitable? That was the one complication; he was constantly fighting his attraction to her. He felt like she had been sent to him to bewitch him. The Campbell had chosen his actress well. It would be a strong man who could resist Mackenzie. It also made her story that much harder to believe as truth.

Her story. He couldn't understand what she hoped to gain with a tale such as that? It was beyond anything he'd ever imagined. How could she ask him to believe such a tale? But some of her idiosyncrasies could be explained that way; her clothing, her manner of speech, her behavior, her blue toenails. There was something very obviously different about her, but was it this fanciful tale?

Nay, he couldn't believe anything she said.

But when she had answered his questions about the future of the Highlands, she had answered that they would not be free…was that because she was telling the truth, or because she was on the side of the Campbell? He narrowed his eyes as he thought of the plot to invade his castle from the inside out. He'd like to believe that the prisoner was lying, but to what end? It made no sense. The prisoner, named MacAllistair, had said that Mackenzie and the Campbell were already married, and the amulet had further supported the story. Supper would be served in less than an hour, and already a plan was forming; he would get the information he needed from Mackenzie. But first, he would speak to this MacAllistair himself.

When he'd spoken with the Campbell's man, he hadn't learned anything his own men hadn't already found out. In fact, the story told was almost verbatim to what his men had said. He did, however, deduce that the man was lying. About what, he did not know. But he would figure it out. That one flaw gave Connor a slight glimmer of hope that Mackenzie might be telling the truth. He wanted to believe that she had not lied to him. Everything in him wanted to believe that. It mattered, no he corrected, *she* mattered, much more than she should.

Chapter Twelve

The sorcerer Morvern was meticulously sifting through ancient scrolls, reading ancient languages, and praying for a miracle. He feared John Campbell had more than "dabbled" in the black arts that he himself had always avoided.

Gregor hurried into their dark work space. The only light came from several tallow candles scattered about the room. There were no windows here, no light, only dark. They were not using the rooms set up for them in the tower; that would give them away.

"Father, I think I have found a way to bar the dark magic from entering the MacRae's castle. It is something akin to a protection spell, only rather than protecting one person, it shall protect the whole of his keep."

"Tell me," the firm command belied the frail voice.

"If we use the charm we placed on the amulet, and add a greater amount of rosehips and lavender, it is said to protect a lady. Have you discovered a way to kill him yet?"

"No, my son, the dark arts blind our magicks to him. I have only defensive spells as of yet. So far I can only trap him or freeze him momentarily. Although, mayhap a moment would be all we need?" Morvern trailed off into his own train of thoughts, as happened to a man of his years.

His son interrupted his musings. "Perhaps we can trap him in the amulet somehow?"

"Perhaps…you work on that. I must needs unbind his dark works from this castle. Only then will we have a chance to defeat him."

"Aye, father, I shall begin immediately."

"Yes, yes, of course. Let us hasten. I fear that Lord Campbell is a lost cause, and while we cannot save him from himself anymore, we certainly can and must vanquish him."

"But how? His anger at the abduction of his bride-to-be grows with each passing minute. He wants vengeance. If we let him be for much longer, I fear he will try to kill both the MacRae and the girl. Are you sure that he does not know of her true identity?"

"As of yet, no. He has been too focused on the MacRae to investigate into her background. For now, he is satisfied that she is who we say. However, while his anger is directed at Connor MacRae, I would not assume that he will let the Stewart lass live til All Hallows Eve. His heart blackens daily and I fear he will forget his plan and try only for total destruction."

"Then we must protect her while we can, else she will surely feel his wrath." Gregor was uncharacteristically compassionate toward the

Stewart lass. He shrewdly guessed what his father had not said, "You have foreseen that she loves the MacRae." It was a statement.

"Aye."

"Did you know that he would attack our carriage that night?"

"Aye, it was inevitable."

"Then why the pretense of the marriage? Why did we not just tell her that she would be delivered into the hands of Connor MacRae? That they were destined to be together?"

"We told her what was necessary, no more, no less. She will need to think that this was the plan from the start. She needs to fall in love without us prompting her. Do not forget, she is not of our time, her world does not believe in magic and true love is a lost concept. And she needed to remain innocent else Connor MacRae would not trust her, let alone allow himself to love her."

"So if they are destined to love each other, if bringing the two of them together was the plan all along, what of our plan to distract Lord Campbell?"

"He is distracted, is he not? Hell-bent on vengeance, he has momentarily forgotten his plot to use our magicks as a means for his dark purposes."

"Then we had best hurry, Father, for Lord Campbell is not a patient man. He is getting closer each day to using the dark arts to defeat Laird MacRae."

"Then let us cast your protection spell without haste. And we had better pray."

Chapter Thirteen

When Connor knocked on Mackenzie's door, he was in a much better mood than before. He didn't want to admit to himself that part of it was the prospect of seeing Mackenzie again. He'd missed her over the past couple of days. He had missed her smile. He had missed her laugh. He had even missed her flash of impatience when he ordered her about. Connor didn't wait for her to answer his knock, he never did. Usually, Connor just walked right in. He frowned as he realized that she wasn't too far off the mark at accusing him of allowing her no privacy.

She was sitting in a chair by the fire, with her legs tucked up under her skirts and her arms wrapped around them. She looked over her shoulder at him, stood gracefully, and walked to stand a couple of feet in front of him. Her eyes were blank, on her face she wore a careful expression of neutrality. Connor didn't like this. Something was wrong. Normally she would have greeted him with a smile, or a heated comment. He found both her anger and her joy to his liking, in fact he found *her* to his liking, *dammit!* He liked her. He liked how she always had something to say, and how she seemed determined to question everything. While he had not liked to have his orders questioned, even that had become endearing. And now that he was finally leaning towards believing her, she changed.

It was obvious she must be distancing herself from him, but what he did not understand was why?

And with that thought in the forefront of his mind, he wondered why she was behaving like this? As if she was empty, or *broken*. He sucked in a deep breath, and stared at her blank face. He wanted to shake her a little. He wanted to kiss her until she moaned into his mouth. He wanted to throw her down onto the bed and force her to confront this all-consuming desire. He wanted *her*. How could he bring that fire back into her eyes?

"Shall we?" Connor offered her his arm.

Wordlessly, Mackenzie placed her hand through his arm. She didn't meet his gaze, instead keeping her face turned forward.

"How are you feeling?" He was worried about her now.

"Well, thank you."

He tried again, "We have a piper tonight; he'll entertain us as we dine."

"That's nice."

Her tone was polite, uninterested, that was all. Where was all the passion, the emotion? Where was *Mackenzie?*

* * * *

Mackenzie had taken the past hour *sans* Connor to re-prioritize herself. Obviously he hadn't believed her crazy tale. Well, she wasn't sure she believed it yet! But for a moment there, he had looked at her as though she might not be entirely insane, and Mackenzie had pinned all her hopes on the brief flash in his eyes. Unfortunately, he went back to being rational. It hurt having him think those horrid thoughts about her being in league with the bad guys. But it really didn't matter what he thought of her, if he wouldn't believe anything she said, why bother trying anymore, right? So she gave up. She gave up caring about her "mission," or caring about who started a fight or a war. Mackenzie gave up hope that she would be rescued, or that she would ever see her own time again. She gave up hope that Connor would ever believe her, and she gave up hope that he wanted her for anything other than to warm his bed. That was surprisingly the hardest thing to give up on. But she did. And when hope was gone, there wasn't anything left. Mackenzie was numb. But numb was okay; she couldn't feel pain when she was numb.

It was a complication that she went up in flames every time he touched her, but maybe she could avoid touching him? Hmm…not likely. Well, she'd just concentrate on getting through dinner, and worry about everything else later, as it came at her. She would live moment-to-moment. It was easier than trying to think ahead; to think of what else the crazy fates were going to throw at her.

It had been what, a week since she'd officially gone insane? Time had become just as meaningless as everything else. She had expended so much energy on hope, and on trying to get Connor to believe her, that she was barely hanging on to her sanity. The instincts for survival were the only things functioning in her overwrought brain, and even those were down to the bare minimum. Eat, sleep, breathe. Her last go-round with Connor had emotionally drained her, and she was running on empty. So she stared at him balefully, and slipped her arm through his as they walked down the hallway to the stairs.

Dinner went by in her new-found haze. She ate the food, but tasted nothing. She listened to the music, but heard nothing. And she sat next to Connor, intensely aware of the heat passing from him to her, and futilely tried her hardest to remain unaffected.

The next few days passed in the welcome fog of numbness. Connor now let her go where she pleased in the castle. She still wasn't allowed outside. Only once, when she glanced out the window in the library and saw Connor with a tender look on his face, conversing with a beautiful woman with long auburn hair, did she feel any of the pain she'd been hiding from herself. But ever the survivor, she resolutely turned her face back to the book she'd been pretending to read and tried to forget the soft, unguarded expression Connor had worn when he'd looked at the girl. He had never looked at her like that; as if he'd cared for her. She refused to feel jealousy for something that had never been hers. She vaguely remembered wishing once that he would look at her like that; with his guard down. But Mackenzie tamped the memory down, and tried not to think.

It was too hard to keep her traitorous thoughts from straying to Connor, so she went back to her room and tried to take a nap. Sleep came quickly to her. Mackenzie hadn't been sleeping well, so she constantly felt tired, and drank a lot of the strong coffee she'd begun to like. She'd found out through Bronwyn that they actually had coffee houses here in 18th century Britain. What she wouldn't give to see one! The first primordial beginnings of trendy café! She had smiled for the first time in days when Bronwyn had shared this information with her. Apparently, when coffee was first introduced to Britain during the 17th century, it was a drink enjoyed by everyone. While the rich would enjoy coffee almost ceremonially in their social clubs, the poor saw coffee as an essential nutrient, a hot drink to replace a hot meal. She just needed the caffeine.

This time, the dream that woke her was as close to an actual nightmare as she'd ever had. It was the man with the ice cold blue eyes again…she was now assuming that he was her "fiancé," John Campbell. He and Connor were fighting in a strange dark place but she could tell it was inside somewhere with high arched ceilings.

It had begun the same as always, but when she glanced across the beautiful room at Connor, she realized he was in chains, as he looked at her balefully. She looked down at herself and noticed that there was something cool and metallic in her hands. She couldn't figure out all the pieces yet, the way some dreams are. Then Connor's chains turned to snakes and he leaped out of them. He ran to the man, sword drawn and Mackenzie screamed.

Her fear wasn't for herself, it was for Connor. In the dream, while Connor had a sword, the Campbell had fire. Mackenzie couldn't explain how he controlled the fire; it seemed to come from his fingertips, but her instincts were shouting to her that Connor would die in this fight. And she was running. She knew how to stop it, the fight, the feud, her purpose here…she knew it all. If only she could get there in time! But she couldn't; she kept running and running, but she never was able to gain any distance. She woke screaming, and pulled a pillow over her face to stifle the sound. She sat up drenched in sweat, and with her hair sticking to her face. Her ragged breathing and staccato heartbeat wouldn't slow.

The sound of her door being thrown open tore a soft scream from her throat. She cut it off by clamping a hand over her mouth as she saw Connor leap through the open door, sword drawn. His eyes were scanning the room, looking for something. She realized that he must have heard her screaming.

He turned his eyes to her and his voice was rough, "Are ye hurt?"

She quietly cleared her throat and said, "No, I'm sorry. It was a dream." She said once more, this time to herself, "It was only a dream."

He sheathed his sword and came to stand in front of Mackenzie, who still sat in her bed, tangled in the unavoidable skirts that came with this century. His eyes searched hers for a moment before he dropped to his knee, so he was at eye level with Mackenzie.

"A dream?" He said it softly, but seriously.

"A…a bad dream." Mackenzie suddenly wanted nothing more than to throw her arms around the man whom she'd been ignoring for the past few days. She wanted to feel him warm and safe, even if it would only hurt her in return. She'd known that she had feelings for Connor, but the dreams had shown her just how deep her feelings went. Her fingers ached to touch his face, to smooth the worry away from his brow. So instead, she swung her legs over the side of the bed, and straightened her skirts. She kept her eyes on her hands.

"Can you tell me of the dream?" Her eyes flew to his.

"You mean you actually want to know?" She didn't want him to know how central to her dreams he was. She could say she didn't remember it. No, he could tell when she was lying. Quickly she mentally edited the dream; it was about blood and death, probably brought on from what she'd seen in her short time here...that could work.

"Aye, lass, I'd like to ken what had you screamin' like a banshee."

"Oh," she flushed, wondering who else had heard her screams.

"Please?" It was the softening of his eyes that had Mackenzie telling him the truth. Mostly.

"Umm…it was mainly about…you…" she looked at her hands again, and fidgeted with her skirts. "You were going to be killed," she whispered it, her lips barely moving with the admission.

"Look at me," he commanded. She didn't move. "Mackenzie?" Her lashes fluttered, but she forced her eyes to remain down. A long finger under her chin tilted her face until she had to look at him. "I'm fine. See?" He spread his arms wide.

"But you won't be." Now she'd done it. She hadn't meant to tell him this.

His eyes narrowed, "What do you mean?"

"Nothing. Don't worry about it." Mackenzie tried to play it off. "I'm okay, so thanks for checking on me." She was beginning to feel again. The friendly numbness was nowhere to be found. She needed him to leave so she could collect herself…or cry.

"There's something you're no' telling me."

Why was he so observant? "It was just a dream, Connor." Mackenzie stood and tried to step around him, but he stood as well, and stopped her with a hand on her shoulder.

"What are you hiding from me?"

"It's not important." Mackenzie swung her hair to hide her face. Connor swept it aside and behind her shoulder, his fingers brushing her neck.

"If it has you screaming like that, then yes, 'tis."

His gentle tone made Mackenzie angry, angrier than when he was pushy and arrogant. Why couldn't he just leave it alone? Why did he choose now to be nice and caring? It made her voice sharp, "But you never believe me, so why should this be any different?"

He stiffened at the bitterness in her tone. "Why wouldn't I believe a dream?"

"Fine," she snapped. He asked for it. "Sometimes I have dreams that aren't really dreams at all. They're, I don't know, premonitions, or something."

He sucked in a quick breath, "You have visions?"

"No. Well, yes. Kinda. It's hard to explain. Like, I've been having the same dream since I was a teenager, but I'm only just now starting to understand it. I think it was about me coming here," she glanced at him before adding, "to your time."

"What was it, this dream from your childhood?"

"I think about my marriage to John Campbell."

"What makes you think that?"

"I'm not sure, but it's the only thing that makes sense. I keep seeing myself in a crowded hall, with everyone in costumes, er, I mean gowns, and I'm staring at him. And I know that I'm going to die, and that he's the one who's going to kill me. Yet I walk towards him anyway." She shrugged. "That's all."

"There's more." His eyes were shrewd. Again, Mackenzie wondered why he had to be so damn observant.

She sighed, "Usually my dreams only predict death. Like when my grandmother died, or my parents, I knew that they were dead before the police told us."

"Us?"

"My brother Braden and me."

"You've a brother? I thought you were an only child."

"For all intents and purposes, here, I am."

He ignored that, "So what was in your dream that has you thinking that I will die?"

Her eyes squinted in concentration. Trying to remember the dream that was becoming less and less real with each passing moment was like trying to look through a dimly lit room. "You were fighting the man with the cold eyes. He had control over fire. I'm not sure what happens…I just know that he will win. Everything we do, bringing me here, it's useless. I'm useless." Mackenzie threw her hands up in the air. She was so frustrated. The whole point of being dragged through time was to save Connor and his people, and she couldn't do anything! And now he would die because of her. She had to stop this.

"And the man with the cold eyes, this is the Campbell?"

"I'm not sure. I think so, but I've never seen John Campbell before. This man is tall, blond, blue eyes."

"That sounds like him. What do you mean when you say he had control over fire?"

"I don't know. It was like it came from his sword, or his hands, I'm not sure! This is so frustrating!" Her voice rose with her irritation. "It's hard to explain, but I'll dream it again, over and over and over. It never stops until someone dies!" She controlled her voice, "The dreams usually have to be pieced together…it takes several before I can really figure it all out."

"And you ken that this is a vision, rather than simply a nightmare?"

She snorted, "Last night I dreamt that I was being chased by a giant cheeseburger, so yeah, I can tell the difference."

"A what?"

"Never mind. In answer to your question, yes, I know when the dreams are important. They feel real. Even in the dream, they feel *real.*" She ran a hand through her tangled curls and exhaled roughly, "I can't explain it right."

Connor stared at her without speaking for a moment before asking her, "Will you tell me when you figure out how he controls the fire?"

"Sure, if you want me to…wait! Seriously? Does this mean you believe me?" Her jaw fell open.

"Aye, Mackenzie, I do."

"Really?" And she smiled so widely, her smile blinded him. And it fell just as quickly, replaced with suspicion. "Why?"

"My mother had visions."

"Oh. But you still think I am in cahoots with John Campbell."

"Aye, and I'm truly sorry about that."

"But you believe that I'm trying to help now." She was trying to understand his thinking.

"Aye, but I still think that I was set up to abduct you; there is just too much that does no' make sense."

"Like what? Maybe I can help?"

Connor didn't answer right away, as if he was trying to decide how much to tell her. "The Campbell's man told me that you two were married last month, and that you are here to help him find a way into my home; to destroy my clan."

Mackenzie burst into laughter. "Seriously?" she gasped between chuckles. "That is what you think? And I thought I was naïve." When she had composed herself, she said, "So does this man have any proof that I was married last month?" She couldn't keep the smile off her face.

"The pendant that you wore; 'tis only given to Campbell brides on their wedding night."

"And you never thought that the men who brought me here might have stolen it for me?"

"Nay, I hadn't. But it matters not, because you canna prove you are not what they say."

"But what if I could prove I am who *I* say I am?" Mackenzie had stepped closer to him in her newfound hope.

Connor's eyes suddenly had a fevered light in them, "Can you?"

Mackenzie thought of her purse, and mentally smacked herself. *Duh! The answer had been there all along!* She could have saved herself a ton of heartache if she'd thought of it earlier. She smiled and opened her mouth to say that as a matter of fact, she could, when a knock sounded at her door.

Bronwyn entered with a tray of biscuits and a cup of coffee causing Mackenzie to smile. She and Bronwyn had become friends, despite all the nasty gossip. And for Bronwyn to remember she liked coffee in the afternoon was touching. But Bronwyn jumped as she saw Connor standing in front of Mackenzie.

"Oh, me Laird! I dinna ken ye'd be in here. Me Lady, here's yer coffee. I'll just be leavin' it on the table here and take my leave." She practically scampered out into the hallway.

When Mackenzie turned her face back to Connor she was shocked. He was frowning at the door. What was wrong? What was he angry about this time?

"Is everything okay?"

"When did you last eat?" She hadn't expected that to be the problem.

Her brow furrowed, "I don't know, breakfast?" It came out as a question; his line of questioning had her confused.

"And you haven't been eating in the hall at suppertime, have you?"

"I didn't know I should." Where was he going with this?

"I doona want you to think you're unwelcome," he murmured.

Mackenzie laughed at that. "Connor, I'm just happy that I'm not in the dungeon, or wherever you would keep prisoners."

"Is that how you think of yourself, as a prisoner?" His blue eyes were intense.

"You don't?" She challenged.

"I've no' been verra welcoming, have I?" Connor shook his head to himself.

"It's okay. I know you don't like me." She shrugged, hoping he wouldn't hear the sadness in her voice. "Don't worry about it. Besides," she smiled, "I'm not cooped up in my room anymore; I get to wander around the castle now. It's nice. I like the library." Her smile looked genuine, but it didn't meet her eyes. "But maybe I could go on walks outside?" she hinted.

He focused on the first part of her comment, "You think I doona like you?" He was surprised, but he said it softly.

"It's not a big deal. Really." *Really, it was*. She shrugged again, and looked away.

"It is to me."

She looked back at him, "Look, I understand, okay? I'm your ticket to picking a fight or whatever. That's all. I mean, you're barely civil to me, so I get it. I only hope that you will let me go after it's all over."

"You want to leave?" The surprise on his face was almost comical to Mackenzie.

"What am I going to do, stay here forever?"

"You ken I want you."

Her eyebrows flew up, surprised by his bluntness. "Yes."

"And still you think I doona care for you."

"Lust and love are two very different things." Now what had made her say that?

"Love?" He arched a brow and she flushed.

Trying to seem nonchalant, Mackenzie played it off, "It's an expression."

Connor was quiet for a long time. Long pauses made her nervous and she was about to break the silence when he finally spoke, "It seems I have a lot to apologize for."

"You? Apologize?" Mackenzie couldn't keep the disbelief from her face.

Connor looked into her wide shocked eyes and demanded, "Come to supper with me tonight."

Mackenzie was too surprised to do anything but stare. Her mouth may have been hanging open; to be honest, she couldn't tell. He wanted her to go to dinner with him? Was this like a date type of dinner? Or was it an "I feel guilty about keeping you prisoner" type of dinner? Definitely the latter. She doubted that dinner had the same connotation here that it did in her time. She didn't want his sympathy. And he was still waiting for an answer.

"No, thank you." Mackenzie said it as softly and demurely as she could.

His eyebrows flew up in disbelief. "You'd rather stay in here?"

"I'd rather not have your pity."

"Now you think I pity you?" He sounded as if he couldn't decide whether to be amused or annoyed.

"You're going to tell me that you don't feel guilty for keeping me trapped here? And that inviting me to dine with you isn't a way to assuage that guilt?"

"Verily, I am sorry that I have no' been more," he seemed to struggle with the last word, "cordial. Would you give me the pleasure of joining me for supper?"

"That was very polite, Connor, but still, no."

"It is entirely maddening to try to hold a conversation with you. Most women would agree to accompany me to dine, and enjoy a pleasant evening."

"I'm not most women," she said tartly, a little miffed that he wanted her to behave like one of the mindless girls who apparently worshipped at his feet.

Connor was thoughtful for a second, "Nay, that you're no', are you? Hmm…"

"And don't expect me to pretend to be."

He looked surprised that she would jump to that conclusion. "I'd never ask you to change, Mackenzie, it's not your nature. Regardless, would you sup with me?"

Mackenzie thought for a moment, "You're not going to give up, are you?"

"Nay."

She sighed, "All right, let's go." She walked ahead of him, so she didn't see his smile.

Chapter Fourteen

Dinner was a quiet event with just the two of them in a more intimate and formal dining room than the Great Hall. Connor sat across from

Mackenzie and she enjoyed the food for the first time since she could remember. It was some kind of meat, mutton probably, and an array of potatoes, vegetables and bread. She drank wine, and by the end of dinner was feeling a little tipsy. Mackenzie didn't know how many cups she'd had because her glass had never been empty. And when Connor looked at her over his own glass of wine, it had been easy to pretend that he felt about her the way she felt about him. She knew by now that she was really close to falling in love with him. And as much as it hurt for him to believe the worst in her, she couldn't help her feelings. It was like she was on the edge of a cliff and the ground was falling out from under her. To fall would be the easy way; falling in love with Connor. But trying to hold on with the earth crumbling out from under her was so hard. She knew that she was fighting a losing battle by trying to keep her heart out of this. When she looked at him over the table, candles glowing and wine flowing, Mackenzie knew that she would lose that battle tonight.

Connor asked Mackenzie if she was finished, and came around the table to stand behind Mackenzie's chair. He held her chair as she stood, and then offered his arm to her. She kept his gaze as he led her to the French doors, and they stepped outside.

"Walk with me."

She nodded and kept her eyes on his. They started along the battlement, and wandered slowly, the only sound the swish of her skirts. The weather had gotten much colder than when she'd first arrived in Scotland, but standing next to Connor she didn't feel the cold. All she could feel was the incredible heat coming off his body.

It had been days since they had had any contact with each other, but if she had hoped time would change her reactions to his proximity, she was wrong. Every time their arms brushed, and where her fingers lightly curled around his bicep, that heat scorched right through to her bones. Mackenzie lifted her skirts to climb down the stairs, and shivered as the wind that swept off the water crept up her skirts to her bare legs (she hadn't liked the wool stockings that women here favored, and instead went bare-legged). Connor took her hand with his and wrapped his other arm around her waist.

At first, Mackenzie didn't realize that they had stopped walking, but she felt the wind much stronger on her face now that they were in the courtyard. A sudden arctic blast tore the pins from her hair and whipped it across her face. In a surprisingly tender gesture, Connor caught a few strands and tucked them behind her ear. It unraveled her willpower that much more. When he faced her now, there was no animosity, no anger, there was only hunger. It wasn't the emotion she'd hoped for, but it was enough.

For now. It would have to be.

Whether he saw her willpower crumble, or he would have kissed her anyway, Mackenzie didn't know. But the gentle pressure of his lips on hers was enough to make her forget that she didn't want this. She wanted him, and that was enough. She wanted to forget all of the pain and stress of the past week. As strong as she'd always thought she was, she felt so incredibly fragile, like anything could break her right now. And Connor felt strong, and warm, and real. Would it be so wrong if she took shelter in his solid strength?

Connor's lips seduced her. They teased hers open and his tongue took over the seduction. First it traced the outline of hers, and she could feel his breath on her lips. It darted in and tangled with hers. She thought she might go insane if he couldn't stop this burning inside her. Finally he braided his hand into her hair and plunged his tongue into her mouth, leaving no doubt as to what he wanted. His other hand reached down the front of her gown and he rubbed his thumb across her nipple, rolling it into a tight peak. He smiled against her lips at her gasp, and he lowered his head to her breast and flicked his tongue across her tight bead. This time she moaned, and leaned her head back so he could feast more fully on her body. But he withdrew his hand and wrapped his arms around her, once more taking her mouth in a fierce passionate kiss.

He pressed her against the wall of the castle, and she didn't even feel the cold stones at her back. There was only the heat between the two of them, and the feel of his body against hers. The fever in her veins. When Connor wrapped his arms around her waist and lifted her to meet his lips, she shuddered and forgot how to breathe. He'd lifted her slightly, one hand under her thigh, to grind her against the hard length of his arousal. Mackenzie gasped. She'd had boyfriends before, but none could ever compare with what she felt with Connor. She had always stopped them before it got too far. It wasn't that she was saving herself for marriage, but she just had never felt that spark; like there had been some crucial piece missing in her previous relationships. And she'd never quite understood what that was. Until she'd met Connor. This all-encompassing desire was what she'd been waiting for. And Connor felt it too. She knew he wanted her, and had since that first moment in the meadow. She hoped once more that it would be enough for her, because he had just taken her will and made it his own.

But Connor pulled back and gazed deeply into her eyes.

"What?" Mackenzie mouthed; she had no breath for words.

He smiled slightly and said, "Unless you'd like for me to take you here against the wall in front of God and everyone, mayhap we should go inside."

Mackenzie turned her startled gaze to the empty courtyard. Truthfully she'd forgotten where they were. "Oh," it seemed anticlimactic, but it was all she could manage.

His quiet laughter shook her body with his. She could tell that he knew she'd been completely oblivious to their surroundings. *Damn him.* He could have taken her right up against the wall of the keep and she wouldn't have minded one bit. Oh well, she'd stopped caring about what he thought of her. Her pride had fallen with her willpower at dinner, and it was now enough that he desired her. This place and time was messing with her sense of self. She doubted she'd recognize the person she saw in the mirror anymore. She was slightly torn between what she wanted more—Connor or her pride. Before she had a chance to say anything else, he made the decision for her; Connor scooped her up into his arms and strode through a door she hadn't noticed before.

* * * *

Connor placed her on her feet next to her bed and stood back to stare at her for a moment. Mackenzie assumed that it was a chance for her to say no, or to tell him to stop, but she gazed boldly right back at him. She didn't want to stop him this time. She could tell when he recognized her assent, that she wasn't going to stop him, because he inhaled sharply and stiffened slightly. He had expected her refusal again, but the look in her eyes was acceptance enough, and he slowly pulled her to him.

He groaned as his head descended to hers, yet his lips were surprisingly gentle. Mackenzie pressed herself closer to him, her hands gripping his upper arms. She wanted the feel of skin on skin. The previously cold air now felt unbearably hot and sultry. The heat that Connor brought with him was seeping through her layers of clothing into her skin. She desperately needed to feel his skin, and he must have felt the same because he had her simple kirtle and gown unlaced and off in one smooth motion while his hands made quick work of her stays.

His lips were on hers before she could slip off her shift, her hands trapped between their bodies as he crushed her to him. She was clutching the front of his shirt when her knees gave out, but his arms were like steel, and he held her tightly. Connor's large hand cupped her bottom, to bring her closer against his bulging arousal, his other had moved up to tangle in her hair. He groaned quietly into her mouth, his rock-hard muscles tightening against her soft skin. He lifted her up and onto the bed, one hand at her waist, the other under her thigh. Connor's weight pressed her into the soft mattress, and she welcomed the solid strength of him. His hand bunched the material at her thigh as he kissed her deeply, moving one hand to the small of her back. He pulled her to a sitting position and pulled it up until he could slip the shift off over her head. Pressing her back into the bed, he dipped his head to the hollow of her throat, and Mackenzie arched her neck back into the pillows. He trailed his lips down her collarbone and found her breast. But he only traced along the valley in between her breasts, then lower to her flat belly, lingering on her belly ring, until his mouth found purchase at the v between her legs. Even though Mackenzie knew what he was going to do, the feel of his tongue darting out to taste her shocked her, and she shuddered in response.

Her eyes flew to his. Connor held her gaze and flicked his tongue out again, and again. Mackenzie moaned and her eyes rolled back into her head. It was the most intimate, erotic moment of her life. Connor's hands gripped her hips to hold her still, and he plunged his tongue inside her. Mackenzie gasped and her hips lifted slightly off the bed. But Connor pressed her back into the mattress and his tongue mated with her in such splendid agony. She wanted more. Mackenzie's hands were clutching the pillow behind her head, and she moved them to Connor's shoulders to pull his mouth back to hers. Instead, he moved his lips to her collarbone, and replaced his mouth with his fingers, slipping one inside Mackenzie. Her fingernails raked down his back, and she writhed against his fingers. He glided it in and out and slipped another finger in. Mackenzie moaned and whipped her head back and forth against her pillow. Connor knew what she wanted, but why was he withholding it?

"Why are you here, Mackenzie?"

Her eyes fluttered, "Huh?" Words made no sense to her right now.

Connor moved his fingers again, and pressed his lips to her throat, "What is it you want from me?"

"I...oh God, Connor...I want..."she squirmed against his hand, "this, you, oh I want you..." She clenched her thighs around him.

"Why are you really here?" she could feel the movement of his lips against her skin and the warmth of his breath as he spoke. It both tingled and aroused.

"I want," her eyes were dazed, and she ran a hand over her face, "umm...I want to help you..." His fingers never stopped and she was so close; what was he doing to her? "I can help..." *So close...* "Oh I can't think...I can distract him...buy you time to kill him...oh please Connor!" Mackenzie was pressing his hand tightly against her, pleading through dazed eyes.

Connor flicked his thumb across her swollen bud and gave her the release she so desperately craved. As she shuddered and stilled, Connor shrugged out of his clothes with a wicked smile playing about his lips, "I'm no' finished with you yet."

Mackenzie didn't even have time to ponder his words; she barely caught a glimpse of his glorious naked body, before he plunged into her with one swift stroke. Mackenzie bit her lip to keep from crying out. It hurt. A lot. It was as if he was trying to split her in two. Was it supposed to hurt this much? But then Connor moved, and oh, it felt so wonderful. He filled her, as he sheathed himself to the hilt. And when he lifted almost all the way out, she pressed her hands to the small of his back to bring him back down. It was unnecessary; he'd already plunged down into her again, and again, and again. He took her with long, deep, slow strokes, as if he could spend the whole night doing only that. She was climbing up, higher and higher. Mackenzie thought that she couldn't take it anymore. Connor's mouth claimed hers as she felt that first glorious wave of ecstasy hit. Then another, and another until she exploded and it felt like she was falling. She could feel Connor driving himself into her over and over until she felt his pulsing release as she fell back to Earth.

There was something timeless about being in a castle with Connor. It made her think of all of the men and women who had and who would make love in this room. She was a girl out of her own time, but feeling like she belonged nonetheless.

Chapter Fifteen

Connor was speechless. He'd never before felt this kind of intimacy with another woman. He traced his fingers down her back, they were still joined, not wanting to move yet. But Connor rolled his weight off her and tucked her into his side, while their breathing slowed. He had never wanted to hold a woman all night long, but he felt that with her, he could do just that and enjoy it. Hell, he felt as if he could hold her in his arms forever. He wanted to. He'd known that it would be good with Mackenzie, the explosive passion between them left little doubt, but what they had just shared was amazing. It wasn't just the sex, but he'd felt a wholeness, a completeness, he couldn't quite define. What he had just experienced with Mackenzie made him feel like he'd been missing something with every other woman he'd lain with. He'd once told her she'd never crave another man's touch, but in reality it was he who would never want another; Connor wanted only her.

It was all so new and fascinating, and frustrating...his life had been so clear before; clan chief, marry suitable girl, have heirs. Simple. And now it was muddled. He was confused. He still trailed his fingers gently up and down her side, from hip to shoulder. She had her hand idly tracing designs on his chest. Her touch was almost pleasure personified. He felt himself harden, and thought that this next time would be even more intense, since he could devote himself strictly to the act.

And besides, now he had his answers. He was finally starting to believe she might be an innocent in all this. Nothing made sense, though, not her story, not the story from the man sitting in a cell downstairs, and not his own thoughts, which were now envisioning Mackenzie having a place in his home, and dare he think it? His heart.

"Is it always like that?" Her soft query snapped his brows down over his nose.

"Nay, no' always." Never for him. Why would she ask something like that? Unless she was...No. It wasn't possible. She couldn't be. The way she dressed belied any innocence. Add that to her behavior, and her connection to the Campbell... He propped himself up on one elbow, so he could more fully see her expression. "Mackenzie, were you a virgin?"

Her eyes dropped from his, but he noticed the flash of hurt in their green depths first. She was quiet for a long time. "Was I not...good?" Her voice broke on the last word.

He inhaled sharply and said, "Is that what you are thinking about? That I wasn't satisfied?" He didn't mean to sound angry, but it was a ludicrous thought in the face of what he'd just done. He had wanted her as he'd wanted no other, but if he'd known she was a maid, well, he would have tried to dredge up some self-control. He'd thought he was bedding his enemy's wife. And while he had feelings for her that he didn't want to think about, it was still no more than scratching an itch. At least, that's what he'd told himself. And whilst her connection to the Campbell was far from cleared up, however, he now knew that she was a maid, or at least had been. He frowned.

He saw one tear slip out from her closed eyelid, and slide down her cheek. Catching it with his thumb, he silently castigated himself for not taking more care with her. He had no experience with maidens. He'd recklessly taken his own pleasure; he must have hurt her at some point. "Och, was I too rough with you, lass?"

Her eyes opened wide and met his briefly, before lowering again. "No. No, nothing like that."

She must be lying, but why? Why didn't she say what she was surely thinking? That he was a barbarian for taking her maidenhead like that. She deserved better. His thoughts were suddenly fierce and possessive. She deserved better than the Campbell. He could only imagine how her soft, beautiful body would be treated. Not to mention her spirit. The anger rolled off him in waves. Mackenzie sat up and faced away from him. He stared at her back. Connor was momentarily distracted by the colorful flowers painted onto her lower back. He'd never seen anything painted onto someone's skin. It was strange and beautiful. He reached out a finger and gently traced the petals. Mackenzie stiffened. Of course. He pulled his hand back; she must hate him so much now that even his touch disgusted her. It was understandable. He hated himself at the moment.

"Are you hurt?"

Mackenzie turned bright eyes to look at him, and had an even brighter smile on her face. "I'm fine." And she stood, pulling her *sark* over her head.

"Doona lie to me." Connor was anxious to know what she was thinking.

Her face crumpled, and she turned quickly to avoid his probing gaze.

"If you are hurt, please tell me." His voice was strained. Connor stood as well, and turned her back to face him, his hands at her shoulders. Her eyes were bright with unshed tears. Oh, what a rogue he'd been! He crushed her to him tightly, "Please doona cry."

She mumbled against his chest, "I'm not hurt."

He pulled back slightly so he could look at her. "I doona understand. Why are you crying?"

"I'm not." Her watery denial was pathetic.

"Close enough." His voice was curt now with the anxiety of watching her cry. Christ, he hated a woman's tears.

"It's nothing, really." This soft, tremulous assurance did nothing to help ease his anxiety.

"Tell me, please," his voice was rough with emotion.

"It's just, I mean, I know that it wasn't the same for you, but, it was amazing for me, and I know that I'm not experienced with these things, but…" Mackenzie couldn't finish; she bit her lip and looked at her hands on his chest.

Connor brushed his thumb under her lip until her teeth let go. His heart was beating erratically from this newfound emotion. And as gently as he could, he said, "I am sorry that I hurt you. Please know that I am just as revolted with myself as you must be." His thumb and forefinger gripped her chin and forced her gaze to meet his. "I did no' mean to hurt you."

"I know. I'm not hurt." Mackenzie looked surprised at his apology.

She was so frustrating. Of course he'd hurt her. Why wouldn't she just say what she was thinking? He sighed mentally and asked instead, "Why did you no' tell me you were a maid?"

Mackenzie's eyes dropped and stayed fixed on her hands, "You wouldn't have believed me."

The softly spoken remark stung. It was true, but it still hurt.

"You're right." It pained him to choke out the words. He had to make her understand. But understand what? He didn't really understand himself what had happened to change his feelings for her so swiftly.

Mackenzie didn't know that this had been more for him, but he didn't want to think about that when she was obviously upset about the whole thing. Her wide, guileless eyes finally met his, and they looked concerned. But concerned about what?

"Are you alright?" Her voice showed no hint of anger.

She was concerned about *him*? That was surprising. She never did what he expected. Maybe that was some of the draw to her, that unpredictability? Whether she was who she said, or not, she was unlike any woman he'd ever known. Or maybe the attraction was in knowing that she belonged to another, he really didn't have an answer.

He looked into her concerned eyes, and said, "Nay, lass, I'm no' alright. I'm ashamed to have treated ye such." She had given herself to him so fully, and he'd treated her as if she were just some conquest to warm his bed.

Surprise flashed on her features momentarily, but was quickly replaced with understanding. "Oh, I'm okay." Her eyes searched his. "Is that really what you're thinking about?"

"Aye. Aren't you?" She *should* be. He'd behaved odiously towards her.

"No, I..." she broke off and flushed.

"What? Please, tell me what you are thinking."

"I..." she cleared her throat, pasting a bright smile on her face, "I just wanted you to know that I really am fine." She paused before continuing, "And that it was incredible for me." Connor smiled slightly at her soft admission. He could tell that wasn't what she'd been planning on saying, but he let it go. He didn't want to see the hurt return to eyes.

"Why dinna you tell me you were a virgin?" he asked again, desperate for an answer.

"I don't know...it never came up. 'Hey how's the weather? By the way I'm a virgin.' It doesn't quite flow into conversation, now does it?" Her eyes were teasing him.

He chuckled, and relaxed; this time the smile on her face was authentic. "Well, at least I ken you've never lain with the Campbell." Another chuckle slipped out. "Verily, he'll be furious when he finds out I've bedded his betrothed."

Mackenzie stilled. "What?"

Connor looked confused. "What?"

Her breath stopped, and her eyes lost their teasing light. "Is that what this was for you? Some perverse test?" Mackenzie's breathing started up again with a sharply indrawn breath, and her eyes narrowed. "Or is it just about who can 'bed' me first? Wow. Well, congratulations, Connor, you win. You beat the Campbell."

"Nay, I..."

Mackenzie pulled out of his embrace and stepped backwards a few paces. Connor reached for her, but Mackenzie skittered back as if his touch might burn her.

"Don't you touch me!" Her voice rose with the hysteria she was trying to suppress. Her eyes were wild, but they cooled and narrowed with understanding, and she sucked in a quick hiss of air. "Is that why, before, when you asked me my purpose here? Oh that's rich. You're a cruel man, Connor MacRae. I'm so outta here."

Mackenzie picked up her gown and slipped it over her shift, the hell with the stays. The hell with him! All she wanted was to be away from him. Before Connor could reach her, Mackenzie had bolted out the door. Cursing her fingers for being so clumsy with the laces, Mackenzie ran through the hallway holding the gown to her chest.

Chapter Sixteen

She didn't know where she was running, just that she needed out. Out of the castle, out of everything. Mackenzie wanted to go home. She ran through the art gallery where she'd first seen Connor in the painting. The room was so familiar, and yet slightly different. She paused at the tapestry where Morvern and Gregor had revealed the secret tunnel. The secret passage! Mackenzie excitedly reached for the medallion she wore around her neck, thinking only of going home. Oh, right, she'd thrown it at Connor. Well, she'd try the passage anyway. She felt around for the lever, and it swung open. *Yes!* As soon as she took her first step in, she released her hold on the gown to feel along the wall for the exit tunnel. She'd only taken a few tentative steps in the dark passageway when a pair of hands pressed her roughly against the wall. Connor! He'd obviously caught up with her.

"And where do you think you're going?" he breathed against her ear. Gripping her shoulders, he turned her around to face him, and as dark as it was in the tunnel, Mackenzie could see his eyes; they were snapping angry darts at her.

"Well?" he demanded.

"I'm leaving." Mackenzie squeezed her eyes shut and chanted *There's no place like home, there's no place like home* to herself.

If he was surprised, he hid it well. He barked a short laugh. "And where would you go? To the Campbell?"

Mackenzie opened her eyes and lifted her chin, "As if you care."

His eyes turned liquid. "Aye, I care, lass." His voice had lowered and his soft burr caressed her. "You're mine now, sweeting."

"I am *not* yours, like a piece of chattel!" Mackenzie fumed. "I belong to no one!" She glared mutinously at Connor.

Connor dipped his head, and trailed his lips from her neck to her shoulder where her unlaced gown had slipped down. Curse her inability to dress herself in these complicated gowns! Curse her traitorous body for warming to his lips! Curse Connor! Her head fell back against the cool stone wall as he reached her collarbone.

"Mine," he repeated against her décolletage.

Mackenzie's eyes flew open. "Bastard," she breathed. She could actually feel his lips curve into a smile against her skin before he straightened up.

"Come." Connor's warm fingers grasped her elbow and he steered her out of the secret passage. Once they were back in the gallery, Mackenzie dug her heels in and shook his hand loose, dropping one side of her dress off of her shoulder again in the process.

"No."

Connor's eyes narrowed. He looked menacing. Mackenzie suddenly regretted defying him. He took a step towards her and stopped inches away from her; Mackenzie could feel the heat wave crash over her when he was close. But whatever he'd been about to say was interrupted by a man whistling and walking past the gallery. Connor's eyes swiftly took in the whistler, and Mackenzie's state of undress. In less than a second, he'd looked up, back, wrapped an arm around her waist, and shoved her behind his body. He waited until the man was out of sight, and pulled Mackenzie around to face him.

"Shall I lace your gown, *my Lady?*" His hands were at her waist, cinching the laces tight before she could say anything. His voice was mocking, "You seem to have forgotten your stays and petticoats in your haste. Come, we shall have you properly dressed in no time." His hands finished lacing her up and they lingered at her breasts. Mackenzie stepped away from his hands, angry at the way her body responded. She backed away slowly, and she could see by his eyes that Connor knew, he just knew she'd run.

"By all means, Mackenzie, go. I'd enjoy throwing you over my shoulder again. So please run; I'll just fetch you back." His voice was amused, but his eyes were tight.

It burst out of her, "Why? Why do I matter so much? Surely there are others who will share your bed? Others more fair and ladylike? Why me?"

"You are fair enough. And mayhap I doona want ladylike."

"Oh, well," she fanned herself with her hand. "My, my, you'll turn my head with all this flattery," Mackenzie sarcastically pressed a hand to her chest in her best Scarlett O'Hara impression.

Connor closed the distance she had put between them, and wrapped his arm around her waist. He brought her close to him so that her breasts brushed his chest, one of her thighs tangled with his, and he looked deeply into her eyes, "You're fire in bed."

Her head reared back as if he'd slapped her. "And is that all that matters? That I'm a good lay?" Her eyes searched his for any hint of feeling. They were hard sapphires. She laughed bitterly, "And to think, I was worried that I wasn't good enough." She met his eyes, not bothering to hide the hurt. "Wow, thanks Connor for being such a willing tutor. Maybe next we can try something new. A different position perhaps?" Venom dripped from every word.

A long finger traced her pouting lower lip. "Such vulgar language from such a beautiful mouth. Need I remind you to hold your tongue?" His soft voice carried the implicit threat, but Mackenzie didn't care.

"Go to hell!" She pushed futilely at his iron chest, desperate to escape before the tears started to fall again.

The whistler was coming back through, and Connor pulled her towards the shadows. "Mayhap we should take this elsewhere." It wasn't a request, it was a command.

"I'm not going anywhere with you," she fumed. Mackenzie wanted to run back to her room and slam the door in his face.

"Stop me then." Connor dared her, his arms around her tightening in anticipation.

She pushed at his chest once more. "What is your *problem?*"

"My problem is a lass who doesn't ken her place," his eyes narrowed in response.

"My *place?*" She echoed, astonished. One hand lifted to cover her eyes, and her shock was obvious even through the sarcasm, "And just where is my place in all this? I'd love to know," she laughed bitterly, "because so far the only place I seem to belong is in your bed!" She flung her arms out and they landed on Connor's rock hard chest with a thud.

"I'll no' argue with you here. 'Tis no' proper."

"Good, then let me go," and she tugged at his hold to emphasize her point.

He smiled, "Hmm...I think no'," and he lifted her effortlessly over his shoulder and strode towards the tower stairs. Her fists pummeled his back in vain.

"Put me down you arrogant jerk!"

"Aye, my Lady, as soon as we are someplace more private."

She didn't quit her struggle as he took the stairs two at a time—not even slowing under her weight. He kicked the door to his room open and dropped her on his bed. He murmured, "My Lady," with a slight mocking bow. Mackenzie gritted her teeth.

"Your bed? Very mature, Connor." She rolled her eyes, hoping he wouldn't see that she was terrified to be in his bed. She knew she wouldn't be able to resist him if he tried something, and it was humiliating.

"Who am I to argue that your place is in my bed?" The blue sapphire of his eyes had turned molten again, the color was that of the ocean and she felt like she was trying to keep her head above water. She was going to drown. Infuriatingly, that thought still couldn't put out the fire he'd started. He leaned down over her until their faces were just inches away, placing an arm on either side of her body. Mackenzie hated that his proximity alone caused her breathing to increase. "Keep it warm for me, lass." He stepped back and pulled his brooch and plaid off.

Her eyes widened, "What are you doing?"

"I am getting ready for bed." He arched an eyebrow, as he pulled his linen shirt off. Mackenzie tried really hard not to look at his naked chest, but it was difficult not to. He was incredible. And he was laughing at her. She slid off the bed, and ran for the side door to her room. Mackenzie gave in to the urge and childishly slammed it shut, looking for a bolt, or a lock of some form. Of course there was none. *Stupid pre-*

women's lib era! Connor stepped through the door and she backed up as he advanced on her.

"Doona do that again." He kept walking towards her.

"Do what?" Mackenzie kept backing away from him until the backs of her knees hit the bed.

"Shut me out." He stopped in front of Mackenzie.

"Why? Again, why do I matter? Is it just sex?" Her eyes searched his looking for some small measure of feeling. His earlier words came back to her: *He'll be furious when he finds out I've bedded ye.* The Campbell. That was all this had ever been about. She glumly realized that she had been played. "Or is it because I was to be your enemy's bride? But you got me first; to the victor go the spoils, right? And I'm the prize? Is that why you want me? God, I'm stupid. To think, I almost imagined you actually cared for me! I am an idiot." She turned her head and prayed that she wouldn't cry. Not now, not in front of him.

"I do care for you Mackenzie," his voice had gentled and he turned her around to face him.

"Sure. Sure you do," she muttered drily.

"Is it so hard to believe that?"

"If you care for someone, you don't boss them around, Connor. You don't use them as a means to an end. You don't keep them prisoner, you respect them. And most importantly, when you care for someone, you trust them. Can you honestly tell me you trust me?"

Connor was silent.

"I didn't think so. Now, if you don't mind, *my Laird*, I'm really tired and I'd like to go to bed." *And cry my eyes out*, she mentally added.

He recognized the change in her tone, the dismissal, and his eyes flashed with the implication. He responded similarly, "Of course *my Lady*...but you're sleeping in my bed."

Her eyebrows shot sky-high. "The hell I am!"

His eyebrows snapped down over his nose. "The hell you're no'. I refuse to let you out of my sight. For all I ken, you'll try to run again!"

"If you'd quit insulting me, maybe I'd stay."

"I tell you I care for you and you accuse me of insulting you?" Connor was incredulous.

"Your actions speak louder than your words, Connor. You slept with me to provoke your enemy. I can't ignore that."

"I dinna. And I doona regret what we did, do you?" he challenged, his blue eyes intense.

"It doesn't matter. It happened. It's over." She glanced sharply at him, "And it won't happen again."

"Either way, you are still sleeping in my bed tonight."

"I promise not to run, okay?" she was almost begging. "I swear it." Staying the night in his bed would only exacerbate the situation. He was silent, appraising. She almost desperately pleaded, "Does my word mean nothing to you?" Mackenzie didn't give Connor a chance to respond, instead, answering herself softly, "Oh, right, I forgot. You don't trust me."

"'Tis na that I doona trust you…"

"Whatever Connor." She interrupted, not letting him finish his sentence. Mackenzie stomped to the chair and sat down with a huff…on her purse! "Oh for the love of…how could I forget?" Her eyes were eager as she yanked it out from under her, but she made her voice uninterested, "Connor, I was wondering, what if I could offer you undeniable proof that I am who I say I am? Would you trust me then?"

"I would be interested to see what proof you have that would fit in a bag that small." Despite himself, he stepped closer.

Mackenzie stood, brushed past him and dumped the contents of her purse on the bed. As she pawed through the many lip glosses and spare change that never quite made it into her wallet, she finally held her camera aloft, much like Arthur when he'd pulled the sword from the stone, she thought. "Here! All the proof you'll ever need"

"How does that prove your story?"

"It's a digital camera! It takes photographs. See look," Mackenzie clicked it on and pressed the Review button. "See these are all the photos from my trip! Here's me in the airport, me in the car, me in front of the castle, see no moat! It's all grass and flowers now. Oh! And here's my room; see? A T.V. and my laptop!" Her excitement got the better of her and she was leaning in close to Connor so he could see the camera's screen. When she glanced at his face in triumph, certain she'd proved her case, she sighed. Connor had no clue what she was showing him. So, she clicked her camera to Auto, and pointed it at Connor, "Say cheese," she muttered and she snapped a picture of a very annoyed Connor. The flash startled him though and when she turned the screen to him, she could see his shock. "See?" She felt smug.

"What kind of witchery is this?" Connor crossed himself and stepped back.

Mackenzie sighed, an impatient and frustrated sound. "It's modern 21st century technology, that's all. Here, watch." Mackenzie turned the camera on herself and snapped a picture. "See? It's easy. No harm done." Mackenzie tried a different approach. She'd explain it very slowly and simply. "Above my bed is a painting, right? What if you were not an artist? But this landscape is so beautiful that you would want to always remember how it looked? In my time, you would take a photograph." Mackenzie walked to the window, opened the glass, and took a picture of the cliffs and ocean. "Now, I will always have a picture of the way the ocean looked right now, at this moment." She paused, "Is this making any sense to you?"

Connor stepped close enough to look, but not did not touch it. "This is trickery."

"Hardly." Mackenzie snorted. "Would you like to try?" Mackenzie held out the camera as a peace offering.

"So what exactly does this prove?" He made no move to take the camera.

Mackenzie sighed and put it on the bed. "It proves that I am from 200 years in the future!" He was so stubborn! How could he *still* not believe her?

"It proves that you have powerful magic."

"Ugh, seriously?" Mackenzie shoved her hair roughly out of her face. "You can believe in magic, but not time travel? You're so closed-minded! Here, let's see what else I have." She found her cell phone and turned it on. "Here's a cellular phone. It allows you to talk to people from far away. I know, I know, it would be more impressive if it had service. But it still has camera capability, and ringtones, and texts I've saved, and I don't know, here." She threw it on the bed next to the camera. "Hmm…what else; lip gloss, pen, tampon, more lip gloss gum, ooh! My wallet! Here look, money, some pictures, my driver's license…Ew, don't look at the picture. Holy cow! My i-pod! Sweet! Here!" Mackenzie held out the i-Pod, but Connor remained frozen. She turned up the music as loud as possible since he wouldn't move to put the ear buds in, and pressed Play. She winced as a heavy metal song came through. "Sorry, my friend Jenna was messing with my playlists." He was looking at her as if she had two heads. "Okay, hmm…how about this song?" Mackenzie changed it to the haunting melody her favorite song. "You still can't even believe me after all of this?" She wasn't really asking him, but rather trying to understand his thoughts. "Why? Why is it so easy for you to believe the worst in me, but not the obvious?"

Connor spoke at that point, "What exactly is the obvious?"

"Let's see, my clothes when you first met me, my speech, my demeanor," she was ticking them off on her fingers as she went along, "pretty much everything strange or unexplainable about me. Doesn't this make any sense to you at all?" Her eyes were searching his unreadable expression, hoping for some small glimpse of his thoughts. Nothing. She heaved a resigned sigh, ready to give up; it wasn't worth the effort if he wouldn't even budge his narrow-minded view of the world. "Wow, okay, never mind Connor. I'll just go back to being your prisoner and you can live in ignorance of what's actually happening and life will be just peachy."

His voice sounded tired, "Mackenzie, can you no' give me a few moments to think through this?" He lifted the still playing i-pod from her bed and glanced at the album cover on the screen, staring at it as if he could find the answers to all his questions on it.

"It is a lot of information to process," Mackenzie conceded.

"Why do I hear noise from this? How?"

"It's music, not noise. In the same way that my camera can record a still image of something, and we can see it whenever we want, we have the technology," at his blank look, she swiftly amended, "I mean, the *ability* to record music and play it back whenever we want. Let me see if I can find something less offensive to your ears." She had to have some classical music on her somewhere. "Do you know this one? It's a traditional hymn. You might recognize it."

Connor tentatively placed one ear bud in his ear, and Mackenzie leaned close to do the same. She scrolled through her playlists until she found what she was looking for, and pressed Play. It was set to bagpipes, so she hoped Connor would at least show some reaction to that.

"I hear the pipes…but how? Where are the instruments?" He pulled the ear bud out of his ear and then tugged at the one in Mackenzie's before taking it gingerly from her hands. "What is this?" He was turning it over in his hands.

"An mp3 player. And I don't know how it works, I only know how to work it." She smiled wryly at her technological handicap.

"I ken the words; 'tis a poem. The tune is unfamiliar though." He seemed to be softening to her cause.

"Here, let's go back to the camera again." Mackenzie turned off the iPod, and picked up her camera. "Do you want to see some more pictures of your castle 200 years from now?"

"It still stands?"

He was starting to believe her! Mackenzie tried to reign in her excitement and had trouble keeping her voice neutral. "Yes, it's just slightly different, and bigger. There's indoor plumbing and electricity. But a lot of it is the same. Here's a picture of my friend Jenna and me in the dining room, umm...your ballroom. Oh! And would you believe that this is where I first saw you? It's a picture of the oil painting of you hanging in the Billeting room."

He murmured, "I never liked that painting." Connor was holding the camera gingerly now, as if it might bite him, and scrolling through the memory. He paused when he came across a picture of Mackenzie and some girlfriends at the beach. "What are you wearing?" His eyes popped out a bit.

"A bikini. Umm…a bathing suit. You know, for swimming?"

"Women are allowed out in public like this?" He was astonished. "But you are *naked!*"

"No we're not!" Mackenzie defended herself. Besides, Jenna's string bikini was way more revealing than her modest tankini. "It's a different time, Connor," Mackenzie said softly. "Look. All the girls are wearing something similar. Don't you remember what I was wearing the night we met?"

His eyes briefly darkened, "Aye, I recall the way your legs looked in those shortened knee-breeches."

"You're such a guy!" She laughed, and for the first time in a long time, it was a wholly carefree sound. Mackenzie couldn't believe how light she felt; as if a heavy, pressing weight had just been lifted, and she hadn't been aware of it until it was removed. All of her anger at Connor had lifted with the weight as well, and she didn't even care that she was supposed to be mad at him. She was thrilled; he seemed to finally believe her. Or at least he was starting to, which was as much as she could ask.

Chapter Seventeen

How could Connor deny what he was seeing here? If Mackenzie had been telling the truth from the beginning, then that meant that MacAllistair had lied to him about her role in this scheme. To what end? What was the purpose? When he'd first met her, he'd thought of her eyes as an open book and he'd wanted to read them; he'd wanted to know her secrets. Well now he did; in fact, he knew everything she'd been hiding from him. He wanted to believe her, but it was a difficult tale to take as truth. She was being exceptionally nice to him, despite his high-handed demeanor. He'd behaved abominably towards her, and he knew she'd been offended by his actions.

Well, he could right this one injustice, "I should have believed ye from the first. I should know by now that your eyes never lie." Connor brushed his thumb under her eye and smiled slightly. Mackenzie lowered her lashes and a faint pink stained her cheekbones. She expelled the breath she hadn't even known she'd been holding, and turned her cheek into his hand. Briefly closing her eyes, she brushed her lips to his open palm. When her lashes fluttered open, Connor's eyes weren't confused anymore, they were hungry.

She stepped back quickly, and brushed at her skirts. "So," she said brusquely, "What do we do now?" And then more softly, "And where does this leave us?"

Connor knew she felt the same hunger he did, but he respected her desire for space, and he stepped past her to set down the camera. He ignored her first question, and answered her with, "That's up to you Mackenzie. However, for your own protection I'd prefer ye slept in my bed." Connor expected her to protest again, so he was mildly surprised when his request wasn't immediately rebuffed.

"What do you mean for my own protection?" Her green eyes were narrowed in suspicion.

"The Campbell has tried several tactics to separate you from my..." he choked off the word "possession," knowing she would resent the implications, and settled for "protection, and I am" he paused, again searching for a word that wouldn't get her back up, "concerned that if I leave you unprotected, he might succeed."

To his dismay, her deep green eyes were merely curious, not afraid. She should be afraid. "Hmm…Do you really think he's going to try something again?"

"Yes. He's gotten men in past my guard before." This bothered Connor much more than he'd let on. In fact, he'd had to ream his men earlier that week for the lapse in surveillance, and he didn't like to punish men he'd known since he was a bairn. " 'Tis impossible to tell when, but I do expect another and stronger attempt."

"Alright then, say I share your bed again. Are there," she paused significantly raising a delicate brow, "expectations?"

He looked resigned, "I never know what to expect from you."

Her eyes relaxed, and she told Connor, "See? Isn't it so much easier when you let me know your reasoning?"

"I shouldn't have to explain myself to you, I am laird of this clan and you should trust my judgment," he grumbled. Actually, it wasn't as annoying as it used to be, explaining himself to her. She really wasn't used to following commands, so he was at least able to understand her position now. That line of thinking made him wonder, "Might I ask you a question, Mackenzie?"

"Of course," the surprise coloring her tone almost made him smile.

"Well, earlier you had said that you have been having the same dream since ye were a child. Why do you think that you have been dreaming of the Campbell?"

Connor didn't like the idea of his sworn enemy in the dreams of this woman who was slowly carving a place for herself in his life. And heart. Not wanting to admit it to himself, Connor was also a little jealous. While he had been in her dreams as well, it wasn't in the capacity he wanted.

"I don't know. Maybe to prepare me for coming here? Then again, I don't think anything could have prepared me for all this," she muttered. Mackenzie was enjoying this new-found honesty between them, and it made her more willing to speak her true thoughts and feelings. "I think, that maybe I am more than just a tool to start a war, or end one, depending on how you look at things. I think I was sent here to save you." She felt her cheeks warm as she admitted this, but she kept his gaze.

"To save me?" He was more than surprised, he was incredulous.

Mackenzie almost laughed, as it was, she felt her lips twitch and had to fight back the smile. "How could a mere woman ever save you, you ask? I'll tell you: I have some ideas."

"I have never thought you a 'mere woman' Mackenzie." Connor's eyes smoldered as he said this, and Mackenzie had to force herself to breathe.

But she had to keep the conversation flowing. She looked away from his all too intense gaze and thought about her dreams. She felt useless. Unless… She'd been so frustrated and unsure, but now she thought of a new plan.

"You need to let me go to him. I can stop him." As she said it, she knew it was true. Her dreams were becoming clearer about that aspect. She just didn't know how… yet.

"What? You want to go to him?" Connor roared. "I'll no' give you over to him. Nor will I give him that much power."

Mackenzie didn't want to lose their new camaraderie, so she quickly tried to appease him, "Okay, okay, calm down. It was just a suggestion."

Connor was still livid. Mackenzie had another thought, "Could we get a message to Morvern? The sorcerer who brought me here?"

"I've a man inside his stables, so 'tis possible." His voice was still angry, but he was curious, "Why? What are you plotting?"

"Let me get some paper and a pen." Mackenzie rifled through the contents of her purse until she found a pad and a pen. As she hastily scribbled the note, she realized that this would look out of place to the messenger. "No, no, this is all wrong. Do you have a piece of paper and a…quill is it?"

"Aye, in the desk over there. What are ye planning lass?"

"Lass…I'm probably only a couple years younger than you, y'know?"

Connor raised his eyebrows at her muttered comment. "Ye'd prefer I didn't call ye lass?"

"Hmm…no, I…it doesn't matter. It just makes me feel like a child."

"It is a term of endearment." Mackenzie glanced up at Connor. He sounded hurt.

"Oh, Connor, I didn't mean to insult you. In my time, it is used for girls, small children. I'm twenty three, hardly a little girl." She cocked her head to the side, "How old are you?"

"I am seven and twenty."

"In my day, you'd be over 200 years old." She smiled wryly, and mentally did the math, "245 years old to be precise."

Connor ignored her attempts at humor. "What are you writing?"

"Come and see." Mackenzie indicated he should read over her shoulder. "It's only an idea, really. But first we need to find out what the two sorcerers are doing, and to see what they've discovered. They told me they needed access to a certain sacred text or something. The plan was that I would monopolize the Campbell's time and attention with details for the wedding, and they would get their hands on said texts. Let's find out what they know."

Mackenzie finished her note and couldn't believe how awful her handwriting looked in the fresh ink. Oh well, at least Morvern would know it was hers; no lady of this time would have such sloppy cursive.

She handed it to Connor who squinted and looked at it this way and that. "I doona think they will be able to read it; your script is barely legible." "Hey, it's my first time with a quill, cut me some slack!" Mackenzie defended her handwriting. She liked her cursive. With a ballpoint pen, it was loopy and girly, and normally much easier to read. She watched as Connor sealed it in wax.

"I'll send it to my man with instructions that no one is to receive it but the wizard."

"Okay, thanks. We won't do anything until we hear back from them, and see what we're up against. How long should this all take?"

"It depends on how difficult it will be for my man to gain access inside the castle. I hope no more than a few days." Connor strode to the door and left before Mackenzie could blink.

Mackenzie could hear him walk down the hallway and call for Robbie. Apparently it didn't bother anyone that he wasn't wearing a shirt. They spoke in hushed tones, and Connor was back before Mackenzie had time to sit down on her bed. She was putting everything back in her purse when he walked back through the open door. His hand was on hers as she picked up her camera.

"May I?"

"Of course," Mackenzie was shocked he wanted to see it.

Connor turned the camera on, and pointed it at Mackenzie. She'd been looking down at her purse so she hadn't realized that he was snapping pictures of her. The flash had her looking up at him.

"Oh! Connor, you should have told me; I would have smiled."

"Amazing. It is a miraculous thing."

Mackenzie smiled at his enthusiasm. "You'd love to see a computer, or a movie. I bet you'd love all those Scottish historical movies."

"What is a movie?" He rolled the word on his tongue as if he were tasting it.

"Hmm...How can I explain this? Okay, it's like a play, except it is captured by a camera. You can watch it whenever you want to. Wait, here..." Mackenzie snatched her camera back and clicked it to Review. She scrolled through it until she found what she'd been searching for; she and Jenna had goofed around with it when they'd first checked into their rooms. Jenna was using an awful Scottish accent and telling Mackenzie that she was "A Highland warrior come to rescue the princess " all the while brandishing her cell phone like a sword. It was almost humiliating to watch, but Connor just shook his head and reverently touched the screen with a fingertip.

"And this is a 'movie'?" His eyes never left the screen as he asked this.

"Yeah, it's a video Jenna and I took when we first got to Scotland. Umm, the day before you and I...met." Mackenzie had packed everything back into her purse and looked up at Connor with a smile. She really liked this honesty thing. It made her feel much more than relieved; she felt at ease for the first time since she'd arrived.

Connor reached out and stroked her cheek and Mackenzie's eyes widened slightly, before she dropped them to look at her hands. While the honesty was a nice change, it was still too hard to look into Connor's eyes knowing how much she felt for him. She was very much in danger of falling in love with him. Although she didn't want to admit it to herself, she was already there. Mackenzie knew how expressive her eyes were, and she didn't want him to see the depth of her feelings for him. That was the last thing she wanted, and while she knew they'd be sharing a bed tonight, she was going to try to keep it at just that; just sex. She refused to let Connor know how far gone she really was. It wasn't just the fear of rejection, she already knew he didn't feel the same; it was more the intimacy of it all.

Connor's fingers were still on her face, burning a path from her cheekbone to her lips, where they paused and he traced her lips briefly before he tilted her chin up so she would meet his gaze. She bit back a gasp at the dark molten blue that his eyes had turned. There was no doubt as to what he wanted. She wanted it too. But she didn't know if her heart would survive.

Bending down, he swung her up into his arms and strode through the connecting door. Mackenzie could feel how hot his skin was through her dress. That heat was amazing and it had become such a part of Connor, like an arm or a leg. It felt natural.

Sliding her down the length of his body, slowly and deliberately, Connor gently placed Mackenzie on her bare feet in his room. This time, she was the aggressor, knowing what he wanted and wanting it too. She was emboldened by the knowledge that they were going to end up in his bed, Mackenzie stared into his eyes as she unlaced her gown and let it drop to the floor. Stepping out of it, she crossed her arms at her waist and bunched up the material, pulling the shift up over her head tossing it on the growing pile of clothes. Connor's eyes betrayed the surprise he felt as Mackenzie stripped down and advanced on him. He deftly slipped off his trews and silently pulled her to him. He whispered her name against her lips before he claimed them as his own.

Chapter Eighteen

Mackenzie woke up to the worst of her nightmares yet. Connor was shaking her shoulder hard enough to rattle her teeth together.

"Mackenzie, lass? Wake up. 'Tis naught but a dream."

Her lashes fluttered and she sat bolt upright before she stared into his deep blue very concerned eyes.

"Huh? Where am I?" Her eyes were searching the dark room almost frantically. As her heart rate slowed, she remembered that she was in Connor's room, or in his bed to be precise. "Oh, it was another dream. Okay. Wow, they're starting to become more and more real." She looked back at Connor, smiling ruefully, "I'm sorry. Was I screaming again?"

"Nay, you were talking in your sleep though. You woke me up when you spoke my name. What was this one about?" Connor was very serious.

"I'm not sure. That's odd. Usually I remember because they're so vivid, but this one's fading so quickly. Umm..." She pinched the bridge of her nose and furrowed her brow. She could feel the dampness on her cheeks. She'd been crying in her sleep. "There was fire again, and snakes, and you..." she looked up at him again. "But I think there was something I needed to do. That's the strongest part of it; I needed to *do* something or *know* something." She fell back against the pillows with a huff. "It's just so *frustrating* feeling helpless."

"You're not helpless, Mackenzie." Connor quietly said.

"I feel it," she muttered. "Plus, I'm stuck here and I can't get home, I have no freedom and I'm powerless! I am supposed to help and I am completely useless! Ugh, ugh, ugh!"

Connor's soft voice sounded mildly sad, "Is it really so bad here?"

"Oh! Connor! I didn't mean it to come out like that." She sighed and ran an agitated hand through her hair as she sat up. Connor sat up as well. "It's just that, imagine for a minute that you are told you have the power to help defeat an evil warlord who is terrorizing the locals, but you don't know how you are supposed to do this, and you don't know who is really a friend or foe, and to top it off, you are suddenly completely happy to stay in the temporary state of bliss that you've just discovered. It's a hard position to be in, Connor, especially when I could be just as happy here, in your bed, for the entire time I'm supposed to be engaged to another man. Why is that, I wonder? Hmm?" Mackenzie ended her mini-rant with an admission she hadn't meant to say, but now that it was out there, she let it sit for a moment. When she spoke again, it was very softly. "And what will happen when Halloween comes and I have to go back to my time? Will I even be able to go home without those wizards? There are so many unanswered questions and every day, I have that much less time to help. So, you asked me if it's really that bad? The short answer is no, it's absolutely wonderful here in your bed." She smiled up at him, "But, when the sun rises, I have all of those other thoughts interrupting the happiness that I have here."

Connor had remained silent through her rambling and slightly confusing explanation, so when he spoke, it stunned her that he understood. "Sweeting, I hadn't realized that you carried so much on your shoulders." He had an arm around her and pulled her against him into his embrace. "We will hear from the sorcerers soon enough and mayhap they will give you some of the answers you seek."

"Thank you," Mackenzie murmured softly against his chest.

"For what?" Connor sounded genuinely surprised, and Mackenzie smiled against his skin.

"For believing me, and for trying to see my perspective. I really appreciate the effort. It means a lot to me that you care."

"I do, you know. I care about ye, more than I should in fact. And I am truly sorry that I didn't believe you sooner." His voice was inexplicably tender, his accent more pronounced.

Mackenzie snuggled deeper into his chest and mumbled "I don't believe it."

"Believe it. Now, what shall we do until we receive word?"

At the hungry light in his eyes, Mackenzie said, "You're insatiable, my Laird. Besides, I'm not completely sure I've forgiven you for all that business earlier." The teasing look in her eyes belied the stern tone.

Connor smiled and almost purred, "My apologies, my Lady. Allow me to convince you of my remorse." He reached for Mackenzie but she danced out of his reach.

"Oh really? And how's that?"

Connor made a move again, but Mackenzie rolled over the bed so that it stood between them.

"You'll see."

Connor lunged across the bed, but Mackenzie dashed around to where he'd been standing, their positions reversed.

She's quick, he thought as he lunged after her again. This time he caught her by the wrist and pulled her on top of him as if she weighed nothing.

An indelicate "Oof" came out of her as she sprawled across his hard body. Mackenzie's hair spilled around them and Connor ran his hand through her curls, leaving one to tangle in them, while the other roamed her body.

"You're awfully high-handed, now aren't you?" she frowned at him, their lips a half an inch away.

"Mmm..." Connor brushed his mouth against hers and said, "If I am, 'tis for your own good."

Mackenzie slapped a hand on his chest, "For my own..." She never finished her thought as his lips touched hers again, this time more demanding.

"You talk too much."

Connor felt Mackenzie's body melt into his in surrender, and he felt his own body tighten in response. The anticipation of feeling her body beneath his left him breathing hard. He rolled so that she was underneath him, and ran his hands down her body to her thighs. He pulled her sark up to her waist so he could skim his fingers along the satin of her thighs.

She was already wet and open, waiting. His fingers had barely touched her dewy soft core when the knock came. He tore his lips from hers and growled,

"Aye?"

"Me Laird?" It was Duncan, one of the watchmen. "I'm sorry to interrupt, but you're needed in the yard."

Connor rested his forehead against hers and Mackenzie expelled a long breath. When her eyes met his, he was surprised by the understanding he saw there. Most women would have pouted, or feigned insult, but there was nothing sullen about his Mackenzie.

She simply said, "Go."

"Are ye sure, sweeting? I can be," he paused, "late." Mackenzie laughed as he wagged his eyebrows at her.

"Far be it for me to be the reason you're late." She gentled her voice, "Go, it sounds like they need you." As he bent down to kiss her, his hands wandered back down to her thighs. Her mumbled, "Connor, it sounded urgent," was lost in the kiss.

"Mm…hmm…" his lips had followed his hands down to her thighs and he spread her legs. When she murmured her protest, he silenced her protests by flicking his tongue across her. Mackenzie gasped and writhed, but Connor held her hips and brought her to climax quickly by sucking gently.

As Mackenzie lay there, looking pleasantly mussed and sated, he stood up and threw on his shirt and fixed his plaid. With a cocky grin he said, "I'll be back soon to finish that." He walked to the door and paused. He looked pensive.

"You're going to be late," Mackenzie reminded him sitting up and adjusting her shift, pulling the blankets up.

"I am. But 'twas worth it. I meant what I said earlier. I do care for ye sweeting. I'd much appreciate your word that ye'll no' run from me again." He waited for her response, unsure of what to expect.

"Oh," Mackenzie looked down at her hands as they fidgeted with the blankets. "Umm…I have no reason to run anymore." She wouldn't meet his gaze, but even without the benefit of reading her eyes, he could tell what this admission cost her. He felt awful about leaving her right now. Honestly he didn't want to leave her. He strode back to the bed and kissed her deeply, drinking from her lips until she was gasping. He felt a little smug about the affect he had on her. That was one thing he'd never doubted about her; her reaction to him had always been genuine.

He left her to see what was so urgent in the yard, but as he walked, he thought about the reaction women had always had to him. He had never really given much thought to it, but now he wondered how many women had only been with him because he was the laird and an earl, and how many had actually cared for him. It was hard to be objective and introspective at the same time. He felt that Mackenzie cared for him.

She had given him her innocence. His brow furrowed, actually he had taken it. Connor still felt guilty about that. Although she had been willing, he knew he had seduced her. He wished that there was a way to right that. Before he reached the training yard, a thought occurred to him; maybe he could right that wrong after all

Chapter Nineteen

Mackenzie watched as Connor left and she idly wondered why his men needed him at, she looked at her watch, five am. Ugh. That seemed to be the average wakeup time around here, though. Connor had said he'd be back soon, but his concept of time differed slightly from Mackenzie's. Mackenzie chuckled at the words "concept of time." Her whole concept of time was completely changed. She would never look at the science fiction novels Jenna loved with disdain again.

Maybe she'd explore the castle some more today. She picked up her clothes and walked to her room. Since Bronwyn usually didn't come with her breakfast tray until seven, Mackenzie had to make do with dressing herself. She wandered toward her trunk of gowns and pulled out a deep blue gown...she thought since the bodice laced up the front, she could manage. Besides, it was the exact color of Connor's eyes. After a couple failed attempts at lacing up her stays, she flung them on the bed, and dug out her bra. She pulled a fresh shift on and then the petticoats and gown. She twisted and turned in the tall oval mirror and thought that the bra gave her a nice natural look, rather than the seemingly in fashion boobs-smooshed-up-to-her-chin-about-to-fall-out look. Vainly, she swiped on some of her favorite "Very Berry" lip gloss and tucked her purse back into the chair where she seemed to keep forgetting it was.

Before she left, she grabbed her camera and stuffed it in her skirts so no one would see it. She wanted to take as many pictures as possible for when she went back to her own time. If she made it back to her own time. That thought wasn't as entirely sad as it previously had been. For some reason, the idea of staying here was now voluntary rather than forced. Perhaps because of Connor's recent declaration?

She felt kind of like a spy, sneaking pictures of the castle before the War. After WWI, the bombed parts had been rebuilt in a more gaudy style, with lots of gilded pieces, if she remembered correctly. While the castle of her time was furnished with lots of antiques, she didn't think any of them were original to the castle. They'd been touted as being from the castle's heyday. Supposedly the only pieces that had been kept and passed down from laird to laird was Connor's bedroom furniture; his room was now dubbed the "Laird's Suite." Mackenzie hadn't seen it though; she and Jenna had more modest rooms in the new wing.

Mackenzie took the stairs that led out of the tower, but instead of turning towards the Hall, she turned the opposite direction. She didn't know where she was headed, but she was exploring after all, so she meandered slowly around the first floor snapping pictures when no one was looking. She wished she'd grabbed a brochure or something with a map of the castle, but she'd never picked one up on the tour. She did remember vague bits from her unfinished tour, but nothing was where she thought it would be. Thinking logically, she started on the bottom floor, and tried every door she came across. Most were locked. She ended up in what she assumed was the laird's private office, or solar in this time. She walked to the window and looked out at the yard. Mackenzie folded her arms over her chest against the chill coming from the window. The nice weather she'd had on her first day was apparently out of the ordinary for the Highlands, and it had progressively cooled down each day.

She saw his men in the yard, but when her eyes scanned for Connor, he was nowhere to be found. Where was he, if it was so urgent, that he wasn't among his men? She looked for Robbie and Dougal, two of the only men she knew by name. They weren't there either. Her curiosity piqued, Mackenzie walked purposefully out to the main Hall, this time, though, she was looking for Connor.

When she got to the Hall, she realized that something was different. Usually there was a lot of hustle and bustle, or at the very least, people. No one was there. So she went through to the next room, and found the private dining room she and Connor had shared the night before. Also empty. Something was going down. This was weird. Mackenzie didn't like this.

Just then, a man came striding in through the doors with such a huge plate of food that Mackenzie could only describe it as a platter. He looked so much like Connor that at first she thought he *was* Connor. They shared the same height, build, hair, even the same deep blue sapphire-colored eyes. When the man saw Mackenzie staring at him, his eyes widened slightly, in surprise, she guessed.

"My Lady, what are ye doin' down here?" His brogue was a little thicker and more pronounced than Connor's.

"Umm..." she stalled. It was disconcerting to look into the same blue eyes that she'd become so familiar with. "I'm looking for Connor."

"Perhaps I can be of service?"

"Perhaps you can tell me your name?" she replied a little tartly.

The man chuckled at her spirit. "Ah, apologies, my Lady, I have been away and we've no' been properly introduced. I am Liam, Connor's younger and better looking brother." His genuine smile and good humor won over Mackenzie much quicker than she'd have expected. "I regret to inform ye that he is with someone at present, mayhap I could help? What is it ye'd be wantin' to talk to me brother about?"

Liam's face was slightly softer than his brother's, but other than that, they really did look alike. Mackenzie realized that she was staring again.

"Oh, I was just wondering if I might go for a ride this morning. I thought it would be best to speak with him about it first."

Liam was looking at her as if he were trying to figure out whether she was friend or foe. Whatever he saw, he must have decided he liked, because his expression went from pensive to cocky.

"I doona see why that should pose a problem. And pray tell, my lady, what is your name?"

"Mackenzie." She knew better by now; she should have said her full name. Liam's eyes lost all warmth.

"You are Mackenzie?" He looked like he wanted to draw his sword.

"Yes. Oh wait, no, not the way you mean," she bit her lip and rephrased, "I am a Stewart. My first name is Mackenzie." She watched Liam thaw slightly.

"Your Christian name is Mackenzie?" He drew it out slowly as if he was trying to reconcile the opposing thoughts of Mackenzie as both his enemy and his ally.

She was annoyed at that, and didn't bother to hide the huffy remark, "Yes, you got a problem with that?"

Liam's eyebrows shot sky high. He noticed her haughty tone, no doubt.

"I'm sorry," Mackenzie sighed. "I've been a little on edge. Perhaps it's because I haven't eaten yet." It was a sorry excuse, but it seemed to work. Besides, she *was* hungry.

"Then by all means, let us get ye some food. I have cold mutton and potatoes on my plate." Mackenzie must have made a face, because Liam amended, "Or we could try the kitchen. I ken that there is some cheese and fresh bread in the cupboard. Shall we?" Liam offered her his arm. He gave off the same kind of heat that his brother did; Mackenzie could feel it through her clothing. It wasn't altogether unpleasant on this chilly morning.

In the kitchen, Liam handed her a hunk of warm brown bread and kept rummaging until he found some cheese and some fresh apples. Mackenzie took them gratefully. She must've burned more calories last night than sleeping alone, she blushed at the thought. Liam looked questioningly at her, but said nothing, and Mackenzie was instantly grateful for that as well.

"So how did ye come to stay here?"

Mackenzie's eyes flew to Liam's and she said, "You mean Connor hasn't told you?"

"Nay, my Lady, I ken that ye have been sharing the Laird and Lady's chambers, but that is all. I've only arrived home this morning."

"You've heard we share what?" Mackenzie's eyes popped open wide and heat flooded her face. Liam looked amused by her flustered appearance.

"That ye've shared the…"

"I heard what you said," Mackenzie interrupted Liam. "I just hadn't realized that's what they were called. The rooms I mean." She was trying to salvage her faux pas.

"Ye thought I'd heard ye share a bed with my brother." He was teasing her again, but he was right.

Mackenzie actually choked on her bread at that. Between coughing fits, and Liam pounding her on the back, she tried to explain, but then decided that she might as well admit it. So once her voice was working, she lifted her chin and rasped out, "And if I am?"

Liam gave her a friendly smile and simply shrugged, saying, "Connor's a grown man. He can do as he pleases." Liam looked Mackenzie up and down, making her feel as if she were naked. "I'd seduce ye meself if I dinna ken his claim on ye."

Mackenzie's cheeks were stained with the faint pink of the blush she tried in vain to fight back. But she batted her eyes coyly and smiled, playing along. "Perhaps I've picked the wrong brother."

Liam laughed long and hard at that. It was a pleasant sound; rich and deep. Mackenzie had yet to hear Connor really laugh like that; unguarded and carefree. Liam was much more easygoing than his older brother.

"Aye lass, ye did. Ye should have met me first. I'd show ye a proper Highland welcome." He waggled his eyebrows at her.

Before Mackenzie could ask what he meant, or if she even wanted to know what he meant by that, Connor walked into the kitchen. While she jumped, looking slightly guilty, he surprised her by laughing.

"I see ye've met my brother Liam. Is he trying to convince ye that he'd be the better brother?" Connor put his arm around Liam's shoulders and squeezed.

"Yes, he…"

Connor interrupted, "He asked the first girl I ever kissed if she would marry him the second I introduced them. He fancies himself a charmer."

Liam chuckled and said, "I am charming, my brother. But I'd rather not waste me charms on the likes of you; 'tis only for the lassies."

Connor fondly punched Liam in the shoulder, "Whoever told ye ye were charming, well, they lied."

Mackenzie had to make sure to keep her mouth closed in fear her jaw would drop; she'd never seen Connor like this. She liked it. He seemed…happy.

"Liam, what do ye think of my betrothed?"

"I like her Connor, but careful she doesn't come to her senses and fall for me charms." He winked at her. They reminded Mackenzie of little kids who were up to no good. The mischievous smiles they both wore were so different from what she'd come to expect around the keep.

Mackenzie had to laugh at the exchange, but it died in her throat. Wait-- *Betrothed?* Connor held her eyes as he said it. Mackenzie's jaw dropped. Liam must have sensed the change in the atmosphere because he tactfully excused himself and left the two of them alone.

"We're getting married?" She was thoroughly confused.

"Aye, sweeting. I've been speaking with the bishop and he has agreed to marry us on the morn." His voice was tender.

Even through her shock, his assumption that Mackenzie would just acquiesce grated on her nerves. "Did you ever think to ask me if I'd even want to marry you?"

His brows drew down over his eyes. "Ye mean that ye doona want to marry me? But ye gave me your innocence." As if that alone was explanation enough.

"I'd like to be asked, to have a choice in the matter. I mean, in my time, people fall in love, and then the man proposes. Women aren't just told 'You're getting married tomorrow' whether they are virgins or not."

He smiled at her rant; he understood that she wanted the freedom to say no. It was important to her. "Might I try once more? Mackenzie of the clan Stewart, will ye give me your hand in marriage and agree to marry me on the morrow?"

Her eyes widened, but she persisted. "We can't get married, Connor. I mean, I'm leaving in a couple of weeks." Mackenzie's voice rose slightly. His eyes tightened.

Connor switched tactics: logic. "I've heard talk that the Campbell wants to steal back his missing bride. If we are married, then he'll no' be able to legally take ye. It doesn't mean he won't try yet, but 'twill make it harder."

"Oh," Mackenzie felt disappointment flood her body. But what did she expect Connor to do? Drop to one knee declaring his love? "Well, I guess that makes sense, in a sensible sort of way." Mackenzie tried not to pout.

"Good it's settled."

"Just one more thing…" Her brows were knit in concentration.

"Aye?"

"What'll I wear?"

* * * *

Connor bit back a smile as they walked out of the kitchen. *Women.* He wanted to roll his eyes. He held his arm out for her as they left the Hall. He led her towards the outer doors, thinking they might take a walk. She cared for him, of that he was certain. Once the fog of doubt had cleared, it was obvious. But he also knew that she wasn't in love with him, yet. This was just the beginning, however and he hoped that she would learn to love him. They matched well in bed, and most marriages were based on less, far less. If she felt even a fraction of what he felt for her, when the time came, mayhap Mackenzie wouldn't want to leave.

When his man Duncan had pulled him from his chambers early this morning he'd only been told he was needed, he hadn't known why. But he'd guessed. He'd heard rumors that the Campbell was plotting a counter-attack to reclaim his bride. Being that he had yet to even set eyes on Mackenzie, Connor knew that it would be a personal assault against him. Mackenzie had always been right about one thing; she was just the excuse to start the battle. She always had been. From what he'd gleaned from his man on the Campbell's lands, he needed a sacrifice, a virgin. The Campbell planned to use his dark magic to ensure his victory in clearing the MacRae from lands he felt were rightfully his now.

Highland law was imprecise and unclear, usually enforced by chieftain and sword. The clan chiefs dealt out what they considered justice; some were fair, some were not, and some laws were vague, varying from clan to clan. The king was reluctant to meddle in the affairs of the Highlands, where land was scarce and men were territorial. The chiefs dressed up and went to court once a year as required (to model their "good behavior" for all to see), but since the Scottish King James VI had merged Scotland and England, there had been nothing but trouble for the people of the Highlands. King George III, amongst rumors that he had bouts of madness, didn't actively do anything. He preferred to live in his precious Hanover rather than deal with the British politics. So Connor and his fellow chiefs had been stripped of most of their judicial powers, while confiscated lands were "redistributed." The redistribution of certain MacRae lands into Campbell hands had marked the start of the feud.

The Stewarts had given the MacRaes some lands as a marriage tocher several generations back. Connor's ancestor had mistreated the lass and been unfaithful for years. She never gave him an heir so when a leman of his birthed a son, Connor's ancestor had his wife "compromised." Once he'd paid the men who would swear before the clan that it was she who had been unfaithful, he had her hanged. Her last words uttered were that of the curse Mackenzie was here to "break."

So when the Campbell heard that Connor was away, visiting his sister and her newborn bairn, he'd seized the castle and lands that were previously Stewart, but by right MacRae. It had been a short and brutal siege, and if it weren't for the insult to Connor and the deaths of his clansmen, Connor would happily be rid of the lands.

Very few lived on the "accursed lands" and those who do have no livestock or crops; the earth was scorched. That was when the Campbell had sent for his wizards, who in turn brought Mackenzie here. While Connor didn't believe in the power of the curse itself, there was no denying the legend or the connection Mackenzie had to the Stewarts of his time. The power of the curse was in the minds of the simple folk who believed it to be true. This was where the Campbell's marriage to Mackenzie was ingenious; if he could convince the rest of the people that the curse was ended, he might be able to sway their loyalties.

Connor gritted his teeth at the thought of Mackenzie being married to the Campbell. The idea of that man, of any man for that matter, touching her, running his hands along the smooth silk of her skin. Feeling her heart speed as he took her. It made his blood boil and his vision turn red. She was his! The primal claimed resounded throughout the whole of his being. He took several deep breaths to calm himself; he didn't want Mackenzie to ask about his thoughts. Those thoughts, however, continued along the same path as before. He knew now that he could never let Mackenzie go to the Campbell, and he didn't think for one second that the wizards could guarantee her safe return. He knew the Campbell would kill her, if not for the curse, then merely to provoke Connor.

Facing the options of what to do and knowing that he couldn't let Mackenzie leave him, he was struck by the knowledge that the reason he couldn't bear to let her leave him was because he was in love with her. Once that realization hit, it seemed so obvious. How had he not seen this sooner? His chest swelled with the new emotion. He loved her deeply and irrevocably. His life would be forever changed and if she weren't in his life, well, it would be meaningless. So, he'd devised a plan that both kept her safe, here, with him, and would insult the Campbell a bit more. The bishop had stopped by the Isle of Donan for the night on his way to marry a couple on the neighboring MacLeod lands. Fate had dropped this in his lap and he would not ignore it.

When he had chanced upon his brother and Mackenzie in the kitchen, they'd looked so natural there talking to each other as if they were old friends, despite the slightly guilty look on Mackenzie's face. He smiled to himself at the remembered image. It felt homey and natural. He hadn't been able to stop himself and he'd announced his intentions right there. He knew Mackenzie would be surprised, but when her deep emerald green gaze had met his, he'd held her eyes in his, and held his breath as well. When she had agreed to the marriage, he'd been so relieved that he hadn't noticed the disappointment flash in her green eyes. He had, however, noticed her particularly feminine comment about not having anything to wear.

Chapter Twenty

Married? She and Connor were getting married? Tomorrow? She almost laughed out loud. This whole experience felt like one big dream.

Maybe that's why she'd been able to take this whole "journey-to-the-past-to-save-hot-guy" thing in her stride. Maybe it really was just a big, elaborate dream. Yeah, that could be it; she was still standing in the Art Gallery of a five star hotel/castle in 2010 Scotland staring at an oil painting of one of the previous lairds. There was nothing wrong with her other than an imagination run amok. Mackenzie sighed, and shook her head slightly, clearing away the logical explanations that made no sense. Interesting how the only explanation that made any kind of sense at all was the far-fetched one full of magic, rather than the rational one involving a head injury and a vivid dream. If she were being truthful, there was no way she could have imagined Connor...his hands, his kisses, his embraces...it was more creative than her imagination could ever create. But how else could she explain magic and portals and time travel? She smiled to herself and thought that marrying Connor was just one more experience to chalk up to the dream. Besides, if she was dreaming, then couldn't she indulge and stay with Connor? Marry Connor? But wow, what a dream! She really couldn't have picked a better match for herself if she *had* imagined him. Besides whom would it harm for her to stay here with Connor?

Her momentary joy was jarred when she grasped that the answer to that was so obvious: herself. She was only hurting herself. Which begged the question: What would happen once the dream ended and reality came crashing down around her? Would she be able to save her heart from the shatter? But Mackenzie shook it off and squared her shoulders instead focusing on the present. In the immediate future, she'd just try to survive the Campbell's next attack, and worry about the survival of her heart later. But for now, as she was happy and harming no one, she decided to enjoy the dream for the next couple weeks, and just take it from there. Who knew? Maybe she wouldn't even be able to get home anyways. That thought actually perked her up for the first time instead of bringing on overwhelming sadness. Interesting....

By this point in her musings, Mackenzie and Connor had wandered in silence through the stone courtyard, each lost in their own thoughts. They had stopped by the sea wall and Connor broke the silence.

"You're quiet. You are never quiet; should I be worried?" It sounded like he was teasing her, but his eyes were serious. Mackenzie wondered what he'd been thinking about.

She smiled sadly and said, "No, I've just been thinking about this whole big mess I've made of things."

Connor pulled her down with him as he sat on one of the stone benches and repeated, "'Mess of things?' What does this mean?" His eyebrows were in a deep v over his nose, and Mackenzie almost laughed aloud at his confused expression.

"It means that I have muddled the plan so much that it is unrecognizable." Mackenzie looked across the courtyard at the main keep. "I mean, here I am, Mackenzie Stewart, from 2010 America. I've never been anything special, completely ordinary, and I am about to marry a Scottish laird in 1792 Scotland. But it gets better! I was literally dragged through time to marry a different man so that I could put an end to all of the bloodshed, but now I can't stop him since I'm here and not there, so I don't even know what he's planning. But I assume it still has my death involved." Mackenzie stood, feeling the familiar frustration grow as she thought of how she'd messed up the plan and began pacing. She gestured with her hands a lot when she was frustrated, and this was no different, "And now you have to marry me to protect me, which I am so sorry about, Connor, you shouldn't be forced to marry me." Mackenzie sat back down on the bench with a huff. "I'm sorry Connor, I don't mean to vent, but I am such a burden and for that I'm sorry as well." She fidgeted with her skirts, not wanting to meet his eyes, afraid she'd see pity there.

But Connor knelt down in front of her and pulled her tense hands apart and into his own. When she still wouldn't look at him, he released her hands and she let them fall limply in her lap. She felt both of his hands frame her face, and he waited for so long that she finally met his gaze.

"Listen to me, Mackenzie Stewart. Ye are no burden and I'll die before I let that Campbell swine lay his hands on ye. Do ye ken? I'll not let him hurt ye. There's no need to be afraid."

"Connor that's sweet, but I..." Connor put his hand over her lips to stop her words.

"Sweeting, I'm going to protect ye whether ye like it or not. And the best way to do that is to marry ye."

"But you shouldn't have to! That's my point!" Again, his hand gently covered her lips.

"I wouldn't do it if I didn't want to, Mackenzie."

"But why would you want to?" Mackenzie hadn't meant it to burst out of her, but there it was. So she waited. And held her breath.

Connor shifted uncomfortably and said "I've already told ye why—to keep ye safe. If ye are my wife then he cannot legally take ye back."

"Oh." Mackenzie knew she sounded like a disappointed child, but she couldn't help it. Her lower lip pouted out and her eyes dropped. Her crestfallen look tugged at Connor's heartstrings. How he ached to take that look from her face...but what could he do?

Something in Mackenzie's face must have given her mood away, because Connor suddenly said, "I've an idea."

"Oh?"

"Tomorrow after the ceremony, I'll show ye some of my lands." Connor smiled as the shock crossed her face, and finished, "And I have a surprise for ye."

"A surprise? What is it? Is it a good surprise?" She could barely contain her excitement and her curiosity.

"Aye, sweeting, it's a good surprise. And if I tell ye what it is, it won't be much of a surprise, now will it?" He was toying with her.

"Please?"

"Well, if ye really can't wait…"

"If I really can't wait…What? Connor, tell me."

"All right, all right." He laughed, holding his hands out so she would stop. "Let us go." He rose and held a hand out for her to help her up.

Mackenzie got to her feet and taking his hand, impatiently tugged, "So, where to?"

Connor laughed. It was a loud boisterous laugh that caught her off guard. She hadn't heard him laugh so freely before, and it was nice. She practically skipped with him as he walked across the courtyard. At the edge of the stones, he covered her eyes with his hands and walked her carefully forward until she felt soft grass beneath her feet. The smell of hay and horses pricked at her nose, and she was breathing hard—but whether that was the excitement or Connor's hands on her face, she couldn't be sure.

He stopped her and commanded, "Keep your eyes closed."

She smiled and replied, "Yes sir."

He grasped her shoulders and pivoted her to face the direction he wanted, saying, "Open your eyes, Mackenzie." And he stepped back to watch her reaction.

Eagerly opening her eyes, Mackenzie stared at a white horse. She glanced from Connor to the mare and back again. "Are we going for a ride? Awesome! I can't wait to get out and feel the wind on my face! Where's your horse?"

"I don't think you understand, Mackenzie," Connor shook his head slightly and grinned at the confusion in her eyes. He spoke very softly, "She's yours."

"She's mine?" Mackenzie's eyes held confusion for just a second more when comprehension hit. "Wait, she's *mine*? As in I get to keep her?" Her eyes goggled at Connor, her mouth fell open. Then she stretched to her tiptoes and threw her arms around his neck, "Do you mean it? Oh Connor, you're the best!"

"The best what?" His eyebrows were knit in confusion but he was smiling at her enthusiasm.

She laughed a blithely carefree laugh, "Silly Connor. It means that you're so, so, so wonderful. Thank you, so much. I love her. What's her name? Can we go for a ride? Where's the tack and gear?"

Connor cut her off by wrapping his arms around her and murmuring in her ear, "You talk too much. You may name her what ye wish, yes we may ride, and I'll have a groom fetch ye a saddle…a men's saddle since I assume ye'll wish to ride astride?"

"I think I'll name her Snow White, since she's all white." *And since I'm in a fairy tale of my own.*

"That's not very creative," he scoffed.

"Well, what's your horse's name?"

He shifted slightly, dropping his arms from around her, and mumbled, "He is Bonnie Prince Charlie." Connor looked uncomfortable.

She laughed, "Nuh uh. I don't believe it. I figured it would be something manly like Angus or Conan or something."

He smiled wryly or he grimaced, "Truly. My sister named him when we were younger."

She was momentarily sidetracked. Tilting her head to one side, she asked, "You have a sister?"

"Aye. Her name is Muireall. She is married to a MacDonald, and lives on the Isle of Skye."

A stable hand brought in a saddle and bridle.

"Oh, the island across the lake? I mean the *loch*," she wryly corrected herself.

"Aye." Connor looked pleasantly surprised that she remembered. "Careful, you're beginning to sound Scottish."

Mackenzie just snickered and murmured, "You should have heard my granny."

"What was that?"

"Nothing. My granny had the thickest brogue I've ever heard." Mackenzie sighed for a moment before telling him, "I really wish I'd paid more attention to her stories and lessons. She tried to teach me about her home, our ancestors, but I never really had time." Mackenzie sighed, "And now she's gone, and it's too late."

Connor enfolded her in his arms, and rested his chin on the top of her head. "It's all right. You are doing magnificently." She glanced up and smiled at him. How Connor's body responded to such a simple embrace was beyond him. His woman had the power to bring him to his knees with nothing more than a look. He forced himself to step back and clear his head, otherwise he might embarrass them both. "Now let's go ride before I throw you down in the hay and ravish you senseless."

"Aye, my Laird," she demurely lowered her lashes and bobbed a graceful curtsey.

Connor had to bite his cheeks to keep from laughing. But she agilely mounted her mare before he could move the mounting block for her and the smile broke through. Until he saw the tantalizing expanse of leg showing as her skirts rode up to her thighs.

"What? What's wrong?" Mackenzie was completely confused by the look on his face.

"If you are to ride astride, then we must cover you up." He was trying to pull her skirts down over her legs.

She laughed, "Oh Connor. Don't be such a prude. Come on, I'll race you!" And she urged her mount out of the stables and into the yard. Connor watched her go, her hips swaying with the motion of the horse.

What a maddening, infuriating, wonderful woman she was. He leaped onto his horse, and rode after her

Chapter Twenty One

They were out the rest of the day, and after their ride, Mackenzie walked to dinner with a smile playing about her full lips. All she could think about was what a softie her rough Highlander was turning out to be. He had such a good heart. Not only was he marrying her to protect her from a very powerful, very ruthless, evil man, but he had just given her the most wonderful gift. Her own horse! What girl didn't want a horse? He was admitting that he trusted her enough to give her her freedom. How could she thank him for everything? It really meant a lot to Mackenzie and she wouldn't forget it. Of course, she was in so deep now that she wouldn't ever forget any of this, nor did she want to. She was completely in love with him and for the first time she admitted to herself how far gone she really was. It was liberating. And she wanted to tell him, but….

Connor had said a couple times that he cared for her; it was a start, right? She didn't want to tell him first unless she was sure of his feelings. Besides, what if he didn't want the complication of her being in love with him? She gnawed on her bottom lip as she worried about that. No, she couldn't tell him…not yet, anyway. But maybe she could make him fall in love with her right back? They were getting married after all.

But still, coming back to reality, how to show Connor what his gift (and the meaning behind the gift–her freedom) had meant to her?

"Connor, I want to thank you for the wonderful gift."

"You just did," he said with a smile.

"No, I mean really thank you. Is there anything I can do for you? Or that you want?" *Me perhaps?*

Connor stopped walking and turned his pensive blue gaze on her, stroking his chin thoughtfully. "Hmm…You want to do something for me…."

"Yes, please. I feel awful that you've given me such a thoughtful present, and I have nothing for you." *I'd give you my heart, if you'd take it.*

"All right, sweeting, I know what I'd like you to give me." He smiled.

Mackenzie stepped forward in earnest, her hands clasped in front of her. "Anything."

"I'd like you to give me a kiss."

She furrowed her brow. "A kiss? Really? That's it?"

"Nothing more, just a kiss."

Mackenzie stepped closer, until they were close enough to touch, and rose onto her tiptoes, placing her hands on his chest. She brushed her lips against his. Connor stood still, not making a move to touch her, or kiss her back. So she pressed her lips to his once more, and her arms crept up around his neck to twine in his hair and she molded her body to his until there was no space between them. Mackenzie was going to tell him with her lips what she couldn't yet tell him with words. Her kiss was gentle, but building, as her tongue teased his lips open. She swept her tongue across his and tugged his bottom lip with her teeth. Connor groaned and his arms slipped around Mackenzie as he took over the kiss. His lips were much more persistent than hers. Where hers gave, his took, where hers were tentative, his were insistent. And they stood there, kissing in the courtyard as the sun set.

Connor broke the kiss first, looking down into her dazed face. "I've another boon to ask of ye."

"I thought you just wanted a kiss?" Mackenzie teased. "Alright, what else?"

"Mackenzie, I'd like to ask if you will marry me tomorrow morn."

"Marry you?" Mackenzie's confused eyes stared into his, looking for some hidden meaning. "But Connor, we *are* getting married tomorrow." She was trying to read his eyes, but those dark blue pools were fathomless, filled with some unnamed emotion.

"Aye sweeting, but I'm asking ye. And ye may answer me how ye wish." His voice was deeper, his accent more pronounced, like when he was frustrated. What did *that* mean?

Mackenzie slowly said, "You're telling me that I can say no, and you'll leave it at that? That I don't *have* to marry you?"

Could this be right? Was he giving her the option to back out? Maybe she'd been wrong before about his feelings leaning toward the romantic. Her heart plummeted. If he was giving her the chance to opt-out, maybe he really didn't want to marry her…of course how could she blame him? She was completely wrong for him, and she didn't even really live here, for crying out loud! She was so stupid for deluding herself into believing he might actually want to do this for emotional reasons.

Or maybe there was another reason. Could he be giving her the chance at her freedom, like with the horse? Her eyebrows drew down over her nose as she took this all in. If that were the case, then Mackenzie was staggered, and her heart swelled in her chest, thumping unevenly. He seemed to know what she needed. He understood her much more than she had previously given him credit for. This rough battle-hardened chauvinist from the eighteenth century seemed to know her very soul. This had to be why she was here, why she'd been in Scotland the very instant that Morvern and Gregor had come for her, why she'd stayed in Connor's castle. Fate! That was the word. She'd never believed in fate before, but now, staring up at Connor in the setting sun, the sea on one side, his castle on the other, there seemed to be no other explanation. It was meant to be.

She needed to know. Then again maybe now was her chance.

"Connor, thank you for knowing I need this." She cradled his face in her soft hands and kissed him so gently, that if it weren't for the heat between them she wouldn't have felt it. She breathed against his lips, "Of course I will marry you. I'd like nothing better than to be your wife." Connor squeezed her to him and stroked her hair from the crown of her head down her back.

"I thought you'd mentioned that in your time, the man asks. It seemed important to you," Connor shrugged.

Mackenzie cut him off with a kiss so passionate, his response felt as if he wanted to press her against the castle wall and take her on the spot. It was a very arousing feeling, having the power to make this Highland warrior lose control like that. Then someone cleared his throat. Liam. They broke apart like two guilty teenagers caught necking.

"Supper is served, Connor."

Mackenzie could see that he was suppressing laughter. Her face warmed and she hoped she looked presentable as they all entered the Banqueting Hall together.

Dinner was lovely. There was a piper and there were some dancers. The steps looked familiar to Mackenzie, and it took her a moment to remember why. They reminded her of when her grandmother had made her learn about her heritage by attending all of the Highland Games. Mackenzie had always been a dancer, so her grandmother had her learn the sword dances.

After several toasts to their upcoming nuptials, Mackenzie was on her way to being good and drunk. Otherwise, she would have never in a million years leaned over to Connor, who was speaking with Liam, and said, "I think I know that one."

His surprise was evident, "You do?"

"Yep, I learned a whole bunch of sword dances, and they aren't that much different. I also learned some Irish dancing too, but I doubt anyone else here has tap shoes." She snorted at the private joke.

Connor just shook his head not knowing what style of shoe was "tap," and asked if she wanted to join in the dance.

"Sure." She was tipsy at best, and when she stood, the assembly went quiet. But Connor stood as well, and helped her down and to the front of the Hall.

"Lady Stewart wishes to join in the sword dance. Fergus? Farquhar? The pipes and drums?"

It took Mackenzie a few wrong steps and a couple shoulder bumps before she caught on, but it was like riding a bicycle. The ballerina in her allowed her steps to be graceful, if not perfect, and luckily the assembly had been drinking as well, so hopefully she didn't look too awful.

Most of the angry and hateful looks had subsided, whether that was from drink or just the passage of time, or even Connor's acceptance of her, Mackenzie didn't know. Everyone here seemed to value not only his position, but his opinion as well. So if she was good enough for him, then perhaps his clansmen felt the same? The few times that Mackenzie had seen Connor interact with the people of his clan, they had looked at him with nothing but respect and sometimes awe. He was a powerful man, and he was a good man. That was something that Mackenzie had never doubted, not even when he'd hated her and believed the worst in her. He put the good of the clan above all else and it was evident in the way he spoke with his people and dealt with their problems. It was also obvious in the toasts to his health, his prosperity, and her…fertility.

When the dance was over and another tune started, Mackenzie, flushed from excitement and wine, looked up to see Connor staring at her. He smiled back at her, but there was something else in his expression…something she couldn't quite put her finger on. Maybe he was surprised that she knew some of the traditional dances. Or maybe, dare she hope, he was impressed. When she took her seat beside Connor, she felt warm. Partly from dancing, partly from wearing way too many clothes, and partly just from his proximity. While sipping yet another glass of wine, Mackenzie suddenly felt extremely overheated. Connor was engrossed in an animated conversation with his brother, so she took the chance to slip out and cool off.

Mackenzie strolled out into the courtyard and wandered to the sea wall, enjoying the ice cold air on her overheated skin. She was gazing at the stars, wondering what it was exactly that Connor wanted from her when she felt a presence behind her. She turned quickly, dismissing her tumultuous thoughts, and came face to face with the business end of a pistol! Good Lord, there was a gun pointed in her face!

Chapter Twenty Two

"My Lady." The standard greeting was not welcoming.

Mackenzie said nothing.

"I can see that ye've made yerself right at home, now, haven't ye?"

When Mackenzie still didn't speak, her mind was running a million miles a second trying to figure a way out of this, he got angry.

"What, nothin' tae say? Ye might be able tae fool the laird, bu' you'll no' fool me. Ye are sent here by the Campbell tae bring our clan tae ruin. Ye are naught but a whore." The man spat at the stones by her feet, but Mackenzie stood her ground. "We donna take lightly to whores around here."

Mackenzie felt she had listened to his ranting long enough and attempted to brush past him. He gripped her upper arm painfully and brought the pistol to her temple. Her eyes widened, but still she said nothing. The man was a dark, squat man missing most of his teeth in the grotesque smile he displayed. As she cast about her mind for a way to distract him, he dragged the mouth of the pistol from her temple to her chin, and then down to her breast. Mackenzie couldn't repress the shudder that racked her body when he settled the pistol against her heart.

"He'll kill you if you hurt me." Mercifully, Mackenzie kept the tremor out of her voice, but still, it didn't sound as strong as she had intended.

"He'll *thank* me for this!"

There was no doubt in her mind that the creepy little man who only came up to her nose was about to pull the trigger. While it wasn't an automatic weapon, she was certain it would do some damage. *Great, I came back in time to get shot by a pistol!* She wanted to groan at the sheer idiocy of it all. Squaring her shoulders, Mackenzie prepared to kick him and run, hoping that if she got shot, at least it wouldn't be without a fight.

Swiftly Mackenzie brought her knee to his groin and while he was doubled over in pain, she ran towards the keep. But she misjudged him and he lunged at her, knocking her to the ground. He was incredibly heavy on top of her, and she couldn't move her arms; they were pinned in between their bodies. Mackenzie kept up her struggle, but something else happened; his eyes changed from hatred to something else.

She screamed at the top of her lungs, only to have him clamp his beefy hand over her mouth. His thick lips replaced his hand and Mackenzie tried to buck him off.

"I like it when they fight. It's more fun. An' I donna see why I can't hae a little fun wi' you afore I go killin' ye."

"Go to hell!"

"Are ye thinkin' that yer too good fer me? The Campbell whore thinks she is too good for me? I'll show ye!"

He brought his hand between them and rubbed her through the material of her gown. Mackenzie did her best not to struggle as it only seemed to arouse him more. But when he had put his hand between them, her hands had been released and she shoved at him as hard as she possibly could, rolling away, hiking up her skirts, and running for her life. She ran about six feet before she slammed into a wall…but arms encircled her waist quickly and she realized it was Connor. She practically fell into his embrace, taking heart from his solid strength.

"What's going on here?" He glanced behind Mackenzie. "Hamish? What are ye doin' out here?"

"Yer woman is a whore, me Laird, and I think I'd be doin' ye an honor tellin' ye the truth afore the wedding."

Connor looked down at Mackenzie, and she could tell he had summed up the situation by the glare leveled at Hamish.

"So you took it upon yourself to take care of the situation?"

Hamish brightened up considerably, that Connor seemed to understand. "Aye, me Laird, that I did."

Mackenzie could see the angry glint in Connor's eyes, and felt nothing short of satisfaction as his voice lowered menacingly, "Then I suggest you leave, now and never return."

"Me Laird?" Hamish was truly surprised at Connor's decision. He shot a murderous glare at Mackenzie.

Connor noted the look, and continued on, this time with his sword pressed into Hamish's throat. "This woman will be my wife tomorrow, and your lady. If you can't live with that, then leave. Now."

Liam had stepped forward and gripped Hamish by his arm, almost dragging him out behind him. Mackenzie released a long breath and looked up at Connor gratefully. They spoke at the same time.

"Kiss me."

"Are you all right?"

"Please, Connor, I need you to kiss me."

He looked confused, but obliged. His warm lips and strong arms reassured Mackenzie that she was still alive. She needed to feel. The things that Connor made her feel were unlike anything she'd ever felt before, and right now, she wanted nothing more than to give up to sensation in Connor's arms.

When he lifted his head, he looked no less confused, but held her tight against his body.

"What happened?"

"I just wanted some fresh air. I was a little warm from the dancing and all." Mackenzie felt stupid but said it anyway. "And then I turned around and he was there with a pistol in my face," she shuddered at the memory. The fun feeling of having a few drinks too many had left, and had been replaced with a hot "I really don't want to vomit" feeling. She must have looked exactly how she felt, because Connor's blue eyes softened and he placed his arm around her shoulders as they walked. Once they had wandered around the whole of the castle, and the island for that matter, they stopped in the moonlit courtyard.

"Are ye well enough to return, sweeting? Or would ye rather retire to bed early?"

"No, that's alright." She took a deep breath and shook off the memories of Hamish lying on top of her. Giving the courtyard one last glance before turning back to the main keep, Mackenzie wandered back with Connor. Her thoughts were still in a turmoil over what had happened, or almost happened, and yet she still couldn't figure out what it was that Connor wanted from her. He'd said that he wanted her to marry him, but she sensed there was something else.

They returned to their seats and Connor picked up his drink while

Mackenzie just looked around, nibbling a piece of bread. Most of the people there were in good spirits, and probably deep in their cups. But at least no one was glaring at her anymore. This brightened her outlook quite a bit. She heard Connor say something to Liam about how she was not who they had thought she was and she looked over at them to find them deep in conversation. Their voices were too low for her to hear what they were saying, but she caught her name on Liam's lips, and he caught her staring at them and nudged Connor with a smile. Liam indicated with a nod of the head that Connor should attend to Mackenzie. She blushed but met his questioning gaze.

"Is everything all right?"

"Oh, yeah, well, I heard my name and glanced over." She sounded a little flustered, but she continued, "That's all." She felt a little guilty about trying to eavesdrop.

Connor smiled, "I was telling Liam how ye are quite an extraordinary lass. He'd heard about your run-in with the Campbell's men last week, and I filled him in on the details."

"Oh." Mackenzie felt the heat creep back up her cheeks to hear Connor speak of her with such respect. She wasn't used to that. Their relationship was new and still tenuous, on her end at least. She didn't know how to respond to that, so she looked away. As she looked around, a hush fell over the crowd. Mackenzie quickly scanned the assembly, and saw an old man struggling to stand, leaning heavily on a walking stick. Mackenzie glanced up at Connor only to find him staring at her over the rim of his cup.

"Are ye having a good time?"

"Oh! Yes, thank you. What's happening?"

But all he said was "Listen."

So she did.

The old man's voice rose above Connor's comment. She recognized him as the clan's *seannachie* from one of her other meals in the Hall. He was the clan's storyteller, and from what she could gather, a sort of genealogist as well.

"Generations before my grandfather lived, when the Mackenzies still roved this isle, these lands were as wild and untamed as any. A MacRae became constable for the first time of the Kingdom of the Seas. And on this land, a mon loved a woman. Together they tamed this isle and the whole of the lands of Kintail. The lands prospered as did their love. The woman bore him many sons, and when the eldest took a wife, he gained the lands to the west in her tocher.

"She couldna give him an heir. The lass birthed him three wee lassies and a stillborn son. He took a leman, and once she gave him a boy, he brought the bairn to be reared as his heir. His weefe, though young, had some spirit in her yet. She didna fancy rearin' another's babe as her own.

"The laird of these lands paid a mon to speak at the clan meeting. He claimed the laird's weefe had been untrue. She was hanged for her sins, but her last words rang out o'er all the lands as a curse. The lands grew barren, and still we hae the Stewart Curse upon us.

"There have yet to be any lassies born to the Stewart line. Til now. And on the morn, a Stewart will marry a MacRae, and the Stewart curse will be done!"

Amidst cheers and applause, the old man sat down, and took a long draught of ale from his mug.

Mackenzie turned to see Connor studying her. Was this why he was so willing to marry her? Was he also trying to end the curse? He didn't strike her as someone who put any stock in curses. Besides, wasn't her marriage to the Campbell supposed to end the curse? A Campbell, not a MacRae? Well, the sorcerers had never really told her the curse; they had only implied she had to break the curse by marrying John Campbell. Mackenzie had assumed the rest. Could she really trust the two wizards? The answer to that was scary; she didn't know. Her heart started pounding as she thought she really didn't know whom to trust anymore, Connor included.

If he was only marrying her to end the stupid curse then wasn't he as bad as the Campbell in using her to his own ends? He'd once accused the Campbell of just that. Ironic that she was now marrying a man for the same reasons. Had Connor lied to her? And if he had, what would she do about it?

How could she be so stupid? Connor had never professed his love by any means, but he had said he cared for her. And that had been enough for her. She had sworn from the beginning that she needed more, but she had fallen for him in spite of herself. Did he know how far gone she was? She peeked up at him from beneath her lashes to see him still watching her changing emotions without giving anything away himself. She felt like an idiot. And to think; she'd been so intent on convincing him to fall in love with her! She *was* an idiot. How could she have not seen this coming? Mackenzie distanced her heart from Connor right then and there. They would get married in the morning, but it would just be a means to an end; *she* would be a means to an end. They wouldn't, however get their happily ever after, because the second that portal opened on Samhain, Mackenzie would go back to her own time, her own country and her life.

While that thought made her sad, Mackenzie refused to acknowledge the emotion, and instead steeled her heart against Connor and forced a smile. She was pulled from her train of thought by Connor's hand on hers.

"You have been quiet, are you not enjoyin' the tale?"

Mackenzie almost choked on her answer. "No, I mean, yes; it's a great story. Quite informative."

Connor's eyes narrowed at her choice of phrasing, but all he said was,

"Perhaps ye should retire early? It has been a taxing night." When she didn't say anything, he stood and pulled her chair out. "Come, I'll walk ye to our chambers."

Connor tucked her arm through his as they left the Hall. He walked her up the tower stairs to the Laird and Lady's chambers, pausing outside his door.

"I ken your thoughts are of tomorrow, and I've a surprise for you."

Momentarily distracted, Mackenzie cocked her head to one side. "Another one?"

"Aye, although, I must admit I'm unsure of what you'll think." He sounded like he genuinely was unsure, and he really wanted her to like whatever it was.

Connor swept the door open and strode in to light a few tallow candles. He paused and turned as Mackenzie walked through the door. She gasped and flitted to the bed. There was a gown of a deep midnight blue with silver embroidery and laces on the stomacher lying on the bed. It was beautiful. He wouldn't have done this for her if he didn't care for her at least a little, right?

Mackenzie held it up to herself and twirled around like a little girl playing dress-up.

"I take it ye approve of the color?"

"Oh, Connor, it's beautiful. I love it." She turned her wide gaze on him and remembered that she was still mad at him. Her eyes turned wary, "But when? And why? I have a trunk full of gowns. Since women don't wear white yet, any one of them would do."

"I commissioned it when we first arrived."

"But that was like a week ago," she persisted. "How long have you been planning this wedding?" she was speculating. It was so thoughtful, but what did it mean? Was there an ulterior motive? Or was it just his arrogance that demanded she look fabulous on his arm at the wedding?

"Since I first looked into your eyes." His thumb brushed underneath her lash line.

"Oh." She blushed "So sure I'd say yes?"

"You couldna say no."

"You're arrogant," she retorted.

"Aye," Connor said without apology. "I am Laird, and third Earl of Kintail. I am allowed to be arrogant."

"Oh, it comes with the title and all that? Hah! I think you've been getting your way for far too long Connor MacRae. Maybe I should have said no."

His smile was smug. "You didn't say nay," he reminded her.

His arrogance or pride or whatever had led to his plotting this marriage brought her initial joy at her new gown to a halt. She felt her hopes plummet as she thought of the reason behind the gown; the curse. She'd meant to keep her own counsel as far as her feelings over the whole blasted curse, and her newly-realized-but-still-in-denial love for Connor, but she'd never been good at hiding her feelings. Maybe it was a blessing that she'd never had to deal with John Campbell, since she was an awful liar and had never really tested her acting skills outside of the high school play senior year.

"Connor?" Mackenzie laid the gown gently on the trunk at the foot of his bed, and waited for his full attention. It was unnecessary; he was already looking at her.

"Aye, Mackenzie?"

"Do you believe in the curse?" She'd meant it to sound casual, but her voice didn't cooperate; it was too intense. It didn't help that she was holding her breath while waiting for him to answer.

She didn't have to wait long; he answered her almost immediately. "Nay, lass, I doona."

"Oh." It came out on a rush of the air she'd been holding. "Good." Her fears were nowhere near allayed. She pressed on, "But don't you think that it's a little convenient that I'm a Stewart and if we get married tomorrow that it ends an ages-old curse? Besides, how can you dismiss it so easily after all that has happened?"

Connor's eyes gentled, "Nay, lass. 'Tis fate. Fate and magic. Magic brought you here to me, and 'tis fate that you are a Stewart and I a MacRae. I saw the chance and I seized it."

"And me," Mackenzie murmured a little staggered by his romantic admission.

Connor's face split into a wide grin. "Aye, and you. I took a chance on abducting a woman I'd ne'er laid eyes on, but I had to ensure the Campbell could not possess you." His voice and eyes hardened, "And he'll no' ha'e you, he'll not touch you. I swear it, Mackenzie, he'll no' hurt you."

She couldn't doubt the fervor and sincerity of his words, but she did doubt the meaning behind them. What had he been planning this whole time? Had marriage been the ultimate goal from the beginning? So, no matter whom he had found in that carriage, would he have married her?

Mackenzie had to know. "So let me get this straight. You knew you were going to marry whoever was in that carriage? No matter who she was or what she looked like?"

"Aye, Mackenzie, for the good o' the clan. It was fate alone that you were in that carriage rather than the pale Englishwoman we were led to believe the Campbell would marry."

Connor almost sneered the word Englishwoman. Funny how being English was worse than being unattractive. Mackenzie had forgotten that his information (as well as the Campbell's) was only that she was from England and a Stewart. Connor had had no idea that when he'd pulled her from the carriage that she would be an American tourist from the year 2008 dressed in shorts and a tank top. Mackenzie inwardly smiled as she imagined Connor yanking a young English maid from the carriage. She felt a quick stab of sympathy as she realized that the unknown girl would have probably fainted dead away at the prospect of being kidnapped by a Highland "barbarian."

His arms were around her, and Connor pulled her tight up against his chest. Mackenzie knew what he wanted, and what her traitorous body wanted as well, but she wasn't sure if she could do this. She wanted to think all of this through; the curse, Connor's plans, and how she felt. His lips were at her neck, tracing their way to the hollow beneath her ear. Mackenzie had trouble thinking. The only thing she was sure of was how she felt in Connor's arms, and she was fairly certain he felt the same inescapable pull of desire. She'd once told herself that it would be enough that he wanted her, and right now she desperately wanted to believe that.

Truthfully, though, she did want to go through with the wedding. She wanted to marry Connor, to bear his children, and grow old with him, but there was no way that was possible since she would be going back to her time in a couple of weeks. There was no happily ever after for them, but perhaps she could be greedy and take the here and now for as long as possible, and screw the Cinderella ending.

So after all that, Mackenzie found herself back where she started; unsure of Connor's feelings for her but knowing she loved him. And now she was rambling on and on in her own head when she should be grasping tenaciously at whatever time she had left with Connor.

He must have sensed it as well, because he said against her neck, "Turn off your mind, Mackenzie. Doona think, just feel...."

His lips brushed her cheek, her temple, her closed eyelids...He bypassed her lips, barely touching the corner of her mouth with his warm breath, continuing instead down her neck and collarbone until he found her nipple through the material of her dress. Mackenzie gave up thinking entirely and surrendered to the magic of Connor's lips.

****

Connor was pleased to see Mackenzie's open joy at the gown. He'd wanted it made in the same color green of her eyes, but his sister had warned him that to be married in green was unlucky, so he'd chosen the color of midnight with the silver accents of the full moon. Just as the night he had first seen her. When she had raced to the bed and picked it up to hold it against her body, Connor had wanted very badly to see her in it. He felt ridiculous.

This was his way of showing her how he felt about her. If he knew her mind better, he would tell her, but she must hear how he spoke to her? And she must see the way he looked at her? He knew his men saw it; they teased him mercilessly on the practice field. But when she'd turned her wide, guileless eyes on him, he saw some hint of suspicion in their green depths.

The only thing he could think of was putting his hands on her body. He would show her with his lips what he couldn't tell her with them.

She deserved more, much more, but she'd be leaving in a few weeks and he didn't want her to go. How could he convince her to stay? How could he even think of asking that of her? Once more, Mackenzie pulled back from him, but he kissed her words away; this was not the time for talking. Connor kissed his way down her delicate neck and found her nipple through the fabric of her gown. He stripped her of the gown, wet from his mouth, and pressed her up against the cold stone of the wall. Her hands wandered impatiently down his back stopping at the small of his back as she tugged at his shirt. Connor tore it off and felt a tingle from skin on skin contact that he'd never before felt. Pressing his arousal into her soft belly he felt her hands clutching his hips. Hoisting one of her long legs up around his hip, he slid into her in one smooth motion, and stifled her gasp with his lips.

They never made it to the bed.

Chapter Twenty Three

Mackenzie awoke on the day of her wedding to an empty bed. The sheets were cold on his side, but the smoldering remains of the fire warmed the room enough for her to slide out of bed. It felt decadent to sleep naked and feel her skin slip against the sheets. Mackenzie had never been one to sleep naked; usually it was just boy-shorts and a tank top. Besides, her roommate usually had a guy over and Mackenzie was tired of being caught in her underwear in her own home. Sleeping nude was definitely a luxury she enjoyed, especially when she was snuggled up to Connor's naked body.

Mackenzie padded barefoot over to the window and looked out over the loch, and the most beautiful October day she'd ever seen. Being a desert rat from Las Vegas, she rarely saw such beautiful scenery, so she drank it in. The fog had cleared—hmm…it must be later than she'd realized. Checking her watch she gasped; it was nine o'clock! The wedding would start in an hour! Just as she started to panic, a knock sounded at the door.

Bronwyn bustled in without waiting for an answer.

"Let's get you ready, dearie. I've a bath ready in your chambers and your gown has been aired out and is ready as well."

Bronwyn scrubbed Mackenzie's body until it glowed and washed her hair with the scented lavender water that Mackenzie loved. When she stepped out of the tub, she caught Bronwyn staring at her naked body with such blatant curiosity that she had to ask,

"What?"

"Oh!" She flushed at the embarrassment of being caught staring. "I dinnae mean to stare, but if it's not too bold, might I ask what that is?"

"Huh?" Mackenzie followed her gaze down. "Oh you mean my belly ring?"

"What is it?" she fingered the jeweled barbell gently.

"Hmm…it's like an earring," Mackenzie touched her earlobes "but it is pierced through my navel. Where I come from, they're the latest fashion."

"Ahh, that's right, the Americas. Are ye missin' yer lands much?"

"Not so much anymore," she smiled thinking of Connor. "But I miss the heat, and the dry air. It's so different here."

Bronwyn, it seemed, had taken offense to Mackenzie's comment. She quickly tried to repair the damage done to her one friend.

"I find these lands to be some of the most beautiful that I've ever seen." At Bronwyn's smile, Mackenzie went on, "I'm not sure I could ever live somewhere without mountains." Bronwyn's face perked up at the mention of her lands.

"Och, aye, dearie, these are some beautiful mountains. Soon they'll have snow covering them, and in the spring you'll see the flowers and heather bloom across the loch and into the moors. Oh aye, it's a lovely sight to behold." Bronwyn sighed happily at the thought of the Highlands in spring.

But, Mackenzie thought, *I won't be here in the spring.* She shook it off before she could depress herself any more, and tried to remember her new philosophy of living in the moment. Bronwyn had finished rubbing scented oils all over her hair and body, and helped her into the gown.

"Married in blue, always be true" Bronwyn quoted.

Mackenzie smiled thinking of the "something old, something new, something borrowed, something blue" adage. Once she was dressed, Bronwyn sat her down to plait her hair, weaving silver ribbons throughout, but leaving some of her hair down so the braids and ribbons laid against her nearly dry curls. Mackenzie desperately wished for makeup or at least some mascara. She briefly pondered trying to sneak a moment alone to swipe on some lip gloss when a knock rapped out on the door.

"Mackenzie?"

It was Connor! Bronwyn called through the closed door, "Me Laird, 'tis bad luck for the groom to see his bride before the wedding!"

Connor's sigh was audible through the heavy door. "'Tis time" was all he said before his footsteps echoed down the hallway.

Mackenzie barely even got the chance to look in the mirror as Bronwyn looked out the door to see if Connor had indeed left. The last thought she had before she was ushered downstairs was that she was glad she'd spent her summer in the pool; her skin still retained a warm golden hue. Between the blue of the gown and her blonde hair, her tan gave her that glow that every bride hoped for on her wedding day.

The wedding. Her wedding. Her wedding to Connor. She'd pictured her wedding day numerous times since she was a child. Doesn't every little girl? But in all those games of pretend, and visions of herself dressed in gauzy white, not once had she ever envisioned herself getting married to a Highland laird during the 1700s. Who would? Bronwyn walked her to the door that led to the courtyard and handed her some blue and purple wildflowers tied with the same silver ribbons that she'd woven throughout her hair.

"Good luck, me lady."

And she opened the doors into the bright day.

Mackenzie stepped out into the sunlight, pausing to allow her eyes to adjust to the sunlit morning. As she looked around, there were faces she didn't recognize, and then there was Connor. He was resplendent in a crisp yellow shirt, open to his chest, with a fresh plaid wrapped around him. His hair was tied back in a leather thong, as was Liam's, who stood beside him. She walked to him, wondering if she should walk slower in the typical step-together, step-together wedding walk, but she figured that this wasn't a typical wedding, so…She walked to Connor at a normal pace, not daring to look away just in case some of the guests still wore angry expressions. When she reached Connor, he grasped her hands in his, and handed the flowers to Liam without ever looking away. He smiled down into her eyes and she smiled shyly back, not sure what to expect. He looked happy. That was good. The bishop began the ceremony and she never took her eyes from Connor's.

* * * *

They were married. There was a delicate diamond and sapphire gold band on her third finger, in case she had any doubt. Mackenzie could hardly remember the ceremony. All she remembered was Connor's warm hands on hers, and his blue eyes sparkling with happiness. It was so new and he seemed so carefree, that she wasn't sure what that meant. Why oh why must she over-analyze everything? She forced herself to focus on the here and now and to stop over-thinking it.

She noticed that they were lined up in the receiving line and she was about to personally greet every single member of the clan. Most of the people whom she greeted were polite; every now and then a face would look hostile, or hold animosity, but she kept a polite smile on her face. A little girl gave her a hug and a kiss on the cheek. Mackenzie's answering smile was genuine, and she felt a quick stab of envy for her mother. Mackenzie had never really wanted children, but suddenly she wanted Connor's children, and she wanted it with an intensity akin to pain. Her attention was diverted to the next little girl; she had pressed something soft into her hand—a handkerchief.

"Oh, it's lovely!" Mackenzie exclaimed, touched by the small token.

No one had ever made her a gift before. It had the name Lady MacRae stitched into several flowers in the corner. It was so intricate, and the child couldn't be more than eight or nine!

"Do you like it? Me mum says the flowers are all askew."

"I love it! And I'll tell you a secret," at the little girl's bright look, Mackenzie bent down, cupped her hand, and whispered, "My embroidery has crooked flowers too."

The little girl giggled and skipped away holding her mother's hand.

Connor leaned in close and spoke in Mackenzie's ear, "That was very gracious of you."

A smile played about Mackenzie's lips as she turned her gaze from the little girl to Connor. "She was sweet. Who is she?"

"She's my niece, Mairi."

"Your niece? Then was that woman…"

"My sister, aye."

"Oh." Mackenzie wrinkled her nose and looked up confused, "Did you introduce us?"

"You were too busy with Mairi," he smiled down at Mackenzie.

"Oh," she blushed, feeling guilty for not meeting Connor's sister.

The next round of well-wishers came by and Mackenzie made a concentrated effort to pay attention this time; Connal, Andrew, Donald, Ian, Isobel, Fiona, Elizabeth, Charlotte…how did Connor keep everybody's names straight? She knew he had grown up here, but wow, there were so many names. It was a little overwhelming.

Once the myriad of people had paraded through the Hall, Mackenzie was allowed a quick respite. She and Connor walked arm in arm through the Hall to their table where Connor heaped her plate full of everything from beef to haggis. With most of the food that she hadn't heard of before, Mackenzie had learnt not to ask, and to just try it first. Haggis was another story. She'd known what it was pre-time travel, but she dug in anyway. Thinking she wouldn't like it, she was surprised that the haggis stew was pretty good. True to her American roots, though, she'd have preferred it with lots of ketchup. If she ever did make it back, maybe she'd order room service and have haggis with ketchup. Mackenzie caught herself daydreaming. Home. Home is where the heart is, right? What if her heart stayed here in eighteenth century Scotland? Would she really want to go back to twenty-first century America? Would she stay, if she could? More importantly, the main question was would Connor want her to stay?

"Are ye no' hungry?" Connor's voice interrupted her now maudlin train of thought.

"Hmm…?"

"I'd be askin' you if you're hungry or not?" He was teasing her but his eyes were concerned. Mackenzie looked down at her plate to see that she'd only been pushing her food around.

"Oh, no not really, I guess. There's just so much food."

"Good," Liam piped up. "I'll take it." He reached across Connor and stabbed her haggis, taking it to his plate.

Mackenzie laughed and teased, "You remind me of my brother."

"How's that?" Liam asked around a mouthful of food.

"Always hungry." They all three laughed at that, but Connor was watching her closely; his eyes missed nothing. Mackenzie added, "And never serious. He was my best friend." She tried not to sound depressed, but it was difficult.

Luckily Liam was flirting with a pretty brunette and hadn't noticed, but Connor did and pressed the issue, "Was?"

Mackenzie fidgeted in her seat and toyed with her bread, crumbling it to bits. Knowing Connor, he wouldn't let it go. She sighed heavily and finally spoke, "He was killed recently." How did one explain a car accident to a man who'd never seen a car?

Connor's warm hand enveloped hers, and she glanced up from beneath her lashes. His gaze trapped her eyes and they stared quietly into each others' eyes for who knew how long before Liam's boisterous laugh interrupted them. Mackenzie blinked and looked away. Wow, she felt like they had just had a "moment" but she didn't know what it meant. Well, she could over-analyze it later. Right now, she just wanted to enjoy her wedding feast.

The idea that there was a feast in her honor right now was a heady thought and it put a genuine smile on her face. When Mackenzie turned back to Connor, the moment was gone, but his response to her smile was encouraging; he squeezed her hand and trailed the fingers of their joined hands down her cheek pausing at her mouth long enough for Mackenzie's lips to tremble slightly.

One man came up to her and toasted her "child-bearing hips," while another toasted their happiness. It continued on like that with well-wishers until many were deep in their cups. While Connor was deep in conversation with some man named Callum, an old man with thinning grey hair paused in front of Mackenzie long enough to remark,

"'Tis doin' me heart well, it is, to see the laird's new weefe so in love wi' him."

"Excuse me?" she gasped.

"There'd be nothin' more beautiful than a woman in love."

"Oh, I'm not, I mean, we're not, umm..." she gave in graciously, "Thank you."

The rest of the celebration was spent in the turmoil of her mind; was it really that obvious that she loved him? She had barely admitted it to herself yet, it was difficult to hear it spoken out loud by a stranger.

When Mackenzie and Connor retired to their chambers, it was well past midnight and the festivities were still going strong. As soon as the door closed behind them Connor turned on Mackenzie with a peculiar gleam in his eyes.

"Did you enjoy yourself tonight?" The intensity of his eyes belied the banal question.

"Yes. Didn't you?" Mackenzie knew Connor's expressions well enough to know that this was not what he wanted to say.

"Aye."

"What? What is it?" She was a little irritated that he was back to speaking with monosyllabic answers.

He just looked at her with an appraising look in his eyes, and a slight smile turning up the corners of his mouth.

"Connor, I know you want to say something to me…just spit it out."

That broke through his brooding silence. "Spit what out?"

She sighed, "It means speak what you are thinking."

"I overheard what Farlan said to you."

"Who?" She looked up at him with her brows knit over her nose. She wasn't playing innocent; she really didn't know. There were just too many names and faces to remember.

"Is it true?" he pressed. "*Are* you in love with me?"

Mackenzie blushed to her roots and hedged, "I'm not sure I know what you mean."

Connor's blue eyes were intense as he stepped closer, but his voice was gentle, "Mackenzie you're a terrible liar."

She sighed and looked away from his sapphire gaze. She knew he'd get it out of her sooner or later, and besides, what was the point in denying it anyways? She drew herself up and glared at him square in the eye.

"I've loved you from the start, Connor MacRae, and I won't apologize for it." While she felt defensive, Mackenzie wanted him to understand she wouldn't press the issue. "I'm not asking anything of you Connor, and I don't expect anything from you…" His fingers silenced her words.

"You're in love with me? Why have you never said anything?" He demanded.

"No one wants to tell someone she loves him, and have him not say it back," her eyes dropped and she said it so softly he had to strain to hear it.

His quickly indrawn breath had her raising her eyes to his. He was looking at her with a look on his face that she had never seen before. It was tender, and incredulous, and there was something else, but she just couldn't decipher it.

He finally spoke, "If you think I doona care for you, then why did you agree to marry me?"

"Umm…it's only temporary, I guess, since I'll be returning to my time on Halloween, or All Hallows Eve, or whatever you call it." She wanted to reassure him that she didn't have any expectations of him. "Plus, even if you don't love me, I still want to be with you, even if it is only for a few weeks." This was hard to admit, how much she wanted to be with him, since she'd never said it out loud before.

"But I've told you I care for you, lass, do you not remember that?"

Mackenzie shrugged, and her lips pouted slightly, "But I never really know what you mean. And let's say you do care for me?" she challenged. "What then, huh? There's nothing we can do about it." Her frustration was evident in her tone, so she tried to gentle it, "I mean, I know I can't stay here, I guess, is what I'm trying to say. And I don't expect you to ask me to stay; I already told you that I am going into this marriage with my eyes open. I'm not an idiot, Connor, I know why you married me and I'm not asking for more than you are prepared to offer."

Connor was irritated, she could tell. "And why did I marry you, exactly?"

Why did he keep questioning her? He wasn't giving anything away himself, but it felt like he was grilling her mercilessly. She was uncomfortable speaking aloud her newly discovered feelings for him, and trying to explain such deep emotions to him was painful knowing he did not reciprocate.

"Like you said, to protect me and stuff." She was depressing herself with the knowledge that he still hadn't said more than he cared for her. And she didn't know if he was merely saying that to be nice.

He had gripped her gently by the shoulders and waited patiently until she met his eyes. Mackenzie noticed that they were a deeper blue than she'd ever seen before. He still didn't speak; he was staring into her eyes, looking for something. It seemed like he wanted an answer, but who knew to what? He could be so frustrating sometimes.

When he spoke, it sounded like he'd chosen his words carefully.

"You mean more to me than any woman ever has." His eyes never once broke contact with hers.

It wasn't "I love you too," but it was a start. She figured that he was trying not to hurt her feelings. She sighed, at least he hadn't said "Thank you" when she'd confessed that she loved him. That was so insulting. Mackenzie held his gaze for a few moments more, but then she dropped her eyes and stepped back from his too-close proximity and that inevitable heat.

"Don't worry about it, Connor," Mackenzie tried to sound blasé and shrugged again, "I told you, it doesn't matter whether you love me back or not, it's only for a few more weeks. Then you can go back to whatever it is you were doing before you kidnapped me." She smiled to show him she wasn't trying to pick a fight, but he wasn't ready to leave the topic yet.

"And are you so anxious to leave?" his voice sounded calm, but his eyes were angry.

No. "I don't have a choice, Connor. The gate only opens once more before the New Year."

"There are always choices, Mackenzie." His voice was low, and gentle, and she wanted to believe a bit sad, but that was purely wishful thinking on her part.

"Not for me." Mackenzie was done talking about leaving. It was too hard and she wanted to memorize her wedding night for later. She turned away from him and tried awkwardly to pull at the laces on her gown; this one laced up the back. She heard a muffled chuckle and glared over her shoulder at Connor.

"Don't laugh at me."

"I wouldn't dare sweeting." He compressed his lips and it looked like he might have been biting them from the inside.

She felt her hair lift off her back and Connor's hands replaced her own.

His "Would ye be wanting some help?" was said against the nape of her neck.

"Please?" She leaned her head back against his shoulder and sighed. It felt so natural to be here, to be doing this. Getting ready for bed with the man she loved; her husband. He slipped his hands around her waist and kissed down her jaw to her neck. She shivered despite the heat that emanated in waves from Connor.

"I knew that you would look exquisite in this." Her gown fell to the floor, and Mackenzie stepped out of it.

"Oh did you now?" She preferred this teasing banter to the serious talk of her imminent departure.

He whirled her around to face him, "Oh, aye Mackenzie, I did." He'd finished with her stays and Mackenzie hadn't even noticed until they too had fallen to the floor. He was so quick at it, that Mackenzie was been about to tease him about how he must have gotten so proficient at undressing a woman, but the look in his eyes halted any words.

Connor dipped his head and kissed from her neck to her collarbone, and down her arm as he slipped the sark off her shoulder revealing the satiny skin beneath. When he got to her fingers, he nipped her ring finger and Mackenzie gasped as he drew it into his mouth and sucked. He raised his eyes back to hers and trapped her gaze in his own. Connor slid her sark down her body and Mackenzie was helpless to do anything but stare into the dark blue pools of molten desire his eyes had become. It was a heady feeling to know that she was the reason his eyes were so dark; she had never before felt so powerful. He wanted her and this time she knew what to do.

Mackenzie unwrapped his plaid from the chieftain brooch and pushed it off his shoulder. Connor held perfectly still and let it fall to the floor with Mackenzie's pile of clothes. Next Mackenzie dragged his shirt over his head; it too joined the growing pile of clothing. Mackenzie couldn't help but marvel at his hard body with all its scars hinting at the power and danger this man carried. She let her fingers trail down from his chest to the patch of hair on his stomach, and lower still. She could feel his muscles clench and his breath stop as she wrapped her fingers around his erection. She quickly found his rhythm and knelt down to press her lips to his lower abs. Trailing her mouth down to where her hand was, she gently licked the tip. She felt a thrill of satisfaction as his hands gripped her shoulders and as her mouth took him in, his fingers tightened. She used both her hand and her mouth to pleasure Connor. He molded a hand to the nape of her neck, holding her in place. She was becoming bolder with her free hand, exploring what made his muscles quiver and his breath hitch, when Connor pulled her roughly up and to him, crushing her lips with his.

He pressed her back against the cold wall and lifted one of her long legs, hitching it around his hip. She was tall enough that he didn't have to lift her. He slipped inside her and Mackenzie reveled in the groan wrenched from him. This was how she liked Connor; out of control. He pushed into her again and again until they were both panting, and Mackenzie was moaning with every breath. She couldn't wait any longer.

"Oh God Connor, I'm so close."

"Just let go, love."

With her back pressed against the cold wall and the heat from Connor's body warming her, Mackenzie shuddered with the force of her orgasm and she melted into Connor's arms as he spent himself in her.

Slowly he withdrew from her and slid her leg down only to gently pick her up and carry her to the bed. He was looking at her like he was waiting for her to say something.

"What?" Mackenzie frowned when he didn't answer. She touched the crease line in between his eyebrows. "What is it?"

"I'm so sorry."

Her frown deepened. "For what?"

"I didn't mean to take you up against the wall like a common whore. You deserve better. I'll be gentle with you. I want to be." Mackenzie thought he sounded as if Connor was promising himself rather than her.

"Oh," she grinned, her breathing still not yet returned to normal. "Don't worry about it; I liked it up against the wall like a common whore."

Her mischievous look had Connor laughing.

"Och do ye lass? Well I should be a gentleman and oblige ye."

Her eyes widened innocently, "Why my Laird, whatever do you mean?"

Connor gripped her by her hips, flipped her over onto her belly, and slid in from behind.

His lips brushed her ear as he whispered, "Let me show you."

Chapter Twenty Four

Connor had slipped out of bed around dawn to fetch his new bride some breakfast. He had noticed she did not rise at dawn like most did, so he thought he would let her sleep. Especially since he hadn't let her sleep much the night before. He'd woken her a couple times during the too short night to find her eager and wet. He smiled at the memory of their last coupling. He had woken her by slipping in from behind while they slept together, snuggled like two spoons in a drawer. Her body had responded immediately even before she was fully awake. Her gasp of surprise and pleasure was all the encouragement he had needed. He had never known anyone who was so willing and giving without asking for anything in return. Not even his love.

She loved him. Connor hadn't wanted to say anything yet—Mackenzie would think he was only saying it in response to her admission. He wanted to make it special when he said it to her, so she would know his heart meant it. Although she now had his name as her own, he wanted to further ensure her bond to him. What it ultimately came down to was that he didn't want her to leave. Perhaps if he got her with child, she wouldn't be able to leave? The thought that he had not taken any precautions with her thus far led to the thought that mayhap she might be with child already.

By the time he entered the dining room, Connor was grinning so wide that a serving girl nervously giggled and peered at him from beneath her lashes before she darted out the door. Liam was eating and flirting with another servant when Connor strode up to the table. He prepared a plate of fresh brown bread and honey with some late season berries.

"Ah the new groom. I see by your smile that ye had a pleasant night."

Connor turned and smiled with an excited light in his eyes. "Aye Liam, although the night was too short, my brother, too short indeed."

They both laughed at the implications.

"Good Connor, ye deserve it. Ye have been too serious of late. Right glad it is I am to see how your new bride has brought such happiness to your eyes."

Connor pulled out a chair and sat down next to his brother. "I think you should know the truth, Liam, about me bonnie bride."

Liam's eyes narrowed, but he merely nodded for Connor to proceed with his tale. Connor knew Liam well enough to know that he would save his judgment until the end. His brother had always been a fair-minded man. Liam had a hot temper, but he had always been a fair man.

"She is not who you think she is, Liam. She's...she is," his uncharacteristic struggle for words had Liam's curiosity piqued. "She is unlike any woman I've ever met. She's the Stewart lass, as I'm sure you ken." Without waiting for Liam to acknowledge him, Connor continued, "I abducted John Campbell's betrothed ere he met her."

"Aye, brother, I had heard that."

Connor interrupted his brother, "She's not English, as our informant led us to believe. Which means the Campbell hasn't any idea she is no' who she should be. The Campbell was told the same as we were, that the Stewart lass would be a spoiled, weak-willed English maid. But she's no' that, Liam, she's so much more." Connor poured a mug of ale and had gulped it down before he'd even set down the jug. How could he make his brother understand? "She's from the Americas, Liam. The Americas. We've been told for generations that the Stewart lass would be Scottish and she's an American."

"Has she got any Scotts blood in her at all?"

"Aye, I believe her grandmother was from the highlands. There's Scotts in her blood. I can feel it. More than that, she can trace her lineage to royalty. But the Campbell doesn't ken more than she is his abducted bride. He needs her blood. He plans to sacrifice her to secure his position through his use of the dark arts. He plans to charm his army with her blood. Her blood is the key to the dark forces. He will transform his army into one merged with the dark magicks he so faithfully worships. Once they are merged he will be nigh unstoppable. But we have her, Liam. We have the Stewart lass, and he will come for her. There was an attempt on her life her first night here. I've been thinking about that a lot, and I believe that it was meant merely as a warning; he knew I'd kill those men. He needs her alive. His deadline is Samhain and then her life is forfeit. We have to keep her safe til then, Liam. We have to!" Connor pounded his fist into the table so hard it drew blood.

Liam finally spoke, "We will keep her safe brother. We canna let the Campbell get his hands on her, that much is evident." He paused thoughtfully, and then his eyes darkened. "The black arts," Liam spat as he said it, his face twisting in a grimace, "I canna believe it. What a snake." His tone changed, "But what are ye plannin' for the lass?"

Connor shifted slightly, almost uncomfortably, "Well, Liam, here's the crux of the matter. There's a wee bit more to the story. My new wife is not only from the America's, but she's from 200 years in the future. She is from the year 2010."

Liam gaped. When he finally spoke it sounded as if he were choking, "She's from…where?"

Connor would've been amused at Liam's expression, except he knew how he felt. "Not where, but when. Approximately 218 years from now. She'll no' even be born til the year nineteen hundred and eighty-seven."

"Be serious, Connor." Liam had regained his composure and his voice was firmer, angry now.

"I am serious, my brother. There'll no' be a Stewart lass born for almost 200 years. The Campbell's magicians took her from her time and brought her here. She was on her way to meet the Campbell when I found her carriage and took her. She says that they were asking for her help to defeat the Campbell."

"Can they be trusted?"

"I'm no' sure. They fed her some tale about breaking the curse, and she agreed to help, but I doona think she knew to just what she was agreeing."

"But what if they were only securing her agreement for pretenses? They could be in league with the Campbell and taking her to him, rather than for their so-called noble purposes. What if their intent is no' for the greater good, but rather for their master's own good?"

"I've thought of that, believe me, Liam, I have. But I've no way of knowing what they are thinking. If I could just speak with them face to face, then I might read their eyes and their intentions." His expression turned black. "If they brought her here to sacrifice her, if they lied to her…they will never get the chance to regret it."

"And what of the curse, Connor? Do ye think this will end it?"

Connor laughed harshly and raked his hand through his hair. "Until recently, Liam, I never believed in the curse. Now, why not? I think that, nay, I *know* that Mackenzie Stewart was brought here for something special, something extraordinary, more than what even she thinks. Whether 'tis ending the curse or defeating the Campbell, I'm no' sure, mayhap she will do it? I'm no' sure of anything anymore, Liam." Connor paused. This next part was the hardest for him to admit. His voice softened and thickened and he spoke slowly, "The only thing I am sure of is that I love her. I love her so much and I am so selfish that I want to keep her here. How can I do that to her? She is set to return to her own time on Samhain, but how can I let her go? How can I tear my own heart out?"

Connor's beseeching look stunned Liam for a second, but he spoke quickly, and softly, not wanting to antagonize Connor.

"Connor, I ken ye are partial to the lass, but what ye speak of, well, it isna possible." He'd said it gently, but Connor's anger was evident.

"I'm no' daft, Liam. I'm no liar, and ye ken I'm no' gullible, that I have to believe what I've seen and heard wi' me own eyes and ears."

"But Connor, ye believe that you're married to a lass from the future?" Liam protested.

"Aye, Liam, I ken how it sounds, but I have proof." And Connor smugly produced Mackenzie's digital camera from his plaid with a flourish. "Here, Liam. Look." Connor snapped his picture and turned it so Liam could see himself and examine the device.

"By all that is holy, what is this?" Liam hissed from between stiff lips. He made no move to take the camera.

"A digital camera. I'm no' sure what that means, but it captures your likeness and displays it. Here, look. These are—what did she call them?—oh, pictures from her time."

Connor hit Review and scrolled through the pictures until he found what he was looking for. "This is our castle," he paused, "218 years from now."

Liam's face had turned white, then red. It settled on a more normal hue as he asked, "What is *that?*" He was indicating the new wing added on to the original keep.

"An expansion. Mackenzie says that our home will be a lodging for travelers one day, an inn of sorts. It is still owned by MacRaes in her time. The current laird still lives there with his family."

"And we know that this is not some of the black magic practiced by the Campbell to have you believe her?"

"I trust her, Liam."

"I ken ye fancy yourself in love wi' her, Connor, but how can ye be so sure?" he pressed.

Connor glared at his brother. "I said I trust her, Liam. Implicitly." His tone brooked no argument, and Liam knew his brother well enough to see that he felt she was true.

Liam slowly shook his head from side to side in amazement and annoyance. Connor found another picture, this one was of Mackenzie and some other girl, and showed his brother the screen with a smile. "Look at how the women dress. Is it no' shameful?"

Liam took in the sheer tank tops and jeans with wide, bugging eyes. "I can see her breasts! Connor, what are they wearing?"

Connor shook his head ruefully and said, "I haven't figured that out yet. Here look at this."

It was a picture of Mackenzie and Jenna when they had landed in the airport. Mackenzie was wearing sunglasses, khaki capris, and a pink twinset, while Jenna wore a blue spaghetti strap sundress, and both girls looked extraordinarily happy. They were posed next to a lit billboard advertising the castle they'd be staying in…Connor's castle.

"What…is…that?" Liam choked out. He was still trying to wrap his mind around the impossibility of Connor's words.

"I've no idea." Connor almost laughed.

Liam scrolled through the hundred or so pictures until he got back to his own. Then he went through them a second time. He slowly released his breath and eyed Connor over the camera.

"Well," his tone was brusque, businesslike, "What shall we do about the Campbell? It's clear he canna have his hands on this." He held up the digital camera. " 'Tis more power than I'd care to see him possess."

"Agreed. I think I've an idea, but I'll be needin' your help, brother."

"Anything, Connor. Whatever ye need."

Connor smiled and said, "As you know, I've a man inside the Campbell's keep, a stable hand. He's been gathering what information he can and feeding lies to his men. I've sent a letter to the Campbell's sorcerers to see if they have any news for me. My plan hangs on that, on them and their help."

"I doona like not knowing part of our plan, or being dependent on those *wizards.*" Liam spat the word, clearly not trusting them.

"Neither do I," soothed Connor, "but what choice have I? We need to know what they know. Mayhap then I can understand what it is I feel as if I am missing. I feel as if there is an obvious solution in front of my nose and I canna see it."

Liam's eyes took on a scheming glint in them and he leaned in toward Connor. "Mayhap there's another way. A back-up plan, so to speak." At the light in his eyes, Connor was intrigued. He leaned closer while Liam described the forming of a plan.

Chapter Twenty Five

The early morning light was coming in the window and it was bright enough to wake Mackenzie. She yawned and stretched luxuriously in bed. It was pure decadence sleeping naked. Connor had been very attentive the night before. He'd woken her several times during the night, each time in a new and exciting way. A small smile curved her lips upward as she remembered some of the ways. She was enjoying married life, that was for sure.

Married. Sheesh. And to a Scottish lord, *laird,* she corrected herself, from the 1700s. Mackenzie smiled at the sheer impossibility of it all. What would she tell her friends? She thought of Jenna, and how she would react to Connor. Mackenzie almost laughed out loud. Jenna would flip! Her smile turned down very quickly into a frown, and she wondered if she would ever see Jenna again. Would she ever be able to tell her about the hunk of a man she'd met and married in the year 1792? Would she even get the chance? Would she see her again at all? Mackenzie got out of bed slowly and grabbed her shift. Pulling it over her head, she thought of the life waiting for her in the twenty-first century. It seemed so distant, so far away, as if it were becoming less and less real to her. She shook her head quickly as if to shake away the realization that the fantasy had become more real than the reality. A short, hysterical laugh slipped from between her lips.

Focusing on the here and now had saved her sanity, but it had also put her in a form of denial. She thought about her "real" life as little as possible. But now, she wondered if she would want to return? She'd been guaranteed safe passage back by Morvern and Gregor, no matter what happened, but she didn't have the amulet anymore, and she didn't have their help anymore. She was alone. They were gone, and she was alone in 1792 Scotland. Well, she mused, not completely alone. Maybe it wouldn't be so bad to be stuck here in the eighteenth century. She could be with Connor; she was happy enough. But was he happy enough with her?

She hoped so. Mackenzie sat down on the edge of the bed with a sigh. And caught a glimpse of herself in the mirror. The shift was getting a little tight around her belly and breasts. Maybe she'd gained a few pounds with the diet of cheese and bread and meat? She'd have to start jogging or something. Mackenzie sighed again and unwillingly turned her thoughts back to her "real" life. She didn't know if Connor would want to keep her around for longer than Halloween. Hopefully, but she really wasn't sure, though. In fact she wasn't sure about much these days. She knew she loved Connor, and she knew he wanted her. She knew it wouldn't be enough for forever, but they might not have forever, so, in the here and now she fought so hard to keep herself in, it was enough. But she also needed to think farther ahead, look at the timeline. She mentally tabulated how much time had passed; almost two weeks...that only left a little over two weeks to save everyone from John Campbell's far reaching dark purposes. The two sorcerers had given her a lot of information in a short amount of time, and all the while she had been in complete disbelief that she was even awake, so now she tried to remember what it was that she was here to do, exactly. She desperately cast about her mind in a furtive attempt to remember the last thing that felt real, tangible, before being dragged across time.

She remembered Jenna's excitement at the first glimpse of the castle. She remembered the night before; the two had ordered room service and watched Scottish films in honor of their trip. After that, Jenna had gotten the tour schedule for the next day, and Mackenzie had arranged their ferry to the neighboring Isle of Skye. Then they had both gone to bed. The next morning and the tour, that's where it got fuzzy. Mackenzie remembered the first time she'd seen Connor, or rather his painting. She never heard one word the tour guide had said about him. Then she'd gone to fetch her sketch pad and a charcoal pencil. Mackenzie vaguely remembered time passing. The only real thing was hearing her name from a foreign voice. And that's where the story twisted and turned until it was unrecognizable.

Following Morvern and Gregor into the secret passageway was both the scariest and the best thing to ever happen to her. She had thought them hotel employees...how on earth had she thought that? It was so obvious that they were out of place, even in the Medieval Castle, they didn't quite fit in. She'd felt anxious and nervous, but they'd seemed innocent enough, until she'd been dragged into the tunnel and then poof! She had been transported across time! And coming full circle, her thoughts brought her to the reason for being here, to stop John Campbell, and the pleasant feelings from the night before were lost in the new overwhelming fear that assailed her nervous system. Mackenzie was scared.

She was scared of what fate had planned for her and these unknown people she was here to help. How could she be the one to do this? And what exactly was it that she could do? She felt like she was in a movie where she had to save the world, but without anyone to guide her through this crazy mission, or whatever she was on. *Hmm...no, more like a bad horror movie where the heroine gets herself killed doing something stupid and predictable, like not turning all the lights on while the audience is screaming at her the whole time.* Mackenzie thought that there was something obvious that she was missing; the missing piece from her dreams. Then it hit her; and she knew. In that instant, Mackenzie understood her recurring non-nightmare—the one she'd been having since she was an adolescent. She was going to be killed. Despite that Morvern and Gregor had assured her safety, and in spite of her love for Connor, or maybe because of it? She knew she had to find her way to the Campbell's keep, and that her death would somehow stop all of the violence that he was planning.

Fate had brought her here, and she was uniformed and alone. She was going to get herself killed. Hopefully she could at least keep Connor out of all this. This evil fate was meant for her, not him. If it was a horrible, painful, awful death she was heading to, then that was her business. She knew he would never let her go alone, but she had to find a way to leave, and she had to be strong enough to leave him. She also needed to find out what Morvern and Gregor had found out, if anything. That was a surprising thought. What if they hadn't made any progress whatsoever? What would she do then? Maybe she could stay here after all? Ah, but that thought begged the question if Connor even wanted her to stay. She needed a plan. And maybe some help.

From all that she had heard, the Campbell was a power-hungry man who used any and all means at his disposal to gain that power and to get what he wanted. Right now, he wanted Mackenzie. Well she would see that he got her. He wanted to use her as a sacrifice? Fine, but she would ensure that it was only she who would be sacrificed, and no one else could get hurt because of her. Perhaps if she was killed before Halloween? Would that mess up his spell? No one to sacrifice, no spell? Hmm...no she didn't believe that. She needed to live beyond Halloween, ensure that he couldn't do anything in retaliation to Connor. Well, she wasn't a virgin anymore. Weren't sacrifices supposed to be virgins? Mackenzie groaned aloud at the overwhelming frustration that was growing inside. She was sick of being a damsel in distress. It was time she did something about it. Slowly, a couple of rough plans started to form in her ever-busy head.

There had to be a way to escape Connor. Now that he trusted her, she could take her horse and try to find her own way. And she was sure that there had to be someone here who would want her gone; who would want the danger she presented taken care of. She needed to find a way to the Campbell's lands, and then she would take her horse and leave Connor. She refused to let him know what she was doing; he was too proud to let a woman fight what he considered "his" fight. What Connor didn't know was that this was Mackenzie's fight, and it always had been. The rightness of that sentiment rang true throughout her body. She felt that maybe this had been her destiny all along; to sacrifice herself for the good of others. And maybe her reward was Connor? She would take it. But first, she needed time, of which there was not enough. And she had to remember all of the Stewart history her grandmother had told her in the form of bedtime stories as a child.

They all had begun with a hero who loved his fair maiden, but none of them ended happily. Real fairy tales didn't always have a happily ever after, isn't that what Granny had always said? Pinching the bridge of her nose, Mackenzie tried to remember. She could almost hear Granny's voice.

In a time before history was written, there was a braw and bonny lad who loved his clan above all. This was the clan Stewart. His father was laird, and one day he would follow his father's path. His father allied many of the warring clans into a time of peace. One of the alliances was to be his son, and their most bloodthirsty enemy. Through marriage to their enemy's daughter, their clan would finally broker the peace the Highlands so desperately needed. And ever dutiful, the son agreed. But one day, whilst out surveying his lands, he met a lass who turned his heart. Och, she was fair indeed, and the laird's son met her each day. And each day he fell ever more in love with her, until finally, the dutiful son refused his duty. His lover had convinced him to run away with her. The father of his betrothed was more than angry, he was furious. In retaliation for the slight, he began the most bloody feud the clans had ever seen. His daughter's honor, therefore his honor, was tarnished.

But what the Stewart's son had never kenned, was that their rival clan never had any intentions of allowing their laird's only daughter to marry a Stewart. He had paid the woman handsomely to seduce the laird's son away from his duty. And with a feud on his hands, the Stewart never had the chance to find his son until it was too late. The lass had led his son directly to their enemy, and to his death. The Stewart was gifted his son's head on a pike. Tis said the Stewart went mad, slaughtering his enemy in his grief, but earning a curse from the rival clans. The curse has been lost to us by now, but don't take them lightly, for curses are all too real. One day, you'll ken what I mean.

What is it about the Scots and curses? Mackenzie wondered idly. The place seemed to abound with them. And what had Granny Stewart meant by one day Mackenzie would see what she meant?

Her thoughts were interrupted as Connor strode through the door with a large plate of fresh brown bread, cheese, and coffee.

"Good morning, Lady MacRae."

His grin was so endearing Mackenzie had to swallow before she could smile in return. Her heart still hurt from the thoughts of impending doom that she was bringing down on his family. The Campbell hadn't tried to do anything in a while, and that new worry put a crease between her brows. And with all these awful thoughts of her death and the death of his people, here he walks in with an impish grin on his face, as if it doesn't bother him at all that she'll be the reason for his death. She was sure if he followed after her, that her other nightmare would come true. Connor would die.

But she smiled back, not without effort, and she prayed her eyes didn't give away her sudden fear and hopelessness. Mackenzie prayed that the hole threatening to open inside her heart stayed closed until she was alone and then she could fall to pieces in private. And she prayed that Connor would understand and maybe one day he could forgive her.

But first, she was going to savor the little time they did have together. And hopefully he wouldn't taste the desperation in her kisses and on her tongue.

Connor set the plate on the bed, behind her and sat down next to her.

"Is everything well? You look as if you're worrying." Connor lightly smoothed the worry from her brow with one long finger.

Mackenzie sighed and closed her eyes, letting Connor push her anxiety away with his touch. As her lids drifted closed, a tiny smile played around the edges of her lips.

"That feels so..." she sighed again, "sweet."

His lips replaced his finger and Mackenzie could feel his breath against her face. Her head was spinning before Connor's lips found hers.

This time, their lovemaking had a frantic edge, at least on Mackenzie's side it did. She felt like she couldn't get enough of Connor, and she was certain that their time was short.

When at last they lay in a tangle of limbs on the bed, Mackenzie listened to Connor's heartbeat slow. Her head was on his chest, her hair splayed out around them. He was running his fingers through her curls, watching the sun glint off them and the question he asked her shouldn't have caught her off guard, yet it did.

"Mackenzie?" He paused and waited for a response.

"Hmm?" she murmured softly, not wanting to ruin the moment.

"What is it you aren't telling me? What are you hiding?"

Her shocked eyes flew to his. She thought she'd hidden her desperation better.

"Nothing?" It sounded like a question. Ugh, she was a terrible liar.

"Mackenzie," he stopped whatever chastisement he had planned and instead softened his tone and said, "I trust you, Mackenzie, and if you for some reason canna tell me, then I'll accept your judgment."

Mackenzie was stunned. Speechless. Wow. Her mouth opened to say something, but no words came out so she closed it. Connor laughed softly at her stunned expression.

He continued as if she had agreed with him, "I am serious. If there is something that you feel you canna tell me, I understand. But then also know that you can tell me anything." His eyes darkened and smoldered. Mackenzie still stared back like a fish gasping for water.

"Umm...Connor. Wow. Thank you. You have been so wonderful to me. I have told you so much more than I ever planned and it's such a relief to know that you believe me and you don't think I'm crazy."

Connor interrupted her and said, "I need to tell you something else, something that I should have told you long ago, but I was too much a coward to tell ye." His voice had thickened and deepened, the way it did when he was upset, and his accent was more pronounced. "I love ye, Mackenzie, I truly do. I am so sorry that I was such a fool before. I should have believed ye from the start, and I have treated ye abominably. Please, can ye forgive me?"

"You...love...me?" Mackenzie tried it out and the words didn't make any sense to her. A myriad of emotions flitted across her face; surprise, joy, anxiety, fear, until her face finally settled on stunned confusion. "But, Connor, you only married me to force the Campbell's hand and to keep me safe. You don't love me."

He was amused at her logic. "Aye, Mackenzie, I do." His eyes tightened and his tone changed. "I should never have hurt ye the way I did. But I canna take it back. I will show ye from this moment on how much I love ye. I need ye in my life, Mackenzie and I doona want ye to leave. I want ye to stay here. With me."

"You want me? To stay?" Her mind was having trouble comprehending this. Mackenzie wanted nothing more from life than to stay here with Connor, but how could she promise that when she was planning on leaving him for his enemy? She couldn't. She was propped up on one elbow staring blankly down at Connor. His hand was still tangled in her hair, so he pulled her down to meet his very tender kiss.

Once she was breathing hard, he broke the kiss, whispering against her lips, "I love you." He kissed her again. "Stay with me?" His lips were on hers once more.

"I don't belong here Connor," she said it softly and looked away, so he wouldn't see how hard it was for her to say.

"I'd disagree, sweeting." Her eyes flew back to his; his voice was so tender.

When Mackenzie pulled away, she stared intently into his eyes for a long moment before a bemused smile touched her lips and she asked him, "You love me?"

His smile was warm, tender. "I do."

"Wow," she breathed. "Just, wow." And she kissed him back.

A long while later, the sun was slanting in from the west, Connor leaned over and trailed his fingers down Mackenzie's ribs and stomach. She raised her eyebrows at him.

His answering smile was boyish; it made him look younger. "Would you be wantin' to go for a ride?"

"On horses? Yay!" Mackenzie clapped her hands in anticipation.

* * * *

Connor smiled at her obvious elation to such a simple thing. It seemed his new wife would be easy to please. Ha! What was he thinking? Nothing was easy in this situation. Still, it was nice to see her joy at the simple things. He had a basket packed for lunch already; it should be in the stables right now, provided his brother had done his part. Connor had planned a day of riding to see some of his favorite places on MacRae lands. He was hoping to take her to a spot he'd gone to a lot as a lad when he'd wanted to be alone. He was beginning to understand some of the little things that made Mackenzie happy, but he wanted to uncover the secrets that made her sad, and those that caused her eyes to look miles away. Every now and then, he would catch her with a slightly sad and wistful gaze. He wanted to know what she was thinking.

Looking at her pull her sark over her head and quickly bundle her hair out of her face, Connor stood and walked slowly over to her. She glanced up at him with a question in her eyes, but he merely unbound her hair and ran his fingers through it.

"I prefer your hair down."

She smiled and told him, "I thought that women were supposed to wear these once they were married." She was holding up the kertch that Bronwyn had given her. Connor took it from her and tossed it across the room.

"I prefer your hair down," he repeated.

She laughed at him saying, "Alright, down it is."

Connor liked to watch her get dressed. It was so intimate. He liked watching her fuss with her hair when she was nervous. He liked how her breasts strained against the thin silk of the sark. He liked how her legs looked as the sark drifted down to the floor, hinting at their shape. He liked watching her fumble with the petticoats; it was endearing. And he liked how she needed him to help her lace up her stays and gown. He felt as if he could watch her all day and not tire of the task. It was staggering how in so little time, Mackenzie had come to absorb his every thought; even the mundane. 'Twas why it was imperative that the Campbell not lay his hands on her and that she stay with him in his time. He had come to love her, and the thought of her leaving him caused him physical pain.

The ride cleared his mind. Every now and then he would pause to point out something he thought would interest Mackenzie. He enjoyed watching her eyes widen as they saw the loch, or narrow as she tried to spot a bird. But he wished that he had had her contraption with him, the camera, was it? Her face was fey-like in its beauty when they came to the spot where he planned their meal.

The trees opened up to showcase the high ragged mountains against the rare sunny sky, with lacy clouds topping their peaks. The mountains were broken by a long three-tiered waterfall splashing noisily into a deep glacial pool. The crystal clear water looked inviting, but when Mackenzie dismounted and ran to it, she discovered it was ice cold, it was October after all, and he chuckled at her quick gasp.

"Oh, Connor it's so beautiful here. Every time I see something here, a tree, the mountains, the water, I think these lands cannot possibly get any more beautiful, and then you show me a magical place like this. It is easy to become caught up in the beauty of the land, isn't it?"

"Aye." But Connor wasn't looking at the land, he was gazing directly at Mackenzie. He knew when she grasped his meaning because she blushed adorably and turned away. Connor reached for the basket he had packed and when he joined Mackenzie it was to discover she had taken off her cloak and thrown it across the damp grass. She was forever surprising Connor. She lay down on the cloak rather than sitting demurely as would the women of his time. He half-smiled to himself and wondered if he would really want her to be like that. The obvious answer was no. He wanted her as she was. Quirks and all. She rolled over onto her side to look at him.

"Aren't you going to sit?" She looked so happy laying down in the pale yellow sunlight.

Connor couldn't resist and teased her, "Are you sure that you are real? You look like a wood sprite, or a nymph."

Her shocked look turned into a dazzling smile.

"What?"

"Nothing, it's just that I've felt like this is some big fairy tale from the first minute...shouldn't that be my line? I feel like I'm going to wake up in my own time any moment now." She paused. "That's why I'm trying to get the most out of every minute I have here." She glanced down, and looked up from beneath her lashes, like she did when she was nervous, he'd noticed. "With you," she breathed.

Connor was awestruck by how such a simple admission from Mackenzie had his heart pumping double-time. She wanted to be here with him. And his body responded to her closeness as he sat down next to her and cupped her face in his hand. Her skin was satin-smooth and soft as down. She turned her cheek into his palm and her eyes drifted shut. His thumb stroked slow circles on her smooth cheeks. He could feel her breath against his hand. It amazed him how such mundane things caused his body to respond to her; her breath coming and going, the breeze fluttering her curls about her face, the way her eyes darkened when she was in the heat of passion…he pressed his lips to hers and reveled in the low gasp that she inhaled as they touched. There was a distinctly male surge of pride flooding through his body as he understood that her reactions were only for him. He knew *she* was only for him. It was as if they had been made for each other. Connor had known from the first that he wanted her, and that the passion simmering beneath the surface once unleashed, would be unlike anything he'd experienced before. What he had never guessed was that the two of them were so right for each other.

"Keep your eyes closed, Mackenzie," he whispered against her full lips.

Connor had a hard time tearing his lips from hers, but he wanted to make her call his name out; he wanted her crazy with desire. He lay down beside her and pressed her back into the soft grass. Slipping her gown to one side, he revealed her shoulder and trailed his lips from her shoulder back up to her ear, nipping lightly, and smiling against her throat as he felt her breath hitch. Connor brushed his lips against the arch of her throat, under her chin, and barely touched the corner of her mouth. He felt her turn slightly to meet his lips, but he just smiled and moved on to her cheeks, and then after kissing each of her eyelids, he touched his lips to the sensitive spot behind her ear. He could feel her pulse pounding beneath his lips and it thrilled him.

Connor loosened her laces and slipped the gown further down off her shoulders. He glanced up to make sure her eyes were still closed, they were, and he took her nipple through the material of her gown. Only when he could feel her tremble in his arms did he slip his fingers under the velvet of her gown. She was breathing heavily now, and he yanked her gown to her waist. Slipping her arms out, she put her arms around his neck and tried to pull him up to meet her lips, but Connor gently pulled her arms from his neck and captured both her wrists with one hand, effectively pinning her to the ground. It also arched her back, giving him a better access to her breasts. He used his free hand to unlace her stays and he lifted her slightly to pull off her *sark*. Her naked body against the deep greens of his lands was intensely beautiful. Connor just looked at Mackenzie for a long moment. So long that Mackenzie opened her wide green eyes to gaze questioningly at him, but Connor merely smiled and swept his free hand over her eyes so they would close again.

His fingers continued the trail his mouth had set, and softly drifted down to her breast, avoiding temptation and just skimming the swell of her breast, they lingered along her hips and slowly traced their way to her soft thighs. He felt them quiver and clench in anticipation, but instead continued down her leg to her calf, gripping it and placing his mouth on her ankle. He dragged his lips so slowly back up the trail his fingers had left that Mackenzie's thighs were quivering when his lips found her.

Connor softly skimmed her inner thighs with his lips, barely brushing against her. When he softly touched his lips to her core, she gasped and arched into his mouth, but he gripped her hips and held her down. He sucked and licked and thrust his tongue into her again and again until she was sobbing for release. Still, Connor refused to give in. He slipped a finger in and moved his mouth to her breast. Mackenzie's chest was heaving in ragged gasps of air as Connor's tongue laved her full breasts. Only when Mackenzie was begging for him to join her did he finally shrug out of his plaid and shirt.

As Connor slid into her, he commanded, "Open your eyes Mackenzie. Look at me, and doona look away." He wanted to see into her eyes as she came.

Her heavy-lidded gaze was glazed over and unfocused and he took her in long, slow strokes until she was writhing beneath him. He felt her muscles tense and tighten around him and whispered,

"Wait. Not yet."

Mackenzie's unfocused gaze cleared and met his, her parted lips were trembling, but she nodded and held on long enough for Connor to rub his thumb across her swollen core. He felt the moment she tightened around him and exploded, right before her eyes darkened to a deep forest green and she cried out his name in release. He joined her and they floated back down to Earth together.

For that split second her eyes were unguarded, Connor had seen what he'd needed to know; Mackenzie was still hiding something from him.

Chapter Twenty Six

Although it was October and snow would fall soon, the cold didn't affect them. Their bodies were slicked in sweat and Connor threw his arm over Mackenzie as she rested her head against his chest. The cool, damp grass actually felt good to Connor. He propped himself up on one elbow and looked down at Mackenzie, who now rested against his arm.

"Mackenzie?"

"Yes?"

"You never answered my question."

A tiny crease appeared between her perfectly arched brows as she looked up at him. He noticed that her eyes looked troubled.

"What question?" She was stalling; she knew what he meant.

"I want you to stay with me, Mackenzie. Here in my time."

Her voice had a tinge of panic to it as she hedged, "But Connor, I can't stay here. I don't belong here." Mackenzie's eyes glanced down while she paused and drew in a deep breath before saying, "I want to go back to my own time."

She was lying, he was sure of it. He just didn't know why. It made no sense. It sounded more like she was trying to convince herself, rather than him. Instead of arguing, as he wanted, he used logic. He knew logic worked better; arguing usually just made her more stubborn. So he merely pointed out a certain factor that he was sure she hadn't thought of.

"But what if you are with child, Mackenzie? What will you do then?" He could tell the soft question was one she hadn't considered. Her eyes widened and he saw both fear and shock in their green depths.

"Pregnant?" she squeaked out. "Oh! I hadn't even thought…I mean, I can't be…I couldn't be…" she trailed off. "Oh," she whispered, "What if I am?" Her panicked eyes flew back to his. "Oh Lord, Connor, what if I am?" Her hand instinctively dropped to her belly. "What would we do?" she whispered to herself. Mackenzie's eyes left his, lost in their own thoughts. He thought he saw a tear fall.

The naked panic Connor saw on her face saddened him. She claimed to love him, but she didn't want his child.

"Would it be so terrible?" Connor softened his voice, trying to hide the misery he felt.

Her eyes refocused on his and she said, "Connor, it's not that I don't want the baby, but what if something happens. What if this wasn't supposed to happen? What if *we* weren't supposed to happen? What if we mess up the whole space-time continuum thingie because we couldn't control ourselves? What if the world ends because we met? I can't even think about this…what if this is wrong?" her strained voice trailed off.

What could be wrong about this? Connor didn't understand what Mackenzie was so upset about. And Connor hadn't missed the fact that she still hadn't committed to staying with him.

When he'd seen that she was still hiding something from him, he'd tried to make her understand that he could be patient and considerate, but she still was intent on keeping her secrets. Well, he would figure them out. And if he hadn't gotten her with child yet, he would. He wanted her tied to him every possible way, to make it harder for her to leave him. He didn't think that she *could* leave him, if she were going to have a baby. His baby. She had pushed his arm away, and stood to dress herself in silence. Connor watched her intently and thought that her sark looked a wee bit tight across her hips and her usually full breasts were straining against the fabric as well. Perhaps she already was with child. He had little knowledge of children, but his sister had complained of swollen breasts early on in her pregnancy.

While Connor didn't understand Mackenzie's reaction to the possibility of a child, he especially didn't understand what she had meant when she'd said that they shouldn't have "happened." He glanced over to her as she fumbled with her stays. She was lost in her own thoughts as

Connor helped lace her up. Since she didn't appear to notice his assistance with her laces, he gathered up the remnants from the meal they'd barely touched, and prepared the horses.

* * * *

Pregnant? Mackenzie couldn't believe that she hadn't thought of that. How could she be so stupid! Of course it was possible. She'd been here for two weeks already, and it's not like she could go pick up a box of condoms or something. It was one thing for the Campbell to kill her, but to kill the baby as well…she couldn't allow that. She wouldn't. But wait, she didn't even know if she was pregnant, so she squared her shoulders and tried to shake off the uneasy feelings. But she knew she was. Now that Connor had brought it to her attention, she knew she was pregnant. Of course she was. She wanted to laugh at the irony and unfairness of it all; she had found everything she'd never even known that she wanted here, two hundred years before she would even be born. She greedily wanted it all, too. How selfish could she be? She had to get to the Campbell's keep and stop his evil plan…but now she knew she had to survive this all. Her hand fell to her stomach again. She would stop him and she would make it out alive, but how? Her eyes darted to Connor. And at what cost?

Connor was silent on the ride home; and for once Mackenzie didn't try to break the silence. She was lost in the tangle of her own thoughts. She had vaguely noticed when he'd packed up their picnic and helped her mount her horse. But it wasn't until they were well on their way home that she felt uneasy. Her horse seemed nervous, and she felt as if she was being watched, but she couldn't focus on anything other than her growing fear. What would happen to her if the Campbell found out she was pregnant? And that it was Connor's baby?

Chapter Twenty Seven

The sound of something whizzing by her ear startled her, causing her horse to rear up, nearly throwing Mackenzie in the process. She held onto both the reins and her horse with a death grip and miraculously stayed astride. Connor was swearing under his breath as he yanked the reins from her hands and urged both horses into a gallop. Mackenzie knew something was wrong, but she had no idea what. Suddenly she was knocked backward, and a fiery pain radiated from her shoulder down her arm to her fingertips. She scrambled to stay mounted and reached with her right hand to feel what was wrong. Her stomach heaved at the warm, wet feeling that was becoming too familiar to her, before she felt the long shaft of an arrow jutting out from her left shoulder.

It took everything Mackenzie had in her to not scream, or faint, or cry. She tried to yank it free, and had to bite her lips to keep from screaming. It must have gone straight through her shoulder, because it hitched as she pulled. She stayed upright on her horse, at full gallop next to Connor.

And he had no idea that she'd been shot.

His face looked angry, and his eyes were roving the trees, but he hadn't glanced at Mackenzie. The way back to his castle was much more direct and much faster than their meandering route from earlier. For that, Mackenzie was intensely grateful. Now, she was not only gripping the horse to stay upright, but she was trying to maintain a grip on her fading consciousness as well. When they were on the stone bridge, within shouting distance of the keep, Connor shouted something to the gate guards and several men flew into action, but Mackenzie saw this through an ever dimming gaze, and heard nothing but the steady ringing in her ears. Once they were inside the yard, Connor jumped down from his horse and turned in time to see Mackenzie finally lose her tenuous grip on her consciousness and slump limply from her mount.

* * * *

When Connor leaped from his horse to make sure Mackenzie was safely inside the yard before the yett slammed down, his blood ran cold. There was an arrow sticking out of her shoulder. He vaguely noticed that it was through and through, which was good, easier. Her eyes rolled back into her head and she slid from the saddle. He was there instantly, catching her before she hit the ground, but the force of her fall knocked him to one knee. His heart and breath had both stopped. It wasn't until he saw her chest moving with rapid, shallow gasps that he calmed enough to lift her and run to the castle, shouting for his brother all the while.

Once inside, Connor rushed her to their room. His brother met him with some whisky and a cauterizing iron. After gently setting an unconscious Mackenzie down on the bed, Connor pulled out his dirk and sliced the sleeve off of her gown, rather than wasting time unlacing the front of her bodice. He delicately slid as much of the sleeve off and did the same to her sark. Her stays weren't in the way, but he yanked them off as well. Mackenzie's face was pale, and her lips were white. His eyes met Liam's as he rolled her to her side. Connor held her down while Liam took his sword and sliced the barb and the fletchings off. He glanced at Connor as he prepared to pull the shaft out of her shoulder. Whatever his brother saw on his face must have been bad, because Liam grimaced before he placed one hand on Mackenzie's shoulder and pulled the shaft straight through. She moaned lightly and her eyes fluttered. Connor's heart stilled at the thought of the pain she must be in. He knew the worst was yet to come. As Liam liberally poured whisky into her wound, Mackenzie strained against Connor's hold. While not squeamish, he could barely watch.

Liam went to the fireplace where the flat end of the cauterizing iron was heating in the fire. Connor gingerly removed any material near her wound and as his brother was about to weld her flesh together, Connor gripped Liam's wrist tightly and met his gaze. Liam wordlessly handed it over to his brother. Connor laid her gently against the pillows, and traded places with Liam. The pain of a thousand daggers through his heart would have been easier to endure than the thought of hurting Mackenzie. She didn't even moan or twitch as he pressed the white hot iron into her soft flesh. The smell was nauseating. Connor had smelled the scent of burning flesh more times than he cared to remember. He and his brother had both cauterized many wounds out on the battlefield, he had even had it performed on him once or twice, but never before had it tightened his chest, or caused him so much pain to watch. Connor wished he could be in her stead.

He had Liam hold her up, her head lolling against his shoulder, and Connor repeated the cauterization on the exit wound. When he had finished, Liam handed her off to Connor, who held her tightly, careful of her wounds while Liam pressed some linen strips into a salve before laying them on Mackenzie's shoulder. Connor finished stripping her down and wrapped the linen strips around her arm and shoulder in a figure eight fashion. There was nothing more to be done. He pulled the covers up to cover her and sat down in the chair by the fire place to wait.

****

Liam's hand on his shoulder brought Connor out of his absorption.

"Any change?"

"Nay, brother, none at all."

"Dougal and Robbie caught the man who shot her."

His eyes flew to Liam's and he grinned in angry joy. "Let's have a chat with him, shall we?"

"We've already begun. Robbie says that he'd be one of the Campbell's men, for sure. All he has gotten from him is that he was aiming for you."

"He had better pray that she wakes soon, else I'll aim for him!" Connor declared it so firmly that had Liam never met Connor before that night, he'd have believed it. "And I won't miss."

Connor's eyes were molten fury. He wanted to beat the truth out of the man with his own two fists, however, the desire to stay with Mackenzie and to be here when she opened her eyes was equally as strong. He didn't want to leave Mackenzie's side. How could he?

Liam's softly said, "Connor, she'll be out for a while, you know this. Fetch Bronwyn and have her stay with her until you're finished."

"Aye, Liam, you're right, I ken ye are, but I canna bring myself to leave her." Connor stared at Mackenzie, silently willing her to open her eyes.

His thoughts moved to the possibility that she might be carrying his child. A wound like this wouldn't ordinarily affect any other body part on a man, but Connor knew little of how a woman's body worked, especially one with child. Women were supposed to be soft, and warm, and delicate. Would her delicate body withstand an infection?

"Brother?" Liam once again intruded on his thoughts.

"I'm coming. Send for Bronwyn, I doona want her left alone. I'll meet you downstairs."

Chapter Twenty Eight

The first thing Mackenzie noticed when she woke up was that her arm hurt. It was as if her left shoulder and arm were on fire. *God, couldn't someone put out the fire?* She couldn't drag her eyelids back yet…it was like trying to claw her way out of a wet blanket. She dimly heard voices, but they sounded far away, as if down a well. Mackenzie listened harder, more intently; all she could make out was her name, though. She tried to understand more, but soon gave up. It was too hard to listen, she wanted to go to back to sleep….

When she woke this time, she was able to open her eyes. It was difficult to focus on anything specific, but it was dark. The fire was going. She sat up and instantly regretted it. Her head swooned, and her arm felt like it was ripping off at her shoulder. Mackenzie fell back against the pillows, gasping from the pain. Oh, right, she'd been shot. With an arrow, of all things! This was surreal. The whole event came back to her quickly; that was good, no head injury, right? She felt warm hands on her forehead, and face. Her eyes desperately searched the dark. It was Connor. He sat on the edge of the bed. Thank goodness he hadn't been hurt. His knuckles were bruised and scratched up, his eyes were frantic; he looked awful. When was it? Had he slept at all?

"Are," she cleared her dry throat and tried again, "Are you alright?" She felt parched.

He looked almost angry. "You want to know if *I'm* alright?"

Was she speaking German? "Yes, you look awful." Every word scratched her parched throat on its way out.

Connor barked a short hard laugh, and ran a hand over his face. "Nay, love, I'm no' alright. You've been shot. Are *you* alright?"

"I'm fine," she said automatically, but at his incredulous look, she added, "My arm hurts. Actually, it feels like it's on fire." Mackenzie frowned as she thought of all the primitive medical resources available. Her frown deepened as she reached over to feel the wound, realizing that the idea of having been crudely stitched up did not appeal to her. All she felt was cloth strips wrapped around her shoulder. She could move her arm, though, so even though the pain was not localized, the injury was.

"Can I have some water?" she still sounded as if she'd been hiking in Death Valley during the height of summer. Her throat hurt almost as much as her shoulder did. Connor handed her a cup of water. Swallowing gratefully, Mackenzie asked, "What happened?"

"Do you no' remember? You were shot with an arrow, Mackenzie."

"I know, I meant, how did you remove the arrow?" She was frustrated that he hadn't known what she meant.

Connor didn't understand her irritation. "We pulled the arrow through and cauterized the wound."

"How?" She persisted. "How did you cauterize the wound?"

Connor didn't answer, so Mackenzie tore the bandages off and felt the tender, puckered skin. She felt sick instantly, understanding that it was a burn. Connor's hands replaced hers on the bandages and he rewrapped her shoulder more delicately than she would have thought possible for such a "braw lad." For a man who lifted a two-handed sword with deadly force, he was extremely gentle. Looking at his face, she could see that he didn't understand her reaction. Of course not; he didn't know the miracle that was modern medicine. She was horrified when she thought of how they had cauterized the wound. But she was more worried about infection; didn't most people who survived arrow wounds die from blood loss or infection? Great. Was it too much to think they'd invented penicillin yet? It had been discovered by a Scotsman, after all.

"Will I survive?" She'd asked it lightly, trying to make him feel better, but she was intensely curious.

"You tell me." His tone was even, but his eyes were tight.

"I feel okay." *Other than the burning fire in my shoulder*. "Did I lose much blood?"

"Nay, the arrow held most of it in."

"Oh. And what are the chances of infection?"

"You doona have a fever, so I am hoping that there won't be any complications with your recovery."

"Oh," she said again. "Wow, I really got shot with an arrow?" She shook her head; this was really weird.

"Aye, and ye gave me the fright of my life." Connor sounded angry; his voice had changed. It was deeper, harder. Mackenzie realized that this was hard for him to admit. He'd said he loved her before they were attacked, and now she was beginning to believe it.

"I'm sorry," she said automatically, but Connor looked annoyed at her apology.

"It's not your fault, Mackenzie. 'Tis I who should apologize to you. I canna believe I exposed you like that. I dinna even bring my sword." He sounded disgusted with himself. "When I saw you slide from the saddle," he covered his eyes with his hand, and spoke in a whisper, "I saw the arrow sticking out from your limp body…" Connor trailed off and removed his hand, his eyes burning into hers. "I thought ye were dead." His voice grew stronger, his brogue thicker, "Why did ye no' scream? Damn it, woman, I had no idea ye'd even been hit!"

"I'm…sorry?" she hadn't known what else to say, her eyebrows knit over her nose. Why was he so mad at her?

He sighed, "For what?"

"I don't know, for whatever made you so mad."

Connor chuckled at her logic, or lack thereof. "Mackenzie, I'm not mad at *you*."

"Then what are you mad about?" She was burning with curiosity.

"Myself. I am furious with myself. I ken what the Campbell is capable of, and I didn't take any precautions. I didn't think at all. Instead, I took you riding, alone, without any weapons or guards. If he had stolen ye back, I'm not sure I could hold a level head. I would have chased after ye and probably gotten both of us killed in the process."

Mackenzie was surprised. He'd always seemed so calm and collected to her. His self-control never lapsed. Except in the bedroom. She smiled at the remembrance of Connor in bed.

"Why are you smiling? This isn't funny."

She blushed and looked away. "No, of course not."

The blush didn't escape Connor's attention. "What are you thinking about?"

"Nothing."

"Tell me," he demanded.

"It's not important." She blushed harder and changed the topic. "And don't feel bad, see I'm fine." Mackenzie tried to rotate her shoulder and it burned like crazy, but she did it.

"Stop, you'll hurt yourself."

"I'm good. See?" She tried to lift her arm above her head.

"Your lips are white."

"Okay," Mackenzie expelled a breath she didn't know she'd been holding. "Wow, that hurt."

"That's what I thought." Connor sounded a little superior.

"Alright Mr. I-told-you-so," Mackenzie said a little tartly, "I admit it hurts. Happy now?"

"Why would I be happy that you are injured?" He looked confused and annoyed.

She rolled her eyes, "It's called sarcasm, Connor. Ugh. I suppose that this will scar pretty badly?" She grimaced, indicating her shoulder.

Connor pulled his shirt free of his plaid, lifted it, and showed her a small puckered scar. "Like so."

"You've been shot before?!" She was appalled.

He seemed amused. "Of course."

Mackenzie's fingers traced the scar on his stomach. She thrilled when his muscles tightened in response to her touch. Truthfully, she was not immune either, with the familiar heavy sensation spreading to her limbs as she ran her fingers over his granite hard body. Her curious fingers moved on to other scars, now, intrigued as to how he got each one. She paused as she reached a large, straight scar on his chest.

"And this one?" she asked tapping it lightly with her index finger.

"A sword." He seemed to like this game. His eyes were watching her face as she trailed her fingers along his skin.

She looked at him aghast. "You've been struck by a sword?"

"Many times." Was he *proud* of that fact? Typical man; proud of his battle wounds.

"Where else?" Mackenzie thought back to the first time she'd seen him training in the yard without his shirt on. She'd thought him beautiful, and thought that the scars proved him a real warrior, not some prissy lord who ordered his men about. He fought side-by-side with his men. She'd been intrigued, and now she wanted to know how he got all of the scars that freckled his body.

Connor pulled his shirt over his head, and his warm hand enveloped hers, brushing her fingers across his chest to his arm, "Here." He continued up his arm and over his shoulder to place her fingers on his back. "Here." He turned around slightly, so she could see where he led her fingers this time. "Here." He'd run her fingers across a long, white line that looked as if someone had tried to slice him in two from shoulder blade to waist. Mackenzie gasped. He turned to face her, and with her hand still firmly encased in his, he trailed her fingers down his arm and traced them along a pink line on his right forearm. "And here." His eyes held hers.

It was the scar from where she'd stabbed him the night they'd met. Mackenzie blushed to her hairline and dropped her eyes.

"I'm so sorry, Connor. I never should have stabbed you. I feel just awful about that."

"It's alright, love, see?"

"Yeah, but I *stabbed* you!" She sounded horrified. "I was just so scared and my mind was still reeling from the whole time travel thing, and I am sorry."

"Mackenzie, stop." Connor placed a finger against her lips and said, "I abducted you, if you recall."

"Yes, but..." she tried to say against his finger, but Connor pressed his lips to hers to silence her. When he pulled back, Mackenzie resumed her apology. "I'm so sorry, Connor. If I'd had any idea what meeting you would have led to, I'd have come along willingly."

"I doubt that." He raised his eyebrows at her.

She smiled. "Are you insinuating that I'm difficult?"

He smiled back. "Aye lass, stubborn to the end." His answering smile was brief, though, and his expression changed until he looked as though he was in pain.

"What? What is it?" Mackenzie rested her hand on his cheek, feeling his dark stubble graze her palm.

He placed his hand on her stomach, not meeting her eyes. "How long before you know whether you are with child?"

"Oh." She hadn't expected that. "Umm…" Mackenzie mentally counted her cycle. "About a week, maybe a little less, but it's unnecessary. I am certain that I'm pregnant."

Connor's face lit up with joy. He tenderly laid his ear to her belly and didn't move. When he did move, he slowly turned his face into her body and kissed her stomach. Mackenzie's breath hitched and broke into a silent sob. He was so happy at the prospect of a child, of *their* child, and she was going to run off to his enemy as soon as she was healed. What would that do to him?

An idea started to form…

"Connor, I want to ask a favor of you."

He lifted his head and looked up at her, "Anything," he vowed. His sapphire eyes were still full of wonder from her announcement.

"I'd like you to teach me to use a sword."

His whole body tensed, and his eyes darkened so much that in the dim light from the fire, they looked black. God help her if he discovered her plan. He'd said earlier that he wouldn't be able to think straight had she been taken, and she believed him. Well, she'd leave him a note telling him of her plans, so he could think rationally. She hoped she could make it to the Campbell's lands before he could stop her, because there was no doubt in her mind that he would stop her.

"Why would you need to use a sword?"

"So if something happens, I can defend myself," she didn't want to say it, but she forced the words out, "and the baby."

His face took on a strained look, "Do ye not think I can protect ye?"

"It's not like that, Connor." She was saying this all wrong.

"Then how is it?" he demanded.

"I just would feel better if I knew enough to defend myself. I don't like feeling helpless. And I don't like feeling like a target, either. I need to know how to defend myself, and our baby."

"That is precisely why you shouldn't learn. What if something happened to the baby?"

"Connor, learning how to use a sword isn't going to hurt the baby."

"How do you know?"

"It doesn't work that way. Maybe if I took a blow to the gut, I could lose the baby, but just working with a sword, I should be fine. Besides, I'm not really even pregnant, not yet anyways. I'm like a week pregnant. My period isn't even late yet. Please? Teach me how to use a sword? Just the basics?"

He was silent, and still angry, but she persisted. "Please?"

After a long pause, he said, "Alright, Mackenzie."

He'd caved?

"Stand up."

"Now?" Oh, she got it. He hadn't caved, not really, he was going to make this difficult.

"Aye, you want to learn, so stand up."

Mackenzie stood up and it hurt like hell. Of course Connor knew that. Connor strode to the trunk at the foot of his bed, and pulled out two very large swords. Flipping one over, he held the blade and handed Mackenzie the hilt. She was grateful that it had been her left shoulder that was injured, but it was still awkward for her to hold the heavy sword with only one hand. Holding the sword like she'd seen in movies was apparently the wrong way, because Connor immediately flicked his sword at hers and sent in clattering across the floor.

"Go get it," Connor ordered.

Mackenzie was in her shift, one sleeve, slipping down from where she assumed that Connor had cut it off to patch her up. She was favoring her left arm, clutching it to her chest, as she picked up the heavy sword. She turned around to Connor and he was ready for her. He knocked it out of her hand again.

"How am I supposed to learn if you keep knocking it out of my hand?" she was annoyed and didn't bother to hide it.

"You should learn to keep a tighter grip on your weapon. Again."

She sighed and picked it up. This time when she turned, she was prepared. When Connor attacked her, she kept hold of her sword. Her arm radiated the shock from his blow, though she kept quiet, he must have seen it in her eyes. He came at her again, and she raised her sword to block his blow, but he surprised her by pressing the tip of the sword to her chest. She glared at him.

"I am not trying to attack your sword, Mackenzie. I am attacking you. The sword is merely a tool. You should always place it where you expect me to strike. Anticipate."

He pulled back, and said, "Again."

Connor swung his sword at her midsection, and when she blocked the shot, the pain from his force all landed in her wrist. She grimaced, but this time it was she who said, "Again. Do it again." After a grand total of fifteen minutes, Mackenzie was in pain. Intense pain. She gritted her teeth and panted out, "Again, come at me again."

Connor softened. He didn't like to see her in pain. "Mackenzie, love, it's alright to stop. You've nothing to prove."

"Again," she said between her teeth.

"Nay. You're spent."

"Again!" she commanded.

Connor effortlessly swung his sword at Mackenzie, sending hers skittering across the floor, and he pressed his sword into her neck, softly saying, "You're done."

Her eyes narrowed. "You've been holding back!" she accused.

"Of course." He sounded so arrogant and high-handed.

"Why?" Mackenzie demanded.

"You can hardly stand and ye want me to treat ye as I would one of my men? You should lie down."

Mackenzie was angry; she didn't like being seen as weak. "Don't tell me what to do," she fumed.

"Stop being so stubborn, woman, and lie down," Connor ordered.

"Make me," she taunted.

Connor raised his eyebrows to the sky and he just stared at her, incredulously. "I beg your pardon?"

"You heard me."

Connor was staring at her as if she were daft. Mackenzie picked up her sword and this time she lunged at him. She caught him by surprise, but he still managed to knock her sword from her hand, and instead of taunting her with his sword, he instead picked her up and dropped her onto the bed.

"You are not strong enough to practice yet. Wait at least until ye are recovered from your wound."

Truthfully she was exhausted and could use a couple Tylenols, but she couldn't give in gracefully. "Fine," she snapped. "But I'm serious, Connor, I want to learn." At his amused look, probably thinking that it was funny the little woman wanted to play with the menfolk, she ground her teeth in frustration. It irritated her, but she changed her tone. "Look, I don't expect to be able to take you or anything, but I want a fighting chance."

"Take me where?"

"It means to beat you. I don't expect to be able to beat you, but again, I'd like to not be a sitting duck. Please, Connor."

Connor sighed and sat down next to her on the bed. She was sitting with her knees pulled up to her chest and her arms wrapped around them. He pulled her left hand from her knees and gently extended it until she flinched.

"You are injured, and there is no shame in waiting until you are recovered." He released the tension he had put on her arm. "I'm not saying that I won't teach you, but I won't hurt you anymore, and not tonight."

Connor kept hold on her left hand, but softly placed it back on her knee. Mackenzie sighed, a short frustrated sound, and grumbled, "This sucks."

Connor looked at her with a slight smile and said, "You speak so strangely."

"I guess I forget sometimes. Besides, I'm not really clear on how I should act, or speak. Oh well, at least around you I don't have to mind myself." She smiled up at Connor, and then lay back against the pillows, still cradling her injured arm. "Tomorrow, then?" She yawned involuntarily. "You'll work with me? At the very least, maybe I could go for a run...I miss working out. I like kickboxing."

"Why would ye want to kick some boxes?"

"It's a way of fighting."

Connor sighed. "You are quite determined to learn?"

"Definitely."

"Then, aye, tomorrow. If your arm is feeling better. You were hit with an arrow just yester morn. It is acceptable for you to rest, to recuperate. Now, I think you ought to sleep for a while longer."

"You're bossy," Mackenzie grumbled.

"And you're stubborn," he countered. His eyes were soft, though, and he lay down next to her. "It'll be dark for a few more hours yet, try to sleep."

"What about you? Aren't you going to sleep too?"

"Nay, love, I've some business to tend to. We caught the man who shot you." His eyes had darkened as he thought of the shooter. "And I'd be glad to talk to him again." He flexed his fingers in anticipation.

"What did he say?" She sat up in her haste, and the burning in her arm intensified with the sudden movement. Gasping she fell back against the pillows again and waited for Connor to say something.

He just pressed his lips to her forehead and said, "Rest."

"Wait! That's it? You're not even going to tell me what he said? Was he sent by the Campbell? Was it because we're married? What happened? You have to tell me!"

Connor sighed and gazed at her for a moment before nodding. "All right, aye, he is one of the Campbell's men, and he has indeed heard that I wed you. He was aiming for me, the foolish, inept archer! He was supposed to kill me and then he would steal you away while I lay there bleeding. He had very little information for me that I didn't already know. But I have heard that the Campbell is growing mad with anticipation of the ritual he wants to perform on you. He is slipping ever deeper into his madness, and he is making mistakes. This is good, because if he is not in his right mind, then I can easily outwit him; however it is also bad, for if he is slowly going insane, then he will be unpredictable and he will more readily use the dark forces to which he has sold his soul."

It was the longest speech Mackenzie had heard him speak. And the thoughts of the Campbell being mad were frightening to her, because her plan was to run to him as soon as she was in the shape to do so. She was going to learn to at least defend herself first, but that was still her plan, nevertheless. And if Connor was worried about this man using his delusions as an excuse to delve deeper into the black arts, then Mackenzie was worried even more so.

"Now," Connor said, "Will ye please get some sleep?"

"Will you stay with me until I fall asleep?" She really didn't want to lose any of the precious time she had left with him. Her two weeks were shortly becoming days, if her plan worked it would mean even less time, and she didn't want to be alone.

Connor slid into bed beside her and settled her against his chest. "Aye, my love, I'll stay."

He'd called her *my love*, she was ecstatic. The last thing Mackenzie remembered was the even thumping of Connor's heart lulling her to sleep.

Chapter Twenty Nine

Another nightmare. She was sitting next to the man with the cold eyes, only now his eyes were wild, excited. He held her hand in a painfully tight grip, but she kept her face smooth. They were watching as the prisoner was being dragged in. Mackenzie had to fight to keep herself in her seat; it was Connor! He was shackled and it looked as if he'd been beaten. How had he been captured? The Campbell stood and dragged Mackenzie up before the guests.

He addressed the crowd, "We gather today to celebrate my impending marriage," he glanced at Mackenzie, whose eyes were on Connor. "And as a wedding gift to you, my dear, I shall kill your husband. Tomorrow you will be free to marry me."

Mackenzie stifled a horror-stricken gasp.

"Now watch as your husband dies!"

Mackenzie tried desperately to feign indifference, but all to no avail. Her stricken eyes never left Connor's bruised face. She begged his forgiveness with her eyes as he glared at her with hate and distrust. He thought she'd betrayed him. Her heart broke and shattered into a million tiny pieces at the thought not only of Connor's death, but of him thinking she would ever betray him. How was she supposed to fix this? There had to be a way. Mackenzie racked her brain for some way out of this. The dagger! She'd stuffed it under her sleeve, and tied it to her forearm with a leather thong. If she could just get to it without attracting attention....

Mackenzie pretended to be bored with the whole procession, and yawned, fanning her mouth, then pretended to scratch an itch on her arm, slowly, so slowly, she slid her hand under her sleeve and in one quick motion, she yanked out the dagger and plunged it into the back of his neck. Her hands were covered in warm, red blood. Mackenzie screamed as she yanked the dagger back out of his neck and he lurched at her, knocking them both down. She was pinned to the ground as she watched him gurgle his last breath. His eyes were dead before the rest of him was, or perhaps they always had been dead, and Mackenzie woke up screaming bloody murder in Connor's bed.

This had been the most detailed of all of her dreams. Nothing was left to innuendo, and the Campbell had spoken this time! Mackenzie had to keep Connor away from the Campbell. Her dream was telling her that he would come after her if she ran, and if he did that, he would be killed. Mackenzie felt it was her job to vanquish the Campbell, now, and not Connor's, as the wizards had originally hoped. Their vision was flawed. Not only were they wrong in being able to guarantee her safety, but this was her fight, not Connor's, just as she had thought all along.

She was shaking from the dream, and freezing cold. She glanced around Connor's room and saw that the fire had died sometime during the night. She wondered when Connor had left her, and what he was doing now. Now that she understood her dream more fully, she didn't like not knowing where he was. For all she knew, he was out riding alone where the Campbell's men could capture him. Mackenzie took several deep breaths to calm herself, and checked her watch. It was six in the morning. The household would definitely be up and about, so Mackenzie slid out of bed and found the simplest of her gowns; this one laced in the front, and she skipped the stays. Hopefully no one would notice. Donning a clean shift was harder than she'd expected. It still hurt like crazy to lift her arm above her head, and the wound was very tender to the touch. She managed it, though, and as long as she pulled her dress on from the bottom up, her arm didn't hurt too much. This one was green, almost the same emerald color as her eyes. It was very flattering, to say the least, even without the cinching provided by the stays. Mackenzie pinned her hair quickly up in a loose chignon, and headed for the door.

Dashing down the stairs, she heard her name. She froze and waited, but she realized that it was just Connor and Liam. About to continue down the stairs, she paused again as she heard Connor say,

"Aye, brother, but what am I to do? Even if she isn't who she says she is, she is my wife, and she thinks she is with child. If there is a MacRae bairn growing in her belly, I'll no' let him have it. Or her."

"Could she be lying about the child?"

Connor's voice was curt, "No."

Liam sighed and he sounded resigned when he responded, "Then we shall keep to our plan. The wizards' reply is too vague to count on their help. We must rely solely on ourselves. Are the men ready for this?"

"As ready as I can make them."

"Then we go in blind. I doona like it Connor. And while I am glad to see ye so happy, I doona like how tied ye are to this woman. She has a hold on ye, Connor, whether ye realize that or no'."

"I ken your feelings, Liam. But as I have stated, she is my wife, and the Lady of this keep, and that means she is your sister now, Liam. And we protect our family."

Liam sighed again, and muttered something in Erse. Mackenzie was beginning to understand Erse a little more, since most here spoke it to each other, but she had little opportunity to use it when she spent all her time with Connor. But by his tone she assumed that what Liam had said was a string of curses. This time when Mackenzie walked down the stairs, she stepped loudly and tried to make a little bit of noise, so they wouldn't guess that she'd been eavesdropping.

"Mackenzie?" Connor sounded surprised. "What are you doing out of bed? I thought we'd agreed you would rest."

"I got hungry, and we agreed that if I were up to it, you'd teach me to use a sword."

Liam stared at her as if he were torn between wanting to laugh, and wanting to be the one to teach her to fight; he probably wouldn't pull any punches, Mackenzie thought. Connor stared at her as if he wanted to throw her over his shoulder and put her back in bed.

"You promised," she accused, pouting a little.

Connor's face relaxed, and he said, "Are you up to it?" She nodded. "Liam? Your sword?"

Liam obliged, and leaned against the post of the stairs to watch.

Connor handed Mackenzie the sword, and said, "Use both hands."

Her eyes grew round, but she gripped the sword with both hands, and tensed. Connor came at her with a mighty blow and she nearly lost a grip on her sword, her left arm screamed in pain. Liam looked like he was suppressing a laugh. Mackenzie flushed, but gripped the sword with her right hand.

"Use both hands, Mackenzie. We aren't fencing. If you are determined to learn, you'll learn properly."

Liam laughed this time and taunted, "Are ye sure she has any Scots blood in her at all? She is too tame."

Mackenzie's eyes narrowed and she grasped the hilt of the sword with both hands, preparing for Connor's attack. This time she anticipated his next move and parried with one of her own. It took both men by surprise, as she clashed swords with Connor, and held her own for all of five minutes. Really, though, it wasn't Connor she wanted to fight, it was Liam. He was so smug, sitting there throwing insults her way whenever she did something wrong. After one particularly cruel insult, she retorted, "Hey, I got shot with an arrow. At least I'm trying here. All you're doing is talking. Are you all talk, or have you got any game to back up that mouth?"

She felt incredibly stupid for goading him, because his eyes flashed the same way Connor's did when he was angry.

"Is that a challenge? I doona feel 'twould be a fair fight, lass."

She knew he was right. But maybe she could hustle him a bit. She knew a couple of self-defense throws, maybe in hand-to-hand…

"All right, forget the swords. You and me, Liam one on one."

Connor's eyebrows rose, and he stepped forward to object, but Mackenzie glared at him and murmured "Don't you dare," under her breath.

"I'll no' fight a lass."

"Afraid?" she taunted.

He glared at her scoffed, "Of a wee daft lass? Nay."

"Fine," and Mackenzie turned around to look at Connor. Liam took the advantage and came at her from behind. The second she felt his arm cross her right shoulder, she shifted her weight into his hip and pulled his arm out and down. By shifting her weight, his balance was thrown and she flipped him neatly over her shoulder. Luckily, the throw was an easy one not dependant at all on strength. Just balance. Once he was down, Mackenzie grabbed the sword lying on the ground and pressed it into his neck.

"Do you give?"

Liam swore.

"That's no way to speak to a lady." Connor interrupted, clearly enjoying this.

"She's no lady," Liam spit out from between clenched teeth.

"I couldn't agree more," Mackenzie quipped. She handed Connor the sword and offered Liam her hand. He grasped her hand, and yanked her down on top of him.

"Hey," she protested.

Connor's hands spanned her waist, and he lifted her up, wrapping an arm around her as he tucked her into his side. "Enough. The both of you. Liam, leave her be, Mackenzie, you've proven your point. How is the shoulder?"

"Fine."

"Truly?" He glared at her.

She sighed, "All right; no it hurts like hell."

"Aye, no more until you're healed." He quickly changed the subject, "Let us find some food for you. Did you no' say you were hungry?" He pulled her with him as he turned for the kitchen without waiting for her response.

When they left for the kitchen, Liam was staring after them, deep in thought. What Mackenzie would give to be able to read his mind right now. Her best guesses were that he was either really mad, or really impressed. That thought made her smile, but Connor steered her into the kitchen interrupting her train of thought.

"Was that entirely necessary?"

"He started it." Mackenzie sounded like a five year old, and she knew it. She sighed. "Should I go apologize?"

Connor grinned and said, "Nay, he could use the lesson in humility."

She smiled back at him as he drizzled honey on some brown bread for her. "Yum, carbs," she murmured to herself as she took a bite. "Which reminds me, Connor, since you won't teach me to fight until I heal, would it be alright if I started running?"

"Running?" He looked at her as if she'd grown a second head. "Where would ye be runnin' to?" he asked quizzically.

She smiled patiently; she didn't mind explaining all of her anachronisms. "It means that I'd like to run a couple miles every day to stay in shape."

He still didn't get it.

"My point is that I would need to wear pants, er, breeches. Would that be all right?"

"Let me understand this; you want to wear breeches to run around outside?"

"Well when you put it like that I just sound like a raving lunatic. Hmm…how can I explain this? Why do you and your men practice all the time?"

"To be prepared, and to be at the ready for an attack from an enemy clan."

"Right, to stay in shape, so I'd like to run to stay in shape. I'm losing all my muscle tone." Mackenzie patted the soft curve of her abdomen.

His eyes softened. "But, what if ye are with child? Should ye really be runnin' around outside?"

"Well I have to do something! I'm tired of waiting around for something to happen. This is so frustrating!" And she needed to be in shape if she were going to put her plan in action.

Connor grew serious. "But Mackenzie, what would you do if there were an attack? You would not be out there fighting with my men. Even if I could train you to use a sword properly in time, even if you were healed, you still would not be fighting alongside my men."

"But what if someone got in? It's happened before," she reminded him, instantly regretting it.

Connor's eyes grew tight at the reminder, but all he said was, "Still, you would only serve to get in the way. Either I, or one of my men, would get hurt trying to protect you, and that's not especially helpful."

Mackenzie exhaled a short frustrated breath and snapped, "Fine. But you'll see. Something will happen and you'll think 'Gee, I sure wish Mackenzie knew how to use a sword.' Like in the meadow that one day. I helped you and you know it!"

Connor laughed at her. "Aye, you were helpful, but it won't happen again; I'll not let you outside without an escort of my men at all times. Besides, you hadn't been injured then. Your priority is to heal. Let me take care of everything else."

She sighed again, this time in resignation. "Fine." Mackenzie asked him about something she'd overheard earlier. "Connor? Have you heard anything from the sorcerers?"

His eyes looked uncomfortable, just for a moment. In fact, if she didn't know his expressions so well, she might have missed it.

"Nay, sweeting, not yet."

Why would he lie? She'd overheard him with Liam; he'd said that the sorcerers wouldn't be helpful, and Liam was worried about their allegiance and their motivation, but it had sounded like her letter had indeed gotten a response. Mackenzie guarded her expression and looked down, concentrating on her food, so Connor wouldn't read what she was really thinking on her expressive face. But it seemed so ridiculous to lie about such a small thing…what was he thinking? Why was this important? Well, she could ask the sorcerers herself when she saw them. Providing that all went well and she healed quickly, she would see them soon.

Mackenzie had come to the conclusion that Liam didn't like her much. Ever since Connor had told his brother of her secret, Liam had been standoffish at best, and downright rude at other times. Perhaps he would be her best bet for helping her get away? She was about to bank on it. That and the hope that he wouldn't tell his brother.

The thought of Connor catching her sent shivers down her spine.

She quickly changed her train of thought so Connor wouldn't guess, and she looked around the kitchen. It was nothing like the remodeled kitchen of her time. She remembered that it had been remodeled in the thirties, and it was so much larger than this cozy kitchen with no stove, microwave, or refrigerator.

"Shall we?" Connor's voice interrupted her musings.

"Where are we going?"

"I thought ye might like to ride. We can take a few of my men and I'll show you the borders of MacRae land."

Thinking it an excellent idea, Mackenzie jumped at the chance to get a feel for the area. If she was about to go riding off on her own, it would help to see where she was going. Taking Connor's proffered hand, she gripped it tightly, wondering how much time they had left before she would leave. If this was their last day together she wanted to savor everything.

Chapter Thirty

During the ride, Mackenzie had ample time to think about how she would gain Liam's cooperation. She would appeal to his distrust of her. Tracking him down was easy enough; he reminded her of her brother, so she checked the kitchen. He was there eating and teasing a serving girl. Just like her brother. She smiled, but when he saw her hovering in the doorway, he stiffened, and she figured it was time.

"Liam? I was wondering if you could spare a minute of your time?"

Liam glared at Mackenzie for a moment before finally answering her.

"What is it you'd be wantin'?"

"Privately, please."

Liam never relaxed his glare but gave her a curt nod and strode away without looking to see if she was behind him. Mackenzie scrambled to keep up. He rounded on her as soon as they were out of earshot of the men, and stood there expectantly.

Mackenzie fidgeted, shifting her weight from one foot to the other, unsure of how to begin.

"Umm…well, I was wondering if you would help me with something…" she trailed off at his incredulous look. If this weren't so serious, she might've laughed at his expression. "It is something that would benefit you as well…" again she stopped at the look on his face; he was looking at her as if she disgusted him.

His eyebrows rose sardonically, and he spat out, "I'll no' hurt my brother by lying with ye. Only a lying, whoring, shrew of a woman would suggest such a thing." The scorn and derision were so hurtful, that even though Mackenzie would never suggest that, she had to bite her lip to keep it from quivering. Regardless, though, she could feel the moisture building behind her eyes.

She kept her tone even. "I don't mean that, Liam, I need to leave. I need your help to sneak away, and I need you to keep Connor from chasing after me. He cannot follow me."

"You're going back to the Campbell." Liam was surprised, but his voice was flat. Nowhere in his eyes was the fun, flirtatious man she'd met the first time. And he'd said "back;" he truly believed that she was here to hurt Connor and his people.

"Yes." She didn't even try to change his mind. He'd never believe her and it wasn't worth the effort to try to explain. Just as stubborn as his brother. She sighed and said, "I need to leave. Will you help me?"

"If it gets you away from my brother, then yes. And you will leave and never come back?" He wanted this to be clear.

She lowered her eyes to hide the pain and softly said yes.

"Then I'll help you." Liam paused before asking, "What of the child?"

Mackenzie took a deep breath and lied again, "There is no child."

Liam sneered at her, "I thought not. I told him."

She reminded herself that his opinion didn't matter. She needed to do this. But she couldn't help it, she had to try.

"Liam, I will go and you will never see me again, but I need you to understand that I love your brother with everything that I am, and I don't want to hurt him. Please believe me when I say that this will be for the good of the clan, and I will do everything I can to help. You may not understand all of this yet, but one day you will. I can't tell you everything, not yet anyway, but rest assured that I will free your lands of the curse and that is all you need to know."

He didn't look convinced, but Mackenzie didn't care, not anymore. She was about to hurt Connor in an unforgivable move, and she was not looking forward to riding alone through an unknown land to her possible demise. She got lost in her hometown all the time, let alone in a foreign wilderness without GPS or cell phones.

"This is my plan. I need you to tell Connor that we are going for a ride. I will need directions and some food— I think I can get that. And then when you ride home, tell him I slipped away while you were going to the bathroom or something, I don't care, just tell him not to follow me. He will die if he follows me. He cannot keep a cool head, and if he rushes after me without thinking it through, he will die.

"Please, Liam, whatever you choose to believe, you must believe that Connor will be killed if he follows me."

"He will go after you."

"Not if you tell him where to look. Take him the opposite direction, at the very least, buy me time to get away, and if he figures out where I've gone, then maybe he'll at least have cooled down enough to think rationally."

Liam stared appraisingly at her, and finally said, "And just why would I do this for you? I doona owe you any favors. It will hurt my brother. I doona relish the thought of lying to him, either."

Mackenzie looked at Liam, trying to read his poker face; it was so similar to Connor's, that maybe she could decipher what was in his eyes. Eventually she spoke, "You don't like me, do you." It wasn't a question, she was just expecting him to confirm her belief.

He did. "Nay, I think my brother should have picked a sane woman who had no connections to his enemy."

Even though Mackenzie had anticipated his response, it still stung. She sucked in a quick breath and her whole body stiffened. "Wow," she breathed out, "You don't pull any punches. I'm assuming that Connor has told you everything about me." Mackenzie didn't wait for Liam to respond, she kept going. "And I think that you believe I am trying to help the Campbell bring down your clan. Well, I'll let you in on a secret, Liam; I have never met the man who will kill me by the end of the month." He looked taken aback, but he hid it quickly. She laughed blackly, "Ah, yes, I know he wants my blood. But I have a few tricks up my sleeve too. So, Liam, believe what you want, help me or don't, but by tomorrow night I will be in the Campbell's keep, and whether your family survives intact is up to you. I have done all that I can here, and for me to fulfill my purpose, I need to leave. So, it's up to you." She paused, judging his reaction, before adding, "Will you help me?"

Liam glared past her, over her shoulder, and she had started to get nervous, fidgeting again, before he spoke.

"You will need to leave early in the morning; it is a full-day's ride to the Campbell lands."

She gasped, "You'll help me?"

"Aye, but you'll ne'er return, agreed?"

"Scout's honor, I mean, yes, I'll leave and never come back." As if she *could* come back.

"Then we should go tell my brother that tomorrow we will go for a ride so we can get to know each other."

Her hands were clammy, and her stomach was filled with butterflies, but she nodded. She would do this. She had to.

* * * *

Mackenzie was pacing around Connor's room, trying to figure out how to word a letter that said "I love you, but I am going to run away to your enemy and leave you forever. PS I didn't betray you."

She wasn't having much luck with it. Her heart hurt at the thought of putting pen to paper. Or quill to parchment, rather. She took a deep breath and picked up the quill. Her hand shook so much that she spilled ink all over the parchment. Taking another deep breath, she tried to steady her shaking hand, and wrote his name out. It was barely legible. Mackenzie cheated; she ran to her purse and took out her ballpoint pen. At least this way he would be able to read it. Another deep breath.

Connor,

I am sorry, so sorry. You have no idea. I have to do this. Please understand that I can handle this. I know how to defeat him now; my dreams have been telling me all along. Please don't follow after me. He will kill you. I know that it is against your nature to sit idly by and do nothing, but if you at least give me a couple of days, I can kill him myself. It has been for me to do all along; the sorcerers were wrong. It's not for you to do. I am sure you can think up a brilliant plan to defeat his men, and I am hoping that I will have killed him by then. Your lands will be safe, and you can have your other castle back. Trust me. And please, please, please forgive me,

I love you, and I always will,
Mackenzie

Mackenzie folded the note over and printed his name on the front. With shaking hands and tears streaming, she twisted her ring off and placed it gently on the note. The pain from leaving the ring was so great, that she doubled over and put her head between her knees. What could it hurt to keep it, right? She stood up and snatched her ring back, shoving it on the third finger of her right hand, that way the Campbell wouldn't guess its significance. Taking a steadying breath, Mackenzie tried to gather her things. She wanted to leave her technological toys here, with Connor, that way the Campbell wouldn't be able to guess her secret, or have anything modern in his possession. Her purse only contained lip glosses, gum, hairspray, a lighter from the airport, her wallet, and other mundane girlie things found in a woman's purse. She left behind her i-Pod, cell phone, and camera.

Her ring glinted in the sunlight and she just couldn't bring herself to keep it. Connor was going to think the worst, no matter what, but maybe if she left the ring, he would know that it had never been about tricking him into marriage, or into bed. This was so hard. Another deep breath, and as she placed the ring on top of the note, the pain intensified. A knock on the door startled her.

"My Lady, it is time." Liam's voice through the door made her jump.

Mackenzie picked up her purse and turned to look at Connor's room—his bed, the trunk where she'd found the amulet she needed, the bed again. She choked back a sob and ran out of the room, leaving her heart with the ring.

Chapter Thirty One

Liam rode with her in silence until they reached the border of MacRae lands. They were overlooking a small forested area nearby the loch, and Liam pointed straight ahead.

"Ride until you exit the trees. Once you're clear, you should be able to see the castle from there. Ride directly toward it without stopping. Stop for nothing and for no one, y'ken?" He waited for her nod. He obviously didn't want her killed by highwaymen; that was a good sign. "If you are stopped, tell them you are the Campbell's bride, and they ought to let you go free." He smiled a grim smile, "If they doona, then I'd get to prayin' were I you."

Mackenzie nodded again, and bit her lip as she gazed out into the distance, squinting as she tried in vain to see her destination; the castle she was riding towards. She glanced back to Liam, and wondered what he was thinking. Placing the palm of her hand ever so gently on his cheek, ignoring him when he stiffened under her touch, she dropped all pretenses.

"Thank you, Liam. I promise that I won't darken your doorstep again. And I also promise that with everything I am, you will have your lands back."

Looking out over the trees again, she mentally prepared to leave Connor's lands. A few snowflakes flurried around her, sticking to her eyelashes. She dropped her hand to her stomach and whispered, "We will make it out alive, I swear it."

Mackenzie straightened her spine and prepared to ride away from Liam, from Connor, and from the only true home she'd had in a long time. Liam's surprised voice stopped her cold.

"You are with child!" he accused her.

Her eyes were wide when she looked back at Liam. He knew.

"Don't tell him, please," she pleaded. Mackenzie bit her lip, unable to meet his gaze, so like his brother's. "He deserves not to know."

Liam gazed at her thoughtfully for a moment before nodding.

Mackenzie knew that Connor was going to be angry enough about her leaving him, that he didn't need to know she was pregnant. He'd be so angry about putting herself in danger, let alone with their child. She sighed and she nudged her mount forward. Liam's hand on her arm stunned her. She stopped and swung back to him, her eyebrows raised expectantly.

"Wait."

She did.

Liam's blue eyes were boring into hers. What did he want? Her hands tightened on the reins, and Mackenzie tried to be patient. Finally, unable to take the gaze that was so like Connor's, she demanded, "What?"

He took in a breath as if he was going to ask her something, but he exhaled slowly instead. After a short pause he sarcastically asked her, "What will your betrothed say when he finds you are with child, and it is not his?"

Her eyes snapped and flashed with her anger, but she reined it in, and rather than telling him where he could go, she calmly and coldly told him, "That is my business." She swung her horse toward the trees again, and once again Liam's voice cut across her thoughts.

"Wait, that's not what I meant."

Mackenzie didn't bother to hide her irritation. "Then what did you mean, Liam? You've already made your opinion of me clear more than once, this is no different."

"Did you…are you…" he was struggling for words. Under different circumstances, Mackenzie might have found it endearing. "Are you really everything my brother believes you to be?" He looked uncomfortable in asking, as if he was admitting some great embarrassment.

She thawed a little. "Yes. And even if you never trust me or believe anything that I've said, believe that I love your brother with everything I am. Everything I am doing now, Liam, is for Connor. Remember that. And keep him away as long as possible." She turned before he could stop her again, and without a backward glance, urged her horse forward.

Once she had ridden down the gently sloping hill, the trees encroached on her as if their branches were outstretched hands coming for Mackenzie. She was frightened of riding alone, and once she was in the thickest part of the woods where daylight barely filtered through the canopy, she was frightened of the dark. For someone who had grown up in the sparse desert of Las Vegas, the dark, cool green forest was intimidating. Knowing that it was snowing only scared her more; she didn't like the idea of snow unless she had a hot chocolate and was sitting by a fire. The fact that she was in a strange forest with snow falling added to the isolation.

With only the soft snuffling of the horse, and her thoughts for company, Mackenzie thought over her last night with Connor. It had of course been wonderful, and awful. Seeing his disappointed face when she'd lied and told him she wasn't pregnant was heart wrenching. All she'd wanted to do was to make love all night long, but she'd had to fake a period so he wouldn't catch on. Luckily, like most guys, he hadn't wanted any details, so she was able to just smile when he mentioned trying for a "wee bairn" after her flux. If it broke her heart to lie to him, then leaving him would rip it out, stomp on it, crush it, and pulverize her tender heart.

She'd been riding for almost a whole day now, and she ought to be able to see the castle soon enough, providing that Liam hadn't given her wrong directions on purpose, letting her wander around the woods until she starved, or froze, or was eaten by wolves.

Soon she was able to see a dim light coming from ahead. Once the trees broke, and she was able to clearly see the land in front of her, she gasped. Apparently, the snow had fallen much thicker and faster than she'd imagined; the trees must have sheltered her from the brunt of the snowfall. There was easily six inches of fresh powder covering the normally soft green ground. And it was still falling. Mackenzie pulled her wool cloak closer around herself and pressed on.

Chapter Thirty Two

Connor glared at his brother. "What do you mean she slipped away?" he demanded. They were downstairs in his private solar, where Connor preferred to conduct most of his business.

"I'm not sure, Connor, she just was behind me one minute and the next she wasn't. I'm sorry."

"You're sorry?" The words made little sense to Connor. He should have gone with them, but the chance for them to reconcile the competitive streak was too tempting. His anger at Liam for not keeping a closer eye on her was tempered only by his fear for Mackenzie. "She's not familiar with our lands, she must be lost, and so scared." Connor's gut clenched with the idea of Mackenzie alone and afraid in the cold. He glanced out the window at the rapidly falling snow. The snows had come late this season, and it looked as if nature was trying to make up for it.

He was on his feet in an instant. Liam's hand stopped him as he headed for the door.

"Ye canna go out in that," Liam indicated the increasing snow.

"If she is out there, how do ye think she will fare? We may be accustomed to this, but she isn't." Connor's voice took on a strained quality. "She'll be dead before sunrise." His voice broke slightly on the word dead.

Liam tried to soothe Connor, "She probably just rode ahead to see the loch. You ken how she liked to look at the loch and the neighboring isles."

"And what? That makes it alright that she is missing in a snowstorm?! Liam, I am surprised at your callousness. This isn't like you. There is a woman out there, in the snow, lost and alone, and you want me to wait idly by until she comes prancing home? What is in your mind?"

"Aye, of course, Connor, you're right. Let's get the men and I'll show you where we were when I noticed she was missing."

While they were on their way to the stables, Connor felt something was wrong. Liam's explanation was lacking, and his behavior was unlike his normal self. Why would he lie about Mackenzie's disappearance? It made no sense. Something was niggling in the back of his head, but he couldn't figure it out. Connor mounted his destrier, and glanced automatically toward the stall where Mackenzie's horse should have been. Snow White, she'd named her, for the fairy tale character. The princess who had a wicked queen after her, who tricked her into eating a poisoned apple, and then fell into a deep sleep…the Campbell! He didn't understand why the story made him connect the two, but it did.

"She's gone to him," he breathed.

Connor had barely voiced the words, but he watched as Liam's back stiffened in response. Liam was in on it! "And you kenned it!" Connor accused Liam.

Liam slowly turned toward his brother, and paused, allowing a loaded silence to hang between them before confirming it.

"Aye."

Connor's anger made him see red. "Did you think that I wouldn't figure it out?" He was almost yelling now, and had to work to modulate his voice. "Why Liam? You ken I'm in love with her. She's my wife, and whether you understand what that means or not, she's your sister now. How could ye do this?"

"It was what she wanted." Liam was interrupted by Connor.

"And that makes it alright? You know better, Liam. So she tricked you into helping her? Why wouldn't ye come to me? Why would you do this? Why?"

"She's no' good for you Connor. Can't you see the hold she's got on you? It's unnatural. And if she's in league with the Campbell, all that will happen is that our clan will fall. For the good of the clan, Connor, you ken that. We were raised to put the clan first. Ever since you abducted that *woman*," he sneered the word, "you've gone soft. She has you believin' her lies."

"She has a name. It is Mackenzie. And I have done nothing wrong. What happened to you Liam?" Connor sadly shook his head back and forth. "You are my brother. You are supposed to support me no matter what, or who, my choice is."

Connor saw the pain in his brother's eyes, but all Liam said was, "We can't go after her. She should be at the Campbell's keep by now. We can't go now."

Connor had to take several deep breaths before he could speak again. The thought of Mackenzie in the hands of that vile, disgusting snake had his heart racing. She was so soft, and warm, and spirited. What would happen to her? Lord Campbell would delight in breaking her. When he spoke again, it was very soft.

"He's going to kill her, Liam. And you just hand-delivered her to his door."

"You don't know that is what he has planned for her. That's what she wants you to believe. And you have believed everything she has told you. All the lies…" Connor cut him off again.

"She hasn't lied to me Liam."

"Are you so certain? She lied when she told you that she wasn't with child."

Connor sucked in a sharp gasp. "What?"

"She is pregnant, Connor, and she has gone off to our enemy with your child in her belly. That is an unforgivable lie. What will the Campbell do with a MacRae babe?"

"You're lying!" But Connor could see that he wasn't.

"We need to form a plan of attack, but not for rescue. We need to kill the Campbell. Now I say we continue with our original plan. We shall get the MacDonalds and the MacLeods to help, and storm the Campbell's keep. He won't be able to withstand such a force."

"You have this all worked out I see." Connor sounded calm, but inside he was fuming.

Liam shrugged.

Connor was livid that his brother had gone to such lengths to help Mackenzie escape and now he wanted to leave her to the Campbell's clutches. "And what of the dark forces with which he has tampered?"

"We will deal with that if it arises."

"So, you are willing to let my wife, my *pregnant* wife, die at the hands of our enemy, while we wait for help to arrive?" Connor knew he sounded incredulous, but didn't care. This was an asinine plan, and Liam was better than this.

"I have already spoken with the MacLeods, and they will help. The MacDonalds have said any enemy of the Campbell's is their ally. It is done. We should wait a day or two and then amass our men. It will be simple."

"I am ashamed of ye, brother." His words found their mark and Liam stiffened.

"While you might be happy to rush in after your woman, I prefer to wait for reinforcements. My plan is sound, Connor, and no matter how angry you are, you must see that. And if you refuse to see my way, then think about it like this; if she is who you say she is, mayhap it is a good thing to have her there. She can do what she was brought here to do. And if those magicians were telling the truth, then they will protect her." He sounded so smug. It rankled to hear his brother speak so dismissively of the woman he loved.

"If she dies, Liam, I'll never forgive you." Connor's eyes burned with the sincerity of his words.

He turned and stalked out of the stable. Ignoring the blinding snow, he strode to the castle and threw open the door. Once in his room, he grabbed the whisky from the table, and throwing the stopper across the room, ignored the shattering crystal as he gulped down the fiery liquid. Connor dragged his hand over his face. How could his own brother do this to him? And Mackenzie. How could she run off to his enemy? He remembered an earlier conversation with her where she'd asked for his help to get her to the Campbell. At his ire, she'd quickly dropped the subject, but obviously had not stopped thinking about it. He should have taken her more seriously. Connor had been pacing, and paused to set the whisky down. That was when he saw it.

Mackenzie's ring. The ring he'd placed on her finger the day they'd been married was sitting on a piece of paper, glinting in the firelight. Gently he picked up her ring, and placed it on his smallest finger. He opened the note she'd left him and with each word, his grip tightened until he'd crushed the parchment. Crumpling it into a ball, he tossed it across the room too. She couldn't even take the ring? What game was she playing at? Her logic was beyond him. Usually he understood her motivations, but this? Leaving someone who loved her for someone who only wanted to kill her? What was in her head?

His anger at Mackenzie slowly cooled and it was all he could do to not rush out and snatch her up. But he had to think, he had to plan. His stomach was tense with worry for her. The idea of the Campbell, his most hated enemy hurting her, touching her, with his hands on her body...Connor saw red.

He couldn't let Mackenzie sacrifice herself, that much was evident. But he didn't think he could wait until his brother's plan came to fruition. But what could he do? He still had his man inside the Campbell's stables, perhaps he could sneak in and steal Mackenzie back before his brother attacked. His fear that Mackenzie would be killed in the ensuing battle was almost as sharp as his fear of what the Campbell would do to her.

There had to be something he could do. Connor slammed his fist down on the dresser so hard that the glasses and the whisky decanter rattled. He stared morosely down at his hand splayed on the dresser. Her camera and the music device were sitting there as well. He glared at them a while longer as a plan began to form. Staring at the items on the dresser and seeing nothing, he began to plot.

Chapter Thirty Three

Mackenzie had been closed in her room for several days when the wizards finally showed up. The only contact she'd had with anyone had been a servant who never spoke and who barely met her eyes.

When she had first arrived at Urquhart Castle on Loch Ness, it had been interesting, to say the least. She had been stopped as she approached the main entrance, which had, no joke, a moat! When the guards had heard her call out her name "Isabella Stewart," they had immediately called for their master, and the Campbell himself had greeted her. He sounded cordial enough, but she knew better. Behind that carefully cultivated façade, lay the black heart of a man going mad in his thirst for power.

When she finally met him in the flesh, and she saw his cold face, lit up with excitement that his wayward bride had finally arrived, there was no doubt left in her mind that he was the man of her dreams, so to speak. Ripped from her nightmares, she balked at the thought of willingly entering his castle. Mackenzie squared her shoulders and urged Snow White forward.

The Campbell had been the picture of hospitality, until he escorted her to her chambers. Upon entering her room, he had rounded on her and his face had lost any traces of its former friendliness. Here was the face of her nightmares; cold, empty. What had she gotten herself into? His words chilled her.

"Forgive the locks, my dear," he indicated the intricate locks on the door–all locked from the outside. "They are necessary to ensure your safety."

"My safety?" Mackenzie asked with wide, innocent eyes. She knew it was to keep her from escaping.

"Yes, my dear, we can't have your husband coming after you, now can we."

"My husband?" she was genuinely startled. He hadn't mentioned Connor other than to say how disappointed he must be to find Mackenzie missing. Disappointed was not the word.

"Now you didn't think that little detail would escape my attention, did you?" He spoke condescendingly, Mackenzie almost expected him to pat her on the head. He was polite, but there was nothing in his eyes. Just cold, barren, ice blue emptiness.

Mackenzie pretended to shudder. She had a role to play.

"That barbarian is not my husband. It was so scary. My father will be happy to hear that I have arrived safely." Hopefully he would believe her to be no more than a simple girl who wanted to please her father.

The smile he smiled as she denounced Connor made her hair stand on end. He reminded her of a snake about to devour its prey.

"Your father has paid handsomely for this match," Mackenzie wondered who had really paid him, "he will be pleased indeed. I am the most powerful man in the Highlands, and after we are married, and I have killed the MacRae for insulting me, I will be the most powerful man in the country. Your father should be happy I chose you."

She hid her pain at the thought of Connor's death, and instead asked if she could have some books to help pass the time, and perhaps a tour of the castle.

"I shall have one of my servants bring you something to read, but a tour, I think not. I can't have you wandering about unattended. I also cannot discount the fact that you may be here under false pretenses. What if you were to run back to the MacRae and let him know everything you have found out?" He clucked his tongue. "Oh, no, that wouldn't do at all. Now, please, behave yourself and I shall see you in a few days for the feast in our honor. Then we shall be married the following day."

He turned on his heel and left, locking all of the locks in place from the outside. Mackenzie didn't bother trying to open the door, she was here, where she needed to be. No matter how scary or unnerving that was, she was here.

So for the next few days, Mackenzie had nothing more than books and staring out the window to pass the time. It reminded her of when Connor had locked her away. What was it about men of this era locking women in towers? Maybe this is where all the fairy tales came from. Too bad she didn't have hair like Repunzel, or a fairy godmother like Cinderella. Ironically, though she had two wizards on her side, however they weren't able to send her home yet, so it wasn't the same as a fairy tale.

When the wizards showed up in her room, it was through some form of teleportation, because one second she was alone, and the next they were standing in the middle of her room. Her gasp was audible.

"We apologize for the unannounced entrance, my Lady, but Lord Campbell has banned anyone from entering your room. He alone holds the keys."

"No, that's fine. I'm curious to see what you have found out." No need to tell them that she knew they couldn't save her. No one could. She was on her own.

"Much, my Lady." Gregor's eyes were lit up with the barely contained excitement. "We have discovered what we need to defeat him; but we need your blood."

Mackenzie's eyes popped out. "Excuse me?!"

It was Morvern who spoke, trying to reassure Mackenzie, "What my hasty son means, my Lady, is that if we could but have a few drops of your blood, the blood of the first female born to the Stewart line for 200 years, we would be able to charm a weapon for you, to protect you." Morvern laid his cold, paper-thin hands on her still flat belly, "and your wee bairn."

Mackenzie gasped again. "What?" she choked out. It felt as if her airways had been constricted.

"We know that you carry the child of the MacRae. Your child has a powerful parentage and his destiny is to unite the clans of the highlands."

"His?"

Morvern smiled. His crinkly skin creased with the effort. "Yes, 'he.' Your child will be a lad."

"Father, enough. We must act quickly."

"Yes, yes." He waved his hand dismissively in Gregor's direction. "My son is anxious lest Lord Campbell find us here. His dark powers have now surpassed our own, and we must kill him before Samhain. Now please, hold out your hand."

Mackenzie obliged and Gregor took a dagger and stabbed her index finger rather ruthlessly, she felt, and the blood spilled into a small vial. She yanked her hand back and wrapped it in the linen strip handed to her.

Addressing Morvern only, Mackenzie asked, "So you have my blood, now what?"

"We will charm the dagger and you will hide it under your gown. Then after the wedding feast, when everyone is deep in their cups, you must stab him with it. But a warning first, my Lady, his blood will burn you, should any of it touch your skin."

Mackenzie cut him off, "Okay, so don't touch, simple enough, but how will this charm be any different from the other dagger?"

"The other one only would protect you, this one will kill him. We have discovered that your blood is the only thing strong enough to accomplish that feat. His dark powers have made him nigh invincible."

"Great, simple." She muttered.

"Do not fret, my Lady. You are for whom this dark task was meant; you will prevail."

Morvern was trying to placate Mackenzie, but she knew nothing could do that. She would relax her frayed nerves when this dirty deed was done. Then she could go back to her own time, and—and what? she asked herself. Pine away for Connor, a man who would have died 200 years before? Raise a child on her own? Oh Lord, the baby? What would become of the baby? Would he even be able to cross over into her time? Or would she lose him as she was losing Connor? Taking a deep breath, Mackenzie tried to focus on what Morvern was telling her; he hadn't stopped talking during her panic attack.

"...and when you see the MacRae, you must not pay heed."

What was this? Connor? What had she missed?

"Excuse me, but what was that about Con—about the MacRae?"

"He will try to reclaim his wayward bride, but it is not meant to be; you must resist him."

"Oh," Mackenzie knew she sounded sad. "Of course not, I mean, I wouldn't want to endanger him. Or anyone else. Umm...is he really going to come here? I thought he would remain at his castle."

Morvern exchanged a shrewd look with his son, and his whispery voice somehow echoed in the room, "Do not mistake your worth. The MacRae will chase after you until he retrieves you. He will follow until he finds you." His voice was intense by the end of his speech, and Mackenzie wondered what he actually was trying to say. His son was gaping at him as if he had revealed too much. Unfortunately for her, Mackenzie had no clue what that might be.

"Do not underestimate Lord Campbell's reaction either. If you are not successful, then he will come after you. Please understand there is no place on Earth, no *time* on Earth, where he cannot find you. And he *will* hunt you."

Her eyes wide, and her breathing accelerated, Mackenzie stared at them for a moment, letting his words sink in. Eventually she was able to make her voice even.

"In other words, if he is not killed, then he will come after me through time, and...and then what? Will he kill me? Pull me back through time? What?"

"Most likely, he will kill you where he finds you, and once he lays eyes on your world, he will want to rule it as well. Or, in the worst possible case, he would bring back your weapons and use them here. We can *not* allow that to happen. He must be defeated, and it must be tonight." Gregor, ever blunt, forced Mackenzie to understand that there were indeed things that were worse than her own death.

Beneath the calm exterior she was afraid. Mackenzie felt as if her knees were shaking so violently that it should be audible. "What you are telling me is that if he is not killed by the time I go back through the gate, then the world will end. Great, super." Where was a superhero when she needed one?

A simple and all-encompassing "Yes" was all that she got out of Gregor.

"Great. So what do I do now?"

"You wait. We will be back soon to bring you the dagger, and if anything else reveals itself to us, we will let you know. Before we go, though, we will set up a warning, so to speak. Gregor?"

He handed his father a large purple crystal.

"Amethyst," Morvern explained at Mackenzie's bewildered expression. "Its mate is down the hall, and whenever Lord Campbell walks by it, this one will light up. It will give you advanced warning of just a few moments, but you may better prepare yourself."

"Thanks." Mackenzie sat down on the one chair, and prepared to wait.

Morvern paused and said, "Do not be sad. All will work out in the end, and everything will be as it should be."

"You sound so sure."

"Naturally. I have faith, my Lady, and faith in you. Good will prevail. You will be surprised at how things work out." He smiled and was gone. They both were. She shook her head and tried to calm herself as she waited. But waited for what? She had no idea.

Chapter Thirty Four

"Father, if the MacRae and the Stewart lass are meant to be, why did you tell her it wasn't?"

They had hidden themselves away in their workroom, and were working on charming the dagger that they desperately hoped would kill their master.

"She needs to believe she must go back to her own time, or she won't go, and the MacRae needs to believe she willingly sacrificed herself for the good of his clan, or he will never understand how she loves him. If all goes as planned, she will save our lands, return to her time, and the MacRae will come to us. We will help him cross times, of course, and then she will understand how much she means to him. A man who is willing to give up his lands, title, position, his time, why would she resist that?"

"Why do you take it upon yourself to do this?"

"The world has so few true champions of good, we must do all we can to help. Pass me the vial of her blood, we must make quick work of this."

* * * *

After the wizards had returned the dagger to her, she stood in her room, looking out the window at the loch. It was Loch Ness, and she idly wondered about the Loch Ness Monster and if it really existed. After everything she had been through in the past few weeks, she was a believer. It was then that she heard a noise behind her, next to the fireplace. A scraping, shuffling sound. Mackenzie gasped, her hand flying to her throat, as the wall opened and the dark shape of a man stepped silently out. Mackenzie ran for the dagger, unsure of what she would do with it.

"I'd appreciate if you didn't stab me again." The all too familiar voice sounded almost amused.

"Connor?" she gasped. Mackenzie was so relieved that it was him and not the Campbell returning, but she was worried for him. He shouldn't be here. She ran to him, but stopped short of throwing herself into his arms. So many emotions flitted across her face, as she tried to control what she felt.

"Aye, lass."

"How did you get in here? What are you doing here? You have to leave. Now." She tried to shove him back through the opening in the wall. His rock hard muscles didn't so much as budge.

"I didn't come all this way to leave now."

"Why *did* you come?" she retorted coldly. It was so hard to be angry with him when all she felt was fear.

"Liam told me that you lied to me."

"There's a big surprise. About what?"

"He said that you are with child."

"Oh, that. Well he's wrong." His penetrating gaze unnerved her, so she turned away and walked back to the window.

"Don't lie to me lass." Connor strode over to her and gripped her chin in between his strong fingers, forcing her to meet his probing sapphire gaze. "Are you carrying my child?"

She instantly denied it, "No, Connor, I'm not pregnant."

"I don't believe you." His voice was thick.

"Believe what you want. I don't care anymore." Mackenzie shook her chin loose and looked away from his too intense gaze.

"What is it? What are you thinking?"

"I'm thinking that you are unwelcome and need to leave. Now." This was killing her to be so cold to him. But she needed him as far away from here as possible, even if it meant sacrificing her own heart and making Connor believe the absolute worst of her. She was a hideous person for having love and pushing it away. So many people dreamed about this kind of love, and here, she had it, and was stomping on it. He had to accept that she was a cold, selfish person who'd never had any feelings for him.

Connor gripped her face between his hands and stared deeply into her eyes for a long moment before pressing his warm lips to her tight mouth.

"I still don't believe you. You are a terrible liar." He was so gentle with her.

A bright purple light caught her attention from the corner of the room. The crystals! *Oh crap, he was coming!* Mackenzie's mind flew in several different directions at once. Her eyes locked on Connor's, then back to the crystal.

"He's coming," she hissed at him. "You need to leave or he'll kill you!"

"The Campbell? Let him come." Connor flexed his fingers into fists, and then released them. He seemed so confident that he could win. Mackenzie was saddened by the knowledge that if he faced the Campbell, he would die.

"No, Connor," her eyes were wild as she pleaded with him. She pressed her hands to his chest and shoved once more, but he didn't budge an inch. "You need to go."

"I'm no' a coward." Connor seemed angry that she would insinuate he should run, but it was necessary.

"You're also not stupid. Connor, you cannot beat him. Not here, not now. *Please*, hide! We're running out of time!"

Connor took in the naked fear on her face and grudgingly nodded. He stepped back into the wall and the door swung shut almost noiselessly. What was she going to do?

Seconds within Connor hiding, John Campbell unlocked her door and walked in.

Chapter Thirty Five

"Come my dear, we have guests."

Mackenzie was stunned. They had guests? Who? And why did he want her down there? So far, he'd seemed content to leave her locked away in her room. She looked down at the Campbell's waiting hand, and up into his cold eyes, and suddenly felt grateful for the dagger she'd hidden up her sleeve.

"There's a good girl," he complimented her as she placed her hand in his. He was so condescending; she felt like a dog. Would he pat her on the head next? The difference between this man and Connor was staggering. There was no heat in his hands, no warmth in his eyes. Connor was all heat. He was cold.

This man had a sick sense of humor. Their "guests" were in the dungeon. They were all of the clan MacRae. They all looked so weak, she thought. Dirty, half-starved, obviously either beaten or tortured, or both. As the Campbell proudly displayed his "guests" and his warm "hospitality," Mackenzie tried not to wrinkle her nose against the smell. At the end of the small, cramped tunnel was a slightly larger cell. Mackenzie steeled herself for another tortured soul, but gasped as she saw what looked like a small child cringing away from the bars.

"Oh!" She tried to run to the bars, but the Campbell yanked her back.

"Oh no, my dear. We mustn't touch."

"What are you doing? Why is he here?" Mackenzie demanded.

"He was caught in the battle this morning. He was trying to fight off my men," his grin was patronizing.

"What battle?" Mackenzie asked slowly, afraid to hear the answer.

"My men nearly decimated the MacDonald clan today. We caught them quite unawares. There were no prisoners, save this." He indicated the boy.

"But he's just a child," she protested.

A slow, evil grin slowly spread across his face, twisting and contorting it. "Exactly."

"I don't understand." Her eyebrows were knit over her nose and she stared at him, uncomprehendingly.

"When I execute *it*, the MacRae will finally understand how serious I am about eliminating his kind from the Highlands. I shall usher in a new era. One where our progeny rule the Highlands, and these lowly clan 'chieftains' will follow my orders. I will be the most powerful man in Scotland, and soon I will be more powerful than the king himself!"

Mackenzie quietly thought about that. She couldn't think of anything a lady of this time would say, so she settled for something a woman of her time would say.

"It won't work, you know." She tried to keep her tone neutral.

"Pardon, my dear?" So polite.

"You'll never beat him. You can't. He's stronger than you and he's better than you." She instantly regretted the words. His eyes were no longer cold, they were crazed. The eyes of a madman.

"You will not speak so disrespectfully."

He slapped her across the face, and Mackenzie staggered back from the blow. She hadn't seen his temper before and she was irritated with herself for not holding her tongue. He grabbed her by the upper arm, making her wince—it was her sore arm—and dragged her back to her room. The whole time he ranted and raved about how he would kill Connor, and how he was better than any Scottish dog who probably didn't even know who is mother was. This time, Mackenzie was smart enough to keep silent. When he had thrown her into her room and slammed the door behind him, Mackenzie childishly stuck her tongue out at the door. It made her feel slightly better. She rubbed her arm, and glared at the fireplace.

After what felt like the longest night of her life, Mackenzie just wanted to sleep. Upon returning to her room, she flopped down on the bed and waited for Connor to sneak back in. She knew he wouldn't give up, so she'd assumed he would be waiting to pounce on her as soon as she walked in the door. He never showed, though. Mackenzie didn't want to admit how disappointed she was, so she tried to think positively. Maybe he went back home. That was as comforting as it was disappointing since she knew he'd be safe there, but it was still hard to be happy that she'd never see him again.

After she finally passed out from exhaustion, Mackenzie dreamed. The nightmare was becoming more and more real. Maybe it was because she knew all the players now, or maybe it was because she was finally living it. Either way, it was now coming true.

Her dream was the same one over and over and over this night. It never deviated. She was waiting for some brilliant twist or idea to help her, but nothing changed.

She was in a large room, a ballroom, she thought. The man she now knew as John Campbell held her hand tightly, but she kept her face smooth, not showing her discomfort. Mackenzie was aware she was dreaming this time, and she waited for them to drag Connor in. He was shackled and it looked as if he'd been beaten. How had he been captured? The Campbell stood and dragged Mackenzie up before the guests.

He addressed the crowd, "We gather today to celebrate my impending marriage," he glanced at Mackenzie, whose eyes were on Connor. "And as a wedding gift to you, my dear, I shall kill your husband. Tomorrow you will be free to marry me."

Even though she knew he'd say it, Mackenzie stifled a horror-stricken gasp.

"Now watch as your husband dies!" he gleefully shouted.

Mackenzie tried desperately to feign indifference, but all to no avail. Her stricken eyes never left Connor's bruised face. She begged his forgiveness with her eyes as he glared at her with hate and distrust. He thought she'd betrayed him. Her heart broke and shattered into a million tiny pieces at the thought not only of Connor's death, but of him thinking she would ever betray him. How was she supposed to fix this? There had to be a way. Mackenzie racked her brain for some way out of this. The dagger! She'd hidden it under her long sleeves. If she could just get to it without attracting attention....

Mackenzie feigned boredom with the whole procession, and yawned, fanning her mouth, then pretended to scratch an itch on her arm, slowly, so slowly, she slid her hand under her sleeve and in one quick motion, she yanked out the dagger and plunged it into the back of his neck. Her hands were covered in warm, red blood. Mackenzie screamed as she yanked the dagger back out of his neck and he lurched at her, knocking them both down. She was pinned to the ground as she watched him gurgle his last breath.

When she woke, she knew how Connor had been captured. He'd been here waiting for her. It was her fault. This new bit of information didn't help ease her anxiety level at all. She sat up in bed and ran her hand through her hair. So Connor had probably been discovered in her room, or in the secret passageway. No wonder he hadn't been waiting for her after her little "tour" with the Campbell, he'd been busy getting himself captured!

Now she had to find a way to save not only herself, but Connor too! Mackenzie groaned aloud. What were the fates trying to throw at her now? This was so frustrating. The man she loved was trapped most likely in the dungeon by the man she had feared her whole life, and not only did she have to save Connor, but she also had to kill the Campbell. All before the end of the month which was only in two days! She flopped back onto the pillows and sighed. What was she going to do?

If her dreams were correct, she would stab the Campbell at the feast the next night. The main problem was that she still hadn't figured out why she'd had the dreams of Connor and the Campbell fighting. Or how he had used the fire against Connor. Pinching the bridge of her nose, she closed her eyes and tried to see the dream again. She saw it vividly; she fell asleep again. But the next dream didn't change, or the next.

Upon waking in the morning, she was more discouraged than ever. So much was riding on tonight, and she felt so unprepared. Her nerves were stretched to their limits, and every small noise had her jumping. She waited for her breakfast to be delivered and for once didn't try to make conversation with the servant who helped her get dressed. After the servant left, Mackenzie tied the dagger to her arm under her sleeve, and mentally prepared herself for the day. Nothing worked though, so she finally got proactive. Mackenzie tried to find the lever to release the door to the secret passage. If she did nothing else right, she wanted to sneak some food to the poor child in the dungeon. At the very least, she had to try.

She fumbled around the fireplace, until her fingers were black from the dirt, and she leaned her forehead against the mantle in defeat. And was eye level with a brick that stuck out slightly. *Oh what the hell*, she thought, and pulled. Success! The door swung open and she wrapped the breakfast she'd been too anxious to eat in a handkerchief before stepping into the dark tunnel. She felt around until she found the release and the door swung shut leaving her in the dark.

* * * *

He and his brother had played with their cousins as children in this castle; he knew all of the medieval tunnels and passageways. Connor had known that Mackenzie would be difficult, but when he'd stepped into her room, he hadn't expected her to be so hostile. She had told him to leave. And she had lied about the baby. He knew she was lying; she was a terrible liar. But he knew she thought she could defeat John Campbell alone. It hurt that she didn't want his help. Even with the magician's on her side, he knew it was a lost cause. She had been hiding something from him for a while, and he had thought it was her plan to leave and run to his enemy. But after seeing her here, he knew there was more. She wasn't telling him everything. And what had she meant when she'd told him that he could not beat him. *Not here, not now* she had said. When?

At her request, he'd hidden when the Campbell had come. It went against everything in his nature to hide, but when her eyes had begged him to leave, he'd done as she requested. He'd known she was lying about not caring any more. She cared enough that she didn't want him to die. But what else was she lying about? His brother had thought she'd betrayed them to the Campbell, but he knew her better than that. Liam was wrong. Mackenzie would never betray them. The fact that the MacDonalds had been attacked this morn was simply a coincidence. Besides, Mackenzie hadn't known any of their plans, so how could she have told the Campbell?

After seeing the truth in her eyes, he knew she was carrying his child. What would happen to that child if she stayed here with the Campbell?

Connor had to force himself to stay in the tunnels when he heard the voice of his enemy in his wife's bedchamber. The tips of his fingers were raw from holding himself in place by gripping the rocky walls. After they left, he followed through the tunnels, bypassing some to get around common areas. He followed as far as the great hall, when a noise caused him to whirl around.

Connor barely missed a blow to the back of the head in the form of the butt of a sword as he spun towards the noise. He drew his own sword in time to block the next attack, and ran the man through, but there were several men behind their fallen comrade. Connor fought until he was outmaneuvered and even then he still took one man down. But he blacked out after that, and the next thing he knew, he awoke in the dungeon.

Connor groaned and felt the lump on the back of his head. He quickly took stock of his battered body, but there wasn't anything that wouldn't mend. He'd had worse. Nothing was broken and there were no gashes. Just a headache and sore muscles. He was chained to the wall with about four feet of slack. He looked around for a way to escape. He thought he could get out of the shackles. He hadn't been completely disarmed; there was a hunting knife in his boot. If he could spring the locking mechanism in the shackles, he might be able to free himself. As he reached for it, he saw a slight movement out of the corner of his eye. He rounded on it with his knife drawn.

It was a small child! A very frightened child, at that. He squinted in the dark to make out features, but all he could see was fear. Connor stuffed the knife into his waistband.

"Hello there, and what might your name be?"

No response.

"It's alright, I'll no' hurt ye," Connor spoke as soothingly as he could. "How came you to be here in this place?"

Connor cajoled and pleaded with the boy to speak, but unto no avail. Eventually Connor gave up and went to work picking the lock on his shackles. The small voice that broke through his concentration surprised him.

"I am called Pip, sir."

Connor's surprised gaze met the small boy's. "Pip? Is that your given name?"

"No sir. Me mum calls me Ronald."

"Ronald? Well I've a cousin named Ronald."

"Truly?"

"Aye, lad. And he's almost as handsome as you."

The lad smiled.

"Now can ye tell me how ye happened to come in a place such as this?"

"The bad man came and he killed me da' and me brother Collum. I picked up me da's sword and tried to fight them off." He shook his head, "There were too many. The captain told me that since I showed such courage, I could come with them. But they want me to join them, and I spat at his feet. So they brought me here."

"You're a very brave lad. Now, Ronald, I have a way of getting out of this, but I'll need your help."

"My help?" his eyes goggled.

"Aye, lad." Connor picked the lock on his shackles and went to work on the iron bars that held them prisoner. "I'll be needin' ye to look out for me, and let me know if anyone is a comin'. Can you do that?"

"Aye sir. I can." The little boy scrambled up and ran to the bars, peering out into the dark tunnel.

Connor had just set to working on the lock, when the boy whispered "My Laird, there's someone coming."

Connor stepped back against the wall and put the chains back on his wrists, but he didn't latch them. He tensed and waited. The footsteps got closer. They sounded too light to be that of the jailor. But who else would it be?

A shadowy figure stepped out.

Chapter Thirty Six

Mackenzie fumbled her way through the passages, stumbling and tripping in the dark closed-in space. She was beginning to get nervous; she still hadn't found the dungeon, and she didn't want the Campbell to find her missing. If Connor had made his way in through a secret tunnel, the Campbell obviously didn't know it existed or it would have been guarded, and she didn't want to be the one to expose the network of tunnels to him. It could be a valuable tool for the opposing clans in accessing the Campbell.

Eventually Mackenzie found herself in the lowest levels of the castle; she had to be near the dungeon. Seeing a light up ahead, Mackenzie followed it, pausing to make sure it was safe to continue. It was. She stepped carefully out into the dim light outside the castle walls. Wow, she'd found her way out. She took in a deep breath and released it slowly. Mackenzie was so tempted to take off and run; the self-preservation instinct kicked in. She took another deep breath and reminded herself of why she would stay. Why she had to stay.

Turning back into the dim tunnel, she stepped back into her prison.

Mackenzie did find the dungeon, and the small boy in the far cell. It was easier to sneak him her food, than she'd dreamed. And while the boy was skittish at first, when she offered him her untouched breakfast, he nearly jumped up for it. She spoke quietly with him and turned to leave, so that she could get back to her room. She learned his name was Pip, and that he had been merely defending his mother when the Campbell's men had captured him and dragged him to this hellhole of a prison. What kind of man brings a child to a dungeon with the intention of executing him? She knew the answer though; he wasn't a man, but a snake. An evil and frightening snake.

A movement in the back of the cell had her whirling about in shock. Connor! Her hand flew to her throat and she froze.

"Hullo, love, miss me?"

"Connor?"

"Who else?"

"What are you doing down here?"

Connor held up his free hands, "Escaping. And you?" He glanced down at the boy greedily gobbling up the food she brought. "Bringing joy to the less fortunate?" His eyes darkened as he reached out from his cell and yanked her to the bars by the laces on her kirtle. "Or a quick tussle before I'm executed?"

Mackenzie had never seen Connor like this, hostile and angry, and it was her fault. This whole damn mess was her blasted fault! She tried to calm her pounding heart and her heavy breathing. Gently disentangling herself from his grip, she stepped back and hardened her gaze and her heart.

"I am truly sorry at that, Connor, but I cannot help you with either."

She registered the shock and pain on his face before she turned and ran. But it was better if he hated her. Easier.

She found her way back to her room much quicker than it took her to find the dungeon. Thankfully no one seemed to notice that she'd been missing for about an hour. She sat idly staring out the window for the rest of the afternoon, when her silent servant came in, eyes downcast, to prepare her for her pre-wedding day feast. And even though her whole life had been leading up to this moment, in truth nothing could prepare her for what this night held.

* * * *

Connor couldn't believe her! She had left him in this prison! She had turned and run. What was going on? He heard booted footsteps and motioned the young lad to keep to the shadows. He placed his hands behind his back, loosely in the manacles.

The Campbell walked in and gently pulled at the fingers of his gloves, taking each glove off and meticulously folding them into his jacket pockets. Being English, he had no desire to dress like the Scots did. He took a castle and its lands that did not belong to him, he insulted the people by raping the servants, and having anyone who opposed him slaughtered.

"Ah, Connor MacRae, welcome to Urquhart Castle. Or should I say welcome *back*?" He was taunting him. "I trust your accommodations are to your liking?" And the laugh that followed didn't sound human. It was the wild laughter of an animal. It was the laugh of a madman.

"Your wife belongs to me now. You really put a kink in my plans when you abducted her, you know. And marrying her? Quite a wily move on your part. I must say that I underestimated you. I never thought you'd be bold enough to take something that belongs to me. While ingenious, it was futile to try to bind her to you through marriage. A completely pointless effort. She and I will marry on the morn."

Connor knew that he planned on executing him as soon as he possibly could. He didn't bother to ask what was to become of his people, his clan. He knew that the Campbell would decimate them; they would be hunted. His lands and his keep would be plundered and his people killed or beaten until they agreed to serve the Campbell.

"What, no witty remark? No parting words? I'm disappointed in you. I expected better out of the fabled MacRae laird. It must be difficult to think that I will soon have what you cannot."

"I will kill you." Connor said it calmly, conversationally, but his jaw was tight, and his eyes were glaring murderously at his hated enemy.

The Campbell laughed. "No, I'm afraid you won't. I will however, have your wife. She is such a tempting morsel, isn't she?"

At his smug declaration, Connor saw red. The idea of his hands on Mackenzie, of him touching her, running his hands down the soft smooth satin of her skin...

He couldn't let his enemy see how much it got to him. So he forced his tone cool and aloof.

"Did she tell you of the babe?"

"What?" That stopped him cold.

"I see your bonnie wee bride has yet to tell you I got her with child."

"No! She can't be!" His rage was showing through his carefully cultivated façade. He took a deep breath in through his nose, and calmed himself, not without effort. "Well, even if you speak the truth, and I'm not entirely sure you do, the child will be mine. Your death will quite an auspicious occasion; proof that no one can defy me and survive. With you dead, there will be no one who would dare oppose me! And I doubt even *she* would care."

"What are you talking about?"

"Why it was she who gave me the information and location of your allies."

"You're lying!" Connor knew Mackenzie wouldn't do that.

"Ah, but I'm not. How do you think I found your reinforcements so easily?" He laughed again. "Did you really think that you could defeat me? That I wouldn't be expecting such a pitiful move on your part? You know, I'd expected more from you." He clucked his tongue, "Such a disappointment."

Connor couldn't believe that Mackenzie would betray him like that.

He knew she wouldn't. Whatever game she was playing, she was not heartless, and she would never knowingly allow innocent people to be slaughtered. But how else could he explain the Campbell's knowledge of his men? Or the intimate knowledge of his wife. Or Mackenzie leaving him to rot.

The Campbell continued on, "And as for the child, if you are telling me the truth, well, of course the child will be reared here under my tutelage and guidance. He will become the son of the most powerful man in the Highlands, and I will generously mold him to my image. What more could you want for your son?" He laughed sadistically as Connor clenched the chains on his wrists until they cut into his palms. He had to remind himself not to give away that his hands were free.

"You're mad!" He glared at his enemy.

"No, I am enlightened. I have seen the way and it is not living by the sword, or the way of men. It is through me! I am a god!" he crowed. "Once you are out of the way, I will rule all of Kintail and reclaim the title of Lord of the Isles. The fragile king will have nothing to say, and there will be nothing he can do. Even his son is too wrapped up in American politics to care what happens here in the barbarous lands of Northern Scotland! Rumors of his father's madness are abundant...."

Connor cut him off, "You are calling the king mad? Is that no' a wee hypocritical of you?"

"I am not mad!" he hissed and backhanded Connor across the cheekbone.

It didn't hurt, however Connor knew the blow was meant to injure naught but his pride. It was incredibly demeaning.

A slow smile replaced the anger on his face as he glared at Connor.

"I trust you'll enjoy your last meal, for within the hour, you will be executed in front of *my* bride."

Connor said nothing, his gaze never leaving his enemy's empty eyes, and his mind constantly working.

Chapter Thirty Seven

John Campbell came to her room as before, and they walked to the Hall in silence. Mackenzie tried not to betray her nerves by her shaking hands. While he gripped one, she clutched her long flowing sleeve with the other so as not to fidget. They entered the Ballroom, and she recognized the colorful scene from her dreams, and it frightened her. At least this time, she was an active participant in the scene before her, rather than just waiting helplessly for the dream to finish. This was real. It was more than real, it was reality, and everything hinged on this one night, this one act. She must kill him before he could execute Connor. She had the advantage of foresight, but she still felt as if it hadn't quite "clicked" for her yet; Mackenzie was still unsure.

Beneath her satin-clad feet, Mackenzie could feel the floor vibrating with the music that had started when they walked in the room. Keeping her face serene, Mackenzie stomped down all of the fears she felt, trying to be as calm as she hoped she appeared.

Standing on the raised dais, he looked out and addressed the crowd. "My guests, you have come to witness my long awaited marriage. The clan MacKenzie is in attendance, and I see several acquaintances from court, oh this shall be festive indeed. Please, enjoy my hospitality; eat, drink, dance, for what a joyous occasion this is." He raised both hands and as he did Mackenzie's eyes widened when all of the hundreds of candles flared and then settled down to a normal flame. The control over fire! Mackenzie wanted to yank her hand free and run, but she tried to take a steadying breath and instead feigned boredom, sat down next to him, and waited.

Before he joined her, the Campbell leaned over to her, his breath brushing her ear as he spoke, "My dear, I have quite a wedding present for you." He paused, waiting for her to look at him. Mackenzie didn't disappoint. When her wide green eyes met his ice cold blue ones, he continued, "You will be widowed before you are married!"

Her stomach fluttered as his words sank in; he was going to kill Connor! Mackenzie had pointlessly hoped that he had made it back to his own lands, knowing full well that he was here in the possession of the Campbell. She had to keep her reactions from showing. *Stay calm, stay calm* she chanted to herself.

"I am pleased to see you understand. I have your husband in my possession, and I will do you the favor of dispatching him tonight."

Mackenzie bit the inside of her cheeks to keep from telling him go to the devil.

"First we shall have him displayed as he is; broken and disgraced.

Then, my men will show him the true meaning of hospitality."

She couldn't keep calm anymore. "You bastard!"

"I am shocked. Are you not pleased with my wedding gift to you?"

"You're disgusting."

He merely laughed, obviously enjoying the play of emotions in her eyes. He still held her hand and his grip was becoming painful. It was as she had predicted; everything was as she had predicted. The colors of the gowns and the candles, it was overwhelming. Everything was too bright and too sharp. They sat, and her dream spun out before her.

The Campbell called out, "Bring out the prisoner."

Mackenzie knew it would be Connor, yet she was still shocked at how badly beaten he was. His right eye was swelling and from his lip and nose poured blood. It looked as though his face had borne the brunt of the attack. Although his shirt was torn and bloodied, it appeared as if the blood was from his still bleeding face. He was shoved to his knees, in disgrace. Mackenzie saw that there were a few fresh wounds on his back as well and almost gagged as she understood that they were from a whip. Connor had been flogged!

If he hadn't come to find her this never would have happened, if she could have kept her hormones in check he would never have come after her and he could be safe in his own castle right now. This was all her fault. She met Connor's eyes, and even as they beat him in front of everyone, he kept his gaze on hers. When the Campbell announced, "We gather today to celebrate my impending marriage," he glanced at Mackenzie, whose eyes never left Connor.

He then addressed the crowd, "And as a wedding gift to my lovely bride, I shall kill Connor MacRae." He turned back to Mackenzie, but still spoke loudly enough that it was intended for the ears of the crowd, "Tomorrow you will be free to marry me." He jerked his chin in the direction of Connor, and several men descended upon him. Standing and yanking Mackenzie up next to him, he crowed, "Now watch as your husband dies!"

Her dream was unfolding before her eyes, but for the first time since she was a child, she wasn't scared anymore. Mackenzie's nerves steadied. Of course she wasn't nervous, this is why she had been born; it was who she was. Every part of her felt the calm settle over her as she accepted and understood what she must now do. Suddenly Mackenzie felt powerful. More than powerful; she felt electricity rather than blood running through her veins. She felt strong, and she felt as if everything had just slowed down. All of the too sharp colors, all of the too bright lights; it all became muted background. Everything was in slow motion, and it was only she who felt the normal passage of time. All of the noise quieted to a dull roar akin to waves crashing, and all of the anxiety and fear had fled.

While Connor vainly fought off more men than one man could

humanly withstand, she vaguely noticed he had a hand free, Mackenzie turned her head to see the Campbell cheering them on and hurling insults at Connor. Now was her time. With the events in the room running in slow motion, Mackenzie was able to notice everything. She saw several heads turn away from the horror of an unarmed man being slaughtered, she saw several men running to help, and she saw a group of men rushing in from the back of the room.

There was a man dressed in a plaid forcing his way through the crowd with his sword raised above his head. Liam! There was enough of a distraction that the men who were to kill Connor were now protecting their own backs. Hopefully that would provide him with enough time to catch a breath or be rescued or grab a sword, or *something*. Mackenzie reached her hand up toward her sleeve when the Campbell impulsively grabbed her from behind. He held her by the front of her neck, her back pulled against his body. Again, she was struck by how there was no heat emanating from him, none at all. He pressed his sword into the hollow of her throat. Yet, for the first time, she wasn't afraid. She knew what to do.

* * * *

Connor had been beaten and tortured in futile attempts to humiliate him. Nothing could hurt him now, not after hearing how Mackenzie had betrayed him. Liam had been right about her all along, and Connor had been too blinded by her lies to see it. What a fool he was! To see Mackenzie on the arm of his sworn enemy was beyond humiliating. He had known that he would be dragged into the room in chains, they had re-shackled him, but he had managed to free a hand. But to watch his wife, the woman he had loved, the only woman he had loved, stand next to that English pig! It was more than he could endure.

He watched as the Campbell whispered in her ear, and he watched as she guiltily met his gaze, and he thought she was a much better actress than he had ever imagined. For the first time since meeting her, her eyes were unreadable. When the Campbell ordered his death with nothing more than a jerk of the chin, he saw her green eyes widen, and he thought he saw fear for a moment, but it was only one unguarded moment. After seeing her guard slip, Connor felt a little smug; he hoped she remembered the look in his eyes as he was killed. He wanted his face seared into her memory for all time. Connor made sure his gaze never wavered once the men set upon him. The only thing that tore his eyes from hers was his brother's voice.

Liam was pushing through the crowd of English nobles with his sword drawn and his men in close pursuit. The men who were supposed to kill him now had to protect their own lives. This gave Connor a small chance to breathe. With his deep breath came clarity. He kicked the man behind him as his brother made his way to where he was standing. Connor shouted for a sword, and Liam instead shouted back to hold his arms out. Connor did, and Liam swung his mighty claymore at the shackles breaking the chain on his first blow. Connor then pulled a still-sheathed sword from a guest who was cowering from the mêlée and ran through the first man he saw. He had to get to Mackenzie; he would kill her himself for this treachery.

He fought through whoever crossed his path until he reached the platform where Mackenzie and her "real" love stood. It was only then, staring up at her, that he noticed the sword at her throat. So the Campbell would play it that way, well Connor didn't care anymore. He shoved the last person out of his way and leaped up onto the dais.

"I'll slit her throat." The Campbell's empty threat didn't worry Connor.

"Do it," Connor taunted. "I don't care. I'm here for you, not her."

"I'm surprised. Where's your chivalry? Aren't you here to save your lady-love from the evil tyrant?" the sarcasm was almost condescending.

"Nay, I am here for your blood and nothing more." Connor watched Mackenzie flinch as his words hit their mark. Good, it was time she felt something for what she had done. Betraying him was one thing, but so many men had died because of her. Let her have that on her conscience.

"I apologize that your wish will not be fulfilled. But I have more important things to do than to fight with a Scottish barbarian. Is that word too large? A Highland brute."

Connor ground his teeth together, but otherwise ignored the insult. He pressed the tip of his sword to the Campbell's chest, who then neatly stepped behind Mackenzie, using her as a human shield. The pig couldn't even face him; he had no honor.

"Mackenzie, would you be so kind as to move?" He said it as if he they were old friends, rather than she the woman of his enemy.

The Campbell's eyes became wild, his voice a growl.

"What did he call you?"

Mackenzie couldn't even choke out her name. Connor felt a twinge of sympathy for her, but he tamped it down. "Oh, did she not tell you her given name is Mackenzie? Hmm…seems like something a man ought to know about the woman he is about to marry."

Mackenzie gave a quiet choking sound, and her lips turned blue. Connor didn't understand. That meant that the Campbell was really gripping her throat hard enough to choke her. Why would he do that to his accomplice? He must truly be an evil man. As angry as Connor was about Mackenzie's betrayal, he didn't want the Campbell to hurt her. He was saving that for himself.

Connor continued to goad him, "Aye, you doona even ken her name, I claimed her virtue, and she carries a MacRae babe in her belly. 'Twould seem you doona ken her at all."

"She will be mine! Make no mistake about that!"

"You can have her. I have taken what I wanted. Oh, and might I say she was quite willing. I hope you enjoy her as much as I did. She's quite pleasing in bed; enthusiastic, if you will." Connor ignored the feeble glare Mackenzie managed. He hoped each insult stung.

It looked as if the Campbell had tightened his grip on her throat, and Mackenzie's eyes started to flutter as if she were having a hard time keeping them open.

But Mackenzie wasn't giving in easily. She looked as if she might faint any minute, but to her credit she stepped on his foot and elbowed him in the ribs. It was a move Connor knew well; she had used it on him once. Only this time, she staggered backwards, and could hardly stay upright, her hands resting on her bruised throat. Connor saw the outlines of fingers forming on her fair skin, and felt ill. Despite all of the anger and betrayal, he was still in love with her.

* * * *

Mackenzie was seeing stars and her eyes started to roll back into her head. The blackness threatened to engulf her, the ringing in her ears drowned out whatever Connor and the Campbell were saying. She just wanted to close her eyes...No! She must succeed! Mackenzie took every last ounce of energy she could muster and stomped down hard on his foot. She elbowed him in the ribs and when his grip relaxed slightly, she tore his fingers from her throat. She stumbled backwards, and every breath she sucked into her raw throat burned.

"Go, Connor," she rasped out of her abused throat. "Leave. Get out of here." Why couldn't he just swallow his pride and let her take care of this?

"Yes, *Connor*, get out of here." The look on his face was that of pure hatred. Mackenzie had never before seen a look such as that. "You are unwanted by even your wife, or should I say *my fiancée*?" The Campbell really thought he was indestructible. Well, Mackenzie thought, she could change that. She knew what she had to do.

Connor's eyes flashed the way they did when he was angry. Mackenzie thought that if the Campbell was distracted enough maybe she could get to her dagger without being seen. The Campbell rounded on her and yanked her against him by the upper arm. His crazed eyes were glaring into hers.

"You whoring shrew! How dare you lie with another man! You belong to me, and you will behave accordingly. You will do as I say, and you will do what I want."

She glared right back at him. As if to emphasize his point, he pulled her up to his face and pressed his cold, lifeless lips to hers. Mackenzie wanted to gag. Instead, she waited for him to pull back and she punched him as hard as she could in the mouth.

The Campbell was a man who was used to paying men to do his dirty work. He very rarely had to deal with anyone on his own, and to be hit in the face by a woman was more than insulting; it was infuriating.

Mackenzie saw his eyes change, and instinctively tried to free her arm. Unfortunately it was her left arm, and the Campbell yanked it forward. Mackenzie was hard-pressed not to scream. As it was, she paled and bit her lips to keep the sound from escaping. He slapped her across the face in front of everyone. It was humiliating and degrading. And as she glared back at him, she could see Liam making his way to where they were. That gave her an idea. She could throw the Campbell with a similar throw to the one she'd used on Liam. Excellent.

The Campbell still had a death grip on her arm, so she just needed to unbalance him slightly. When Connor stepped forward, the Campbell turned his attention back toward him. Mackenzie seized her chance and pulled him in, and hooked her leg behind his knee, dropping him instantly. She hadn't planned on him keeping hold of her arm though, and she fell on top of him. She mustered up all her strength, freed herself, and ran. She could only hope that he would follow her and not stay to fight Connor. At the very least, she could keep Connor out of this.

She ran out of the Hall and tried every door she came to, pulling futilely on their handles. She hid in the first unlocked room she found. It was dark, but there was moonlight, and since the moon was full, she could see well enough. It seemed to be a study of some sorts, with a couch and chairs scattered around the room. The shadows cast by the furniture closed in on her. She could hear nothing over her heart pounding in her ears. Mackenzie concentrated on slowing her loud breathing and her incredibly loud heartbeat. She heard someone pulling on door handles. He was getting closer. But who?

If it was the Campbell, this could be her chance. Her only chance. If it was Connor, how would she keep him safe? And how would she know who it was until it was too late?

Before Mackenzie could try to distinguish the footsteps, suddenly Morvern and Gregor were standing in the room with her! She almost screamed as they appeared out of thin air. Controlling her reaction, Mackenzie stifled the scream and ran up to them.

"What do I do?" she begged.

"Sadly we cannot help you, save to cast a protection spell around you and the MacRae. Neither one of you will die tonight, however, we cannot otherwise guarantee your safety."

"So, let me get this straight...you can bring me through time, but you can't keep me safe?"

"We merely predicted the gate's opening, we ourselves did not open it." Gregor always seemed a bit snippy to Mackenzie, and tonight was no exception.

"I can hear someone; who is it? Who will come through that door first?" There was so much that Mackenzie needed to know right now, but first and foremost, if it was Connor, she didn't want to attack him.

Before they could answer, the door opened, and they vanished. The

Campbell stepped into the shadowy room, and Mackenzie held her breath and stepped back against the wall, trying to blend in. Footstep by footstep, he entered the room, each step drawing him closer to Mackenzie. She was becoming lightheaded with the lack of oxygen, but if she could do this…

She was clutching the dagger to her chest, but slowly started to raise it. When he passed by, she hoped to plunge it deep into his neck. He stepped past where she was standing, and he walked towards the fireplace. Mackenzie stepped behind him, matching her footfall to his. A shuffling noise in the hallway caught his attention, and as he turned to see what it was, Mackenzie brought the knife down on him.

Chapter Thirty Eight

Mackenzie's aim was true, but the Campbell caught her forearm in a painful grip and bent it backward until the dagger clattered to the stone floor. A small yelp slipped through her lips, which she was biting against the pain. When he jerked her arm back farther, she panted with the agony. His other hand came to grip her throat once more, although this time it wasn't so tight. She pulled uselessly at his merciless hold.

"Foolish, obstinate girl. Did you really think that I wouldn't find you?" What surprised Mackenzie was that he sounded…amused. "I told you, you belong to me." His light tone changed without warning, it was abruptly ominous. "And I will have you." His face was inches from hers, twisted in anger.

Mackenzie barely sucked in enough breath to whisper, "Never."

He laughed. The deranged lunatic actually laughed at her.

"You will follow orders or I will have your lover killed. Painfully."

Mackenzie ceased her struggle and her hand fell limp against his.

"Ah, I see that caught your attention. My men have your 'husband' as we speak."

Mackenzie couldn't fully believe the sorcerers when they had said she and Connor would be protected from harm, but neither could she believe the Campbell. Her eyes searched his in the dark. Even with the light of the silvery moon, she could only see the emptiness that had consumed him. If her life was forfeit, so be it, but she would be damned if Connor would die as well.

"You lie."

He raised his eyebrows. "Do I?"

While Mackenzie had been studying his eyes, the Campbell had simultaneously been backing her up. He stopped her when the backs of her knees hit something—the couch in the center of the room. He pushed her by her neck, his grip never releasing her arm, until she was lying down on the couch. She was starting to panic. She could feel her eyes widen, and her heart accelerate. She hadn't been afraid before, but now, there was no doubt in her mind as to what was about to happen.

"You will stay silent, do you understand?"

Mackenzie nodded as best she could with his hand on her throat. He ripped her gown from her shoulders and tore through her stays and sark. His hand was at her breast, kneading it painfully. He groaned in anticipation. His mouth was all over her; her face, her neck, and when his cold, lifeless lips pressed against her breast, she shuddered in revulsion.

"That's right," he said mistaking her disgust for passion. "Just relax. You are about to become part of history. Our child will usher in the new race between the black arts and mankind." His lips had moved to her neck and were dry and cold against her throat.

God, he really thinks he's going to rule the world, doesn't he? Mackenzie was quickly realizing that he was absolutely insane.

His hand was creeping up her leg, pulling up her skirts. Oh Lord, she knew what he was going to do, and she trembled in fear. He was squeezing her abused throat so tightly that she was having trouble breathing. If only she would black out before he violated her. Her heavy eyes flew open and she gave herself a mental smack. How dare she give up now! He would not win. When his fingers touched the smooth flesh of her inner thighs, he moaned. She felt her stomach heave. The fingers of her enemy were touching her where only Connor had, and as she thought of him, she found there was some fight left in her after all.

Mackenzie had one hand on his at her throat, she'd tried to pry it off, but it had been impossible. While the Campbell was not as big as Connor, he was still very strong. But so was Mackenzie, and she refused to give up. She raked her fingernails across his cheek as he tried to pry her legs apart. He hissed at her! He'd actually hissed at her!

"Don't do that again. I can make this pleasant for both of us, or I can make this pleasant for myself." He smiled as she grasped his meaning.

Well, he would have to take her the hard way, there was no chance that she was giving up without a fight. His cruel fingers moved from her neck only to slap her across the face again. The blow rattled her teeth together, but she refused to show her pain. Glaring up at him, she was barely able to whisper through her swollen throat, "I will kill you."

He laughed. The rat-bastard was laughing at her. "No, my dear, you won't." His hand was once more at her throat, pinning her down, while his other hand still tried to open her legs. Mackenzie couldn't even get enough air to scream.

She had always known her death would be by his hand, but that had been before. Before she had met Connor, before she had found love, before she had found something worth fighting for, worth living for. She refused to die. She placed both of her hands on his chest and shoved as hard as she could. He didn't loosen his death grip on her throat. She reversed the tables and placed both of her hands around *his* neck, squeezing as hard as she could. She registered the change in his eyes from lust to aggravation. He pulled his hand from her thighs at least, but he successfully pried her fingers from his neck.

The Campbell chuckled darkly. "I am afraid you'll be disappointed if you think that will kill me." He laughed again, an evil, frightening sound, as he gathered both of her hands in his, successfully restraining her. He ran his eyes down her body, and the lust returned. She could feel the evidence against her hip. "You are beautiful, my dear. I hope your Highlander hears how I tasted you, and how I enjoyed your favors. It will be the start of a beautiful war."

Suddenly, his weight was gone. She heard the thud as he landed on the ground. Squinting in the dark, Mackenzie made out the shape of another man in the room. He was standing above the Campbell, sword drawn. She recognized his stance, the way he held his sword; it was Connor. She could tell without seeing his face. Fumbling to cover herself, Mackenzie tried to pull her stays back up. They now resembled a strapless corset. Her sark stayed on one shoulder, but the other was fluttering loosely around the top of her stays. The gown was a lost cause; there was no salvaging the sleeve, so she pulled her arm out and tied both of the sleeves around her waist, 90s grunge style. In the seconds that Mackenzie had fixed her clothing, Connor had his sword at the Campbell's throat. Still, ever arrogant, the Campbell taunted him and goaded him endlessly. He still thought he could win.

This scene was too familiar. Mackenzie vaguely remembered a dream from a few weeks back. Connor and the Campbell fighting in a dark room with arched ceilings. This is where the fire had come into play. Oh no! Connor!

"Connor, no! Let him go!" She distracted Connor enough that he stepped back just as a spray of fire flew from the Campbell's fingertips barely missing where he had just stood.

"You protect him?" Connor snarled, his disgust apparent.

She didn't have time to explain. He obviously couldn't tell that she was protecting him, not the Campbell. When the Campbell turned on her, he was smiling. It was the cold smile of a snake, and it chilled her to her soul.

"I knew you'd warm up to me, my dear."

Mackenzie glared, but kept silent. She needed to think. And fast. The Campbell reached for her again, but she side-stepped his grasp. She could see the glint of her dagger on the floor, but it was on the other side of Connor and the Campbell. There was no way she could get to it without attracting attention to what she was doing. Meanwhile the Campbell had grabbed Mackenzie's upper arm in a painfully tight grip and yanked her up against his body, intent on pressing his mouth to hers once more. This time Mackenzie let him, and she opened her mouth to his thin, cold lips. The second his tongue slithered into her mouth she bit down as hard as she could, until she tasted blood. When she released him, he backhanded her. It snapped her head back, and the force of it threw her to the floor. When he went to reach for her again, Connor swung his sword down, slicing into his arm, but the man didn't flinch, or bleed, or anything! Instead he laughed, and she saw his wound heal in a fashion any movie special effects director would envy.

What manner of man was he? He wasn't. He had sold his soul to the dark forces, and in return had become indestructible. No wonder he had been so arrogant. He knew he couldn't be killed. The glint of the dagger drew her gaze again. Except by her dagger! Her blood had always been the key, and the sorcerers had used her blood to charm that dagger so it would succeed where Connor could not. She had to reach it!

Connor and the Campbell were fighting. Well, Connor was hacking at him, but he wasn't falling or bleeding.

Mackenzie made a run for it, and prayed this would work. She made it to her dagger just in time; the Campbell had gotten bored letting Connor chop at his impenetrable skin, and threw fire at him once more. Mackenzie brought the dagger down and into his shoulder. It worked! The scream he let had her covering her ears, and backing away.

"It's not possible!" he screeched. He turned wild, frenzied eyes on Mackenzie and howled with rage. "How? How did you do it?" He was advancing on her with wild eyes. "I am invincible. I am a god. No mortal has the power to destroy me!" He was raving.

Mackenzie waited for him to close the distance between them and swung the dagger once more, aiming for his heart, but he pivoted out of the way and she grazed his upper arm. Once again he howled as if he was being burned. And then he did something truly surprising: he turned and fled.

Mackenzie was cradling her arm for some of his blood had spattered onto her skin; it felt as if it was melting the flesh from bone. But she had to go after him.

"Mackenzie, I—" Connor began, but Mackenzie didn't have time and bolted for the door.

Running past Connor was easier than she'd thought it would be. He let her go. Mackenzie was running on instinct and adrenaline alone, hoping she was following the Campbell's trail. She felt that she was going in circles, and she felt as if every time she climbed a flight of stairs, she never really went up. This was reminding her of a dream as well. She knew she had to be somewhere for something important, but her memory was fading and she couldn't remember where she was supposed to go, or for what? She had slowed her run to a walk as she looked around the suddenly unfamiliar walls.

The voice of Morvern broke through her confusion, though.

"Remember you are here for the Campbell. You must not be distracted. See through his deceptions. You are the Stewart lass, you alone must defeat him. For the good of your people, for the good of your child. You must press on."

That's right! She was in Urquhart Castle, and she had to find John Campbell. She was the only one who could kill him. She was no longer confused, but she still didn't know which way to go. Morvern interceded once more. He showed her to the tower stairway. She kept climbing until she reached the balustrade, and she could see her enemy standing with his back to her, his arms raised to the full moon low in the sky.

Her every movement was in slow motion, it was similar to in the Hall. She knew this would be the end of it all. It was as if her vision had centered on the Campbell and everything else was blacked out. She was vaguely aware of someone coming up behind her, but nothing could distract her from her purpose. She walked toward the Campbell, seeing only him and the target his back presented. She would slit his throat. He hadn't turned at the sound of her approach, but still she walked toward his position. As she came up behind him and raised her dagger, she heard her name called from behind her, but she ignored it. Nothing could sway her from her mission. Stabbing him at the base of the neck, Mackenzie hoped to snap his spine with the blade, but as she pulled the blade out, his blood ran down his back and he turned surprised eyes on her.

He gurgled out an unintelligible response, and managed to say, "How? You should not be seeing me." He staggered to one knee and almost collapsed. He stumbled up and backward until he came to the low wall, his momentum carrying him over.

The Campbell had fallen off the top of his keep, and landed in front of the confused partygoers on the main floor. Mackenzie's wide eyes blinked rapidly, and her vision cleared. The bloodlust was gone, replaced with calm rational thinking. And the knowledge that someone else was up on the balustrade with her.

Mackenzie stepped as far back as she could from the grisly scene so far below. Turning, she saw Connor, with a look on his face that she had never before seen. She wanted to sit down and cry. She couldn't deal with him. She couldn't deal with him thinking she had betrayed him or their people. She had come to think of them as her people now, too, and she had saved them from the rule of a tyrant who would have killed or enslaved them. Instead of peace, or pride in her accomplishment, she was ready to break. She was so fragile that the idea of confronting Connor, made her hands shake. She had to get out of here.

Connor caught her arm and swung her around to face him. His steely eyes bored into hers, seeing everything she had in her soul. Her green eyes filled with unshed tears as she held his gaze. Let him see what he wanted, she didn't care anymore.

"How did you do that?"

Mackenzie couldn't answer him.

He shook her slightly in frustration, and asked, "Why did you tell him the location of my men? They were slaughtered like animals! How could you do that? No matter your feelings for me, how could you do that to those innocent people?"

Still she couldn't make her voice work.

"You owe me an explanation!"

"I don't owe you anything," Mackenzie whispered. "I've given you everything I have, and I've got nothing left to give! Just let me go, Connor." She'd expended so much energy on trying to defeat the Campbell, that she was spent. Now, she just wanted to survive. She knew her heart wouldn't make it out intact, but she could still spare their child. So she shook his hand off of her arm, and ran.

Mackenzie ran as fast as she could away from Connor, not stopping until she had run down several flights of stairs. Once down the winding staircase, Morvern and Gregor appeared in front of her. Both had huge smiles on their faces; even Gregor, who never smiled. His plain face looked almost attractive when he was happy.

"We knew you could do it," Morvern clasped her hand, the one with the burn marks from the blood, and ran a light touch over her skin. When his hand had passed, the burn was gone.

"Thank you." Mackenzie was rubbing her arm where the burn had been.

"No, my Lady, it is we who thank you." Gregor bowed to her. She had done the impossible, and in turn earned his respect. Not that it mattered, the one person whose opinion meant anything at all was lost to her for all time.

"My Lady, you must come with us now, if you would like to go home."

Home. Where was that again? Home is where the heart is, there's no place like home. Home! Home! Home! It didn't even sound like a real word anymore, *home*. She was done!

Morvern's ancient face looked shrewdly on her as he asked her, "That is, *if* you would like to go back to your own time?"

Mackenzie found her voice and mumbled that she did want to go back to her time; she couldn't bear to say *home*. She heard footsteps close behind her, and knew it would be Connor. Her eyes flew to Morvern's, pleading with him silently, and he smiled knowingly. He touched her shoulder, and they were suddenly in the Great Hall, chaos reigning around them as people shoved and pushed to catch a glimpse of the Campbell. When they noticed she had entered the room, a hush descended over the crowd. All knew it was she who had killed him. The two wizards led her through the crowd, which parted like the Red

Sea. As she came up next to them, some people touched her shoulder, her arm, reverently and tentatively.

It was unnerving to see so many people staring at her with such gratitude. Even Liam was looking at her with acknowledgement of her deed. She had to pass him to leave, and as she did, he stopped her with his hand on her shoulder.

"My Lady?"

"Yes?" She still didn't have much volume to her voice after nearly being strangled twice. Fortunately it was dead silent, so she was heard.

"I am sorry for my actions. I was wrong in my judgment of ye. Please accept my apology."

Mackenzie whispered, "Of course, Liam. You were trying to protect your brother." She managed a tiny smile. "No hard feelings."

"You are more generous than I would be, were our places reversed. Thank you."

She bowed her head, as the tears were threatening to spill, and tried to leave.

"Please, wait."

She looked up at Liam.

"What of my brother?"

"He's on his way down. He's not injured."

"I meant, what of you and my brother?"

"He...he doesn't want me." Her lips trembled as she whispered the words.

"He said that?"

"He didn't have to," Mackenzie barely got the words out, they seemed stuck in her throat.

"And the babe?"

"I am leaving for my" she choked on the word *home*, and quickly substituted "time." She placed her hand over Liam's which still rested on her shoulder. "Keep him safe for me Liam? And tell him that I wish him only happiness." Her watery eyes met his, as she begged for him to promise.

He was surprised. "Aye, my Lady." Liam dropped to one knee and bowed his head with respect.

One by one, the rest of the audience did the same, with the exception of a few groupings of prisoners being held by Connor's men. Mackenzie was overwhelmed by the reaction of the people.

Morvern's voice crackled through the silence, "We must be on our way. The gate closes at midnight."

Mackenzie expelled a long breath and looked around the room just in time to see Connor entering the room, looking furious. Gasping, she turned away, and followed them out of the keep

Chapter Thirty Nine

Connor watched Mackenzie hurry after the two sorcerers. It tore his heart out of his chest to see her leave. She was walking out of his life forever, and she was taking his child. The whole room had bowed to her, Connor had been chasing her all over the castle, and she was able to walk away. His brother had even bowed to her! What in blazes was Liam thinking? He despised Mackenzie! Connor made his way over to his brother, and choked out the words he had never wanted to believe.

"You were right Liam, she lied to me and betrayed us all. She couldn't even stay to face me. She ran like a coward."

"No, she didn't. I was wrong, Connor. She loves you more than you ken, more than I believed. I didna want to understand, but now I do. She saved us all. She saved our clan, and we have our lands back. The Stewart curse is broken, Lord Campbell is dead, and all has been righted. Surely you must see that? Now go, get your wife back."

"Liam, I canna fathom what you are thinking. She gave him the location of our men! They were slaughtered like animals."

His eyes hardened, but he calmly said, "No, Connor, that was due to a traitor among our men." They shared a knowing look.

"Hamish?"

"Aye. The girl told him nothing. Hurry, brother, find your woman before she goes back to her time."

"Her time?" Connor was momentarily stunned by what his brother was implying. "Are ye tellin' me you believe her?"

"Aye, brother, I do. I'm sorry I didna believe you from the start. I am surprised that you canna see how she saved your thick neck by killing that sorry excuse for a man."

"She's saved me in more ways than one, Liam," Connor said quietly putting his hand on his brother's shoulder.

"Then you must go to her."

Connor stared at his brother for only a fraction of a second more before turning and running out the wide double doors. His horse was still waiting for him and Connor leaped onto his back and dug in his heels. As he rode, he thought.

When he had seen the Campbell forcing himself on Mackenzie, the red haze of bloodlust clouded his sight and his thought. All he had been able to clearly think was *Mine. She's mine.* The primal claim he felt over her resonated throughout his body. Without thought, Connor had raced in and ripped the Campbell off of his wife, throwing him across the room. He had immediately thrown a couple of punches into his face, yet it served only to hurt his hands. It was as if the Campbell had skin of iron. An armor or shield of some sort that allowed no blows to touch him. He had even laughed at Connor, and insulted him further as Connor tried unsuccessfully to breach his shield.

Before he could kill the swine, Mackenzie had placed herself in between them and ordered him to stop. Connor couldn't believe her! She would defend that vile snake? Her betrayal went deeper than he'd originally thought. At that moment, flames shot from the Campbell's fingertips, directly where Connor had been standing. It jogged a memory loose from a few weeks back; the memory of her dream. Mackenzie had been frightened that Connor would die at the hand of the Campbell. Could that be why she'd placed herself in front of his sword?

After he had thrown Mackenzie to the ground, Connor saw the opportunity and took it. He brought down his mighty sword and sliced through the Campbell's forearm. In a blow that should have severed his forearm, the Campbell didn't even flinch. The dark forces healed him unnaturally, and at that moment, opposite his fight and across the room, Mackenzie had rushed behind the Campbell and picked something up off of the ground. Connor couldn't tell what it was, since he was presently engaged with the Campbell. But Mackenzie drove her dagger directly into his shoulder. Her small dirk found purchase! How had his sword done nothing, but she had made him bleed? The Campbell seemed even more shocked than he. The Campbell turned around and fled like the coward he was. Mackenzie met Connor's eyes briefly, but she too ran out of the room.

He followed her, but stopped short. For there, in the hallway, Mackenzie seemed to be blindly running, and yet she never went anywhere. It was the strangest thing, and suddenly, as if she had been shaken from a spell, she ran up the tower stairs. Connor followed behind at a slower pace, unsure of how to handle the situation. He wasn't certain of anything anymore. When he reached the balustrade, he arrived in time to see Mackenzie kill the Campbell. It had been incredible; she had walked slowly to him and deliberately plunged her small dirk into his neck. He hadn't even fought back. Once she turned from the macabre scene below them, her eyes widened at Connor's presence. After she had noticed him standing there, watching her, she tried to run again. This time he caught her, though, and forced her to meet his gaze.

She had a lot to answer for.

And yet she turned tear-filled eyes on him and told him to let her go. She turned and fled. But Connor was damned if he'd let her walk out on him again. He chased after her, only to have the wizards intercede on her behalf. Once more Connor was left alone. He ran down to the Hall, intent on meeting with his men to find her, when the scene that greeted his eyes stopped him cold.

Watching Mackenzie walk out of the doors, walk out of his life, had been the hardest thing he'd ever been through. It tore him in two to see her leave. And for his clan, his kin, his own brother to bow to her as if she were royalty. *What the hell had just happened?* For Liam to have a change of heart was unlike his brother, especially for it to happen so quickly. But it seemed he'd been wrong about Mackenzie, and her motives. From the start, she had proclaimed her innocence, and the desire to help. He had wanted to believe her, *had* believed her, mayhap he should have believed *in* her? He had never known anyone like her. But of course he hadn't; she hadn't been born yet. There would be a good 200 years before she would exist.

Connor almost halted his mount when he realized that she would be going back to her own time. Her own life, as she had once stated. It was a sobering thought for Connor, since he knew nothing about her time, or her life there. He knew very little about her, he realized, except he knew how she had helped his people, a people she'd never before met, out of the goodness of her heart. He knew how she tried to hide the grief when she spoke of her brother. And he knew that she was the bravest, sweetest, most passionate person he'd ever met. And Connor knew without a doubt that he wanted her forever. Letting her walk out of his life was unacceptable and unfathomable. Just the thought of never seeing her again constricted his chest. But did she want him back? She was leaving him. He had broken her faith in him.

He would get her back. He had to. His life was meaningless without her in it, and it might be too late to tell her that. Connor rode his mount harder, faster, until he could see the borders of his own lands.

By now, Connor was on his own lands, and had ridden through the night, chasing after the woman he loved. His keep was close. He was certain that this was the way she had gone.

As he approached the gate, he saw the two wizards. Perfect!

"Hullo! You there. Where is she?"

"Mistress Stewart? Why she has returned home. Charming lass, it's a shame to see her leave. Amazing how she has saved us all, is it not?" The elder of the two men spoke to Connor as if he knew something more than he was saying.

"Bring her back," Connor commanded. He softened his tone. "Please."

"We cannot. I am afraid that the gate is closed. The gate will not open again until after Yule, on the New Year. Only then can one pass through the gate, and we do not yet understand in what time it would open."

"You must, please. I need her. She carries my child."

"And you want the child?"

"Aye. I want her." He paused, "I love her."

"Well then, let us see what we can do."

Chapter Forty

The next couple of months were hell. Connor did nothing, he went nowhere. Nothing brought him any kind of joy. It was as if when Mackenzie left, she had taken his heart with her. Liam had been understanding at first, but Connor's foul mood had eventually gotten to him, and soon, even he left Connor alone.

The sorcerers no longer came to see him with details of their progress.

He was utterly and completely without hope.

At first, the idea of trying to go through the gate to retrieve her was appealing, but as the sorcerers worked, they could make no progress in how to control the time of the opening, or the ability to bring him back.

His love for Mackenzie was a pressing weight on his chest, constricting until he felt as if he couldn't breathe. This was wrong. Love was supposed to be light, not this dismal darkness in his soul. It was almost Yule, but he had little interest in the celebration; Connor had little interest in anything. Even as the concept of bringing Mackenzie back faded farther and farther into oblivion, Connor could not rouse himself from his self-imposed isolation.

While the Yuletide festivities resounded throughout his keep, Connor drank himself into a stupor. It was unlike him, but lately he didn't know who he was anymore. His whole life had been for the good of the clan, he'd been reared to be chief. But what good was he, what good were his instincts, if he hadn't trusted them on even the most basic level? His heart. Had he trusted his heart, mayhap Mackenzie would still be here. He passed out in front of the fire, and he dreamed. For the first time since Mackenzie had run from him, he dreamed.

In his dream, he was a ghost, a wraith, moving in and out of time without the sense or feel for it. He saw decades come and go, and centuries pass, but he felt nothing, he was nothing. And then a light in his darkness. A beautiful girl with honey colored curls and emerald green eyes was sitting before the fireplace, his plaid wrapped about her shoulders as a shawl. But this was wrong; she was sad. The girl with fey-like beauty should not be sad. And she was crying. For the first time in a long time, Connor felt something more than the soul-blackening depression he'd wallowed in. Connor felt alive.

Walking slowly toward the girl, he moved around in front of her. Still she gazed deeply into the fire. When he knelt down before her, she sighed. The sound struck him in his heart—a heart that had not beaten for centuries now jump started at the simple sound of her breath. She spoke!

"Oh, Connor. I am so sorry." Her voice broke and her lower lip trembled with the tears. "If only you knew…"

Knew what? She never finished. Connor was yanked back into his own time, but this wasn't real either. The same girl who had haunted him for too long now sat in front of the fireplace in his chambers. Only this time, she smiled as she held two young children with blue eyes and blonde curls on her lap. They were reading a story, and when she looked up at where he stood watching, her lips curved upward in a smile so sweet, the ice around his heart melted. Could she see him?

"Mind his head," she indicated the warm bundle in his arms.

Another babe! And this one had her emerald green eyes!

Could it be? Was it truly his child? Nay, his children? And the look she gave him was so tender and loving...how could this be?

Once more Connor was ripped from the scene, from the beautiful woman who held his heart. When he regained consciousness, it was in his own chambers. Alone.

Connor threw the whisky bottle across the room and slammed out of his chambers. Storming through his own castle, he made it to the stables before his brother came running out to see what he was about.

"What are you doing? Connor it is well past midnight!"

"I am going to retrieve my woman."

Liam sucked in a quick breath. "The wizards?"

"Nay, they have yet to figure anything out that can be of use."

Liam eyed him carefully before suggesting, "Connor come on back in, we'll have some coffee, and you can relax."

"I'm not drunk, Liam, for the first time I am thinking clearly." The ferocity of his statement brooked no argument. He gave his brother a knowing look, "I'm not daft either."

"Never said ye were."

Connor rode until he found the dwelling he sought. He threw the door open, scaring the room's only two inhabitants.

"My Laird!" Morvern's startled voice broke the silence left behind after Connor had stormed into the room.

"Any progress?"

Not needing to ask to what he referred, Morvern answered, "Regrettably not, my Laird. Is there anything else with which we can offer our assistance?"

"Aye. You can follow me. We will try this now."

Gregor gasped. "Now?!"

Connor grimly stared him down, "Aye. Now."

They rode back to his castle, and upon arrival, Connor stopped them, demanding the location of the gate. Morvern showed them to the stone door that no one save Connor and his family knew of, and marched through until they stood in a tunnel that led into the Gallery. It was only then that Gregor announced his displeasure.

"But my Laird," protested Gregor, "It'll not open for another week. We also cannot guarantee your location." He stopped at the fierce look in Connor's eyes.

"Open it."

"But we cannot…"

"Open it."

Morvern and his son exchanged a look and began the incantation to open the gate. To Connor, it seemed that neither one believed it would open, since both had said it would only work as the last day of the year changed into the next. The shock and surprise on both of their faces might have been humorous to Connor in a former life, yet right now, no trace of amusement could be found.

Connor walked straight ahead of him, only pausing to ask when it would open again.

* * * *

"Father, I thought it wouldn't open til the beginning of the new year?"

"I discovered long ago that we can open it at will."

"Then why make the MacRae wait? It is obvious to any that he is in agony without the Stewart girl."

"He needed to know how much she meant to him, and the only way was for him to be without her until it became too much. His love is stronger now, and he will do what he can to keep her. He needed to see what he was losing." His shrewd eyes met his son's as he confessed, "'Tis why I sent him the dream."

"The dream?" Gregor answered vaguely. His father was really quite crafty, to orchestrate all of this.

"Aye, I sent the MacRae a dream tonight showing him exactly what he was missing in his life, and what his life would become. He would become nothing, ghosting through centuries until he found her, but by then it would be too late."

Gregor shook his head, but instead of interrogating his father further, he said, "You have planned this from the beginning, have you not?"

Morvern's dark eyes twinkled, "Aye, my son, and now we shall wait. Come morning all will be as it should."

Chapter Forty One

Mackenzie woke up to the sound of pouring rain washing away yet another dream of him. Too bad it couldn't wash away the pain as well. Her time in Scotland was almost through. She and Jenna would leave the following afternoon, and probably never return. She was torn. Mackenzie desperately wanted to go home; to be among the familiar and comforting. But going back home meant leaving Connor. She didn't want to leave; she felt like the only connection she had to Connor was here, staying in his home. When she went home, to her life, it would make everything that she'd experienced that much more dreamlike, and that much less real. As it was, she already felt like the past month was nothing more than a product of her overactive imagination. Especially since she'd returned to her own time at the exact moment she'd met Morvern and Gregor, the two men who had changed her life so drastically. Only this time, when she had wandered back to the Gallery, she had been alone.

Meeting up with Jenna and the rest of the tour group as they toured the castle had been unbearable. The pain she was suffering hadn't even been allowed a good cry in her room. Jenna kept glancing at Mackenzie with a worried glint in her eyes, but Mackenzie just kept her head averted and pretended to look around, as if she had not lived in the castle for the past month.

Feigning excitement at every antique or painting was wearing her down. As the tour ended back in the lobby (to her it was still the glorious foyer of Connor's time), she couldn't force herself to laugh and flirt casually with Jenna and her new Italian boy toys. She not so politely excused herself, but if she thought Jenna would just let her go, she was mistaken.

"Kenzie, what's wrong? I've never seen you like this."

"It's nothing," she even dredged up a smile. "Really."

"You're a crappy liar, Kenzie. What is going on?" The knowing look of her best friend who was like a sister to her was too much. She couldn't stay here.

"Umm...I'm going to wander around a bit. You go have fun with those boys of yours." Her attempt at humor failed miserably.

Jenna narrowed her unusually shrewd eyes on Mackenzie and stared at her, lips pursed, for a long, uncomfortable moment.

"You're going to go ogle that painting again, aren't you?"

Mackenzie's eyes widened and she nearly flinched. "No, I'm not in the mood for any ogling." *Ever.*

"I'm surprised at you. There's always room for ogling."

"I think I'm just going to go for a walk." She had already started to walk away from her best friend, so Jenna couldn't try to stop her again. She wanted to be alone. Maybe she could rent a horse for the day and ride.

The idea of going for a ride was so appealing, that Mackenzie couldn't dislodge it from her brain. She ran to her room and changed into jeans and a button up shirt, throwing her jacket on as she hurried downstairs. Once at the concierge desk, she inquired about renting a horse and was delighted to discover that the stables were still behind the main keep, and that she could indeed rent a horse for the day. Her mood improved at the thought of riding a horse.

* * * *

Mackenzie had been riding all day. She'd gotten to know Connor's lands pretty well during the past month, and even though so much of the surrounding lands had changed in the past 200 years, it was still achingly familiar.

She had ridden across the stone bridge to the town across the sea, and found several charming shops. One shop had a variety of local wares, one of which was a beautiful lavender wool shawl in the window. Mackenzie inquired about it, and once they settled on a reasonable price, she bought it. It reminded her of a gown she'd once worn. It ripped at her heart to think about it. Pushing the memory out of her head, she focused on paying for it and the loose weave poncho she picked out for Jenna.

On her way out of the shop, the display in an antique store caught her eye. There was a brooch and plaid wrapped around a mannequin in the same tartan as the MacRae clan. It looked too new to have been Connor's, but she had to know.

But as she walked in, something was glinting gold in the back of the shop. She ignored the shopkeeper's greeting and kept walking until she saw it was a locket. Opening the locket, she gasped, and it slipped from her suddenly numb fingers.

"Is everything alright, dear?" The shopkeeper's gentle question jogged Mackenzie out of her stupor.

"Oh, yes, thank you." She felt the heat creeping up her face.

"Ah, the laird's locket." The shopkeeper indicated the locket Mackenzie had picked back up.

"The what?"

"It is said that one of the lairds had that locket commissioned for his bride, but she went missing a few weeks after they were married. It was quite the scandal, for she was said to have helped to defeat his enemy before she disappeared. No one knows what happened to her, and the laird supposedly wasted away in despair, waiting for her to come back for him."

"What a sad story. If this is part of such a tragic tale, why is it here, and not on display in the castle?"

"Well, if you look inside, there is a photograph."

"Yes." Mackenzie could see that; it was her!

"Well, it can't be the laird's wife, because it would have been a miniature, rather than a modern photograph. So no one knows what to make of that, and the few times it has been sold, each patron has brought it back. They say it is cursed."

"I'll take it."

"I thought you might say that, dear. But don't you even want to know the price?"

"It doesn't matter. If you take plastic, I'll take the locket."

The shopkeeper smiled fondly and said, "I'm sorry my dear, but I don't accept credit cards."

Mackenzie could feel her face fall.

"However, I think that this locket belongs to you." She tapped the picture inside the delicate gold oval. "She has the look of you." As Mackenzie's shocked gaze met hers, she smiled knowingly and said, "In fact, I think you'd be doing me a service, taking it off me hands."

"What are you saying?" she gasped.

"That when you meet that laird of yours, you promise me that you'll hold on tight and never let him go. D'ye ken? You love him well, and he'll love you in return. And *that* shall be a true happily ever after."

Mackenzie could do nothing but stutter and gape like a fish. She pulled herself together enough to thank the kind woman, and when she left, she could have sworn she felt as if she were being watched.

Arriving back at the castle well after dark, Mackenzie turned in her rented horse, and had to force herself not to run to her room. Once safely in her room, she finally dared to open the locket again. There it was! It was a picture of her. One that had been in her wallet as of yesterday. It had been a picture of her and Jenna from a trip to Cancun they once took. She'd folded it in half so it would fit in her small wallet.

Mackenzie grabbed her purse and rifled through her wallet. It was nowhere to be found. The only logical explanation was that Connor had snagged it when she wasn't looking, and had kept it. But why? And when? Was this before or after he'd suspected her of betraying his clan? And what did this mean? How much truth was in the story about a laird pining away while waiting for the woman he loved to return to him? Her mind was all over the place, trying to make sense of this new discovery. She thought Jenna had mentioned that the castle was haunted by a man who'd died waiting for his lady love…that couldn't have been Connor? Right?

She jumped onto her laptop and searched for all of the history surrounding the castle of Eilean Donan. She found pages for the castle, about the clan MacRae, and plenty about the current owners, but nothing about Connor. She tried searching for him alone, but she only got the basics; name rank and serial number. She had his date of birth and (gulp) the date of his death. He hadn't lived much more than a few years past her departure. Oh, this was torture! How could she go on knowing how much he had loved her…and how she had left him! Mackenzie felt as if her heart had been ripped out of her chest and smashed with a sledgehammer. What had she done? She forced herself to continue reading. She needed to know everything about him, if he had, she choked on the thought, married again….

Mackenzie fell asleep at her computer, but her dreams were not pleasant. They were visions of Connor drinking himself into a stupor, and ignoring everything around him. In one dream, he'd held the locket and stared at it silently for what felt like eons. When Mackenzie woke up, she felt hot. Really hot. She ran a hand over her face, feeling the imprint of her keyboard on her cheeks, and looked blearily around. Something was standing in the corner, no, not something, someone!

Connor!

But as she turned, there was nothing. God, this place was messing with her mind. Of course she hadn't seen Connor. He was long dead. What did she think, that his ghost would come and haunt her? Her heart tightened because she *had* hoped that. On some level, she had wanted that.

She climbed into bed, only pausing to yank off her jeans, and she fell back into the mattress with a frustrated sound. Her dreams only served to frustrate her more; dreams of Connor, of course. In all of them, he was an angry embittered shell of the wonderful man she had known. And however briefly she had known him, she felt as if she'd known him forever.

The next week was hard, but she didn't know which was more difficult to get through; her days without Connor, or her nights, reliving her heartbreak through her all-too vivid dreams.

Jenna had had little patience for Mackenzie's mood swings, and Mackenzie still hadn't been able to bring herself to tell Jenna what had happened. So Jenna spent a lot of time with her new Italian friends.

Initially, Mackenzie had tried to pass her time in the Gallery, staring at the life-sized portrait of Connor. But after only a few minutes, the tears would start up, and she would rush out of the room as if the devil himself were chasing her. Once she had thought she'd seen Connor standing across the room, but when she looked fully at where she'd thought he'd been, there was nothing. Of course. Maybe the locket *was* haunted. But for her it was haunted with nothing but memories. After the first two tries, she gave up. She couldn't bear to look at the oil painting of Connor; it hurt too much. So she avoided the Gallery like the plague.

However, on her last night, Mackenzie forced herself to stand in the Gallery that she'd so avidly avoided, and stared at the canvas. She had to say goodbye. That was something she would regret for the rest of her life. She had never said goodbye to Connor. While she would treasure every memory she had of him, she still felt nothing but sorrow at the way they had parted. Her attention was captured by the painting once more, and she stared into his eyes. His eyes that could pierce right into her soul and see everything.

She'd taken so many pictures that first day, that she didn't feel the need to photograph it anymore. Today she sat with her pad and charcoal pencils to sketch. She let the tears fall onto the paper, and idly watched the smudges they made. And then Mackenzie could feel the heat coming from him. Her eyes flew to the painting. Was she going insane? It actually felt like Connor was in the room with her! Ignoring the tingling sensation that said she was being watched, she purposefully dropped her eyes to her drawing, and focused. This wasn't the first time she'd thought Connor was in the room with her. Again, though, Mackenzie felt heat. This had been a bad idea. She had to get out of here. She stood quickly, trying not to trip in her heels, and gathered her pencils and pad, stuffing it all in her bag. With one last look at the painting, she prepared herself mentally to leave him.

"I've never liked that painting." The deep baritone had a hint of amusement in it.

Mackenzie froze.

"Are you real?" she whispered to the empty room.

"Aye, lass, flesh and blood." His voice was rougher now.

She stared at the canvas, not knowing what to expect, but his voice had come from *behind* her. Not from the painting. Mackenzie turned toward her hallucination slowly, not sure what to expect her obviously fractured mind to have created. But when she turned and saw him, she gasped and took a step back. He looked so real. Her mind must be playing tricks on her. This couldn't be real. Her fingers timidly reached out to his cheek, but she didn't even make it halfway before she snatched her hand back. She took a deep breath and reached out to him again. His cheek was solid and so warm. Mackenzie desperately wanted to believe he was real, but how could she? He had died 200 years ago! She knew--she'd searched him on the internet.

Yet, here he was, standing in front of her as if the past week had never happened. It made no sense; but then again, none of it ever had. None of it was logical. The hell with logic! Mackenzie threw herself at him and tightened her arms around his neck.

"I take it you're happy to see me?" She could hear the smile in his voice.

"Oh! Connor! You're here! You're really here!" Mackenzie buried her face in his neck and breathed in his scent, the scent of heather, and horse, and man. "But how?" was all she could manage; her thoughts were slightly incoherent.

"After you left, I tried to stop you. I raced back as fast as I could, but I was too late. The wizards found me...."

She cut him off, "They sent you through? Oh no...how long do we have"

"Until sunrise tomorrow."

"It's not enough time. Why are we always fighting against time?" Mackenzie was quickly becoming hysterical.

Connors arms tightened around her, and although his voice was soothing, his eyes were tight. "It'll work out. It has to. At least we found each other, for however short a time, at least we had that."

"And I'm acting like a stupid girl. You're right." She smiled a watery smile and wiped her eyes with the back of her hand. "Come on. Let's go." She took his hand from around her waist, and dragged him towards the door.

"Where are we going?"

"My room." Mackenzie flashed a brilliant smile at him, and winked.

"But you chambers are that way," Connor pointed down towards the tower.

"Umm...not in this time, remember? I have a room in the new wing."

"'Kenzie! 'Kenzie!"

Her wide eyes flew to Connor, and then back to the source of her irritation: Jenna.

"Mackenzie Isabella Stewart, don't you dare ignore me!" Jenna was screeching at Mackenzie from across the room. "I got that hottie Italian to agree to a double date, so don't you let me down tonight." Jenna was tottering to Mackenzie in stilettos and stopped dead when she saw Connor standing next to her. "Oh my goodness! 'Kenzie, you've been holding out on me!" She was eyeing Mackenzie shrewdly. "Well, I guess you can stand up Fabrizio...again...you seem to have your own plans."

Mackenzie sighed, in no mood for explanations. Her time with Connor was too short as it was. "Jenna, this is Connor. Connor, Jenna"

Connor took her proffered hand, but rather than shake it, he bowed slightly and said, "I am pleased to make your acquaintance."

Jenna giggled, "He's a keeper! Here I am chasing down the Italians, and you go and get yourself a regular hottie Scottie! Wow, just wow. By the way, love the kilt!" Jenna winked at Connor, and Mackenzie glared at Jenna.

Connor bent down to whisper to her, "Who's Scottie?"

Mackenzie had already turned and was towing Connor behind her. She wanted to be away from Jenna before she could notice the resemblance between Connor and the oil painting hanging behind her.

"I'll talk to you later, Jenna!"

When they reached her room, Mackenzie dragged Connor in and threw herself at him before the door was even shut.

After their first heated, passionate reunion, Connor had pulled Mackenzie up against him, and thrown an arm over her. His fingers were tracing her ribcage when he suddenly stilled.

She propped her head on his chest and looked up. "What? What is it?"

"Where did you get that?" Connor was holding the locket she wore and staring at it as if he had seen a ghost.

"Oh, that's right. I wanted to ask you about this. I found it in an antique shop in the village. There's a story that goes with it. Supposedly this necklace is haunted by its first owner: a man who had it made for his wife. But she apparently disappeared before he could give it to her. Then he pined away for his lady wife until he died, and now he haunts anyone who buys the necklace. The woman in the shop wouldn't even let me pay for it. She said it was meant for me."

"I had that made for you after our wedding night. I was going to give it to you after you told me about the babe, but you were gone by then."

The pain in Connor's eyes ripped at her heart. "Oh, Connor, I am so sorry that I left you." Tears started to fall of their own volition, and Connor gently wiped them away.

"Doona be sad, lass. We are here together now."

She gave him a watery smile, and softly told him what she should have told him a long time ago –200 years ago to be exact.

"I love you, my wonderful, caring, more-than-I-deserve husband."

He smiled, "As I love you, my wonderful, caring, exactly-what-I-deserve wife."

"You arrogant—," she never got to finish her sentence as Connor's mouth was on hers once more.

* * * *

Mackenzie was smiling at Connor as she wolfed down a cheeseburger that she'd ordered from room service.

"What?" He was eyeing his cheeseburger warily as if it might bite him.

"Nothing," she said around bites. "It's just that I never in a million years thought I'd be sitting in bed eating cheeseburgers in the middle of the night with you. It's funny, that's all."

Ever brave, Connor bit into his burger. He seemed pleasantly surprised at the taste, and quickly ate the rest in three bites.

"Here." Mackenzie handed him a soda to wash it down.

He more readily accepted the drink and guzzled half of it in one gulp.

She arched an eyebrow, "Thirsty?"

She was really enjoying having Connor here in her bed, in her time. She wanted to show him all of the new and cool technological advances they'd had in the past 200 years or so, but she doubted they'd leave her room. Especially if they only had until sunrise. Mackenzie tried not to frown as she pushed the thought of him leaving out of her mind, and instead concentrated only on the here and now.

"What?"

"I was thinking that I wish we had more time, or that I could go with you or you could stay here. There has to be some way we can stay together. Especially now."

"Why especially now?"

Mackenzie shimmied off the bed naked and ran to her suitcase. She held up a small white stick. "See?"

Connor didn't know what he was looking at. "See what?"

She walked over to him and stood in between his legs. "You were right; I'm pregnant." Her smile was brilliant.

He smiled and then immediately his smile fell, his lips compressed into a thin line.

"What? Aren't you happy?"

Connor placed his hand against her cheek, and he stared deeply into her eyes for so long, she lost track. "Are *you* happy?" He kept his intense gaze on her as she wondered what he could possibly mean.

Her eyebrows drew down over her nose. "I *was* until you said that, and now I'm not sure what to think…" she trailed off at the look on his face.

"Mackenzie, I wasn't certain you'd even want me back in your life. I…are you…" He paused to gather his thoughts, and Mackenzie would have smiled at the thought of Connor being unsure about anything, if she hadn't been worried about why he was searching for words. He always seemed so confident. It was unnerving to see him at a loss for words.

"Spit it out, Connor."

He smiled a little. "I am sorry for doubting you. You were only trying to save my people, yet you are not even from my time. Why?" His gaze was intense, his eyes searching. "Why did you decide to help us? To help me?"

"I wanted to help."

"I want a real answer, Mackenzie. Why did you help us? It wasn't your fight."

She took a deep breath. "You're wrong; it *was* my fight. It always *was* my fight. I only came to realize that after meeting you. I have been having the same dream over and over since I was a child. I couldn't ignore that. And I have never had a better reason to fight for anything before." She dropped a hand to her belly, and placed her other hand on his heart, feeling his heartbeat thud under her fingers, savoring it. "I want this baby, Connor. Whether we are together or not, I want this baby."

He placed his hand over hers, and said, "I want this child as well. And I want you." His eyes bored into hers. "I doona want to lose you."

"But how? How can we possibly manage this?"

His features softened, "With love, lass anything is possible."

It made so much sense, of course anything was possible. She had crossed time to meet him, she had fulfilled her destiny in vanquishing the Campbell, and now he had crossed time to find her! The shopkeeper's words came back to her, *When you meet that laird of yours, you promise me that you'll hold on tight and never let him go…* Of course they would stay together. It was so obvious. She would go with him.

Before she could tell him her idea, his fingers had found their way to her hips, and pulled her in between his legs. He was nuzzling her neck with his lips. What had she been thinking again? Connor's lips found their way to her breast, and the wet heat of his tongue on her nipple erased any lingering thoughts about anything except the bulging erection under the sheet draped across his lap.

Connor pulled Mackenzie in tighter against his body. With her standing before him, he was at the perfect level to worship her breasts. Her head fall back, and he could feel her growing frustration. He smiled against her skin.

"What's so funny?" she demanded.

He smiled wickedly and turned her so she faced away from him.

"What are you—"

"Ssh…" Connor brought her down on his throbbing erection and savored the gasp of both shock and pleasure. He held her there, sitting on him, for a moment, enjoying the feel of filling her. After a moment, he gripped her hips and brought her down on him again and again and again, until she cried out his name then he brought her down hard once more as he pulsed his own release. Mackenzie leaned back against his chest and cupped his cheek. Turning her head she brought his lips down to meet her kiss.

"That was utterly and deliciously sinful," she sighed against his lips. He could kiss this woman forever. The honey of her lips was a drug to him, and he could already feel himself hardening for her.

She turned wide eyes on him, the green was liquid from their most recent bout of lovemaking. He loved to see her like this; tousled, eyes languid and heavy, her lips ripe from his kisses….

"I love you."

She smiled brilliantly at his tender declaration. "As I love you."

Connor was suddenly fierce. "I canna be without you. The past few months have been the darkest of my life. I *will not* be without you." He could see that he had startled her with his sudden change of mood, but he would not live without her. He squared his shoulders. "I will stay here."

"No, you can't, Connor."

Connor's heart froze; she didn't want him to stay with her? Had he misjudged her affections?

"You can't go from being the Earl of Kintail, Laird of the MacRae clan, to just living with me. It's not fair. You're an earl for crying out loud! You would lose your title, your lands, your family, your home…"

She was worried about his pride? Damn his pride! "Being your husband is enough for me."

"You say that now, but what about in a year? Five years? You'll go mad with nothing to do, living in a big city, no land, no horses, it's not the same."

"I just want to be with you. I will do everything I can to make you happy." He had to find out what she was thinking. "Are you saying you don't want to be with me?"

"Of course I want to be with you, you overbearing, arrogant, wonderful man! That is why you can't stay here in my time."

What kind of madness was she spouting? "Blast it woman! What are you saying?"

"You can't stay in my time," Mackenzie gave him an enigmatic smile and softly cupped his face with her hand. Staring deeply into his eyes, she told him, "That is why I will go back with you."

Connor felt as if he'd been punched in the gut. She wanted to go back with him! She truly did want him as he wanted her: forever. But how could he let her leave her home? Was it fair?

"You would do that? Leave this marvelous place? I can't ask you to leave all this. To leave your home." He had dropped his eyes from hers, so she wouldn't see what this had cost him, but her tone had him looking back up at her.

"You're not. I offered. I'm going." It was final. "Try to stop me," she teased. "Besides, my home is with you, by your side. It always has been. I can't explain how, but I think I have always known that I didn't really belong here. I belong with you."

"You won't miss this?"

"Not a bit." She smiled. "Of course," Her eyes dropped, "If you don't want me to come with you, I won't force myself on you."

Connor wrapped his arms around her and buried his face in her hair, "You'll never leave my side."

"Promise?" she breathed against his lips.

She would drive him crazy like this. His body was already responding to Mackenzie's gentle kiss. How many times had they made love? He'd lost count. By all rights, he should be sated, exhausted, yet his body reacted as if it were their first time.

"Aye." He would enjoy keeping that promise. But before she could work her wicked magic with those lips, he remembered that there was one last thing he needed. "Mackenzie?"

"Hmm?"

"You forgot this."

Green eyes met blue as her confused gaze locked with his. Her eyes focused on something small and glinting in the dim light. Connor's heart stopped for a moment as her eyes widened and she gasped. Her eyes met his once more, only this time, the walls were down, and her eyes shone with emotion.

"My ring."

Her soft response had his heart starting double-time at the emotion in those two words. She took it from him and placed the delicate band on her third finger. Connor's heart swelled at the look on her face. He had never been so aroused in his life as he was right now, watching his woman slide a gold band onto her slim finger. This time, when Mackenzie kissed him, he didn't stop her.

Epilogue

Mackenzie sat before the fire with their eldest boy Collin, and their daughter Kaelyn. The children were completely engrossed with the story of how their father had absconded with his enemy's bride and married her. It always amazed Mackenzie how much they loved to hear the tale of how she and Connor met. She heard a slight rustling sound and glanced up at her husband.

"Mind his head," she smiled at him while Kaelyn played with her hair, and Collin hugged her tightly round the neck trying to recapture her attention. Connor had a bemused look on his face, and to Mackenzie it seemed to be more than just a father looking at his new son.

"What? What are you thinking about?"

Connor looked startled, but he answered her anyway. "I saw this, once, in a dream. I saw what might be and I wanted it. I refused to wait on the wizards and made them send me through that very night. That is how I came to your time; I saw this," he indicated the happy domestic scene," and I knew that nothing would stop me from finding you."

She raised tear-filled eyes to him, and she whispered, "Oh, Connor." Her lip trembled, and Connor placed the baby in his cradle, he then knelt down next to Mackenzie and the kids. He took them all into his embrace and pressed his lips to Mackenzie's. She shuddered. How after all this time, did one kiss from the man still turn her into jelly?

"Let's put the kids to bed," she suggested.

He raised his eyebrows, but said nothing. Instead he scooped both kids up into his strong arms and carried them to their room. Connor came back in to his wife nursing the baby to sleep.

"You're staring."

"Am I?"

"Mmhmm…"

"Mayhap it is because you are so beautiful, and the sight of our babe at your breast makes me want to do wicked things to you."

"Well, I guess it's a good thing he's asleep. Now you can do some of those wicked things you're thinking about."

Connor lifted Mackenzie as if she weighed no more than their children, and he placed her gently on the bed. As his fingers intertwined with hers, he brought her hands over her head, using the weight of his body to press her into the mattress. Mackenzie pressed her hips against his straining erection, kissing his lips more hungrily than ever. And Connor showed her some of the wicked, naughty ideas that had been forming in his head, taking them both to heaven on earth, and beyond.

The End

Made in the USA
Lexington, KY
12 March 2011